LET
ME
LOVE
YOU

ALSO BY BRITTNEY SAHIN

Standalones

Until You Can't
The Story of Us

Falcon Falls Security

The Hunted One
The Broken One
The Guarded One
The Taken One
The Lost Letters

Dublin Nights Series

On the Edge
On the Line
The Real Deal
The Inside Man
The Final Hour

Becoming Us

Someone Like You
My Every Breath

Hidden Truth Series

The Safe Bet
Beyond the Chase
The Hard Truth

LET ME
LOVE YOU

BRITTNEY SAHIN

 Montlake

Published by Montlake, Seattle

www.apub.com

Amazon, the Amazon logo, and Montlake are trademarks of Amazon.com, Inc., or its affiliates.

ISBN-13: 9781662513800 (paperback)
ISBN-13: 9781662513794 (digital)

Cover design by Caroline Teagle Johnson
Cover photography by Wander Aguiar

Printed in the United States of America

LET
ME
LOVE
YOU

PROLOGUE

Maria

Six Years Ago—New York City

"Why aren't they hanging out with us? I thought we were here to celebrate?" I tipped my chin toward the bar, and my sister swiveled on her seat to put eyes on our "bodyguard" and his brothers.

We were sitting at a table inside a nautical-themed bar in Greenwich Village, not too far from where she lived, celebrating my twenty-third birthday.

"I think they're trying to be polite and give us time to chat. This is just our warm-up spot." Natalia turned back to face me while fidgeting with the neckline of her black dress, attempting to hide her cleavage.

"So we're pregaming, huh?" I snatched my espresso martini, ready to take my first sip of the night.

"Something like that." Natalia smiled. "You did fly up here for your birthday, so I want to make sure you enjoy yourself."

"I owe Enzo a huge thank-you for surprising me with a plane ticket."

"He knew how much I missed you."

And here I was hoping he secretly wanted to see me. I almost laughed out loud at the ridiculous idea as my eyes landed on Enzo, our so-called bodyguard for the evening.

I hadn't expected to find him looking at me, and I nearly spilled my drink. My free hand slid up the column of my throat as I counted backward, giving myself three more Mississippi seconds to look at Enzo before focusing on my sister.

"Maria, Maria."

Thank God for the shitty lighting so she couldn't spot the stain of embarrassment on my cheeks. Of course, she'd already read me, her lips twitching with mild amusement. It was her I-caught-your-hand-in-the-cookie-jar type of smile, one she used whenever she knew I was daydreaming. Or in "la-la land," as our mother called it.

"What?" I nervously giggled, casually trying to downplay that I'd been caught lusting over one of the Costa brothers.

When my sister had moved to New York, our parents had reached out to the Costa family, their longtime friends, and asked them to keep an eye on her. Out of the three Costa sons, Enzo had the privilege of being assigned to play the dutiful role of bodyguard on nights like these. She and Enzo had become close friends, practically like family, these last few years, too.

"We may not live near each other right now, but that doesn't mean I forgot your poker face," Natalia teased.

I set down my drink, threading my fingers together on my lap before I spilled both the martini and my naughty thoughts about Enzo. "Speaking of the whole not-living-near-each-other thing . . . I really can't wait for you to come home."

We grew up in a small town outside Charlotte, and while I could see the appeal of New York, I knew I'd never survive more than a week in such a big city; otherwise, I'd probably have moved with her.

"One or two more years, then I'll be back. It's been an experience, that's for sure. Busting my ass working at two restaurants and a bar learning the ropes, all so I—"

"Can open your own place back home," I finished for her, hoping I hadn't made her feel guilty for being away. "I know. I'm sorry. And I'm super excited for you. You've known what you wanted to do since you were ten. And here I am at twenty-three and still clueless."

"You don't need to rush."

"Yeah, I kind of do." My English degree wasn't doing much for me in the workplace. And the extra student-loan debt was now heavy on my shoulders.

"Well, you'll figure out your thing, I'm sure of it."

"I'm working three jobs that barely pay minimum wage to afford my student loans and avoid living with Mom and Dad. All I really care about is reading, and I don't think 'professional reader' is a thing."

"Or is it?" Natalia smirked. "You never know. I mean, you do change your personality based on whatever book you're reading like it's a job."

"I do not." I laughed. *Okay, not totally.* I was more like an empty vessel of nothingness, and books filled me up in ways nothing else seemed to.

Taking another sip to try and dull the worries still fluttering around in my head, I felt the liquid go down the wrong pipe, and I smacked my chest while coughing. *Real smooth, Maria.*

When I set the glass down, I felt him watching me. I chanced a look in Enzo's direction and was met with his concerned gaze.

Enzo mouthed, "You okay?"

How'd he hear me coughing over the loud Bon Jovi song playing? The man really was great at watching over us.

"Good," I mouthed back with a slight nod.

"Oh no." Natalia's knees bumped mine from under the table. "You're doing it again. Making googly eyes with one of the Costa brothers."

"And if I was?" I arched a brow, eyes back on my overprotective sister.

It'd been seven years since I'd seen anyone in the Costa family. The last time I'd been in New York was for a funeral. Not the greatest memory.

"You came out of your shell at dinner last night at the Costas' house. Flirty. Funny. Living in the moment. I loved it." She was stalling. Why? "But redirect that sexy energy elsewhere. You don't know the brothers like I do. Before I moved here, we only saw them a handful of times, and we were younger. And now, well, just trust me when I say you should consider them off-limits."

But out of all the Costa brothers, only one managed to inspire a sonnet of sexy prose to echo through my head like a chorus tonight. A soft hum of pleas to walk straight up to him, fist his shirt, and pull him down for a kiss in front of a room of strangers. The perfect hot birthday kiss.

I thought back to last night and how Enzo had sent his parents' chef home for the evening and put his culinary skills to use. Watching him cook had been nearly as gratifying as eating his food.

Enzo had seemed different in the kitchen than the man in the expensive suit tonight. With his sleeves rolled up, faded denim jeans, and wearing a backward ball cap while he'd chopped veggies, he'd been warmer. Softer. More like the younger version of him I remembered from the few vacations we'd spent together as kids at their third home in the Hamptons.

Some of my best childhood memories were from their house at the beach. Splashing around in the chilly waters and building sandcastles.

Bianca Costa, Enzo's twin sister, babysat us when our parents went out. She was an avid reader and the one who turned me into a fan of books.

And then . . . she was viciously murdered seven years ago at twenty-four, and it was a reminder of why the real world was awful.

I did my best to shuffle my thoughts around, hoping to place my head back in the present. "So, what's their story now?"

"Bianca's death changed them all in a way that . . ." What was it she didn't want to say?

"I mean, of course something like that would change them." I quietly sat with my thoughts for a moment, the tragedy of her death washing over me again.

Bianca had believed in happily-ever-afters. That fairy tales were possible. And she'd want her brothers to fall in love, I was sure of it.

"They're heartbreakers, Maria. That's the easiest way I can put it."

I wasn't looking for love tonight. "I just want a hot birthday kiss. Not a proposal." And preferably from the youngest brother, Enzo.

Last night had been the first time I'd set eyes on him since Bianca's funeral. And what a way to greet him—I'd tripped on a rug inside their fancy foyer and flew right into his muscular arms. He'd circled my waist, and my breasts had smashed against his hard chest.

After that, I began a list in my head of all the naughty things I wanted to do with him, or for him to do *to* me.

"A hot kiss, huh?" Natalia snatched her drink and took a big gulp, clearly hating the idea.

I looked at the Costas again, thinking about our dinner together. The three brothers had sat on one side of the twelve-person table with their parents at each end. Natalia, myself, and the youngest Costa, Isabella, had been opposite the devilishly handsome men.

A few moans of pleasure had escaped my lips with every sinful bite of Enzo's food, drawing his eyes more than once, as well as a slap on my thigh from my sister, since it sounded as though I were orgasming at the table.

While I'd indulged in a *second* helping of the best veal Milanese I'd had in my life, I'd also given the brothers labels in my head.

The Broody Genius was Constantine. He was thirty-five, and he'd spent a good part of his twenties in the navy, leaving only a few months before his sister was killed.

The Playboy was Alessandro. He was thirty-three and had devastatingly good looks with light-gray eyes that pierced through you. He'd also served, but in the army and only four years.

Then there was the Sexy Chef. Enzo had turned thirty-one last month in July, and although he'd originally planned to go to culinary school after high school, he wound up serving in the army for six years.

"Are you done with your inner monologue so I can have your attention again?" Natalia smirked.

"Yeah, I think so." I took a more cautious sip this time. "But I'm still not convinced these men are walking red flags. You'll have to give me more than 'heartbreakers' to scare me away."

"Of course you'd say that," she teased. "You love the bad boys in fiction, but I thought you had enough common sense to avoid them in real life."

"So they're 'bad' now, huh?" Glancing back at them, I saw Constantine appeared to be nursing his drink, Alessandro was flanked by two blondes, and when I cut my gaze Enzo's way, chills scattered over my bare arms.

He adjusted the cuff of his black suit jacket, and I dragged my attention up his shirt to the top few buttons undone. And then farther up. Straight to his dark eyes. Eyes that were on me.

Maybe you are a bad boy, but . . .

"You really think you can convince Enzo to leave his fancy, rich life here to work grueling hours in a kitchen as your head chef one day?" I asked instead of continuing to press her on the kissing-a-Costa thing.

I wet my lips as Enzo squeezed the back of his neck as if frustrated by something or someone, and considering his eyes were still riveted my way . . .

"I hope he will. His mom and sister think Enzo might become the man he was before, um, Bianca died if he gets away from this city," Natalia said, finally drawing my focus to her again. "But this is your birthday." She blinked, probably trying to shake free any negative thoughts. "Let's go somewhere less *Top Gun*–like where we can dance and find you a hot kiss." She abruptly stood while pointing at me. "A non-Costa kiss."

I grumbled, "Fine," then rose as well. "Anyone in New York has to be better than whoever Mom keeps trying to set me up with back home."

"Oh no, is she playing matchmaker again?" Natalia polished off the rest of her martini. "It's bad enough she's begging me to get back with Anthony. I was hoping she'd leave you alone, since you're not as old as I am."

"Okay, you're only twenty-seven, not ancient. And ugh, you didn't tell me she's pushing you to date him again." I wasn't a fan of my sister's pro–hockey player ex. They'd dated for a second in college, but I'd always wondered if Anthony's hot Navy SEAL brother would've been a better match. Of course, he was older than her and always overseas.

"Yeah, you know her. She wants to see me married with kids ASAP. And who is she bugging you to date?"

"Oh, you know, just every banker between Charlotte and New York. She's worried I'll never find a career I love, so she thinks I need a man to support me." I snatched my black clutch from the table and tucked it under my arm. "We have to learn to say no to her, don't we?"

Natalia sighed. "One of these days, we will."

But I was the pessimist, and I doubted we'd stand up to her anytime soon, given the powerful influence she had over us. "I'm going to head to the women's room; then we can go."

"I'll tell the boys we're ready." She tossed a look Alessandro's way. "And try and peel those women off that man."

"Good luck with that," I teased, then headed toward the hallway, hoping to find the restroom. But the moment I rounded the corner, I slammed into someone. "Shit, I'm sorry," I said at the feel of something wet sloshing onto me.

My clutch tumbled to the floor, and we both crouched at the same time to get it, nearly knocking heads.

"I'm the one who spilled my drink all over you," he said, reaching my clutch first. "I should be apologizing." That deep drawl was far more Southern than my home in North Carolina.

We both slowly stood, and I accepted my clutch from him while staring into his incredible blue eyes. "It's my fault. I was walking too fast," I shared, finally checking the stain on my sleeveless gold tank top, and based on the smell, I was wearing whiskey.

"Why don't you come to my office? I can give you some club soda, and we'll see if we can remove the stain."

"Your office?" *Walk off with a stranger?* Nope. That was on my Don't Ever Do list.

"I own the club," he noted, as if sensing my hesitation.

"Oh, um. I can ask one of the bartenders for a napkin and club soda. It's no worries. Thank you, though." I turned to the side, prepared to flee, but then I remembered I wanted a hot New York moment, and if the Costas were off-limits and this man did own the club, well, maybe I could trust him? But he'd have to prove himself first.

When I faced him again, I took a quick inventory of his looks. No Jeffrey Dahmer vibes. Muscular. Midthirties, but the beard could've been aging him. Trusting, and yet, lost-looking eyes. Dark denim jeans and a white button-down shirt. I checked his finger next. No ring.

"What's your name?"

"Hudson." He smiled, as if that were supposed to mean something.

Ohhh. The name of the bar was Hudson's. "So you do own the club?" I relaxed at the thought. But he could have made that up. *Yup. I'd never make it alone in New York.*

He lightly laughed. "I have the code to enter the office to prove it."

"Right. That'll seal the deal, I suppose." I shook my head, a bit embarrassed. "I mean, not like you're going to seal, um . . ." *What am I saying?* He stared back at me with an amused expression. "Show me the way, please. If you still want to."

8

"Oh, I do." He winked, and I wished like hell that sexy wink created butterflies in my stomach the same way one slight look from Enzo managed to. *Come on, give me something. Anything. This man is hot, hot, hot.*

No bad-guy vibes, sure. But also, no wet panties. Damn.

Hudson unlocked the office, proving he wasn't some rando. Then he propped the door open with an anchor-like stopper, which made me feel even better.

At the sight of all the framed photos on one wall, mostly of men and women in uniform, as well as of naval warships, I let go of the last bit of anxiety about being alone with a stranger. "Navy?" I asked as he went to a small bar cart by his desk.

He tossed a look over his shoulder and nodded.

I smiled; then my gaze landed on the bookshelf filled with colorful spines. "And you're a reader, too?"

"That I am." He swapped his glass for club soda.

"The perfect man," I teased.

"Far from perfect, I'm afraid," he returned in a low, rumbly voice.

As he dabbed some of the club soda on a napkin, I decided to shoot my sister a quick text to buy myself some time before Natalia came looking for me.

"I take it you're a reader?" He offered the napkin, and I set my phone and clutch on his desk to accept it.

"A real-life Belle searching for a Beast with a library to share," I said, feeling slightly silly until my words produced a devastatingly handsome smile from him.

And yet, no pitter-patter in my chest.

"Better yet, the Beast after he's a man again." With literary talk from a muscular, handsome man, how was my pulse not jumping?

I went still when a rush of heat climbed up my body, the little hairs on the back of my neck stood, and I followed Hudson's gaze to see the only man capable of provoking such a reaction.

Enzo.

"She's Natalia Romano's sister," Enzo said in a gravelly voice, and he propped his palms on the exterior doorframe.

"I didn't know," Hudson returned in an apologetic-sounding voice.

"I need the room." It was an order, not a request from Enzo, and I looked at Hudson, surprised to see him nodding without question.

"Have a good evening." Hudson tipped his head goodbye, and Enzo stepped aside to allow him to exit.

Then Enzo kicked aside the anchor, and the door thudded shut.

"What just happened? Why'd he leave like that?"

Enzo's eyes shifted to the stain on my tank top. "He's a friend. Do you think I'd let you and your sister hang out somewhere that I didn't—"

"That you didn't what?" I began dabbing at the stain, remembering why I was in the office.

"Deem safe," he bit back. "What were you thinking going into a room alone with some guy you don't know?"

"You just said he's your friend. Based on the military photos, I figured I was in good hands."

"Good hands, huh?" he growled out, and for whatever reason, something I'd said had further pissed him off. "You came in here before you knew that bit of information," he pointed out, and then he began speaking in Italian.

My parents were born in Italy, but they never taught us the language, and I had a feeling it was so they could talk in private without us knowing what they were saying.

Enzo had moved to the US when he was six, and clearly, he was still fluent, even though his accent seemed to show up only when he was upset. Like now.

Enzo stalked closer to me. One angry step after the other until he was within arm's reach of me. "I can't protect you if you go down dark halls with men you don't know. What in God's name were you planning to do with him?"

"First of all," I said, taking a defensive tone and stance, "the *bathroom* was down the dark hall, and I had to pee. And secondly, he spilled his drink on me and offered the club soda." I waved the napkin, hating that it looked like a little white flag of surrender.

Enzo might have intimidated people, but I wouldn't let him scare me. Of course, my experience with "bad boys" and "heartbreakers" was limited to fiction.

He grunted. "He's too old for you."

"And what does his age have to do with anything?"

Agitated, I flicked the napkin at him, and he snatched it from the air and balled it in his hand.

When his eyes dipped to my dressy tank top, I couldn't help but look down, noticing that the whiskey had spilled all over my right breast. The thin material of the top and my sheer bra were wet, which meant my nipple penetrated the two flimsy layers of protection.

"Hudson fucks just to fuck." The way the f-word passed through his lips and hit the air, it was as if the man had reached out and placed his large hand between my legs and skated his finger over my sex.

Holy hell.

But then I remembered what he said and snapped out, "So you're just going to keep riding this train of crazy, I see?"

If Constantine is the broody one . . . then what do you call this? That dark look in Enzo's eyes was almost enough to scare me. But something told me he'd sooner lay down his own life than do anything to jeopardize mine.

Enzo's eyes raked over the length of my body, from my slingback black heels to my black flowy skirt, and then he skipped over my tank top and found my eyes again.

"Fine, maybe I did want something from him. I'm guessing Natalia told you I'm inexperienced and a virgin to ensure you kept men away from me, but I—"

"What did you just say to me?" Enzo hissed as he stepped closer, stealing my breath as he gently cupped my chin.

His long, dark lashes remained still. His espresso-brown eyes focused on me as though I were the bane of his existence.

"Yes." I gulped. "I'm twenty-three, and I've never been laid."

Had a man tried to get me off with his hands back in college? Yeah. Had he been successful? Sadly, no. But that was the most action my body had seen aside from my vibrator.

I had high standards—like a book boyfriend in the flesh. My mom didn't read, so she was clueless about the kind of men I'd ever want to date, which was why her matchmaking skills sucked.

"Virgin?" he mumbled, then said a word in Italian.

Note to self, google the word for virgin *in Italian when home.* Also, did I just stun this man into speechlessness?

He released his hold on my chin, only to run a hand over his bladed jawline, and his anger seemed to intensify based on the slant of his brows and the harsh lines cutting across his forehead.

I had to find the will to continue going head-to-head with him. And it took me channeling Katniss Everdeen from The Hunger Games and her fearlessness to be able to say, "I wasn't planning to let some rando screw me in here, if that's why you look all pissed off right now."

"No? Just back at his penthouse? Up against his glass wall, huh? Your tits on display for all of Manhattan to see while he fuc—" He cut himself off as if realizing he was painting a vivid picture. Little did he know that was now number seven on the list of things I wanted to do with him.

My nipples hardened as a response to his dirty talk, and a little pulse of energy had me tightening my thighs together. This was new for me. I didn't get all hot and bothered by a man unless he was written by a woman and inside a book.

His eyes fell to my skirt like he knew what was happening beneath it. The man freaking snarled at me, as if realizing I was aroused, and why'd it feel like he wanted to take me over his knee and punish me for it?

Well hell, that can be number eight.

A litany of curses left his mouth, a mix of English and Italian, while he tossed the napkin into the trash bin by the desk.

"You're too young," he murmured under his breath. "Too fragile." He abruptly turned, clawing at his black hair, mussing it up.

"What are you talking about? Too young and fragile for what? Hudson?"

"For *me*," he seethed, swiveling back around, breathing hard.

My mouth hung open. The words were trapped behind my shock. And the longer he stared at me with such a dark, heated look, the harder it became for me to think clearly.

He shoved back his suit jacket to draw his hands to his hips, continuing to stare me down. "What do you want, Maria?" He finally broke the silence, which had felt like the only real fragile thing in the room.

What I wanted was for him to remove his jacket and roll his sleeves up to expose the ink on his arms. Unbutton his shirt so I could see the tattoo on his chest.

I wanted to study him. Pretend I had artistic talent so I could sketch this man before me. Capture the emotion on his face. Immortalize in a drawing the way his muscles were no doubt bunched and tense beneath his clothes.

"Maria?" he repeated. "So help me, I don't know what's in your head, but you're walking a tightrope right now by being alone with me."

I swallowed and tore my eyes back to his face. "Why?" I rolled my tongue along the seam of my mouth, and he tipped his head to the side and dragged his thumb along the line of his lips as if he were touching me instead.

"Because I don't fuck virgins, and certainly not one I vowed to their father to protect." His hands snapped into fists at his sides, and I stumbled back, hitting the wall. He lifted his hands as if realizing what he'd done, and it was the first time I saw the muscles in his face go lax. "I would never hurt you." His Adam's apple moved as he carried his attention back to my eyes. "I'm trying to refrain from giving you what you seem to want."

Oh jeez, could he read me that well? I was supposed to be the reader, not be the one read. "What is it that I want?" For some reason, I needed to hear those words more than I needed anything right now.

His hands relaxed at his sides as he stalked toward me, eating up the space between us. He dipped his head to find my gaze as his palms went to the wall over my shoulders.

When he didn't answer, I offered up the truth. "I—I want, um, a birthday kiss." Damn the stammer betraying the confidence I wanted to pretend to have in this moment. "Or maybe for you to take my v-card so I can be done with it already." There. I said it. The real "it" in my head.

"You're sure as hell not kissing or screwing anyone out in that bar." His words rippled through the air and slid under my clothes, hitting me right between the legs. Being told what to do shouldn't have turned me on, and yet . . .

"Does your order extend outside the bar? To all the boroughs of New York?" I shot back, unsure where that spitfire came from.

The side of his lip hitched, a devilish smirk appearing. "You really want me to break my rules, don't you?"

"Would you do it if it meant stopping someone else from touching me?" I challenged, allowing my backbone to remain as stiff and tough as possible. But he wasn't the villain he was trying to portray. I remembered him from our trips to the Hamptons. The sweet boy who'd throw paper airplanes across the room with funny jokes on them to make me laugh. Then that boy went to the army and became a man.

"If you think for one second I'm letting any guy near you tonight, you're gravely mistaken," he growled.

"*Any* man?" I rasped, unsure how long I could remain imprisoned by his hard body with his mouth so close to mine and not draw myself even closer. Not fist his shirt and arch into him. "That include you?"

His eyes fell to my lips, and his brows stitched together. "For a virgin, you like to play with fire. Why is that?" His voice was deep, thick with intent. But the intent to do what?

"I'm not a kid anymore, remember?"

"Trust me, I'm well aware of that fact." He leaned in, his mouth nearly brushing my lips, and it took all my restraint not to kiss him. But like hell would I make the first move. "But I'm bad for you. You have no idea just how bad."

My body had never responded to anyone like this before, and every nerve ending inside me was charged and ready to go. "I don't believe you. The man you're *pretending* to be right now is fake. The real you made dinner last night. You're soft beneath this exterior." I poked his chest. "I don't know why you—" I cut myself off when he pinned his body to mine, letting me feel his rock-hard length, and my eyes widened.

"There's nothing soft about me." One hand left the wall, and he swept my long brown hair away from my face and palmed my cheek.

"You want me?" I murmured the question.

He skated his hand away from my face and along my bare arm, catching my fingers for a moment before he found my hip, and I gasped as he held me tighter. Unable to stop myself, I pressed up in my heels, closed my eyes, and shimmied against him, searching for relief between my legs.

"Open your eyes and look at me while you rub your pussy against my cock," he roughly commanded, snatching my attention, and then my body went still at the realization I'd been doing what he'd said.

"I, um . . ." My hand flattened over his heart, finding it pounding. "What do you really want?" *Please say me.*

"The things I want are impossible."

"What else is impossible?" I was reaching, and I knew that—hoping this man would open up to me like he could with Natalia.

"What I want is for my sister not to be dead," he said in a broken voice, and at that, he let go of me and backed away, and I felt so utterly cold and alone without his proximity. "And that'll never happen." His eyes journeyed over the length of my body before he added, "Just like you and I will never be together."

I processed his pain. Took it in. Absorbed some of it. And then admitted, "She was the best of us all." I closed my eyes, feeling the prick of unexpected tears, such a sharp contrast to the heat still burning between my legs.

I gasped when my back went to the wall again, and I tore my eyes open to find him slamming a hand over my shoulder. "Why are you doing this to me? Why the hell are you making me feel . . ."

"Feel what?" I exhaled.

He lowered his chin, eyes moving down and to the side as if lost in thought. "You shouldn't be in here with me."

"I don't see you backing away," I challenged.

"I can't seem to un-fucking-glue myself from you since you showed up last night," he rasped, eyes returning to my face. "But I won't give you what you *think* you want, because it'd break you, I promise."

"But?" I hoped there was more coming.

"The birthday kiss. I'll give *that* to you. I don't want some asshole putting his mouth on you tonight."

"Oh, I . . ."

"Save your virginity for someone you love. Don't just give it to anyone." There he was, that sweet, nice guy who gave a damn. He was trying to hide him. Conceal him under this facade he'd created. But even now he couldn't help but be him. That made me want to cry for some reason. "You deserve better than what I can give you."

I wasn't sure why he felt that way, but I also wouldn't refuse what he was willing to offer when I so desperately wanted to feel his mouth on mine. "Kiss me, then," I pleaded, reaching for the lapel of his jacket.

He stared deep into my eyes, still unmoving, but when I arched into him to feel his cock, his restraint snapped. Hands darting up to cup my cheeks, he gently caressed my face as he slanted his mouth over mine.

His tongue skimmed the line of my lips, seeking entrance, and I gave it to him.

I moaned, struggling to comprehend how this felt like more than just a hot birthday kiss . . . this was borderline life-altering.

His kiss turned more ravenous, and his hands slid into my hair, holding my head tight as his tongue stroked mine. He kept me pinned to the wall with his entire body, and I melted into him, gripping his forearms. An all-consuming kiss. It was almost as if I could absorb his pain and his passion within the space of those few brief seconds.

I was pretty sure he was equally stunned by whatever was happening between us, because the next thing I knew, he was breaking the kiss. Resting his forehead on mine, he inhaled a shaky breath and took a second to compose himself.

And now, part of me wished he'd never given me that moment . . . because how in the world would I ever find someone to top that kiss? How would I move on from *that*?

He didn't have to take my virginity to steal my heart.

He backed up and tapped his fist against his lips, lightly panting as he stared at me, appearing distraught. "Maria," he began, a look of devastation on his face, "you have to promise me something."

I gasped when he abruptly pulled me back to him, holding me tight to his frame with his hand at my back. "What?"

He brought his mouth to my ear, and my skin became hot and tingly. "Please, for the love of God," he gruffly began, "never offer yourself to me again."

ONE

Maria

"How does it feel to be twenty-nine and a single mom?"

"Jeez, Ma. You could've at least opened up by wishing me a happy birthday first." I turned to locate my favorite bartender, Christian, needing a drink to get through this conversation.

My sister and her husband, Ryan Rossi, threw me this surprise birthday party at her restaurant, Talia's Tuscan Grill. Almost two years ago, my sister's hard work paid off—she opened her own restaurant, and I was so damn proud of her.

There was no place I'd rather spend my birthday. Of course, the place was crowded with a bunch of people I either didn't know or wouldn't trust with a single secret of mine. But if a big, flashy party made my sister happy, I'd smile and make small talk with everyone.

Glancing down at the other end of the bar, I saw three of my old high school friends clamoring for more than just Christian's cocktail skills. *So much for making sure the birthday girl never has an empty glass.*

"You know how we feel about divorce." Mom dropped another not-so-stellar comment on me. Wrapping a hand over my shoulder, she urged me to face her. "We're Catholic. Your father and I think—"

"What, that I should've stayed with Thomas even though he slept with other women?" I finally whirled around, giving up hope on that drink. "Cheating is a sin, Ma. I'm pretty sure that's still frowned upon at the church." I loved her to death, but she needed to let go and stop trying to run my life.

"You didn't let me finish." She dropped a dramatic sigh on me. "I was going to say that your father and I believe in the sanctity of marriage unless your husband is a cheating asshole." She frowned at her accidental slip of a swear word. "Thomas was never right for you, and it was my fault I pushed you to marry him. I steered Natalia the wrong way in the past, too." She showed me her palms as if in surrender. "You should celebrate being single at twenty-nine and enjoy your life. You know, meet new people, date a little. Maybe try some dating sites."

"What?" I fake-laughed. "So I can get asked by a dozen different men my favorite color? No thank you."

"Well, I promise I'm going to do my best not to play matchmaker anymore."

My eyes widened in mock horror. Reaching for her, I joked, "Who are you, and what have you done with my mother?"

She chuckled. "I'm trying to change, my dear daughter." Her Italian accent I loved still clung to her words. "But change takes time."

Speaking of change. I looked around the crowded bar area, searching for one of the few people I *did* want to talk to, but I didn't see Enzo anywhere.

"Maybe not with Enzo, though."

"What?" I whipped my attention back to her.

"Don't 'enjoy' yourself with Enzo, if you catch my drift. I see the way you look at him. He's not good for you."

Ugh, her and the air quotes. What was with everyone trying to warn me away from Enzo?

And great, now my head was back in the past, and my sister's words to refrain from falling for a Costa echoed all around me. I could also see vividly the girl I once was, the one who'd ignored Natalia's warning, standing in Hudson's office with her whiskey-stained shirt, swollen lips, and a semishattered heart.

"Don't get me wrong, I'm grateful for everything he's done for your sister." The beginning of Mom's lecture brought me back to the uncomfortable present, and she snatched her Moscato from the counter.

I painted on a fake smile and bit down on my back teeth to keep my mouth glued shut.

"I'm glad he was able to move here to help her with the restaurant, because he's a phenomenal chef, and talent like that shouldn't be wasted. I know his mother's happy he's turned over a new leaf while living in Charlotte, but . . ." Her hesitant pause was textbook dramatic from her.

I decided to let her unfinished sentence hang in the air while I once again flipped through the pages of my mind, landing on more recent memories, ones Enzo also owned.

To be honest, I'd been a bit shocked a man like Enzo would truly give up his fancy life and the money that came with it in New York to run my sister's kitchen. Of course, I hadn't exactly kept up with his life since our one and only hot moment. When he'd arrived in town two years ago, it'd been the first time I'd seen him since New York on my twenty-third birthday.

It'd also felt like time had stood still when our eyes met, and a rush of energy had moved through the room and slammed into me. I'd heard only the erratic beating of my heart as his eyes journeyed over my pregnant stomach.

And then he'd offered his hand as if we were two strangers who'd never shared a kiss, and I'd nearly vomited.

From that point on, I'd decided if he wanted to act like nothing ever happened, then so be it, and so would I. Plus, I'd been married and pregnant, so it made sense to erase that hot memory from my mind as if it were only an Etch A Sketch drawing.

"Maria, are you even listening to what I'm saying?" Mom snapped her fingers, trying to shake me free from my internal monologue. I swear, in another life I'd be a character in a book or movie and not a living, breathing person.

"You think I don't know why you wouldn't let me invite the Costa family to your wedding to Thomas?" This wasn't a question she expected me to answer, so I continued to keep my mouth shut. "Your taste in men is like mine. Well, before I met your father, at least. I *do* know you, and that's why I've done my best to ensure you avoid the same mistakes I made."

I had to say, I didn't see *that* coming.

"I thought men like Thomas were the safer option for you. I was wrong, but I was just trying to protect you."

I'd never wanted safe when I was younger, I'd wanted the kind of love that was all-consuming. But my search for it had led me to Enzo . . . and he hadn't wanted me. So I gave up on the idea of a book boyfriend materializing in real life to give me a happily-ever-after, and I gave in to Mom.

Not-so-spoiler alert, her picks were all wrong for me. So wrong that, as of two weeks ago, my ex and I had officially divorced after a nine-month separation. In North Carolina, we were supposed to be apart for a year before the paperwork could be finalized. For whatever reason, Thomas finally had a change of heart and confessed the truth to the lawyers and judge about his infidelity. And now I was a free woman earlier than expected.

The crazy thing? Even to this day, Thomas still blamed Enzo for our marriage failing, not the fact he cheated.

"Ever since that man moved to Charlotte, you've changed. Hell, you're probably fucking him at your sister's restaurant," he'd yelled during our blowout fight last November after I'd confessed he'd pocket-dialed me while he'd been out of town and having sex with another woman.

"I stopped loving you long before he came here. And I'm wondering if maybe we never actually loved each other at all." I'd snapped back the ugly truth I'd been hiding from everyone, including myself.

But had I cheated? Not once. I may have been unhappy, but I'd been faithful.

Never crossed any lines. No late-night texts with Enzo, or anyone for that matter. Nope, I'd been a loyal and faithful wife.

"Before your father, I was attracted to the bad boys," Mom revealed; then she turned to the side, putting eyes on my dad as he bounced my daughter, Chiara, on his knee at a corner booth. He cupped the back of her curly-haired head and then nuzzled her ear with his nose, which had her giggling.

"So you're saying you always set me up with guys who preferred golfing and checking their stock portfolios to—"

"Tall, dark-haired men with tattoos who would ruin your life."

"Easy with the stereotypes, Ma." *Damn.* "I take it someone with tattoos broke your heart?"

"Maybe," she said, and the somber look in her eyes told me she might still be mourning the loss of a relationship from more than three decades ago. "I'm not just thinking about you," she went on. "Chiara adores Enzo. And what if he gets bored with Charlotte and leaves? He'll break two hearts, not just one."

Yeah, that reminder poked a hole in my heart. It was hard to believe my daughter was eighteen months old, and Enzo had been in her life since birth. The supposedly "dangerous man" was a baby whisperer, too.

"We're only friends." I hadn't meant to follow that with a sigh of disappointment. "It'd be hard on all of us if he were to up and leave, Natalia especially."

Enzo and I were still not as close as he and my sister were, but he'd never stuck his tongue in her mouth, and I had a feeling he'd kept his distance from me on purpose. Although I wasn't quite sure why, since I had to assume he'd forgotten about our kiss.

"It's not just that. What if this 'new leaf' is temporary? What if he becomes the man he was back in New York?" she pressed.

"You know, you're making a poor case for yourself in the whole change department. If you think he can't change for good, why should I believe you'll stop meddling in my love life?" I rolled my eyes. "Case in point, this entire conversation."

Mom set down her glass, then nervously ran her hands through her chestnut-brown hair, which had streaks of silver and gray at the temples.

"Everything okay over here?" I flinched at the deep voice behind me, then relaxed realizing it was my brother-in-law. He must've picked up on the tension-filled bubble surrounding my mother and me from across the bar.

Facing Ryan, mild panic on my face, I mouthed, "Help me."

"Natalia needs Maria in the kitchen. Mind if I steal her away?" He offered his hand to help me stand.

"Sure, but aren't we singing and cutting the cake soon? Can't have the birthday girl miss that. Plus, Chiara will want to help you blow out the candles," Mom said, pointing to her granddaughter.

"Of course. This should only take a minute or two." Ryan tapped my back twice like a signal to hurry and escape.

"Thank you," I said once in the back hallway. "You're officially my hero." And Ryan really was a hero. He'd served as a Navy SEAL for twenty years, only retiring because it'd been medically necessary. His family had been our next-door neighbors growing up, and now he was happily married to my sister.

It still struck me as strange that Natalia had started seeing Ryan at all, since she'd first dated his brother. Anthony had been all wrong for her. A cheater, too. Mom was to blame for that relationship, of course.

Ryan, though, was far from a bad guy. He'd kept his feelings hidden from my sister for more than a decade, doing his best never to cross any lines even when she was single. Then fate brought them back together.

"Does Natalia really need me?" I asked as he pushed open the kitchen door, and my heart went to my throat at the sight of Enzo. He had his back to me while talking to my sister. His black chef's coat was on, as if he'd been busy in the kitchen even though we were closed tonight for the party and Natalia had hired someone else to cater so no one had to work.

"She does," Ryan replied as Natalia peeked around Enzo, smiled, and waved me over. "Hey, you. How are you holding up?" He went to Natalia and took a knee before her and kissed my sister's pregnant belly before rising to his full height of six-two.

He had stars in his eyes for my sister, acting like he hadn't just seen her and their unborn son five minutes ago, and I freaking loved it.

Natalia smoothed her hand over her abdomen and winced as if she'd been jabbed in the ribs. Her son was as active at six months as Chiara had been in my belly back in the day. "I wanted to show you the cake before we brought it out. Enzo and I collaborated to come up with something special."

"Oh?" I looked around but didn't see anything.

Enzo finally faced me, and his eyes combed over my pink-and-white sundress. He took me in inch by inch, and goose bumps scattered over my bare arms. "I'll get it." He headed for one of the industrial refrigerators on the other side of the kitchen, and I couldn't take my eyes off his tall, muscular body as he sauntered away.

A tall, dark-haired "heartbreaker" inked in tattoos.

"You look pale. You okay?" Natalia stepped forward and set the back of her hand to my cheek as if checking for a fever.

"Mom was just being Mom, and you know how that goes." I sighed, and Natalia pulled her hand back and exchanged a quick look with Ryan. He shrugged, as if not too optimistic Mom would ever truly change, either.

But people do change, right? Maybe not Mom, though.

My gaze switched to Enzo as he pushed a rolling cart in our direction with the sheet cake on top of it.

"What do you think?" Natalia beamed and stepped away from her husband to hook her arm through mine.

I forced my attention up to the other side of the cart where Enzo stood, hands in his pockets, eyes focused on me. "It was your sister's idea. I can't take credit."

"He's being humble." Natalia elbowed me. "What do you think? You're not talking."

I studied the large sheet cake, which had a bookshelf painted on it in frosting. There were books on each shelf with printed titles on the spines.

"Twenty-nine books for your birthday," Natalia continued, since I was still searching for words. "I went through your bookshelf at home. I figured whichever were the most worn were your favorites, so those are the titles I chose. Plus a few throwbacks I remembered you reading as a kid."

"It's incredible," I whispered. "Thank you." *The Hunger Games* was on the top shelf. And I was back in Hudson's office again, remembering when I'd channeled my inner Katniss to face off with the man before me now. "I'm . . ." *Going to cry.* On the middle shelf there was a Baby-sitters Club book, a reminder of Bianca. She'd introduced me to that series one weekend in the Hamptons when I was ten.

"Could we have a minute?" Enzo's rumbly voice had me looking up at him, tears brimming in my eyes; had he read my mind? Did he know I was thinking about his twin?

"Yeah. Just roll the cart out when you're ready so we can sing. I'm sure everyone is excitedly waiting." Natalia smiled, and Ryan took her hand as they left.

My gaze moved to Enzo's fingers as he deftly worked to undo each button of his chef's coat. He tossed the coat onto the counter, and his plain black tee showcased his strong arms and the ink my mom equated with being dangerous to my heart. It was like a clash of good and evil wrapped around his forearms in ink. From rosary beads on the inside of his one arm to skulls, a sword, and other themes of death being swallowed by flames on the other.

I followed his one arm up as his hand dove into his dark hair. It must've had gel in it, because the imperfectly messy look he always had going for him returned to its original place after his hand left his thick locks.

I tipped my head, anxious for him to share his thoughts. "You okay?" But the touch of chaos in his eyes staring back at me had me nervously blurting, "Are you considering offering me another birthday kiss?"

His smooth jaw clenched at my words. I was used to seeing him with facial hair, but he'd shaved the other day, and he was one of the few men who looked hot with or without facial hair.

I held a palm up between us. "Relax, Enzo, I was kidding."

His hand fell somehow gracefully to his side as he asked, "You never told Natalia about that kiss, did you?"

Wait, what? "No, I didn't." I shook my head in surprise. "You remember the kiss?"

His disarming smile caught me off guard as he studied me. "You think there's a chance on God's green earth, in the oceans, or the heavens above that I'd ever forget that night?"

I blinked in surprise at not only his revelation but the way he'd so eloquently delivered the unexpected words. Bianca had been the writer, but maybe he'd always had a way with words, too, even if he'd never admit it. "So," I said around a swallow, "you remember."

He tapped his temple. "It lives rent-fucking-free in my head, Maria. Probably burned into the forefront of my mind for all of eternity. So yeah, I guess you can say I remember."

Taking a step back, I bumped into the rolling cart, stunned into silence.

"But I wanted to talk to you about something, and I'm not sure if you'll want to slap me or, well, kiss me for it." He held his palms between us as if to say, *Up to you.*

"Slap or kiss?" My heartbeat ramped up at the options. "What is it?"

With a contemplative look, he stroked his jawline as if forgetting it was smooth. "The reason why Thomas finally admitted he cheated was because of me."

Ah, shit. My shoulders fell at the news, and I spun away while I grappled with the information.

I flinched as his strong hands came down over my shoulders and lightly gripped them. Okay, maybe there were a few goose bumps on my skin at his touch, too. Especially because his mouth was at my ear when he said, "I've seen your pain. Your frustration. I've heard you telling Natalia how much you want to be free of him for good, and I waited too long to make it happen. I should've forced him to confess sooner."

"And you promised not to get involved." I reached back and patted one of his hands, a request to let me go. He backed away, and I took a moment to process everything before facing him. "You broke your word to me."

His head was bowed, hands on the rolling cart alongside the cake. His broad shoulders relaxed forward.

"Thomas already hates you. But like it or not, he's in my life because of shared custody." I lifted my eyes to the ceiling, trying to prevent the tears from falling. There'd probably be twenty-nine of them, too. "I don't want him making things worse for us. We're friends. Colleagues. Next-door neighbors."

"And you think I fear him?" he asked once our eyes met again.

"I know you don't fear him, but what if he—"

"If that man ever hurt you or Chiara, there'd be no mercy, Maria. No fucking mercy, and you have to know that." That harsh tone of his had chills rolling over my heated skin.

He straightened to his full height of six-three and rounded the cart to stand before me. "He lost you. Lost his perfect family because he's a fucking *idiota*, Maria. And the least he could do was be honest so you could get out of that marriage quicker. I couldn't take seeing you in pain anymore, knowing you wanted to be free of him."

While he stood tall, my shoulders shrank. I wanted to cover my face and hide from this man. A man who made me feel so many different emotions all the time, and I couldn't always make sense of them.

After my split with Thomas, I'd ridiculously hoped one day Enzo and I might have a second chance now that he lived in Charlotte and had swapped his suit for a chef's coat. "And is that what you wanted? Did you want me to be single?"

"I just want you to be happy. You're my friend, and I care about you."

Friend. I let go of a flustered breath, and he circled my forearm, unexpectedly drawing me closer. Swallowing my personal space. Something a *friend* wouldn't do. "The second I left him last year, you moved me into the apartment next to yours, and—"

"Yeah, to watch out for you and Chiara. To keep you safe."

"And did you force your neighbor to move out so I could move in the same way you forced Thomas to confess about the cheating?"

I'd been living next to Enzo in the city since the separation, only five minutes away from the home I'd shared with Thomas. Part of the agreement with Thomas was that I live nearby with our daughter.

Enzo happened to already be living in the area, and when he'd mentioned the place next to his was available, it seemed too good to be true. But it hadn't been fate, it'd been grade-A Enzo interference. He was about as frustrating when it came to my safety as my mother was regarding my love life.

"I'm just trying to protect you," was all the stubborn man would give me. Not a shocker.

"From what? Going down dark halls with strange men?" It was a joke, but he didn't seem to find me funny.

"If I have to, yes." He let go of my wrist but didn't back away. No, he was still so close it wouldn't take much for him to give me yet another birthday kiss. "Listen, I don't want to fight on your birthday."

"Then you should've waited until tomorrow to confess your guilt."

"I'm so sorry, Maria," he rasped. "You're right. I suppose I owe you a birthday do-over."

The sudden distressed look of his hurt my heart, so I admitted, "I'm relieved to be divorced earlier than expected." And of course that was the truth. "I just don't want Thomas causing any more problems for anyone because of whatever you did to convince him." No bruises on Thomas's face recently, so that was a good sign. I didn't think Enzo would hurt Chiara's father even if he wanted to, though. "I know he's not a threat to you because you're . . . you. I don't know. Thank you, I guess?"

I nervously threaded my fingers together, wondering if I ought to tell him something that'd been on my mind ever since I'd signed the divorce papers. We were already having an uncomfortable conversation, why not make it worse?

"What is it?" he asked, reading my thoughts.

"I'm going to start dating again in the near future," I shared. "At the very least, I need rebound sex." *Damn my lack of filter.* But hell, since I'd dug the hole, why not bury myself? "I've only ever been with Thomas, and I—"

"*He* took your virginity? *He* was the only one you . . ." His fingers dove into his hair as he turned toward the cake.

"It could've been you." And I'd lost count of the number of times I'd wished it had been after that hot kiss in New York. "You had rules, though."

He whirled around as if I'd insulted him. Pointing toward the floor, his gaze harsh and nearly cutting, he hissed, "If you'd been with me, you'd never have had sex with anyone else after, that I can assure you."

"You said you'd break my heart," I reminded him, and he prowled my way in two quick steps and gently snatched my chin.

"Do you really think if we'd slept together, I would've been able to walk away from you?" He didn't give me a chance to respond before sharing, "But I wasn't lying about being bad for you, and then you would've been stuck in hell with me, and I couldn't do that to you and . . ."

Another unfinished thought. More secrets he wouldn't reveal to me. And I was tired of it.

"Chiara," I whispered while closing my eyes, and he released me. "She wouldn't exist, either, and as much as I hate the choices I've made, those decisions gave me her." A tear slipped down my face, and I startled at the feel of the pad of his thumb swiping along my cheek.

"I hate that man." His rumbly tone softened when he added, "But I love her."

My chest tightened at how easily he'd admitted his love for my daughter, but I wasn't ready to look him in the eyes as I worked up the nerve to ask, "And me? Do you think you could ever feel anything for me?"

"What makes you think I didn't feel something for you while you were married?" he murmured.

I forced open my eyes. "I don't understand. For the last two years, I didn't think you even remembered our kiss, let alone felt anything for me."

"Maria." He hung his head, robbing me of the view of his gorgeous deep-brown eyes. "You were married, what'd you want me to do? I promised your father I'd protect you, that includes not breaking up your marriage."

And I was thankful for that. Respected him for it. "And what about now? I've been separated since last November, and you haven't made a single move. Don't tell me you were trying to give me time to process the divorce. I won't believe you."

He looked up and reached for me, brushing the pad of his thumb across the line of my lips, and my tongue peeked out. He went still when our eyes locked. "As much as I want to stand here and tell you I'm not the same man I was from that bar six years ago, I can't." He frowned and pulled his thumb away. "Don't let the chef's coat fool you. I still carry my past with me every day like a fucking shadow. So no, the same holds true as it did six years ago. I can't ever have what I want," he said in a solemn tone.

"But you want me?" My body was as frail as my voice right now, and I hated it.

He lifted his eyes to the ceiling and said, "The best I can do is protect you and Chiara the only way I know how."

"And you won't let me judge your past for myself? What if I'm okay with whatever you're keeping from me?" I could hear the panic rising in my voice.

"You won't be," he said without looking at me.

"My sister knows, right? She'd never let you near me if she thought you were dangerous, though."

"Natalia doesn't know everything, trust me." He stole a look at the cake, and I couldn't help but wonder if he was remembering Bianca and her love of reading. Some of my books back home had once belonged to her, and I planned to give those childhood favorites to Chiara one day.

"I hoped one day we'd . . ." *Why waste my words?* "If you truly think there's no chance for us, I don't see how I can live next door to you anymore. I should move out when the lease is up in November."

"No." Enzo abruptly reached for my hand and threaded our fingers together, tugging me his way, and I nearly crashed into his chest. "You can't leave."

"How am I supposed to move on with my life? Date again when what I want is on the other side of the apartment wall?"

That look of chaos returned to his eyes, and now I recognized it as something other than anger. An internal battle of restraint.

Tipping my head toward the rolling cart, I whispered, "Enzo . . . you can't have your cake and eat it, too." His silence only emboldened me, had me feeling the need to stand up for myself. "Promise me you won't give any man I date the third degree, then. Look me in the eyes and tell me you won't stare them down when they show up on my doorstep."

His gaze flicked to the floor between us for a few agonizing seconds. "I can only promise I won't kill any of them." His eyes returned to my face, and the dark expression there had me swallowing as he added, "Unless, of course, it's to keep you safe."

TWO

Enzo

Three Weeks Later

"I came here to work out, not to get my ass whooped." Ryan bent over, holding his abdomen. "I turned forty this year. I'm too old for this shit."

"Yeah, yeah, and I'm thirty-seven, so what?" I slapped a hand over his shoulder, urging him to stand tall, knowing he wasn't too old for anything. He'd still be running ops for DEVGRU, more commonly known as SEAL Team Six, if he hadn't been medically forced into retirement.

"You think I'd let one of my best friends marry a guy who wasn't tough enough to go up against me?" *That* had him upright fast.

"Oh, you *let* Talia marry me, huh? Is that right?"

"That's right." A sly grin slid across my lips, one I hoped would lure my friend into raising his gloves again. I needed to relieve some tension, and since I couldn't do the one thing I wanted to do, I needed to hit something.

Ryan let go of his side, still a little breathless, since we'd been sparring for nearly an hour. "I know what you're trying to do, and it's not going to work." He pointed to the punching bag to our left. "Beat the bag up instead of me. My wife will have both of our heads if we keep at it and I come home with bruises."

I looked around the mostly empty boxing gym. It was Monday evening, and one of the nights the restaurant was closed during the week. I always went a little stir-crazy when I wasn't working. I needed to be doing something with my hands, or I'd wind up . . .

I let go of those thoughts and surrendered, heading for the heavy-weight bag. "Fine."

"Does your stress have anything to do with the fact Maria is going on a date tonight?" he asked once opposite the black bag.

I went still at Ryan's words, and he closed one eye as if preparing for a swing to the face. "She's what?"

"Maybe I wasn't supposed to tell you that?" He snatched the sides of the bag and tipped his head, a request to pound it and not him.

I made a come-hither motion, shaking my head. "Too late. Details. Now."

Maria had told me three weeks ago on her birthday that she had planned to date again, but she hadn't brought up that she *was* dating again. I'd hoped a lot more time would pass before the dreaded day came.

Ryan's shoulders fell, and he let go of the bag. "Talia's gonna have my head anyway, I see." He dragged his gloved hand over his bearded jawline, his eyes on the mat beneath his bare feet. "Tonight is Thomas's night with Chiara, and Maria was asked out, so she said yes. I'm sorry, man. You can't expect her to wait around forever."

I let go of a gruff breath and struck the bag so hard, it nearly slammed into Ryan. He caught it between his palms and looked around it with narrowed eyes.

"I can't be with her." I flicked my wrist, a demand to release the bag so I could hit it again, but he held it hostage between his gloved palms.

"You really think you can watch her date? And what happens when she brings a guy home? You're not going to break down the door and kill the guy?"

The fact she'd been with only one man in her life and it hadn't been me made me insane. But Maria was right, and Chiara wouldn't exist if I'd crossed the line six years ago. "I promised Maria I wouldn't kill anyone."

"No cutting hands off her dates, either?" He smirked, and I knew he remembered the threat I'd made to that son of a bitch last year who'd thought it was okay to put his hands on a woman without consent.

"I wouldn't have *actually* cut off his hands." *Well, probably not.*

Ryan's smile dissolved, turning into a solemn look. "Clearly, you're worried about your past. But I know whatever happened in New York that you *haven't* shared with me can't be dangerous. You'd never have risked coming to Charlotte in the first place if it were. You wouldn't work at Talia's or live next door to Maria if being near you threatened them."

No, my past wasn't dangerous. I wasn't one to leave loose ends. Ryan was right, I'd never jeopardize their safety if I thought I was a risk to be around.

"Don't do what I did and wait too long. Life is short." He released the bag and began removing his gloves, letting me know he was done. "If you're worried about starting a relationship with secrets, then tell her the truth. See how she reacts."

"She doesn't need to know I have blood on my hands," I said in a low voice, referring to one of the things Ryan did know about, the fact my brothers and I killed the man who'd murdered Bianca. Where the justice system had failed my sister, we'd vowed not to. "And there's more to it than that. I just . . ."

"Just what?" Ryan tossed his gloves in his gym bag as a text on my Apple Watch popped up.

Maria: I need to see you. Can you come over?

"It's Maria," I shared as he pulled his shirt over his head. "She needs me."

"She *does* need you. And I hope you come to your senses soon and realize you *are* good enough for her." Ryan patted me twice on the shoulder. "Go. I'll see you later."

I removed my gloves and grabbed a tee from my bag, covering my sweaty chest. "Tell Talia hey, and thanks for taking the, uh, beating today." I smirked.

"Just glad you found out about the dating news after we stopped sparring." He jerked a thumb over his shoulder, telling me to get a move on.

We bumped fists as our goodbye, and once my sneakers were on, I grabbed my phone, slung my bag over my shoulder, and started home.

I sent a group text to my brothers, hoping one of them would calm me down before I faced the little hellion who drove me nuts.

Me: She's going on a date. How do I stop this? My trigger finger is fucking itchy.
Alessandro: You forced us into retirement, remember?

Alessandro was always there for me no matter what he was doing, or "who" he was doing, and I appreciated that. The same was true for Constantine.

Constantine: We made a deal. We all agreed. Don't blame him.
Constantine: Ask Maria out. Make Mom happy. Have babies. Live the good life, brother.
Alessandro: Sure, sure. Do what Boss Man says. But if not, I'll help you dispose of her date's body. Your choice.

I shook my head at their responses, allowing them to continue in the conversation without me.

Constantine: Don't listen to him.

I swiped my key fob to enter my apartment complex and went inside. It wasn't too fancy of a place. No lobby with a security guard, and now that Maria was living next door, I was beginning to wonder if I needed to upgrade our location. Tap into some of the money I told myself I wouldn't touch to get a more secure place and then somehow not let her know the actual cost.

Alessandro: Watch her with another man the way you had to do with Thomas? Genius idea. Your control has its limits, bro. You've waited long enough. You're bound to snap soon.

I finally joined their exchange because he'd struck a nerve on purpose.

Me: What choice did I have? She was married.
Constantine: And she's not now. WTF is wrong with you?
Me: You know my problem. ALL of our problems. What we've done . . .
Constantine: Was exactly what needed to be done. And you know that.
Alessandro: If you're not going to make a move, then I'm going to get back to the two women who are having too much fun without me right now.
Constantine: THAT'S why you bailed on this important dinner meeting I'm now handling alone? Get your ass here PRONTO.
Alessandro: Easy with the caps, bro. One of the three of us needs to get laid.

I laughed as I stepped into the elevator. They'd never change. I missed them, though. And at least I felt a bit calmer now before I faced Maria.

Me: I'll leave you two to argue. Later.

I pocketed my phone and stepped onto our floor a moment later. We had the only two apartments on our level, and yeah, luck had nothing to do with the fact my neighbor abruptly moved out last November, freeing the place for Maria.

I knocked and rang the bell. After no answer, I checked the door handle, which was locked.

Good girl. I grabbed my keys from the gym bag and used the key she'd given me to let myself in.

"Maria?" I dropped my bag in the foyer and went into the living room in search of her.

The bedroom door was open, so I poked my head in, surprised to see Chiara on the bed, since it was her father's night with her.

Chiara's eyes widened as she let go of her favorite stuffed animal. She opened her arms and stood but lost her balance and fell back. "I thought you were with your dad, silly?"

"Enzo!" Maria exclaimed on my way to get Chiara, and I turned to see her exiting her bathroom in only black jeans and a lacy bra, and her tits were trying to escape the damn thing. *Fuck.* "Chiara spilled her juice on me while I was getting ready. I didn't hear you ring, sorry."

"Getting ready for your date?" I let go of a frustrated breath, tense all over again at the fact she had on such a sexy bra for her date. Did that mean she hoped someone would see it?

Maria's brows lifted in surprise. "Who told you?"

"Maybe cover up before we talk?" I rasped, my voice a bit harsh, but she was testing my patience.

She didn't pin her arms to her chest to hide her body as she walked closer to me, and a gorgeous smile slid across her red lips.

"Maria," I hissed, and I turned and reached for Chiara.

I'd accidentally seen Maria in a bra twice while she'd been married. This was by far the most memorable, since she was single and I didn't have to feel guilty about eyeing another man's wife's breasts. Of course, her husband had been an ass, so I'd never felt that bad about seeing her in a bra back then. I'd only been upset that I couldn't swipe the pad of my thumb along the underside of her breast before placing her nipple between my teeth.

Chiara cupped my cheeks and smushed my lips, and my heart dropped like it always did when she exclaimed, "Dah-dah."

I wish, sweetheart. I sighed and faced the storm coming. My Maria. And she'd always been mine, even when she was with Thomas. She owned my mind, heart, and soul. My fucking everything. I just couldn't be with her for reasons I had no clue how to explain.

"Has she called you that before?" She lifted her perfectly shaped brows in question as she buttoned up a silky gold blouse, thankfully hiding her breasts before Chiara witnessed my control snap.

I looked back at Chiara and tried to talk, but she kept squishing my lips, so I nodded my answer. *A few times.*

Maria retreated to the bathroom, presumably to finish getting ready. And I peered at her adorable daughter, shifting Chiara's shoulder-length dark hair away from her face. She had the same dark mass of curly hair as Maria, but Maria's was often styled to be wavier instead. Her ex used to make her straighten it, though, and . . .

I sat on the bed, trying to discard my anger toward Chiara's real "dah-dah" for being such a horrible human being. But the dark, shitty side of me was secretly glad he hadn't been husband of the year. Because if he had, he'd still be with Maria right now. And Alessandro was right, my self-control had its limits. Maria may have been married when I moved here, but her eyes and the way she'd always looked at me betrayed her secret. Her eyes weren't just a window to her soul. They were a mirror of my own thoughts and desires.

And fuck, I didn't just want this woman, I craved her. Needed her like fire needed oxygen. But if I had her, then I'd do what fire did best—ravage and consume her. And then I'd ruin her life, because ruining lives was what I was good at. And *that* was why I was so hell-bent on not giving in to what we both so desperately longed for even though she was now single.

But Alessandro was right, I'd barely survived her relationship with Thomas. How would I handle someone new?

"I'm crazy, huh?" I asked Chiara in a soft voice while holding her little fingers, and she giggled her answer, as if saying, *Yes, you are.* I bounced my leg up and down like I knew she loved as Maria opened the bathroom door.

She folded her arms and leaned into the interior frame, and I took a moment to study her. Her hair was like a bed of silky waves that stopped just shy of her belly button. She wasn't tall or short, about five-six, but in her heels right now, she was tall enough that if I fisted her thick hair and pulled, I could slant my mouth over hers without too much effort.

Her light-brown eyes and long lashes beneath those dark brows always did a number on me. And I could feel her gaze piercing me, so I gave her my attention and did my best not to imagine her on her knees looking up at me with hooded eyes.

"Were you working out when I texted?" I lost sight of her brown irises for a moment as she peered at Chiara bouncing on my thigh.

"I was sparring with Ryan, yeah. We were just finishing up."

"So he told you about my date tonight?"

I nodded, and this news had her straightening, relaxing her arms at her sides as she crossed into the room as if delicately stepping over the invisible line that I'd done my best to maintain between us.

"Never offer yourself to me again," I remembered telling her six years ago, and I'd meant every ugly word. If she wanted a happy life, untainted by the likes of me, then it was best if she never let me have her. Because I *also* meant what I told her three weeks ago, if she were to ever be mine, there wasn't a chance in hell she'd ever be with anyone else. "I thought she was staying with Thomas tonight?" I steered my focus to the issue at hand—her dating someone. "What happened?"

"He had a work thing run late, so he bailed on me." She frowned. "I was hoping you could watch Chiara." At her words, she took her from me.

"You're asking me to watch her while you're on a date?" I slowly stood, and I was wrong, I *still* towered over her, even in her heels. "It's only been five weeks since you've been divorced, maybe you should wait?"

She looked up at me with a stubborn lift of her chin. "And it's been forever since a man has touched me." She flicked her wrist, and her bangle bracelets jangled together.

Yeah, well, I wish no man other than me had ever touched you. And if Chiara wasn't wedged between us, I'd allow my thoughts to turn dark. To picture this woman with her long legs over my shoulders, her heels digging into my back, and those bracelets clinking together, as I plunged in and out of her.

"Dating, are you sure that's what you really want to do? Maybe give those dance lessons a try again?" I suggested.

Last month, she'd taken dance lessons and quit. The month prior, she'd taken a few real-estate classes. She'd been on a quest to find a new passion in her life ever since singledom, and I was all for her doing that. But did dating have to be next on her Things to Try list, as she called it?

"I sucked at dance lessons, and you accidentally walked in on me practicing and nearly fell on your ass laughing. These Italian hips just don't move like they should."

"Oh, I bet they do," I blurted, forgetting myself for a second, and she bit her lip at my suggestive words. *Shit. Fucking. Hell.*

Maria innocently tipped one shoulder as she shared, "I love being a mother, you know that. And running Natalia's catering business is great. But I feel like there's this void inside me still. I've been searching for my thing for years, and I haven't found it."

"A 'thing,' huh?" I poked back in a teasing tone. "Tell me more about this thing you need."

Maria rolled her eyes. "Be serious."

"I am." *Now I am, at least.* Because if finding a new man was going to be her "thing," I'd more than likely lose my mind.

"In the meantime, while I figure myself out, why not have some fun, you know?" There went her other shoulder. A not-so-innocent lift this time because she'd followed it with the word *fun* in relation to dating. "I need to get back on the horse, as the saying goes."

The blood drained from my face. "I don't want to think about you on any horses. Literal or metaphorical."

"No?" Her lips twitched as if fighting a smile.

Did she find me funny? I was serious, dammit. I crowded her personal space even more, but she didn't back away. "You could break your neck riding a real horse."

"And the other kind?" Oh, she was trying to get a rise out of me.

My little fireball. "Someone else's neck will get broken," I shared in a steady voice, letting her know I wasn't joking.

"And you promised you'd behave when I started dating."

She still thought I was joking. I hadn't made myself clear, had I? But she didn't know about my past, so why would she take me seriously? "I promised I wouldn't"—I looked at her sweet daughter, not wanting to discuss murder in front of her—"put your date six feet under." *I said nothing about breaking bones.*

"You'd never really hurt anyone. You're all talk. You might look like some tough guy, but I see how you are with my daughter. You're a softy."

I stepped back and pointed to Chiara in her arms, my heart pounding. "For her, I'm who she needs me to be."

"And who is that, exactly?" She lifted her chin, not backing down from her stubbornness to always press my buttons. She'd been relentless in pushing me to my limits since her birthday, ever since I opened my big mouth and admitted the truth, that I wanted her.

"Her friend. Her protector," I said in a hoarse voice, dying to add *father* to that list.

"And tonight, her babysitter?"

This is a test, isn't it? And if I failed, she'd move out in November. If I didn't prove I could handle this, I'd lose her for good, I could feel it in my bones. But my dumb ass blurted, "So you can get laid?"

"Baby ears," she snapped out. "And it's just dinner."

My gaze fell to her chest, partially hidden by her squirmy daughter playing with her bracelets. "Then why the sexy bra if no one will see it?"

"You saw it," she remarked, and when I looked at her, I saw the stain of embarrassment on her cheeks, as if she hadn't meant to verbalize that thought.

"Dah-dah." Chiara extended her arms for me, and Maria hesitantly handed her back.

"Who is he?" I asked, doing my best to maintain my control, knowing it was becoming increasingly impossible to do.

She fixed her bracelets in place, keeping her eyes away from me as she answered, "I met him at a catering job last week. It was for his company. We were talking while I was there, and he asked me for my number. We've been texting this past week, and tonight we're going to dinner. And since I don't have another night off until next weekend, I don't want to cancel at the last minute, and I—"

"This man ate my food? *And* you've been texting?" My stomach dropped, all the way down to the seventh circle of hell where the soul of Bianca's murderer lived for all of eternity.

"Enzo, you wanted to just be my friend, so be my friend. Okay? Prove to me we really can make this work."

Friend. I repeated the word a few more times in my head, trying to digest it. My idea or not, I hated the thought of just being her friend.

My chin went to the top of Chiara's head as I mulled over how to communicate my desire for her to stay home and never date again. Had I really boxed myself into a new kind of hell, one where I watched her fall in love with someone else?

"What's his name?" My heart was beating so fast, the hard snaps of sound traveled to my ears.

"I'm not giving you details. Let's take it one step at a time."

A dark laugh fell from my lips, one that let her know not to test me. "You think I'm letting you walk out the door without knowing you're safe first?"

"He's safe. You wouldn't have let me cater his office party if he wasn't, right?" she chided, taking Chiara from me while letting out a heavy sigh. "Forget it, I'll find someone else to watch her tonight."

What do I do? I gave her my back, cupping my mouth as I played out the possibilities. If I told her to choose me instead of this corporate dickhead, I'd be lying. Because I wasn't an option. *I'm not a choice.*

I looked down at the ink on my right arm. Good versus evil battled on my skin, and it was a reminder of how I'd spent years taking on the role of judge, juror, and executioner on more than one occasion.

My fingers curled into my palm as I tried to reclaim my sense of control that waned every second we were alone. "Fine," I relented, facing her. "I'll watch Chiara. Go on your date."

She peered at me with curious eyes, as if worried she was walking into a trap. Maybe she was? I wasn't exactly thinking clearly. "Okay, well, I'm meeting him downstairs in ten minutes, and you're sweaty. Maybe shower first?"

"He's not coming to the door?"

"So you can give him the third degree?" She faked a laugh. "No, like hell am I letting him come up here." She waved her hand like a directive. "Go. Shower. And then come back to me." Her tongue flicked between her lips for a quick second, and I wanted to catch it with mine. "Come back here, I mean. Please."

I studied the two of them for a few agonizing seconds, then stalked away from her, hating myself for allowing this moment to happen. But once in the living room, I stopped in my tracks at the sight of the bookshelf, and memories peeled open in my mind.

One of Bianca on her favorite swing at our family home in Long Island with a book on her lap and a bright smile.

Another memory of one of her handwritten letters she'd sent while I'd been deployed. She'd hated emails, preferring the personal touch of ink to paper.

My stomach tightened as I thought back to a few weeks before she'd been viciously killed, when she sent me a selfie holding up a magazine, which housed her first published piece of fiction.

"Technically, it's mostly nonfiction," she'd told me. "In part, a real-life love story. But no one needs to know that." I never did have a chance to ask her whose love story it'd been, because she was murdered.

I closed my eyes at the last memory. Her gravestone. Rest in Peace. My brothers and I knew she'd never have peace if her killer walked the earth. Since the justice system failed to do its part, we'd had no choice but to handle it ourselves.

"You okay?" Maria asked from behind, catching me by surprise.

I opened my eyes, glanced over my shoulder to quietly nod my lie, then left.

Once at my place, I quickly showered and changed. I put on gray sweats, slipped into a pair of kicks, then snatched a white tee from the dryer, since I'd yet to put away my laundry. Hiding my wet hair with a backward ball cap, I returned to Maria's so she could go on her date. *Kill me now.*

Maria was waiting in the living room with Chiara on her lap. Her eyes went to my crotch, and her lips flatlined.

"What?" I looked down, checking to ensure I wasn't hard, and the fact she was going on a date had me about as limp as possible, so no, that wasn't it.

"Gray sweats. Backward hat." She wedged her lip between her teeth and stood. "You do that on purpose?"

"Do what on purpose?" I had no clue what she was talking about, but if my pants and hat were the cause of her doing that sexy thing with her lip, sign me the fuck up, I'd do it every damn day.

"She's been having trouble falling asleep lately," Maria said instead while handing over Chiara.

"I know, you've barely slept in weeks."

"No rocking her to sleep. Just put her in the crib with Stuffy, her favorite bear, and leave the door cracked. I know it'll be hard, but she'll fall asleep after crying a bit."

Watch Chiara beg for me and not pick her up? Ha. No chance. "Sure." Another lie. I was on a roll tonight. "Can I at least know where you're going to dinner? Time you think you'll be home?"

Maria leaned in and kissed Chiara while gently giving her a small squeeze. "Do you plan to come spy on us? You do have a car seat in your Tahoe, so you can't blame me for worrying."

I'd traded my Porsche last year to help Natalia keep the restaurant afloat. I could've easily accessed the millions in my savings account or the money stashed in my safe, but part of my promise to myself to try and change when moving to Charlotte was making it on my own without my family's money.

"I'm not taking your daughter out at night to spy on you, no," I said, trying to reassure her, though it wasn't that crazy of an idea. "So, restaurant name? Time?"

"He didn't tell me where he was taking me. He knows I love sushi, though. And the time? I don't know. I guess it depends on if . . ."

Yeah, I didn't need her to finish that sentence, and she must've noticed I wasn't capable of hearing more.

"Listen, I appreciate you doing this, and I know it's awkward, but maybe this is what we need to happen so we can be certain living next door to one another is something we can keep doing." She paused. "I'm sure you've had women over, but you've been good at—"

"No." I shook my head, and Chiara was the only separation between us now as I stared at her. "And you won't see it, Maria." That was a promise I could easily uphold.

She swallowed at my clipped confession, then looked at Chiara, and I'd swear her eyes were glossy. "Have fun, baby girl."

"Be safe," I forced out, trying to maintain my cool. Having Chiara in my arms was all that was saving me from going downstairs and yanking this new guy from his car to ask him fifty questions.

"Okay," she whispered, then pinched Chiara's cheek.

Then that dark part of me I couldn't contain snapped out. "If I find out he touched you"—I wanted to leave it at that, but I reluctantly growled out—"without your permission . . ."

"I know, I know." Her brows tightened. "A broken something-or-other."

"And, Maria," I added as she turned, so she stole a look back from over her shoulder. "You look beautiful."

She frowned at that for whatever reason, then crushed me as she walked out the door.

I looked at Chiara. "I shouldn't have let her go, right?"

"Mmmm." She smiled and said, "Love you," which sounded more like, "Wuv u."

Fuck. I drew her closer, situating her at my side, and walked us over to the window.

Chiara set her hand on the glass and tapped when she saw her mom exiting the building, heading for a BMW out front waiting.

Maria must've sensed us, because she hesitated outside his car door and looked up.

The prick didn't even get out to open the door. What in God's name was wrong with him?

Maria waved, presumably at Chiara, then slid inside the passenger door.

My stomach dropped as I watched the car pull away. "Let's go see who this guy is, okay?" I carried Chiara over to my apartment and headed straight for my office.

Maria had said he'd been one of our clients last weekend, which would narrow my search to one. I set Chiara on a blanket at the center of my office so I could find the information from the catering event on my laptop.

After locating the owner's name, I went to the painting of our family home in the Hamptons behind my desk. Swallowing hard at the memories connected to it, I removed it from the wall to access an electronic keypad.

After punching in the code, I stepped back and waited for the bookshelf on the other wall to automatically open, revealing a hidden room.

I picked up Chiara and we went inside. "This will just be our little secret, okay?" She smiled and nodded as if she understood me. "But we need to make sure Mama's really safe."

THREE

Maria

The last sight I'd expected to come home to was Enzo in my bed. The light was still on, so I could make out every adorable detail of the moment. Chiara's feet were near his face because she always twisted every which way in her sleep. Enzo's one hand was draped over her abdomen, and his other arm was bent and behind his head. He must've accidentally passed out while waiting for her to fall asleep so he could carry her to the crib.

I slipped off my heels and padded in, trying not to wake either of them. Once in the bathroom with the door shut, I got rid of my clothes and jewelry and went into the walk-in closet.

I contemplated my options for nightwear. *Do I go with cute PJs or sexy ones?* As much as I wanted to slip into something that'd catch Enzo's eye, I went with the safer option. A soft pink cotton nightshirt that went midthigh and read, COFFEE BEFORE TALKIE, which Natalia had given me for one of my recent birthday gifts.

After tossing my hair into a messy bun and scrubbing the makeup from my face, I quietly turned the knob, finding the two of them peacefully where I'd left them. Part of me wanted it to be me there instead.

Get on Enzo's other side and snuggle up next to him, have his big, strong arm over my stomach, holding me for safekeeping.

One cruel minute of watching this picture-perfect moment had my heart beating hard. I finally went to the bed and carefully lifted his heavy arm and laid his hand across his chest.

He stirred. His long, dark lashes fluttered, which had me going still. He brought his hand over the scruff on his jawline and scratched before his arm fell back to his other side.

I gave it a few more seconds to ensure he was still out, then scooped Chiara into my arms. *You wore each other out, huh?*

Once she was back in her crib, and thankfully, she'd remained asleep, I forced myself to do the inevitable, let Enzo know I'd returned, and he could leave us. Leave *me.*

I climbed onto the other side of the bed and shifted the pillows he'd set up as a barrier for Chiara, then lightly touched his arm. He jerked awake as if stunned. It was like a flash of muscle and ink flying over me, and I found myself pinned beneath his hard frame.

Enzo was breathing hard as he continued to brace himself over me. "Maria," he murmured, shaking his head as if still rousing himself from a deep sleep. "Where's Chiara?" His eyes widened in panic.

"In her crib." I touched his chest, attempting to calm whatever bit of worry I'd created for him. "I was trying to wake you."

He looked over at the old-school alarm clock on my nightstand, which was there for aesthetic only. It was twenty minutes after eleven.

"I'm surprised you slept while I was gone," I admitted, wondering if he had any plans to move, considering my pelvic bone touched his body, and if he shifted just a bit, my nightshirt might slide up, revealing my silk panties. He'd already seen the bra. Why not the matching underwear?

"Ryan texted me. He told me you ended your dinner date early and took an Uber to their place to see Natalia. He let me know he'd drive you home afterward," he explained, shifting his hips a bit, and I could feel the heavy weight of his cock resting on me.

I gulped, then whispered, "Of course he did."

"I'd never sleep if I thought you were with . . ." He cut himself off. "You could've sent me a text, you know." He arched a brow, as if guessing why I didn't.

In truth, I'd been a hot mess about going on my first date since the split with Thomas, especially since it wasn't with Enzo.

"Date not go well?"

Boring and not "heartbreaker" material, so Mom would've loved him. "He's a nice guy." *Just not you.* "I wasn't interested, though. Why waste time?" I arched my back the slightest bit, dying for him to relieve the pressure between my thighs but also knowing he'd only hang me out to dry.

"How much did you drink?" His brows slanted as he studied me.

"One glass of wine at dinner. Two with Natalia." I wasn't close to being drunk if that was his concern. Tipsy, sure.

His eyes moved to my nightshirt, and maybe my PJs weren't the "safe option," because I was still braless, and my nipples had to be poking through. There was a slight snarl to his lips, and then he rolled to the side and sat on the edge of the bed, raking his hands through his hair. He snatched his hat and situated it backward on his head before standing. "I'm going to take the monitor and sleep on the couch." He faced me, and his gaze fell to my bare legs.

"Why would you do that?" I shifted, tugging the hem of my nightshirt lower.

"You haven't slept well lately, and I'll wake up with her. You need to sleep."

"You don't need to do that." I sat and tossed my legs to the side of the bed, nearly losing my balance as I stood. He reached for my arm and kept me upright, but now we were so close that I had to look up to find his eyes.

"I know, but I am," he said in a sleepy-sexy voice.

"I don't think that's a good idea." I shook my head, searching for his eyes.

"And why's that?" His gaze narrowed slightly as he tilted his head in question.

"I can't touch myself while you're in the other room." *Oh. My. God.* Where did my filter go around him? "It'd be, um . . ."

"Why do you do this? Play with fire expecting not to get burned?" His jaw tightened as he leaned in closer, eyeing me with that swirl of chaos and desire in his hooded eyes.

Because safe is boring. Safe didn't get my heart beating faster, my sex clenching. But I wasn't about to say all that.

He stepped back, giving me a few inches of breathing room, so the last thing I expected was for him to snatch the hem of my nightshirt and peel it up to my waist.

Like a deer caught in headlights, I froze, unable to move, let alone speak. "What are you doing?" I finally managed, releasing a deep breath.

He tipped his head to the side, his eyes laser-focused on my silk panties. "I'm seeing how wet you are."

Well, I'm officially a hell of a lot wetter now. "And how can you tell only by looking?" But then I remembered my panty set had been nude, and yeah, I was soaked, which meant he could see my arousal.

"It won't take much to get off," he said matter-of-factly while letting go of my nightshirt. "I'll be on the couch while you finger fuck yourself into orgasm, and then you *will* get a good night's sleep after. Don't argue with me," he roughly added, eyes holding mine like a challenge.

"I prefer my vibrator, not my fingers, thank you very much," I bit back, angry at both his order and the fact he was so damn frustrating that he could walk away from me like this. The man had restraint like I'd never seen in my life.

"No." A dark expression crossed his face. "It'll be your hand tonight." He palmed my cheek as if he wished he was touching me somewhere else instead. Or maybe that was me?

"You can't tell me what to do," I reminded him, but that cocky smile cutting across his lips was evidence he knew I actually craved it.

I was twenty-nine and a mother, and most days I felt unsure what in the hell I was doing. And part of me missed having someone guide me. Make the decisions. Take some of the control so I could breathe for five minutes and stop worrying so much about . . . everything.

"You'll do what I say, I know you will." That unwavering confidence only turned me on more.

I had no clue why he wanted me to touch myself. What difference did it make? Well, unless he wanted me to imagine it was his hand on me, and the vibrating metal might interfere with that fantasy. "Pretty bossy for my neighbor."

"I'm damn well more than that," he offered in a low, steady voice.

"What you are is confusing." I clenched my hands at my sides, searching for the strength not to "offer" myself to him, knowing he'd probably reject me, but I was failing miserably. "The only hand I want on my body tonight is yours. So, vibrator it is."

His jaw clenched as he quietly studied me, a nearly vicious look greeting me.

"Just so you know, your restraint speaks volumes," I admitted, shoulders falling. I turned toward the bed and startled when his hands circled my waist and he pinned me against his hard frame.

With his mouth at my ear, he murmured, "If you think for one second it's not taking every ounce of my control not to fuck you right now, you're insane."

Oh God. My ass went back, pressing harder against him like an invitation to do whatever he wanted with me as long as he relieved me of the pain between my legs.

His teeth grazed my earlobe as he kept me locked in place.

"So do it," I challenged, calling his bluff.

The growl at my ear and his warm hand lifting my shirt wasn't what I'd expected, but it was what I needed. The second he slid a finger over my panties along the seam of my sex, I moaned, and my knees buckled. I winded my arm back to hook his neck, trying to draw him even closer.

He feathered his fingers over my panties one more time before he finally shoved his hand down them and touched my smooth sex.

He squeezed my breast with his other hand while roughly pushing two fingers inside me. "Is that what you want? You want to see me lose control?" He was angry, but he wasn't stopping. He wasn't backing down. "God, you're so wet." His hand went still when he asked, "You wanted to make me jealous tonight, didn't you?" His breath fanned over the sensitive part of my ear, causing chills to coat my body.

"No," I whispered as he moved his thumb over the sensitive part of my sex.

"Don't lie to me."

I kept hold of the back of his neck so my legs wouldn't collapse as I shared, "Yes." I peeled my eyes open to look down at his inked arm holding me against him, and he resumed touching me.

"Come for me. Now, Maria," he demanded. "I can't break another rule. I can't fuck you while you've been drinking, and I'm two seconds away from bending you over and showing you how much restraint I clearly *don't* have when it comes to you."

At his words, I rode the heel of his palm as he pumped his fingers in and out of me, and I moved my ass in circles, grinding against his cock as he squeezed my tit nearly to the point of pain.

"That's it," he said into my ear. "Be a good girl and come for me." He nuzzled my neck and lightly nipped my earlobe again.

At his command, my body shuddered, my stomach muscles tightened, and a wave of euphoria tore through me. I bent forward, my arm falling from his neck as I surrendered to the last bit of ecstasy.

I was tender and sensitive as he continued touching me after I'd orgasmed, as if he couldn't stop himself and never wanted to.

When he decided to let me go, I turned to face him, and his dark eyes locked on to mine. He dragged his two fingers beneath his nose as his tongue slipped between his lips. Smelling me. Tasting me.

"Now go to bed," he demanded a moment later, and I lowered my focus to the bulge in his gray sweats. "No," he snapped out. "You drank, and I've already lost my damn mind tonight." He closed the space between us, a fierce look in his eyes. A request not to challenge him this time.

For whatever reason, I did what he told me and got into bed beneath the silvery-gray comforter.

He set a hand by me and bent forward, brushing away the runaway strands that'd escaped my messy bun; then he surprised me by tenderly kissing my forehead.

When he lifted his head, his brown eyes met mine, and instead of kissing me like I hoped, he whispered, "We'll talk about what happened over breakfast," and then he stood and left, taking the monitor with him as promised.

He shot me one last look, hit the light switch, then gently closed the door.

How could I possibly fall asleep after that? Tonight had gone from a failed date to one of the most erotic moments of my life. And the part that crushed me, that stole the chance of a restful sleep . . . was knowing this stubborn man would never let it happen again.

FOUR

Maria

Six thirty? Had I really managed to sleep? I reached for my phone to text Natalia, which was my morning ritual since splitting with Thomas. But I wasn't sure how to start my message. A lot had happened to unpack.

And Enzo touching me, holding me close to him with his mouth at my ear last night, had met my needs when dance, real-estate classes, tai chi, and that date last night hadn't come close to doing it.

Me: Enzo spent the night.

The littles dots popped up, then disappeared a few times. My sister was probably flustered, but I knew she'd be awake. The little man in her tummy kept her up as much as Chiara's sleep issues did for me.

Natalia: That's not what I was expecting for my first text of the day.
Natalia: And this convo demands a phone call.
Me: He slept on the couch insisting he help with Chiara since I haven't been sleeping well.
Natalia: When will he ever realize he's not the villain in the story?

I was starting to wonder if there was a fine line between the classic idea of what it meant to be the villain and hero. My limited-to-fiction knowledge was being shaken up and redefined every moment alone I spent with Enzo. Because if he really was the antihero, as he saw himself, what'd that make me for still desperately wanting him?

Natalia: You need to talk to him. Maybe he'll finally open up?
Me: Yeah, I don't know. I guess I should go face the music, though. See if they're awake. Talk tonight at work?
Natalia: Of course. Love you.
Me: Love you, too.

I tossed the phone onto the bed and went into the bathroom to brush my teeth and cover my flimsy nightshirt with a robe.

I caught sight of my tired eyes in the mirror, and visions of last night cut through my mind. My hand wandered down the length of my abdomen as I remembered his hand between my thighs.

"What are you doing to me?" I whispered, then shook my head and finally went in search of the mystery man.

The living room was empty, but his hat was on the couch. He had to be with Chiara, so I went down the hall to her room and gently opened the door, my heart colliding with my rib cage at the sight before me.

Enzo was asleep on the floor by the crib with his muscular, inked arm stretched out. His hand was wedged between the thin slats of wood, and I stepped closer and confirmed my little girl had her hand wrapped around his finger.

And that sight right there . . . was a void-filler for sure. Because my heart had never felt so full at the image.

He really did love Chiara, and I didn't know how to put into words what that meant to me.

I finally peeled myself away from the room, deciding I'd cook for Enzo for a change and make breakfast.

Once in the kitchen, I grabbed what I needed for an omelet and began chopping a bell pepper but flinched at the feel of a hand skimming my silhouette before going to my hip.

"Enzo," I whispered, my eyes closing at the feel of his cock twitching against my backside.

He brought his mouth to my ear and in a husky voice asked, "Did you sleep well?"

I leaned into him, letting go of the bell pepper and knife. "Better than you, I think. You didn't need to sleep on the floor."

"I can't say no to her, and you know that." He abruptly spun me around, and my eyes flashed open as his palms landed on the counter.

"You're so good at saying no to me, though," I reminded him as his gaze lowered to my pink robe.

"I didn't last night, did I?" He kept his eyes on my body as he added with a slight smirk, "Are you cold, or do you not want me to see your nipples poke through that flimsy shirt again? Are you trying to behave?"

Holy hell. From zero to sixty this morning? I had been prepared for a different Enzo when he woke up. One who'd act like yesterday never happened and it'd been a mistake. "I, um." I swallowed when his eyes journeyed back to my face. "Do you want me to behave?"

He cocked his head as if torn on how to answer that, but I could read the desire written into every line of his face. It'd been there for the last two years, I'd just been living in the land of disbelief so I wasn't unfaithful to a man who never truly had my heart. And it was easy to understand that now, when the man standing before me so clearly owned it.

I reached up and ran a hand through his messy hair. There was just enough to grab hold of, and he angled his head a touch, as if enjoying my fingers running across his scalp. "Maybe you like it when I'm bad, though?"

He lifted his hands from the counter to untie my robe. "I don't know what to do with you," he said in a low, conflicted voice. "I made up my mind last night that there'd be no more repeats of what happened, and then I walked out here and saw you and . . ."

I let go of his hair, searching for his gaze, but he had his eyes down, hidden from me. "And what?" My nipples poked through the fabric as they went hard, and he shifted the robe from my shoulders and pushed it back so it fell to the floor.

"Now all I can think about is making you come, but this time while you sit on my face," he said in a soft tone, almost as if he'd lost whatever interior battle he'd been fighting and was giving in.

His eyes closed, and that harsh line of his lips told a different story. He was *still* resisting. It was a warning to me not to get my hopes up. His hands turned to fists and swooped back alongside me, going to the counter once again to trap me.

He let go of a deep breath and finally looked at me. "Maria, I—" He dropped his words when the bell rang, and his gaze snapped toward the foyer. "Who in the hell would be at your door this early?"

My phone was on silent in the other room. My Apple Watch charging by the bed. If someone had called while I was in the kitchen with my sexy chef, I'd have missed it.

Our "almost a moment" was effectively disrupted, and Enzo went to the door.

I hurried after him, and my body went cold when he swung it open, seeing Thomas there.

My ex had on one of his expensive Tom Ford suits, which was tailored to fit his tall and lean frame. The man had always taken care of himself. Worked out four times a week. Meal prepped. And styled his light-brown hair in just a way to give him a magazine-cover-ready look. He kept his beard trimmed and always smelled nice. He was classically handsome and a little too perfect. He'd always made sure I knew that I wasn't during our marriage.

I self-consciously flung my arms over my chest when I remembered what I was wearing, worried Thomas would see through the flimsy material, and he lost his right to see me when he stuck his tongue between another woman's legs.

"I knew it." Those three words ripped from somewhere deep in Thomas's chest. Words he'd been saving, ready to throw at me. "That's why she wanted the divorce. You're fucking my wife."

I didn't make it two steps before Thomas snapped out a punch, but Enzo snatched his hand before contact was made, and he simply held Thomas's fist in the air like it were a fly he'd caught. "*Ex*-wife," Enzo seethed. "And the only reason I'm not putting you on your ass right now is because your daughter is asleep in the other room."

I touched Enzo's back, hoping to calm him before his control actually did snap. "What are you doing here?"

Thomas had to look around Enzo to put eyes on me. He jerked his hand away and answered, "I've been calling to let you know I was on my way to get Chiara, but it looks like you were busy."

"What do you mean you're here for Chiara?" Noticing Thomas's eyes laser-focused on my breasts, I quickly returned my arms over my chest.

And when Enzo turned to the side and peered at me, his brows slanted in anger, clearly not wanting Thomas to see me, either.

"My mom had a heart attack, and she wants to see her granddaughter," Thomas finally remarked.

"Your robe," Enzo gruffly stated, ignoring Thomas's words.

I wasn't one to obey orders, but I didn't want any blood spilled on my floors, and I had the distinct feeling Enzo might actually lose his mind if Thomas continued to admire my body. And why in the world was he checking me out now? Desire had been absent from his gaze long before our marriage had ended.

"Is your mother okay?" I finally asked, shaking away my thoughts, and then I motioned for him to follow me. I needed a robe, so it would seem.

Enzo shot his muscular arm out, stopping Thomas. "Give her a moment to cover up," he nearly snarled, lifting his chin as if saying, *Don't think about arguing.*

Thomas scowled, apparently in no mood to cower to the intimidating man today like he'd done in the past. Not that I cared, but he'd grown a pair since we'd split. "My mom will be okay," he finally answered, eyes back on me. "She's being discharged from the ER, but I'm taking off work to visit, and I'm bringing Chiara with me."

My arms fell weakly to my sides at the idea of this man taking my daughter away on a trip without me. Enzo shot me daggers, then hissed something in Italian, and before I knew it, he hurried past me and returned within seconds with my robe in hand. *Bossy, bossy.*

"My parents live an hour away. It's not like I'm taking her out of the country. But part of the divorce arrangement is that I get to go on two trips with her a year to see my family. And, well, it's happening now." Thomas's angry stare bounced between Enzo and me as if daring me to challenge him on this *or else.*

"I need time. I can't just . . ." I slipped on the robe and tied the belt, and Enzo seemed to breathe again.

"It's her grandmother. I know you never liked my mom, but this isn't about you, is it?" Thomas snapped.

"Your mom hates me. Hated us together," I reminded him. "God, the number of times she complained I wasn't good enough. Too curvy. Too—"

"Looks like the divorce helped you drop a few pounds," Thomas noted, his eyes moving over my body yet again, probably to piss off Enzo. Such a bad idea. "Though it seems you kept the curves where they matter."

Enzo had Thomas against the wall within a second, a forearm to his windpipe. "Go ahead," Enzo challenged in an eerily low voice, "say that again."

Thomas gripped Enzo's forearm, struggling to breathe. He searched for help from me, but he'd been the idiot to goad a man like Enzo.

Reluctantly, I decided to save him. "Enzo." I grabbed his shoulder and yanked. "Stop."

Enzo's shoulders fell, and he finally released him.

Thomas circled a hand around his throat as if mortified at what had happened. "I'm taking Chiara with me. Don't make me get the lawyers involved," Thomas declared, and that threat was the real knife to the heart. That was the last thing in the world I wanted.

"How many days?" I'd never been away from her for more than forty-eight hours. He had her only two weekends a month. And it was always hell, those forty-eight or so hours.

"As long as nothing critical with work pops up, I'll be there until Sunday." He adjusted the cuffs of his suit jacket and squared his shoulders, as if trying to regain some of his manhood that Enzo had stolen.

But wait. Sunday? Today was Tuesday. *Ohhh hell no.* "Thomas, I understand it's part of our arrangement, but that's a long trip. And I don't feel comfortable with this."

"Well, you have an hour to get comfortable with it, because that's when I'm leaving, and Chiara's coming with me." Thomas turned and shot me a look from over his shoulder. "Bring her to my place by eight, or I'm calling the lawyers, and you'll be the one with trip restraints." He snarled as he headed for the door, and I tried to process everything that'd just happened. Was he really threatening me?

"Tell me what you want me to do." Enzo gently held both my arms, urging me to look at him after the door closed. "Tell me, and I'll do it."

I wasn't sure what he was asking, but it felt like he was suggesting he could "handle" my ex for me in a way that wouldn't involve lawyers. Chills crept up my spine at the thought. But he wouldn't really . . . would he?

My lower lip quivered as his gaze met mine. "Your past really is dark, isn't it?" I whispered as recognition dawned on me. "And I don't mean from your time in the army."

He let go of me and tapped a fist against his lips twice, as if grappling with what to say.

"Dark as in dark-dark?" I couldn't even ask the real question burning hot through my mind. I'd be naive to think he'd never taken a life while in uniform, but had he taken one outside the army?

"The irredeemable kind of dark, Maria," he returned in a low voice, and his pained expression as he stared at me was an answer in itself.

"You killed Bianca's murderer." It was no longer a question occupying that back corner of my mind. It was now a fact. One scribed in blood.

But that meant someone rewrote the history of what happened to her killer, then, right?

His brows slanted over his guilt-filled eyes. But nothing came from his parted lips.

I drew my palm from my collarbone down to my stomach, trying to quell the flutter of nerves unleashing hell there. "I thought karma killed that man." My voice cracked with disbelief. "I remember my parents telling me Bianca's killer had been in a car accident, and he drowned in the Hudson." I waited for Enzo to say something. *Anything.* But he kept quiet, so I went on. "Did you cut his brakes? How'd you do it?"

He dipped his head, catching my eyes, and with grit to his tone, he rasped, "Don't ask questions you're not prepared to have answered." His Adam's apple rolled with a harsh swallow. "Let. It. Go."

"Enzo, please, I need to know if—"

"Yes," he nearly snarled, his nostrils flaring. "I killed him. And I'd do it again in a heartbeat. I don't regret it, not for one second."

"And if Thomas ever hurt me, you really meant what you said on my birthday?" My gaze landed on the words inked beneath the sword on his forearm. "No mercy?"

He nodded, his jaw tightening beneath his dark stubble. "And, Maria?" He gently held my chin. "When it comes to that man . . . I'd enjoy every fucking minute of it," he murmured darkly.

FIVE

Enzo

"I call bullshit. You're trying to scare me. Push me away." Maria's cara-mel-brown eyes glossed over with emotion as she shoved at my chest, but I didn't budge.

I captured her wrists, wet my lips, and prepared to deliver her the ugly words she needed to hear. "If Thomas ever hurt you, you don't think I'd do the same to him as I did to the man who murdered my sister?"

And no, I hadn't cut his brakes. I cut his fucking heart out.

Lacing her fingers with mine, I lowered our hands, holding them at our sides. "The problem is, I'd love nothing more than to break every bone in that man's body just for breathing the same air as you." I leaned in, my eyes still locked on hers. "But . . ."

"He's Chiara's father, you wouldn't do it. You know if you hurt him, it'll hurt her in the long run. Also, you're not a monster, Enzo."

I *was* a monster. And I really would end that man if he ever hurt Maria or Chiara. I'd come close to choking the life from him this morn-ing, too.

Maria adamantly shook her head, as if disagreeing with my unspo-ken thoughts; then she pulled her hands free from my grasp and swiped at the messy strands of hair by her face.

How in the hell was she not walking away from me after what she'd learned? I'd given her a glimmer of the truth, a peek at the darkness inside me, and here she was still rooted in place.

"I wish you would stop trying to keep this wall up between us." A soft sigh left her beautiful mouth. "Just admit it—you're scared to feel something for me."

"I already feel something, *Tesoro*," I shared, even if I shouldn't have.

"*Tesoro?*"

Tesoro, my nickname for her. And until now, I'd only ever called her that in my head. She wasn't a material object, but she was precious. Rare. Someone I'd always value, and, well—"Treasure," I revealed, finishing my thoughts aloud. I set my hands on my hips and bowed my head and, before she could respond, roughly added, "Do you have any idea how close I am to hauling your ass to the bedroom and fucking you so hard you call out to God to come save you from me, *il diavolo*?" I looked up at her, angry at myself for sharing more, for giving her hope only minutes after she learned I was a killer.

She dragged her fingers across her lips as the color rose in her cheeks. And then my little fireball said in a steady voice, "The devil doesn't sleep on the floor next to a crib, nor would he stop himself from taking what he wanted, would he?" Her hand planted on my chest, and I lowered my eyes to her touch. "So, like I said, I call bullshit."

My breathing intensified as the blood rushed south, and all I wanted to do right now was take this woman and make her mine in every possible way.

When I remained quiet, she said in a softer tone, "You could've had me six years ago, and you could've had me last night. The fact you haven't yet is on you. Only you. So be mad at yourself, no one else."

"Believe me, I hate myself enough for the both of us and then some," I snapped; then we both turned at the sound of Chiara crying, and I was shocked she hadn't woken sooner when Thomas had been there.

Maria's shoulders fell, and she pulled her hand from my chest. "I have to get her ready for Thomas's. After this morning, if I don't do what he wants, he'll make my life miserable. I don't want him trying to change the custody agreement or drag me back to court."

"I'd never let that happen," I reminded her, which only earned me a stern look. "Not by killing him," I reluctantly added in case there was any doubt. "Unless—"

"He hurt me," she finished for me, and a sad look that crushed me crossed her face. "He won't, just so we're clear. Thomas was a cheat and a lousy husband, but that's it. Because of Chiara, he's going to be in my life, and you need to learn to accept that if you want to stay in mine, too." She turned to the side, preparing to go to Chiara. "And, Enzo? This whole you-killing-a-killer thing . . . we're not done talking about that."

Once she was gone from sight, I let go of a gruff breath and slipped on my shoes. I snatched my hat and went home, deciding she needed time alone with her daughter. Plus, she needed to process our conversation. Or had that been a fight? Hell, I didn't know what to call it, but I felt horrible. The idea of possibly losing them both had me feeling empty.

Once in my bedroom, I opened the top drawer of my dresser, searching for the small black velvet box I kept hidden in there. I opened it up and removed the rosary chain I hadn't touched since giving up my life in New York two years ago. It'd been Bianca's. She'd been a devout Catholic like our mom. Rarely missing mass unless it was for work.

After tightening my hand around the necklace, my eyes fell to the same beaded rosary tattooed on my forearm. Bianca's initials were in script beneath the cross, and memories from my past burned through my mind. I nearly took a knee as the pain robbed me of the breath from my lungs.

It took a text from my brother to shake me free from whatever zoned-out state I'd fallen into, and I stored the rosary back where it belonged and read my brother's message.

Alessandro: How'd last night go?

I dropped onto my bed, my gaze moving to the mirror over the dresser for a moment, catching sight of my tired eyes. How'd Maria function during the day waking up so many times in the middle of the night to put Chiara back to sleep? I was beat from one night of doing it.

Me: Why are you up so early? I thought you rolled into the office after nine.
Alessandro: Dodging my question, I see.
Me: It didn't go as expected.
Alessandro: Because you did or didn't kill someone?
Me: I played babysitter while she went on a date. Then she came home and I . . .

I wasn't sure how much I wanted to divulge, particularly over text. My brother must've read my thoughts, because the phone rang a second later, and he placed us on FaceTime. "Are you on a stair climber?" That drew an unexpected laugh from me.

"It's good cardio."

"What, having sex with two women last night wasn't enough cardio for you?" I glared at him, his white tee and hair soaked in sweat. Out of all of us Costa kids, Alessandro's complexion was the lightest, and he had sandy-brown hair and silvery-gray eyes. Features that kids used to tease him about when growing up were the same ones that women flocked to him for now. Well, among other reasons.

"Nah, you know how it is. Sex doesn't scratch the itch. Not after the lives we've lived."

"And the stair climber does?" I couldn't help but smile, but at least he was changing my mood.

"Gets my heart going is about all." My brother stopped the machine and swiped a towel over his face. He had his own personal gym inside his penthouse in New York, so there was no risk of anyone overhearing our conversation. "But nothing can replace—"

"That's messed up, you know that, right?" I cut him off. "We shouldn't miss that life."

"The way you're throwing a 'we' has me shocked, bro. I thought you didn't miss anything about New York." He took a moment to drain his water bottle in a few deep gulps. "Well, aside from us. I mean, you miss us, right?"

I rolled my eyes. "Of course I miss you guys. But my being here and living a normal, so-called healthy life makes Mom and Izzy happy."

"You're Mom's baby boy. Her favorite. She never pushed me to move from the city and start new."

"Screw you, man," I teased. "Mom just felt bad for me."

"We all lost a sister, not just you," Alessandro shot back, and yeah, of course I knew that, but it was different for me in a way that I couldn't explain. A twin thing, I supposed.

"Anyway," he said, realizing we both needed a subject change before our moods went dark. "Tell me about the whole you-playing-the-role-of-Mrs.-Doubtfire thing."

I stood and went to the window and opened the blinds, allowing the morning sun to wash the room in natural light.

"Because it sounds like you're the one needing to get laid, brother."

"Oh, really? And meaningless sex is doing wonders at fixing your life, I see," I punched back, eyes still on the window.

Alessandro waited for me to look back at the camera before responding, "Pretty sure it wouldn't be meaningless for you."

Yeah, he was right about that.

"So tell me. Is her date still alive? Need help taking care of him? I can bail on the meeting with Constantine later and hop down there for an assist if you need one."

My brother really did miss the hunt, didn't he? And part of me did, too. I just didn't want to admit it, and certainly not to him on this call.

"Well?" he prompted when I'd yet to reply.

I thought back to last night when I'd done some digging on Maria's date, and the man had been boring but safe. "He's no longer in the picture, but only because she wasn't interested."

"Because she wants you. And you want her."

I turned away from the window, remembering my conversation with Maria before *and* after Thomas's untimely arrival. "Even if I tell her everything, I'll screw up at some point. I don't know how to be who she needs," I admitted. "And I don't want to hurt her." *Plus, who's to say she'll even want me now that she knows I'm a killer?*

"First of all," Alessandro began, his brows snapping together, "like, 'tell her everything' as in *everything*?" The best I could do was nod, so he continued. "Second, you'd never hurt her. That's a nonissue."

"Not physically. You know damn well what I'm talking about. Just because you act like you don't have a heart doesn't mean—"

"Sorry, man. Constantine is beeping in. I should take this."

"Yeah, sure. You hanging up with me to get your ass chewed out by him? Likely story." We all had our hard limits when it came to topics of conversation, and Alessandro discussing his own personal demons was never up for discussion.

The man didn't think he had a heart. My problem? I only had half of one.

Alessandro mumbled something too low to hear, then added, "Just do us all a favor and shit or get off the pot. It's now or never, man. Either be with her or go find someone new to distract yourself with. At the very least, you need a blow job before you blow up."

"Great advice, asshole. Fuck you very much." I waved my hand at the screen, motioning for him to go. "Later." I ended the call and chucked the phone onto my bed.

Alessandro was right about one thing. I was hanging on the edge of my sanity.

My thoughts drifted back to Maria and the way her body had quickly responded to my touch, with her coming hard on my fingers as they were buried deep inside her pussy.

Fuck. My cock went hard at the memory, and I adjusted myself, realizing I'd never survive the day without relief. I needed to get off before I lost all self-control.

But Maria deserved to know the truth before deciding if she could truly love a man like me. And I needed time to be sure there wasn't a chance I'd break her heart.

SIX

Enzo

"WHAT WAS HER NUMBER?" I remembered roaring, demanding to know how many lives the bastard had taken.

His eyes had been cold and dead as he'd blankly stared at me, refusing to answer. I'd wrapped my hand tighter around his throat. "What was her fucking number?" I'd seethed, dragging the knife in my other hand down his sternum.

The bastard had looked down at my knife, then back into my eyes, a gleam evident in them.

Seeing red, I'd snapped and stabbed him. Constantine and Alessandro had reached for me, pulling me back to prevent me from finishing him off.

"You good, Boss Man?"

Blinking a few times, I dropped my eyes to the knife in my hand, and all I could see was blood coating the blade. "What?" I muttered, freeing myself of the thirteen-year-old memory.

"You okay?" my sous-chef, Brandon, asked. "You're off tonight. You've never messed up a dish."

"I messed up a dish?" I let go of the knife and faced him.

"Yeah, man, this doesn't taste right, too much salt." He set a bowl of my signature red Romesco sauce in my hand. "That's not like you."

I snatched a spoon and tasted the sauce meant for tonight's salmon dish, and damn, he was right. But my mind had been messed up ever since the exchange with Thomas that morning, especially the conversation afterward with Maria.

In the back of her head, she had to have known my brothers and I would never have let that animal walk away after what he did, though. Justice had failed my sister. The murderer's lawyers had the case thrown out of trial because of evidence mishandling. No way would we let him walk away and potentially hurt someone else.

We'd wound up arrested for his murder. Constantine had tried to fall on the sword for us, but we wouldn't let him go to jail.

But then we were offered a get-out-of-jail-free card and a fake news story about the man's death in exchange for our souls. Though nothing in life is ever truly free.

"I think I need to step out. Can you take over?" I was in no condition to be cooking.

Before Brandon had a chance to respond, I began walking my fingers down my jacket, preparing to leave.

I heard him say, "Of course," as I tossed my jacket on a chair on my way to the back door.

Once outside, the door to the parking lot thudded shut behind me, drawing the attention of the only two people outside. Facing Maria right now was not the plan. But there she was. And so was Natalia.

Maria had avoided me all day after she'd dropped Chiara off at Thomas's house. She'd texted earlier that she planned to drive herself to the restaurant instead of catching a ride with me, and I didn't argue. She'd needed space, and I'd given it to her, too worried about my state of mind to be around her in the first place.

"Everything okay?" Natalia called out, her hand over her stomach with her back to her husband's truck. A nearby lamppost illuminated both of them, making them look like angels, and there I was standing in the dark like a damn metaphor for something.

"I just needed to step away for a minute," I shared, unsure if I wanted to go to them or escape somewhere else.

"I was about to head in." Natalia started toward me and whispered upon passing by, "She's upset about Chiara being gone. Cheer her up, please."

Yeah, she's upset about more than just that. But I nodded, then waited for Natalia to head inside before I reluctantly ate up the space between myself and the woman who drove me crazy. But the world also seemed to stop spinning whenever she wasn't with me. And that wasn't good for anyone. "You didn't tell her what happened between us?"

Maria fidgeted with the sleeve of her cream-colored blouse as she said, "No, not yet." Her eyes worked up to mine as she leaned against the truck. "I've been doing some thinking today."

"That doesn't sound good," I glibly responded.

She huffed out a deep breath and let go of her sleeve, only to nervously shake her hand at her side. What was she planning to say? "And?"

"You keep telling me you're bad for me. Dangerous. And sometimes I forget that this is real life and not fiction." She wet her lips, drawing my eyes there like a magnet. "And if a guy tells you he's not good for you, well, in real life, you should listen." Her gaze lifted to the clouds overhead in the dark sky. "The thing is, I'm stubborn. I don't listen well. And why can't life imitate art? Or hell, who says art's not actually just a mirror of life?"

I grabbed the back of my neck and squeezed, uncomfortable as I waited for my little fireball to continue. That morning, I told her I'd killed a man, and she was taking it in stride. Acting as though I'd confessed only to stealing someone's recipe or running a stop sign.

"Even in light of what you told me this morning, I'm still here." She sniffled. "I'm willing to risk my heart for you," she declared in a soft voice as her eyes returned to mine. "I'll take the chance you break it if it means you'll give *us* a chance." She was being vulnerable with me, possibly even forgiving me for murder. And I was standing there like an *idiota*, unsure what to do or how to react to that.

I promised her father long ago to protect her and Natalia. But I'd made a promise to myself, too: never let anyone I care about feel anything close to the kind of pain I lived with daily. And if I gave in to my desires, gave in to my feelings for her . . . what if the horrible scenarios that crossed through my mind like a deadly storm came true? What if I hurt her? Lost her forever?

"Maria." Her name came out like a rough plea from my lips. Of course, I had no idea what I was begging her to do. Stop wanting me or *never* stop?

"I tried to open the door to my heart for you on my birthday, and you slammed it shut." Her voice trembled this time. "I'm opening it again for you tonight. Right here in this parking lot. It's up to you whether you want to walk through. This is your last chance. I'll stop being stubborn if you reject me tonight. I'll face reality and move on."

Was this my shit-or-get-off-the-pot moment, as my brother had so eloquently called it?

"You'd risk your heart, but what about Chiara's?" I cut straight through to the meat of what I knew would be the main problem for her. The only counter defense I had left in my arsenal to use against her, to keep this woman from breaking me down to the point where I stopped fighting this thing between us, and I tried to be happy.

"No." She shook her head, tears in her eyes. "You'd kill yourself before hurting my little girl."

Without question. "And you already know what I'm willing to give up if it means keeping you safe." I reached for her, cupping her cheeks, unable to think straight.

Her glossy eyes unleashed a few tears. "Yeah, you're already doing it," she whispered. "Breaking your own heart so you don't risk breaking mine."

My hands slid to her hair, and I set my forehead to hers, playing with the locks by her face as I mustered the strength to keep fighting her on this.

She was offering herself to me, doing what I begged her not to do, but this went way beyond sex. She was offering all of herself to me. Not just her body. Her whole life.

"Maria, what are you doing to me?" My voice broke that time, and her hands covered mine.

She shifted back to stare into my eyes as her lower lip trembled.

"After what you learned about me, I just can't wrap my head around why you still want me," I bluntly said, no point in sugarcoating anything now. "But I need time to think things through before I . . ." I let go of a ragged breath. "Can you give me that?"

Her lips rolled inward, and it took all my strength not to lean in and suck that bottom lip, to not taste her for the first time in six years.

"Okay." The word was more like a breath of air passing between us as she eased her body a bit closer, and my hand brushed against her breast with barely any space between us. "I wish you'd kiss me," she cried like it was meant as a confession for a priest. Only I was far from worthy of hearing anyone's sins. I was a man incapable of redemption, and my soul wouldn't wind up with hers on the other side when my time came.

I pulled my hands free from hers and brought the pad of my thumb along the seam of her lips, and her eyes closed at the contact. "The next time my mouth touches these lips," I began before reaching between her thighs with my other hand, "or *these* lips," I added in a low voice, and her pussy arched into my palm, "you'll first know the truth about me. But not tonight."

She wanted my walls down? Then so be it. But I was terrified that once they came crumbling down, she'd hate me and build them back up herself.

"Give me something," she pleaded, peeling her eyes open. "Either a bit of hope. One of your secrets. Or, at the very least, touch me. After the day I've had, especially with Chiara being out of town, I need something."

My shoulders slumped at her request. *Hope?* That wasn't in my wheelhouse. And my secrets weren't meant for being shared in a parking lot.

I looked around, finding us still alone, so I snatched her wrist and guided her so her back was to my Tahoe on the other side of Ryan's F-150, which served as our shield from the back door of the restaurant. "You want my touch? You want it out here? Like this?"

She licked her lips and nodded.

Of course you do. It disturbed me how easy it was for her to break through my defenses, to get me to do things I'd vowed never to do. "Unzip your pants for me, then," I ordered.

Her palm slipped between us, and she did as she was told.

Hoping like hell no one walked outside and witnessed us, I spun her around so her hands landed on my SUV, and her eyes caught mine in the reflection of the glass.

I set my hand on the window alongside hers while my other wrapped possessively around her body as I'd done last night, pressing my hard length against her ass.

Her parted lips slammed into a tight line the moment my hand dove beneath her pants and panties. I nuzzled her neck with my nose, nearly losing control at how soaked she was. "Fuck my hand," I demanded, wanting her to take from me all that I could give her right now.

She rocked against the heel of my palm; my finger slid up and down her wet sex, and I swept the pad of my thumb in circular motions at her sensitive spot as she moved. But her ass rotating against my cock was going to destroy me, as it'd nearly done last night.

"Why is it that when you touch me, when you're this close to me . . . I feel unstoppable? Powerful somehow? Being with you makes me feel . . ."

Complete?

"You hold the power, *Tesoro*. With me you do. You always have," I admitted, somewhat terrified by that truth.

"Then why won't you give me what we both want?" she begged. "Promise me you will one day." She was on the verge of coming already, I could tell by her shaky inhalations and the way she moved faster against my hand. "Please."

That cry mingled with her desire had me opening my stupid mouth and doing something I hoped I wouldn't regret. "I promise," I whispered.

More breathy moans left her lips; worried someone would come out and hear her, I reached around and covered her mouth with my other hand. Her tongue skirted between her lips, licking my skin, and I nearly unzipped my pants and took my bad girl right there.

I felt the shudder rip through her, and she came so hard, she bent forward and would've whacked her head against my Tahoe if I hadn't caught her.

She had to be dripping down her leg, and I wanted nothing more than to take her inside and clean her up myself. Lick that pussy and see how she tasted.

Frustrated in more ways than one, I snatched a fistful of her hair instead, angling her head to the side to look back at me. "Feel better?"

She nodded, licking her lips, and I was far too tempted to kiss her. I released her hair and stepped back as she fixed her zipper and faced me. "That should've been on my list."

"What list?" I asked as she tucked in her blouse.

"The naughty things I want to do with you," she responded, her tone going shy, which was adorable given what she'd just let me do to her.

My hand went to the SUV over her shoulder, and I was prepared to ask her to elaborate, but her gaze snapped to our left, and her eyes widened.

I turned at the realization we weren't alone, hating myself for not noticing sooner. This woman was a distraction, that was for sure.

"Am I interrupting?" A man stepped into the light. Although shadows crossed his face, it took me less than a second to recognize him, and a sharp, stabbing pain of worry cut through me.

"And you are?" Maria asked once I'd aligned myself alongside her.

"I'm an old friend." The blast from my past finally spoke.

"From?" Maria pressed.

"The army." His lips quirked as if realizing Maria wasn't someone he could lie to and get away with it.

"Why'd that sound like a question?" Maria didn't back down from anyone, did she? Not even me. And that made me nervous. What if she crossed the wrong person one day?

Instead of answering, he offered his hand. "Jesse McAdams."

Maria reluctantly accepted his palm, but I felt her eyes on me.

I was too worried as to why Jesse was there to look at her. "I need you to go inside now," I told her, maintaining eye contact with the former army ranger turned CIA hit man. And last I heard, he now worked in private security.

"Yeah, okay." She gripped my forearm and sent me a reassuring squeeze, as if sensing I needed it, then left us alone.

"I heard rumors you were a chef, but I didn't believe it until this moment." Jesse scratched his beard while he assessed me. "I guess you were always good with a knife."

"What are you doing here?" I asked, cutting to the point, my heart beating erratically at the fact he was there, which meant something was wrong. The pit in my stomach doubled in size when he reached into his pocket and showed me a USB.

"I'm in the middle of a job, and I stumbled across some information you'll want. Although I do have orders not to share it with you. Not yet, at least."

"And yet, here you are," I remarked in a low voice. "Why?"

He handed me the USB, and I held it tightly in my hand, waiting for answers. "My team at Falcon Falls Security is working a case. And a few days ago, we managed to get close enough to a man we were tracking to hack his computer. When we tried to grab him, though he evaded us like Harry fucking Houdini."

Someone got away from you? That was a surprise. "What does any of that have to do with me?"

He pointed to my fist holding the USB. "My team is worried that if I hand that over to you while we're still pursuing him, you'll interfere with our op." He held his palms up. "But I've known you longer than my team leaders, and if it were my sister, I'd want to know now."

My body went cold, even though my heartbeat doubled in speed. "Isabella?" I opened my palm as if the USB were a grenade with the pin pulled.

"No," he said. "This is about your other sister."

Chills like I'd never known before coated my body as I slowly worked my focus back up to look him in the eyes. "What?" The word was a dying breath from my lungs, nothing more. Because *that* was impossible.

"The man we're hunting is a professional cleaner. The kind of guy the mob or a dirty politician calls when—"

"I know what a cleaner does," I roughly bit out.

"Yeah, well, this cleaner also assists with alibis and frame jobs. He doesn't just clean up the crime, he ensures someone else is to blame and all within hours."

I knew what he was getting at, and I refused to accept it. Because that would mean . . .

My head was spinning. Body starting to sweat.

"Someone hired him thirteen years ago to pin Bianca's murder on that other guy," Jesse said, spelling it out for me as if I weren't putting two and two together. "The proof is on that USB. We just don't know who hired him, and trust me, when we grab him, we'll find out."

"No." I shook my head. "I killed her murderer. That asshole followed her home from a nightclub." A million questions raced through my mind, but I held back from asking them.

"And that asshole was framed."

He gave me a few seconds to adjust to the news and the shock, and now I needed to clarify something. Something that had my stomach dropping. "You're trying to tell me we killed an innocent man? I had his life in my hands, and he didn't beg. Didn't try and convince me he didn't kill her."

"Would you have listened?"

Probably not.

"That man wasn't innocent by any means," Jesse added, clearly sensing the panic in my eyes. "Based on the cleaner's records, the cleaner always has a running list of people in New York to pin crimes on at any given time. People who meet certain profiles. So when he gets a request to cover up a crime, he's able to handle the case much quicker because of it." He waited for me to look at him before continuing. "The man he chose to frame was a killer, he just didn't kill your sister."

I turned and set my palms on the SUV, my mind and heart at odds. Some weird fight-or-flight mechanism taking over. "There was evidence at Bianca's place. He lived in the same part of town."

"And the case was dismissed because of evidence tampering or mishandling. Something like that, right? But in reality, the cleaner planted the evidence at her apartment, and based on his files in which he laid out his plan, he even drugged his fall guy so he wouldn't remember the night of her murder. It's possible he even thought he'd committed the crime."

My hands turned to fists as I bowed my head to the window. "You're going to need to run this by me again. Use smaller fucking words, I don't know. Because I'm not understanding." Nothing made sense right now. Not a damn thing.

Jesse was quiet for a moment, and I lifted my head to catch him in the reflection. "Someone else killed your sister and hired this fucker to clean up the mess and provide him a bulletproof alibi, I just don't know who the hell did it. He didn't have any names of who paid him on his laptop. We're trying to track the money trail, but it's thirteen years old, and—"

"And you have another case more recent you're working on, too." I slowly lowered my hands and faced him.

Jesse shifted to the side. "It looks like you're trying to start a new life, same as me, so the last thing I want is to come here and fuck all that up, but—"

"Your team is right. I'm not going to sit back and let someone else handle this." The adrenaline shot through my body as I murmured, "You know exactly what I'm going to do."

"Yeah, I figured you'd say that."

"Any chance you were followed?" I looked around, hoping it was just the news that had me paranoid, feeling as though we were being watched.

Jesse peered back at me, his brows drawing tight. "No tail." He reached into his pocket, producing a folded sheet of paper. "My number. It's a secure line. Text me after you look at the USB and talk to your brothers."

I accepted his number and shoved it into my pocket. "Thank you for breaking orders."

He held his mouth for a moment as if guilty for being the one to share the news with me. "Is she your Ella?" He tipped his head toward the restaurant, and I searched my memory bank for the name, Ella, and then remembered she was Jesse's "the one"—the woman he never thought he could have because of his past, because he'd believed he was too broken.

I forced a nod, then pointed to his hand. "You married Ella?"

Jesse fidgeted with his ring. "Yeah, I finally removed my head from my ass." He held the back of his neck and met my eyes. "I'm guessing you've yet to remove yours?"

"No," I said under my breath. *Not yet.*

I'd been slapped in the face by the fact someone else was responsible for my sister's death, and at the same time . . . Jesse had managed to deliver me hope. If he could change and marry the woman of his dreams, could I?

SEVEN

Maria

I paced Ryan and Natalia's living room, checking my messages for the hundredth time that hour. Still no response from Enzo, which wasn't like him. Of course, it wasn't like him to leave the restaurant during the dinner rush, either. One text to Ryan with orders to bring me to their house instead of letting me go home. Radio silence in the last three hours.

"What do you think that guy told him? That's all that makes sense as to why Enzo would just leave and ignore my calls and texts." I faced my worried sister and her husband, who were on the couch, watching me. "I know you said you don't personally know this Jesse guy, but—"

"If he's who I think he is, yes, we have mutual friends. His sister is married to a SEAL. And his wife's brother is a Team Guy as well," Ryan finished for me, sharing the same sliver of information he'd given me earlier on our drive to their home in Waxhaw, our small hometown, not far from the restaurant. The paint was barely dry on the walls. They'd moved in only last month. It'd taken six months to build, but they'd wanted it finished before their son was born.

"Could you call one of those SEALs? See if they know anything?" The question felt crazy, but I'd already been ripped apart watching

Chiara cry over FaceTime that evening being away from me, and now this.

Enzo had sent me to orgasm heaven, and one visit from an old friend of his and I felt firmly planted in hell. The not knowing was what I couldn't handle. My overthinking brain was overheating from creating far too many what-if scenarios.

Ryan looked at his Apple Watch as if deciding whether calling up a SEAL at eleven at night was a shit idea or not. "Let's give Enzo a chance to call us back and see what he—" He stopped midsentence when Natalia's phone buzzed on her thigh, nearly falling to the floor.

"Is it Enzo?" I dropped onto the couch next to her to try and see the screen.

"I don't recognize the number," my sister responded. "Do I answer?"

"Speakerphone," Ryan instructed.

"It's Constantine Costa," he said once she answered. "How are you?"

My stomach dropped, and my sister looked at me with wide eyes.

"Not so great, considering you're calling me after eleven, and not only have you never called me before, I didn't know you had my number," Natalia quickly responded, and Ryan set his hand on her knee.

"This is about Enzo," I rushed out. "Right?" My heart hammered in my chest. Thwacking hard. "Some guy came to the restaurant tonight; then Enzo up and left without a word. What's happening? Is he okay?"

"Hi, Maria," Constantine responded after a deep breath over the line. "Listen, I'm calling to let you know Alessandro and I plan to fly down tomorrow as soon as we can. Probably in the afternoon. We're coming to get him. But in the meantime, I need someone I trust to keep an eye on him."

Keep an eye on him? Fly here? I was back on my feet again.

"Why? What's going on?" It was Ryan this time, and his concerned gaze sharp on her phone did nothing for my sanity.

I checked my texts, praying for the read receipt to appear so I'd at least know Enzo saw my message.

Nothing.

"Enzo received some disturbing news tonight, and I need to investigate it. Make sense of it. That's all I'm going to share right now. I'll let him tell you if he wants to." Constantine and his cryptic words weren't helping. "Can someone go over to his place and stay with him? He's not in the best state of mind, and I haven't seen my brother drink like this since Bianca died," he added in a low voice, and the blood rushed from my face.

"We're on our way," Natalia said without hesitation, holding her stomach as she stood with Ryan's help.

"Thank you," Constantine solemnly said.

"Of course." I was glad my sister was more put together than I was, capable of fluid responses.

Was Enzo drunk? Constantine was right. I'd never seen him have more than one or two drinks. It made sense, though. Enzo hated losing control.

"I'd offer to go alone, but I know you'll both give me a hard time." Ryan snatched his truck keys.

"Damn straight we would," Natalia fired back, and Ryan grumbled something too low for me to hear, and we followed him to the garage.

It was a quiet thirty-minute drive into the city, only the soft tunes of country music to keep us company while I was lost in my thoughts.

The second we were in my building and on my floor, every intrusive *what if* buzzing around in my head stopped. Anticipation grabbed hold of me, sinking its teeth into my flushed skin.

"I know the navy trained me to be a professional door kicker," Ryan said once we were by Enzo's place, "but tell me one of you has a key so I don't have to knock this thing down."

"Assuming he won't answer?" Natalia asked while producing a key before I had a chance to go for the one on my key chain.

"Affirmative," Ryan gruffly said, accepting the key from her, and then he didn't bother to knock or ring.

The sight that greeted the three of us once Ryan opened up wasn't one I'd prepared myself to see.

The living room was dimly lit by a fire, and Enzo stood in front of his wall of windows with one arm propped over his head, gaze set on the city. He had on a pair of black sweats that hung low on his hips, just the white strip from his boxers visible. His back muscles were on full display, showcasing a lone tattoo on his right shoulder. Even though he knew he was no longer alone, he'd yet to move.

"Enzo," I hesitantly called out, surprised I could get my voice to work.

"My brother shouldn't have called you," Enzo returned in a low tone as he slowly faced us, holding a bottle of something at his side. His eyes locked on to Ryan standing by Natalia just inside the living room. "And you shouldn't have brought her here. I told you to keep her away from me."

"Wait, what?" I looked to Ryan for an explanation. That wasn't remotely close to what he'd told me Enzo had texted him at the restaurant earlier. "What's going on?" I asked, returning my focus to the angry man before me.

Enzo slowly stalked closer to us, bringing the bottle to his lips as he did so. My gaze skated from the ink above his heart, down the hard planes of his abdominal wall, to the vee that disappeared into his black sweats.

Somehow, this was the first time I'd ever seen him without a shirt, and I was taken aback by how strong and hard he truly was. God, the man was positively breathtaking.

We'd never so much as hung out at a pool or beach together, well, not since we were kids. And yeah, he looked a hell of a lot different at thirty-seven than he did at seventeen.

"You need to take your pregnant wife home," Enzo told Ryan in a clipped tone. "You all need to leave."

"Something is wrong, and your brother sent us. We're not going anywhere," Natalia firmly said. "Talk to us. Let us help."

The dark laugh leaving Enzo's mouth had me walking back. "Help me?" He chugged more from the bottle. Most likely whiskey.

"Watch yourself, man," Ryan warned. "We may be friends, but if you piss off my pregnant wife and upset her, I won't hesitate to lay you the fuck out." He stepped before his wife like a shield, and honestly, I had no clue who'd win in a head-to-head match, but I knew neither Natalia nor I wanted to find out.

Enzo only smirked as if he wanted the challenge. "I'm in the mood to fight or to . . ." His gaze cut to me, and I heard the unspoken f-word sail through the air and knock the breath from my lungs.

Natalia hooked her arm through her husband's, and I recognized that as her silent request not to tango with Enzo tonight.

"You're drunk," Ryan said, arms going across his chest. "Sleep it off. Tell us what's going on in the morning. But we're not leaving."

Enzo remained quiet as he drank more, his gaze lingering on me as he did so.

I faced Natalia and pleaded, "I need to talk to him alone."

"I'm his best friend. I'm not leaving," Natalia insisted.

"And he's my . . ." I looked over my shoulder to find him at the window, his back to us again. *My what?* "Take my keys and go next door. You've been on your feet all night. You should sleep. Stay in my room." I snatched my keys from my purse before tossing the small bag onto the armchair by the couch with no plans to leave.

Natalia exchanged a look with Ryan, searching for what to do.

"Please." I shoved the keys into Ryan's hand. "I can handle this." I nodded, hoping to convince the both of them.

I honestly had no clue if I could handle a drunk, angry Enzo, but I was certain he'd throw us all out on our asses in a minute if I didn't reduce the number of us in the room.

Natalia stole a quick look at the brooding man by the window, then squeezed my forearm. "We'll be right next door if you need us."

"Thank you," I mouthed.

"Don't be an ass, Enzo. Talk to her," Ryan bit out before he and Natalia left, and once the door thudded shut, I started for the fire, unsure what to do next.

"Stop," Enzo commanded. "There's glass over there."

I went still and looked at the fireplace, where I'd barely noticed the shards of glass. From the looks of it, he'd angrily hurled more than one glass. "Talk to me," I begged, slowly turning, not expecting to see him inches away, his gaze on me.

The light from the fire bounced off his hard features, and I flinched when he reached out and ran a finger up the column of my throat before tipping my chin. "You shouldn't be here."

"But I am." I hoped he wouldn't notice the nervous swallow, but the slight tip of his head with his eyes focused on my throat meant he had. "Why are you drunk? Why are your brothers flying here?"

He closed his eyes and his hand fell back to his side. He started to bring the bottle to his mouth, but I reached for his forearm, an attempt to stop him. His eyes flashed open, catching mine, and his lips hardened as if I'd defied him.

"Always playing with fire. What will I ever do with you?" he murmured instead of answering me. He pulled his arm away and brought the rim of the bottle to my lips. "Want a taste, baby?"

I had to remind myself he'd been drinking, and I'd never experienced this man at anything less than 100 percent in control. I had no idea what to expect.

He dragged the bottle tip along the line of my lips, forcing them to part, and I was certain he wanted to see my lips wrapped around something and it wasn't the bottle. And I shouldn't have been aroused by that fact. Because the unspoken reason why he was drinking from the bottle still hung in the air between us.

"I want you to stop drinking so you can talk to me. Sober up first if you have to, but—"

"If you want me to stop drinking, then you'll need to distract me." He lowered the bottle to his side.

I wet my lips, growing both hotter and more nervous by the second. "How do you propose I do that?"

The side of his lips hitched. "Tell me about that list of yours. What's on it?" He turned and went to the window, but he set his back to it instead of looking out at the city.

"Why would you care about that right now?" I crossed the space and boldly took the bottle from him, and he didn't stop me. Once the whiskey was at a safe distance away from him, I returned to find him with the back of his head against the glass, eyes steadily on me.

"I'm angry. If you don't want me leaving this apartment and unleashing hell on the first fucker who crosses me," he began while shoving away from the window to stalk closer to me with confident strides, "then distract me."

"With the list?"

He stopped before me and gently cupped my cheek, a contrast to the asshole-like attitude he was trying to portray. "What's number five? Does it go that high?" A dark smile cut across his mouth.

"Higher," I whispered, captivated by the powerful man before me, ready to bend to his will when I normally loved to challenge him at every turn.

"So?" He angled his head, waiting. "Number five?"

Dizzy with need but knowing I'd never act on it, given his state, I closed my eyes, and my entire body heated as I admitted the truth. "That you take me, well, um . . ."

His hand slid into my hair, and he gripped my locks to draw my face closer. I could feel his whiskey breath near my lips, but I didn't give him my gaze like I knew he wanted. "Your ex wouldn't know what to do with an ass like yours. You've never been taken there, have you, *Tesoro*?"

He grabbed hold of my ass, and a shuddery gasp fell from my lips at the feel of his rock-hard cock pressing against me.

"No." That hadn't been what I'd planned to say, but maybe it should've been on the list? "You'd be the first."

"Good." He surprised me by dropping his mouth over mine, only to lightly nip my lower lip as he squeezed my ass, and then he released both my lip and flesh and eased back a step.

I blinked free from my stupor a moment later when realization struck me. "I'm not distracting you." My hand went to his chest. "You're trying to distract *me*. You don't want me to know something."

He dipped his chin to look at my palm over his heart.

"Tell me what Jesse said to you. Who is he really?"

He smirked, his hard gaze meeting mine again. "John Wick."

"Real funny." I thought back to the man I'd met earlier tonight in the parking lot. "I didn't know John wore flannel." I tensed at the fact he didn't seem to be joking about John Wick. "If he's a contract killer, are you?"

"No, I'm a chef." His tone was softer than I'd expected that time.

"And before?"

"Go home, Maria. I'm not doing this tonight. Everything is about to change, and I need one night to—"

"Fall apart before it does?" *And what is going to change?* I wanted to cry, to beg him for the answers he didn't want to give me.

"Yes," he hissed, his chin angrily jutting out. "So leave me alone and let me fall the fuck apart."

I shook my head. "No, I won't let you do that."

"Stay here and watch it happen or go. Those are your choices." When he tried to turn, to escape, I hooked the waistband of his pants with my finger and tugged.

He slowly turned, zeroing in on my face as if he were on the verge of putting me in my place. Quite literally. And I knew where I longed to be. With him. Or maybe beneath him.

But not tonight. I'd never let him take me while he was drunk—not because I didn't want it but because he'd never forgive himself for it afterward.

"Fire," he mouthed, as if warning me I was on the verge of getting burned. "Hell is my playground, not yours."

"Then give me an invitation," I snapped back, tears in my eyes. "Because if you're there right now, then I want to be, too."

"No, you don't."

His dark smile only emboldened me. "Don't tell me what I want."

"You think what you learned this morning is bad, it's just the tip of the iceberg, sweetheart. You wouldn't walk away from me if you knew everything. You'd *run*."

"I don't believe you." *Well, not about the running part, at least.* "I'm here. I'm not going anywhere, so go ahead, give me your best shot. Try and push me away with details about your past and watch me take two steps closer instead."

His lips lifted, showing a hint of his teeth as he hissed like a wounded, frightened animal in the wild.

But silence was all he gave me. *He really is scared I'll leave him, isn't he?*

"Fine," I grumbled, realizing he had no plans to share. "You want a distraction?" I pointed to his bedroom. "Then give me number six."

His expression softened. "What's number six?"

"I'll show you." I huffed out a breath, flicked off the switch for the gas fireplace, then walked into his bedroom and turned on the light.

I spun around to see him hanging just outside his room with his arms folded while he leaned into the interior doorframe, eyes steady on me.

"Tell me." His gaze walked up the length of me, landing last on my lips.

"You need to get off, right? I know we can't have sex tonight, but I also don't want you going outside and 'unleashing hell,' as you called it, so . . . take a shower and get off. Maybe it'll help sober you up a little."

"What's that have to do with your list?"

I peeled off my top and tossed it. My tank top went next. He'd seen me in a bra the other day, but he'd never *seen me* seen me. I went for the clip of my black satin bra, and he kept quiet, watching me but not stopping me. When I freed my tits from the uncomfortable underwire, he pushed away from the doorframe and strode closer, and my breathing only picked up. Hard, hot, and fast.

"What are you doing?" He palmed his dick over his sweats, more than likely not realizing he was doing it as he approached me.

"I'm giving you something to look at while you release all that tension," I explained, feeling a little crazy.

"And that's on your list? Watching me stroke my cock *without* participating?" He reached for me, drawing my chin into his large hand, guiding my eyes up.

I nodded. "You're telling me you've never thought about me while you get off? Because you're all I can think about when I touch myself."

His brows slanted as he lowered his eyes to my breasts, and my nipples weren't just hard because I was chilly. That dark, heated look in his eyes had goose bumps forming all over my exposed skin. "They say that the more orgasms you have, the longer you live," he remarked.

"They do, do they?"

He cupped my breast with his free hand. "You know what that means?" He pinched my nipple, and I chewed on my lip so I didn't cry out from the pleasure of his touch. The walls were thin, and my sister and brother-in-law were next door. "I'll live for an eternity from the number of times I've beat off thinking about you."

My legs tightened on reflex at his confession, and I had to remind myself he was under the influence so I didn't launch myself into his arms.

"So will you give me number six?" I forced my eyes to meet his, and he slid his tongue along the seam of his lips as he rolled my nipple between his thumb and forefinger, eliciting yet another moan from me.

"I'm curious how you went from me taking your ass as number five to watching me jerk off for number six. Feels out of order." A sly smile slid across his lips, almost as if he'd forgotten all about whatever darkness was weighing him down.

"My list isn't exactly arranged on a kink scale from one to ten." Not that number five had been that, but still.

A torn look crossed his face.

"So?" I arched a brow and set my hand over the one cupping my chin. "Will you?"

"Yes," he said as his hand slid over my mouth, and I kissed his palm. "Tonight . . . I'll give you whatever you want."

EIGHT

Maria

Enzo walked into his en suite, turned on the light, and I quietly followed him. Without saying more, he shoved down his sweats and stepped free of them.

As he removed his boxers, I stifled a moan and leaned against the counter. Enzo's body was absolute perfection from head to toe. And his muscular ass . . . Michelangelo couldn't have carved a better one.

He wordlessly stepped into one of the most luxurious showers I'd ever seen, and God, I wanted to join him. But it was more important that he sober up right now and shake off some of his anger. I needed him to talk to me and let me help him with whatever the hell was going on.

Keeping the door open and with the water on, Enzo slowly turned beneath the spray, and I braced the counter on each side of me at the sight.

The girth of that man. His length. The veins that led to the head of his impressive cock. I licked my lips, wishing I could taste him.

He leisurely slid a hand up and down his shaft as I worked my focus up his wall of muscles to find his face. He ran his free hand through his wet hair and messed it up, and his wet lashes only intensified that dark look in his eyes as he stared at me.

"This what you want?" he roughly asked while moving his hand up and down a few more times, and I chewed on the inside of my cheek, trying to summon the strength not to slip my hand down my pants and touch myself as I watched him.

And then a hard knot formed in my stomach and had me gripping my shoulders. I smashed my forearms to my breasts to hide myself. "You wouldn't do this if you hadn't been drinking or weren't so upset. Maybe I—I shouldn't be in here with you?" I gave him my profile, prepared to flee and leave him alone to rub one out.

"So help me, Maria, if you walk out that door, I will slap your ass so hard you won't be able to sit for a week." The abrasive tone of his voice and order had me nervously peeking over at him, finding him still gripping his cock.

"You wouldn't."

"Don't try me, *Tesoro*," he remarked, only further turning me on as I fully faced him. I dragged my eyes up to meet his hard gaze, needing more reassurance from him that he truly wanted this. "It would take an entire bottle and then some for me to completely lose my mental faculties. Even then, that's debatable. I'm *not* drunk. Now, get your sexy ass over here."

His brother had said he'd been heavily drinking, and I'd assumed he was drunk, but he hadn't slurred since I'd arrived.

Smirking, he motioned for me to come closer, but I kept my hands to my shoulders, feeling my body blush with embarrassment.

The man before me was all hard and rigid lines, and I was the opposite. I'd never had washboard abs even before pregnancy, and working to get them now wasn't on my to-do list. I'd rather enjoy cheesecake and eat chips and salsa while binge-watching shows on Netflix.

"Maria?" He peered at me with a question in his eyes. "Don't you tell me that *idiota* ex of yours is in your head right now. If you're thinking about what he said today, so help me . . ." He was no longer beneath the spray of the water, and yet the cooler air striking him didn't make him go remotely limp.

"I'm just . . . well." I gripped my shoulders a touch harder. "You're like this Greek god before me."

"Italian," he shot back, nearly smiling despite whatever grave news he'd received earlier.

But then Thomas and his mother infiltrated my thoughts, and their not-so-kind words painted vicious strokes through my mind. "I'm curvy, Thomas was right." I thought about my stomach next. "Soft." I shook my head. "I have hips. Thighs. An ass. And, well, life's just too short not to eat bread." I shrugged, still holding my shoulders.

His lips twitched as if torn whether he wanted to smile or scowl. The mention of Thomas was probably to blame for the latter. "I love watching you eat, especially my food," he finally said. "And if you think for one second I don't love everything about you just as you are . . ." Instead of finishing his words, he surprised me by swallowing the space between us. "Lower your arms and let me look at what's mine."

The rough command alone would've done me in, but the way he'd snapped out "mine" had me feeling dizzy with desire, as if I were already on the precipice of an orgasm.

"*Tesoro,*" he said in a calmer voice this time, dragging a finger along the contour of my cheek while staring into my eyes. "If you walk away from me, I will snap. I can promise you that." He swallowed. "You're the only one capable of keeping me from . . ." He closed his eyes. "The only one who can save me when this is all over."

Over? "From what?"

"From hell, Maria." His lids slowly parted. "From hell," he repeated in a solemn tone that time.

"Enzo," I whispered, unsure what to say or do. "Talk to me. Now you really are scaring me." I let go of my shoulders to hold his muscular biceps, slick with water droplets. "Tell me what's going on."

He bowed his head to mine and in a shaky voice shared, "The man my brothers and I murdered wasn't responsible for Bianca's death. He was framed."

Your brothers helped you kill him? And wait . . . what? He was innocent? My body went cold at his words as disbelief grabbed hold of me.

"The man was still a killer, just not *her* killer." He eased his head back, and instead of the harsh look that'd been there since the moment I walked into his place tonight, I saw the twenty-four-year-old young man in mourning before me. Sad. Hurt. Angry and broken. "The day Bianca died, though, I died, too. Part of me, at least," he said in a hoarse voice. "That's my problem, don't you see? I only have half of me to give you. And you deserve someone who can give you their whole world, not just a piece."

My lip wobbled at the threat of tears, unsure how to talk without a sob escaping. But before I could find the strength to speak, he shifted away from my touch and went to the shower and turned off the water.

His hands went to his hips as he faced me. "I'm sorry, I was wrong. I can't—"

"I just want to be here for you, Enzo," I cut him off as I stepped before him. "Let me in. Stop pushing me away when it should be obvious by now I'm not going anywhere." *Let me love you.*

He reached for me and drew me against his body a second later, and my tits smashed against his damp skin. He held me tight, setting his chin on top of my head, and I lost track of how long he held me like that before we went into his bedroom.

He offered me a tee of his to sleep in, and he pulled on a pair of boxer briefs while I swapped my work pants for his shirt. His eyes never left my body the entire time I changed, and chills scattered across my skin at the way he looked at me.

Once in bed, he cradled me beneath his comforter, and little did he know he was still giving me the only non-naughty number on my list and the one that meant so much to me: falling asleep in his arms.

NINE

Enzo

With my sweatpants on, I went into the kitchen and chased down two Advil with black coffee, hating the harsh pain in my temples from drinking way more than normal last night. For once in my life, I'd wanted to lose control. And I nearly had with Maria.

Spotting my phone on the counter where I'd left it, I hesitantly flipped it over. The screen lit up with far too many texts I wasn't prepared to face.

I thumbed through the notifications, then shut off the screen, deciding I wanted to see the woman of my dreams asleep in my bed one more time before my world flipped upside down.

Pocketing my phone, I went back into my bedroom armed with my coffee and mixed emotions. How was I going to leave her later?

I leaned into the interior doorframe, studying her. Part of her face was covered by her long, thick hair. She must've been hot, because she'd shoved the covers down, and my white tee was bunched at her hips, showing her long, tan legs and a hint of her panties.

She shifted to her side, propping her hands beneath her face, but she remained peacefully asleep, and my heart ached at the sight of her in my bed, where I wanted her to spend every night for the rest of our lives.

It was almost too painful to see her there, to know what I could have if only I . . .

I stepped back and quietly drew the door shut and settled into an armchair by the fireplace to call Constantine.

"I wasn't drunk," was the first thing I said once he picked up. "You didn't need to worry." But sleeping with Maria in my arms had been what I'd needed, though I hadn't realized it until she showed up with all that determination in her eyes, prepared to fight my battles alongside me. *My fireball.*

"You had me worried," Constantine grumbled. "You're not one to throw back the whiskey like that."

I set the coffee mug aside, but my gaze lingered on the words CHEF'S KISS on it with a pair of red lips by the writing. It'd been one of my gifts from Maria for my birthday. "And you?" I cleared my throat. "What'd you do after I told you what I learned and sent you the cleaner's files?"

Alessandro probably had sex all night to try and handle his tension like I'd nearly done.

But Constantine? My brother was a question mark at times, and I didn't always understand how he could maintain his cool without exploding like I did.

"I worked," he answered in a steady tone.

"Oh, great. Mergers and acquisitions are more important than our—"

"I worked on Bianca's case," he fired back at my shitty sarcasm. "I went through all our old files from the investigation. I spent all night on it."

His words had my shoulders falling. My anger from last night was circling back without Maria in my presence to calm me down. "And?"

"And it doesn't make sense. She had no enemies we were aware of, and she would've told you if something was wrong. You two were close." He paused for a moment. "She didn't have a boyfriend at the time. Not even a lover. Even if she kept them hidden from us, there would have been photos when we packed up her place. Or the guy would've come to the funeral, right?" He hissed a deep, frustrated breath over the line. "And as for work, she'd written a few stories and articles for a magazine, but she wasn't an Erin Brockovich who might wind up with a target on her head. And no one would be stupid enough to come after one of us, knowing our family name."

"Not everyone in the US knows not to mess with us," I reminded him. "But we clearly missed something back then."

"Unless . . . well, her murder wasn't premeditated, and it was still a crime of passion as we'd originally believed. But instead, it was committed by someone else, and he had deep enough pockets or enough power to acquire a cleaner to assist him in the middle of the night to cover up a crime."

"What if she went somewhere after that club? Somewhere before she went home?"

"She punched in her building's security code at around midnight, though. Shortly after we had footage of her leaving that nightclub," he reminded me. "Unless the cleaner tampered with that, too."

"If the guy was that good to fool us back then, it's possible he altered even more than just when she turned off her alarm to enter her apartment."

"I know you're blaming yourself right now, but we were young. Inexperienced. We couldn't have known any of this."

"And you didn't spend all night blaming yourself?" I retorted, and his silence was my answer. Yeah, he felt the full weight of the guilt, same as I did. Because Bianca's killer was still out there.

"CEOs, dirty politicians, criminal groups, and—"

"The alphabet soup of government agencies all use cleaners." I finished his line of thought. "That's a big pool to scour through."

"Which is why we need to interrogate the cleaner ourselves. And I don't think your friend's boss will let us near him."

"Why do I get the feeling you know Jesse's boss?" At his curse in Italian, my body tensed. "What is it?"

"I do know him, and let's just say he's not my greatest fan." Constantine dropped the shit news on me. "His name is Carter Dominick. Former army Delta Force. CIA officer after that. Now coruns Falcon Falls."

I didn't need an introduction. I needed him to get to the point of the problem. "And?"

"Back when I was in college, before I dropped out to join the navy, Dad needed a favor from me. Didn't give me much of a choice." He paused to let the beginning of the storm sink in. "A company was attempting a hostile takeover of our family business. We were smaller back then, and this other corporation was ruthless. The owner was up there with Warren Buffett in terms of his bank account." Another pause that had me uncomfortable. "Dad needed me to try and buy some time to prevent the takeover."

"What could you possibly have done?"

"I was in school with the competitor's daughter, and Dad asked me to try and date her. Get her to fall for me so we could delay the takeover and strategize a way to prevent it from happening."

But how the hell was Carter part of the story? And how much of my brother's life did I not know about? As the oldest son, how much shit had he done to keep our family's business going?

"I was young and did what Dad told me. Did what I thought needed to be done," he explained. "It worked. And they backed off, assuming their daughter and I might marry."

"Tell me you didn't sleep with her." I pinched the bridge of my nose, worried I was going to need to beat the shit out of my older brother for something he'd done two decades ago.

"No, I'm not that much of an asshole," he hissed. "But her best friend was Carter Dominick. When Rebecca found out what I'd done to save the company, she was upset. And let's just say Carter came at me, swinging for retribution."

"I'm surprised her family didn't hold a grudge and do their best to take us down because of all that."

Constantine was quiet for a moment. "There was an accident not long after, leaving Rebecca the only one alive in the family. She was married to Carter, though. And then, um."

My brother didn't ever drop an "um." What in the hell was he going to tell me now?

"Rebecca was viciously murdered in a home invasion in DC, and Carter went rogue from the Agency, not believing it was random. I offered to help him, still feeling guilty for the past, and he told me to go fuck myself and if he ever saw me again, one of us wouldn't be walking away."

"Constantine . . ." What else could I say to that?

"Carter was angry, and although he's had vengeance for his wife's murder, I'm still certain he won't be willing to play nice. Seeing me will dredge up bad memories."

"I knew Dad was ruthless in business, but I didn't think he'd use one of us to get what he wanted."

And if I didn't know about any of that, then what if there was more to Bianca's life she hadn't shared, too? What if she hadn't told me everything while I'd been in the army, worried any distractions might prove deadly in war?

I thought back to my time in the service. I'd enlisted for four years with no plans to continue, but the war was brutal, and the army was desperate. They begged me for any more time I'd be willing to give. Feeling guilty, I offered two more years. And every day, I wished I could take that decision back, because what if Bianca would still be alive had I come home instead?

"If Dad was willing to go to such lengths as to have his own son manipulate a college girl to protect his company, then what if he pissed someone else off and they went after Bianca as retribution?" I asked, hating the idea when my dad had once been a champion of justice, someone my brothers and I had revered.

"He would've told us. He'd ensure the real person responsible for her death was handled—how could he not?"

"Unless he felt guilty?"

"I don't believe it, but we need to talk to him about this no matter what."

And how would our sister Izzy take the news? She was finally happy and had her life together. I didn't want this to cause her to spiral.

I put Constantine on speakerphone so I could reread the last encrypted text exchange I'd had with Jesse before Maria had shown up last night.

Me: I need his name.

Jesse: You'll get it. I promise. But don't forget, others need justice, too.

Me: There won't be anything left of him when I'm done.

Jesse: Which means I should've listened to my team, but it's too late now.

Me: Thirteen years too late.

Jesse: Just hang tight. Please. I'll be in touch tomorrow.

"Make sure Jesse's at your apartment when we arrive this afternoon," Constantine said, as if somehow knowing I was reading my texts. "I'll get the information out of him, since he doesn't seem to want to give it to you."

"Jesse's not someone you fuck with, trust me on that."

"And neither am I," Constantine was quick to respond, and I looked up to see the bedroom door opening.

"I have to go. See you soon." I ended the call at the sight of Maria and set my phone on the table by the chair. "How much of that did you hear?" I'd only placed the call on speaker less than a minute ago, so hopefully not much. She didn't need to know the dark details of what was about to go down.

"Not enough to make sense of anything." She tugged at the hem of my white tee, which went to her midthighs, as she slowly walked my way. "How'd you sleep?"

"Better with you by my side." I tipped my head toward her apartment next door. "Surprised no one broke down the door to check on you, though."

"They know you'd never hurt me," she softly said once within arm's reach.

"Never." I reached for her, forgetting for a moment I was supposed to become the man I was before moving to Charlotte. I'd soon need to tear apart New York until I found the answers I needed.

She sat on my lap and hooked an arm around the back of my neck while her legs dangled off to the side.

My gaze wandered appreciatively over her. From her nipples poking through my white cotton shirt to her shapely legs. I skirted a finger up her smooth thigh, and she nudged her knees apart at my touch.

God, I'd wanted her last night and nearly had given in to stroking my cock while she watched. But I knew I'd wind up pulling her into the shower with me. And I'd been too angry, too upset to be gentle with her.

"Thank you for last night. You helped me in a way I didn't know I needed," I shared, doing my best to maintain my control now.

"That's what friends are for," she murmured as I cupped her cheek with my other hand, and she leaned into my touch.

"Maria?"

"Yeah?" She pointed her big brown eyes at me. So innocent. So beautiful.

"If you ever show your tits to another 'friend' of yours," I began while sliding my hand down the tender column of her throat to swirl my thumb over her nipple, "they won't be able to see after that," I announced in a calm voice, unable to prevent the words from leaving my mouth, because when it came to this woman, I knew there was no going back. No watching her date. Absolutely no sharing.

"Oh, is that so?" She leaned back, maintaining eye contact, then ran her short nails over the ridges of my abdominal wall.

"That's so." My hand on her tit quickly changed course, finding her ass, and I squeezed, probably a bit roughly. But she spread open her legs even farther at the touch, and a small whimper escaped her lips. With everything going on, it was insane for me to want to hook her panties to the side to get a good look at her pussy, wasn't it?

I drew my mouth near hers, on the verge of kissing her despite the fact I'd told her in the parking lot last night she'd need to know my past first before our lips touched.

Seconds away from shifting her so she straddled me while I plunged my tongue inside her mouth, I was stopped by a knock at the door.

Maria groaned at the interruption. "Probably Natalia checking to see if we're awake." She nuzzled her nose against my neck, and my dick twitched. "We could pretend we don't hear her?"

"We shouldn't worry her." *And I need to behave.*

Maria untangled herself from me and stood at the next knock. "I guess you're right."

"Give me a second and just stay in here," I said while standing. "Unless you want your sister to see you wearing my shirt."

She blushed and fidgeted with the loose tee, and then I forced myself to go to the foyer to face Natalia.

I wasn't sure what I'd say to her after she'd witnessed my disastrous state last night, and I'd been an asshole, nearly begging her husband to fight me to release some steam.

I went to the door as the bell rang. I didn't check the peephole, and why would I?

So, when I swung the door open, the last thing I expected to see was three masked men, one of them wielding a bat.

TEN

Enzo

I shot my forearm out, and the bat slammed against it instead of hitting my face, but the other two men charged me in one fast movement, which sent me backward into the foyer, and I lost my balance and hit the wall behind me.

Maria's startled gasp distracted my focus, and I twisted around to see her too damn close to the danger. "Get in my bedroom." The punch to the side of my head snapped my attention back to two of the ass-holes, and they came at me hard.

I snarled, took a knee, and sent my weight forward to grab hold of one of them. I flipped him to his back, then, on my knees, sent a side kick to the second prick's abdomen.

Before either man had a chance to react, I pivoted to locate Maria, finding the man with the bat climbing on top of her. A bat to her throat. A hand on her thigh. And a death wish I was about to grant.

The two men grabbed hold of me before I could go to her, and I used all my strength and adrenaline to wrench myself free and take them down. I was at Maria's side seconds later, kneeling by her as I peeled the fucker from her body.

I had him on his back and under me. Blows and elbows to the face before I circled my hands around his throat, choking the life from him.

Growling out curses in both English and Italian, I kept at it until Maria cried out, "Enzo," just as something hard pressed against my temple. "Don't shoot him, please," she begged.

I went still, terror like I'd never known slicing through me at the idea there was a gun in the room with Maria. I loosened my hands on the man's throat; he'd been moments from death.

"Let him go," the man behind me said, but he had to be kneeling to have his weapon by my head, so I took a second to map out my plan and then lifted my hands, as if planning to surrender. I shifted in one fast movement as I'd been trained, and before he knew it, I had the 9mm in my hand instead.

He stumbled back, falling onto his ass in surprise.

"Who are you?" I barked out while standing. I stepped around the man on the floor and motioned for Maria to get behind me.

And then my world stopped when I saw Natalia walking into the living room with a gun to her back, hands in the air.

"Natalia." Maria started around me, but I snatched her waist with my free hand, stopping her.

"We only came here for you," the man standing behind Natalia said, eyes on me. "Hand over the gun and let my men come to me, and the women can go."

I considered my options, and handing over the weapon wasn't one of them. "And if you don't want his brains all over my floor, you'll lower your firearm," I hissed, keeping my hold on Maria even though it seemed she was determined to trade herself for her pregnant sister.

Natalia shook her head as if in apology. "I had a craving."

Fuck. She was letting me know Ryan wasn't home, and he was probably buying breakfast.

"Come closer. We'll trade," the man offered, flicking his gloved hand.

"Who are you?" I asked again, doing my best to buy time. Calculate my options. And hope Ryan would soon show up and disarm that prick. I'd just been thinking we needed to move to a place with better security, and now this . . .

I checked on the man I'd nearly choked to death, finding him trying to army crawl away. And my gaze snapped to the familiar ink on the back of his neck. The *triscele*, a symbol of Sicily, was there—the head of a Gorgon with serpents wrapped around it. It was the insignia for the New York division of the Sicilian mafia.

"Mafioso?" I whispered in alarm, my body somehow feeling both hot and cold at the same time.

The masked man on the floor halted, and he shifted to his side and grabbed something from his pocket. He flipped open the pocketknife as if that would somehow save him.

It made no sense. But . . . "Giovanni sent you?"

"Wait, what?" The man behind Natalia stumbled back a shocked step. "How do you know that name? You're a chef in Charlotte. You shouldn't know his name unless . . ." His dark gaze fell to the floor.

"Yes, you *idiota*," I rasped. "I'm Lorenzo fucking Costa." I knelt alongside the bastard and snatched the pocketknife from him. "Lower your weapon," I ordered to the one holding Natalia hostage.

The man hesitantly did what I'd instructed, and Natalia rushed toward Maria. They hugged and backed away from the scene.

I could breathe again, but these three men were about to lose their ability to do so in a moment.

"Get in my office. Lock the door," I told Maria and Natalia, and once they were out of sight, I stood tall again, lowering the firearm to my side, knowing the only threat in the room now was me.

"We didn't know," the man by the door said. "We'd never have taken the job if we realized you were *that* Costa." He slowly peeled his mask up because there was no sense hiding his face anymore.

"Giovanni would've known," I coldly remarked. "So who really sent you?" *Is this about Bianca?*

The man tucked his firearm at the back of his jeans and held up a surrendering hand. God, he was practically a child. He couldn't have been any older than I'd been when joining the army.

"Tell me what's going on or I slit his throat." When they all remained quiet, I took a knee again and set the blade to the man's throat, almost hoping for a reason to cut. I nicked him, drawing a little blood, my frustration growing by the second.

"Giovanni doesn't know we're here," the man closest to the door shared. "We take side jobs here and there when we get bored."

Bored? God help these men, because I wasn't sure if their age would be enough to save them from me. "What's your name?"

"Jensen. And the truth is, we were offered a lot of money to show up today to give you a beating. Break your arms. Fingers. Those were our instructions. We only take jobs outside of New York so our boss doesn't find out about our side gigs."

"Who hired you?"

"We don't know, I swear," Jensen replied. "Dark-web kind of thing."

My jaw tightened, and I shifted the knife away from his throat and slowly stood, pointing the 9mm at Jensen. "Call Giovanni."

The guy I'd disarmed, who'd been obediently kneeling, begged, "No, Giovanni will kill us for this."

I grunted and cocked my head. Did I really need to warn him what I'd do if they didn't listen?

Jensen was quick to follow my order, and he approached with caution while placing the call on speakerphone.

"Why the hell are you calling me at seven in the morning?" Giovanni rasped in a sleepy voice. "Someone better be dying."

"Someone is about to," I remarked in a low voice.

"Who is this?" Giovanni slowly asked.

"Lorenzo Costa. Three of your men are at my home in Charlotte. And they were sent here to *try* and beat me up."

A string of Italian curses flooded the line before Giovanni said, "I have nothing to do with this. We have a deal. You know I wouldn't break it."

"And what about your son-in-law, Nico? I heard he's taking over soon." I was testing him. Testing Jensen's story, too.

"Nico knows better than to mess with a Costa." He was quiet before saying, "What did you do, Jensen?"

Jensen looked at me, then back at the phone. "We were just trying to make some money on the side. We never, uh, do anything in New York. I promise." His dark-brown eyes disappeared with every dramatic blink. "I don't know who hired us."

"You have until tomorrow to get me the name of whoever the hell did," I said in a steady, low voice, doing my best not to unleash my anger on the three *idiotas* in the room with me. "The only reason we tolerate your family is because you're my mother's cousin. But believe me when I tell you that won't stop me from burning your entire operation to the ground if I don't have a name by tomorrow."

Giovanni quietly assessed my threat, but he knew better than to fuck with me. Family or not, I meant every word. "What do you plan to do with them? Jensen is my wife's nephew."

I shot a harsh look to the man on the floor clutching his throat, unsure if I could let him walk away from me, but Maria and Natalia were in the other room, and could I kill someone with them here? What would that do to them?

"They're practically kids," I hissed. "I suggest you encourage them to shut down their side operation and knock some sense into them when they get back home. Or I'll hunt them down after they leave here and do it myself." I focused on the man who'd been on top of Maria, my eyes narrowing his way. "If you ever touch a woman inappropriately again, you'll beg me to kill you after what I do to you, understand?"

He wrapped a hand over the small puncture at his throat where I'd nicked him, and he nodded.

"I'm showing them mercy, Giovanni. That's something I don't do." I peered back at the phone. "There won't be any tomorrow if I don't have the name."

"Understood," was all Giovanni said, and then I motioned to Jensen to end the call.

"Leave before I change my mind." My eyes fell to the blood on my white carpet near my feet as I waited for them to go.

A minute or so later, I looked up to see Ryan now there with a brown bag cradled in his arm. The door must've been left open, and he'd assumed Natalia was here, and . . .

Ryan looked at me, then at the 9mm at my side, and the bag fell to the floor as his face went pale. "What the hell happened while I was gone?"

ELEVEN

Maria

"Mafia?" Natalia exclaimed, eyes wide as she spoke with her hands, pacing around the living room. And from the looks of it, that was one secret she hadn't known about.

I honestly wasn't sure what to do or how to process anything that happened before my brother-in-law had shown up with my sister's everything bagels she'd been craving.

So far, all I'd done was put on pants and one of Enzo's hoodies to hide my body. Not that Ryan would check me out, but still.

"I'm not *mafioso*," Enzo said in a low, grumbly voice, and his gaze snapped to me as I stood by the wall of windows. It felt wrong somehow for the sun to be spearing through the room as it was, illuminating the place. "I don't know what you heard through the door, but you're wrong."

Ryan stopped my sister from wearing a hole in the floor and pinned her back to his chest, setting his chin on her head. The fact someone had pointed a gun at her had the tic in his jaw on overdrive ever since he'd arrived. He wanted to wipe the floors with those men's blood, too, didn't he?

And honestly, when we left the office, I'd expected there to be more blood staining the carpet. Enzo had shown restraint, which meant he wasn't the monster he tried to make himself out to be.

"But those men are in the mafia, and they have a connection to you, right?" my sister asked, still searching for answers I wasn't sure Enzo would give.

"I need to call Constantine since I'm now planning to go there instead." Enzo left her question unanswered, and he grabbed his phone and went into his office.

I wasn't sure if space was what he needed, but I had no plans to give it to him. Not after some man got on top of me and set a bat to my throat and my life had flashed before my eyes. Chiara being raised without me wasn't an option.

"Give him a second." Ryan's request had me remaining still. "He's running on adrenaline right now. And he's probably upset that he let three men walk away alive after what they did."

"And are you upset?" Natalia faced him, and I tugged the hoodie strings, my mind spinning every which way.

Ryan tipped her chin and stared down at her. "A man pointed a gun at my pregnant wife, and the only reason I'm not going after him is because I know you won't let me kill him."

"And because you want to be in our son's life instead of prison, right?" Natalia whipped her arms across her chest, glaring at him.

He cocked his head as if unsure prison was a deterrent to murdering anyone who'd dare hurt the woman he loved and his unborn child.

"Ryan," she hissed. "You and Enzo, I swear. Cut from the same cloth." Her attention landed back on me, her arms still tight above her pregnant belly. "Let's go in there before he goes nuclear. He doesn't need space. He needs sense knocked into him."

"I agree." And I was glad we were on the same page.

Ryan trailed right behind us, but we halted the second we entered the office. The bookshelf wasn't in the same place, and there was a six-foot wide-open space in the wall there instead, exposing a second room.

"Did you know about this?" I asked her, pointing to a room where I saw three large screens on the wall, and I knew Enzo wasn't into day-trading like Thomas. So no, those screens weren't for watching the stock market.

"No." Natalia squeezed my arm, motioning to go in.

I hesitantly entered, finding Enzo off to my left by some small control-panel thing, and a second later, what appeared to be a mirror slid down and in its place were at least ten types of guns and an array of knives. *Not* cooking knives.

Holy shit. "What is this?" I whispered in astonishment.

"It's who I really am," Enzo said without turning, and the icy tone of his voice provoked a massive wave of shivers to flow down my spine. "Real life. Not fiction. This is me."

My hip bumped into a nearby table, and my gaze fell to a sheet of paper there. I mindlessly snatched it, my gaze narrowing on the name and photo. *My date?* "Enzo?" I blinked. "What'd you do to my date?"

He slowly turned. "Did he hurt you? Touch you that night?"

"No." I quickly shook my head, terror climbing into my throat, squeezing my vocal cords at the idea Enzo might hurt the man I'd had dinner with the other night if he had so much as put a hand on me.

"Then nothing happened to him, Maria," he casually remarked as if discussing the restaurant's specials for tonight; then he focused back on packing what appeared to be a heavy-duty case full of weapons.

"I thought you left this life behind," Natalia said. "Why would you need this room? The screens? The weapons?"

"Because you just never know," he snapped out; then his shoulders fell as if he regretted his tone. "I know you want answers, but I need to make sure no one else was hired to go after my family in New York."

"And why would anyone come after any of you?" Ryan asked.

Enzo locked the case and faced us, but his eyes landed on the hoodie. I looked down to see NYU in bold letters. Bianca had attended college there. She must've bought it for him, and now . . .

His brows tightened as he kept his gaze focused on the sweatshirt. "It doesn't make sense, not even in light of the news I learned last night," he slowly began. "They were sent here to rough me up. Not kill me. Not warn me about anything. My brothers and I haven't even started poking around to draw attention." His inked arms slid over his muscular chest as he studied us.

"Bianca's death?" Natalia stepped forward, but Ryan went right with her. He knew Enzo would never hurt her, but I had a feeling he was going to be overly protective, even more than normal, after what went down this morning.

"An old friend of mine showed up last night, letting me know he has reason to believe there's more to the story involving the death of my sister. I'm heading to New York to look into it." His gaze slowly went to Natalia. "Brandon can handle the kitchen while I'm gone. I'm sorry, but I have no choice but to leave."

He wasn't just leaving the restaurant, he was leaving me.

"I know you want justice," Natalia began, "but going back down that path is dangerous, and you know it. Let the police handle this. You've been gone from the life for years, even before I asked you to move here, and—"

"I haven't been gone as long as you think," Enzo cut her off. "When my contract ended, I didn't stop taking justice into my own hands."

Contract?

"My brothers and I didn't retire until I came here." He finally shared what appeared to be news to Natalia. "This isn't the time or place to have this conversation. I need to get ready and go." With eyes on Ryan, he added, "They were only after me, but Maria should stay with you until this is over."

"You told me the other day you weren't a danger to them," Ryan remarked.

When was that conversation, and what had brought it on? Would Ryan cooperate? Let Enzo leave the truth hanging?

"You were clearly wrong." Ryan huffed out a deep breath and hooked his arm around his wife, pulling her tight to his side.

Enzo's broad shoulders arched back, and a million regrets seemed to seep from his body, striking me one by one like bullets.

Is being in my life now one of those regrets? "If those men don't tell you who sent them here by tomorrow, what will you do?" From the office, I'd overheard Enzo warn something to some guy named Giovanni over the phone. Thin walls and all.

Enzo's gaze cut to me. "It'll mean war."

"With the mafia?" For once, I was grateful Chiara was with her father.

"With my mother's side of the family," Enzo tersely answered, "yes."

TWELVE

Maria

"No, don't come here. It's a waste of time. Just stay there and send the jet, Constantine," Enzo said into his phone while buttoning his black dress shirt.

I had my back to the wall in his bedroom, and we were alone for the time being. I'd followed him into his room, not giving him a chance to shut me out. He'd been on the phone and slightly distracted, or he probably wouldn't have let me in. But I was done being behind a wall of secrets.

"I know, I'll talk to Jesse. Don't worry," he continued, his eyes finding mine this time as he shoved down his sweats, and I swallowed at the sight of his hard, muscular legs, remembering that hot moment from his bathroom last night.

He still had on the same black boxer briefs he'd slipped into last night, and after expelling a deep, probably-frustrated-with-me breath, he snatched his black dress pants from where he'd laid them out on the bed.

"No, I don't think Giovanni lied. He'd never be stupid enough to send his own people to rough me up, especially not if he was connected to her death back then," I listened to him say, and I had to assume Constantine had floated the idea their mom's cousin was somehow responsible for Bianca's death. "I think this was just a bad fucking coincidence. But it's possible whoever hired the three *idiotas* was trying to make it look like the mafia is to blame for her death to throw us off."

They exchanged a few more words; then he ended the call and tossed his phone on the bed. He zipped his slacks and buttoned them, eyes returning to me.

"You don't think what happened this morning was about Bianca, or you do? I'm not sure where your head is at on this." I kept my back to the wall for stability because my legs were on the verge of giving out.

He adjusted the collar of his shirt, then fidgeted with his sleeves, working one to his elbow, exposing the ink I was so drawn to. "I suppose it's possible, but it just doesn't make sense."

I cocked my head, waiting for him to meet my eyes again. I hated that he felt like a different person right now. Cool and aloof. A man I barely knew. He wasn't the man who'd stood before me vulnerable last night as he asked me to save him from hell.

Three men attacked him this morning, I reminded myself. *Nearly hurt Natalia and me.* Yeah, of course Enzo was off.

He focused on his other sleeve, working it to his elbow while sharing, "Jesse is too good to have been followed. Too good for someone to figure out why he was even at the restaurant last night."

"But because of the timing it's hard to believe it's unrelated?"

"It would have to mean whoever hired the cleaner found out he was on the run, and they preemptively acted, worried I'd find out the truth. But it still doesn't add up. Even if they didn't know about Jesse's talk with me, by coming after me, they put me on alert, and why would they want that?" He finally looked at me and sighed. "I'll figure it out, don't worry."

"That's not what I'm worried about." I finally pushed away from the wall and went to him, but he lifted his palms between us as a request not to touch him, and, well, that sucked.

"Maria, I'm not in the right state of mind right now." He flipped his palms to look at them. "I wanted to kill that man for what he did to you. But he was a fucking kid, and you were in the other room, so I showed him mercy."

"And what's wrong with mercy?" My voice broke that time as I eyed the inked words **No Mercy** on his forearm. "Because that's not something you're accustomed to showing someone?"

His jaw went tight beneath his facial hair, and he shook his head. Did that mean yes or no? "Last night you said you wouldn't run, but after what just happened . . . you should be terrified of me. Why aren't you?"

"You keep telling me I like to play with fire. I guess you're the flame I'm drawn to, and I can't stay away." I candidly admitted the only truth that seemed to make sense.

But was I crazy not to be scared? Was I so head over heels for this man I could get hit in the face with a bunch of red flags and see green instead?

I mean, his mother's family was mafia. And the mafia was afraid of *him*. He had a room of monitors and weapons that didn't belong in a chef's home. Then there was the brutal fact he could kill, and here I was, a person unable to kill a bug without remorse.

And here I am, glued in place.

He was as stuck with me as I was with him, that was all I knew.

Now the tricky part would be making him understand that.

"No," he bit out, as if reading my thoughts. "You're not coming." He slashed his arms through the air and began cursing in Italian, eyes still beholding mine. "Absolutely not."

I chewed on my lip, trying to figure out how to get through to him when he had way more restraint than I did. Was far more stubborn, especially when it came to my safety. "What if someone comes after me to get to you?" That would be my best chance to get him to surrender to my wishes. Yes, I was playing dirty, but in my mind, the man's soul was on the line. His life. If he went back to New York to face those demons without me, and they swallowed him whole, I could lose him forever. "I guess Chiara is safer away from me and with her father right now, too."

He frowned and remained quiet for a few painful seconds before suggesting, "I'll hire Ryan's SEAL buddies who helped him out last year. They can fly in for extra protection."

"Natalia's pregnant. She doesn't need the stress of worrying about having a target on her head because I'm around. It's a bad idea."

He closed the space between us, which forced me to walk backward until I hit the wall again. "Then they can take you somewhere off-the-grid and keep an eye on you." He angled his head as if daring me to challenge him.

"You want me alone in a cabin with a bunch of guys?" My question had him snarling. He was still wound up, so it didn't take much to push him. "And if something happened to me because you weren't personally protecting me, then what?"

"Nothing will ever happen to you. I won't let it." His palms went to the wall on each side of me, and when he leaned closer, I realized he was as hard as I was wet.

Was there something wrong with the both of us that we were aroused right now? But this man always had me hot and bothered, and I didn't know how to turn it off.

"Then prove it." I lifted my chin. "Protect me yourself."

He scowled, and I'd swear, it felt like he wanted to punish me. Throw me on his bed, bend me over, and take a belt to my ass.

"Why do you do this to me?" he rasped.

"I'm trying to save you." And that was the truth. "It's a lot easier to bring you back from hell if I'm already there with you. After all of this, what if . . ." No, there was no chance I could let him leave without me. "It's Wednesday," I said with a nod. "You have until Sunday to get justice."

"Sunday?" He angled his head. "Why then?"

"I'm coming with you, and Chiara's with her father until then."
I swallowed, worried he'd see the bit of fear in my eyes. "That's your
deadline for revenge."

"Deadline for revenge," he growled out. "And you think you can
handle the things I plan to do in the name of justice?"

I rolled my lips inward, attempting to summon the answer he
needed to hear, hoping I'd truly be able to stomach the "things" he
planned to do.

But then I thought about Bianca, and I stared him in the eyes as I
murmured, "If someone out there is responsible for your sister dying . . ."
My eyelids fluttered closed as I said as confidently as possible, "I'll light
the match you need to burn down their entire world."

At the feel of my arms whooshing up over my head, my eyes startled open. Enzo had my wrists pinned to the wall. He was leaning in
so close we were practically one, and every hard ridge and slope of his
body touched me.

"You don't mean that," he gruffly said, his hot breath on my face.
"You don't understand what it's like to take a life. And I never want you
to know that feeling, do you hear me?" With his forearms over mine
still, he laced our fingers, locking our hands together against the wall.
"Maria, so help me, tell me you understand."

"I—I understand," I whispered. "But I'm still coming with you." I
wouldn't back down from that.

His gaze narrowed as his grip strengthened a touch. "You make
me crazy," he said in a nearly broken voice just before he did it. Finally
kissed me. Six long years of waiting to feel his lips again.

With his restraint snapping, our soft groans mingled together as
we kissed. My body seemed to meld with his as he slid his tongue into
my mouth, twining his with mine like a battle he was desperate to win.
I gave in and let him dictate the movements because the man had an
expert tongue, and he could lead me nearly anywhere with it.

"Maria," he said between soft kisses that turned erotic again, and I wanted to grab him. Hold his hair. Touch him. But with my arms locked over my head, I was at his mercy.

He tore his lips from mine a minute or so later, only to drag them along my jawline. Then he trailed his mouth down the side of my neck, sucking and nipping at my skin in a few places as if he wanted to devour every inch of me.

His teeth grazed my flesh before he lifted his mouth to my face and found my lips again, and a nearly bruising, punishing kiss followed and had me spiraling.

When our lips finally broke, I whispered, "I'll take that as a yes. I'm coming with you."

He brought his mouth to my ear, coaxing more goose bumps to erupt beneath the hoodie. "I told you, you have power over me, *Tesoro*. I don't know how to say no to you." He let go of my hands, which allowed me to finally touch him.

I fisted his black dress shirt with both hands, and once our eyes met, I begged, "Then don't."

THIRTEEN

Enzo

"You're absolutely certain no one knows you came to see me about the files?" I may have been talking to Jesse, but I couldn't rip my focus away from Maria inside the private hangar at the Charlotte Douglas Airport. She was talking to her sister, and they were exchanging a few words before we boarded my family's jet. From the moment we'd shared that Maria was coming with me, Natalia had been trying to convince her to stay. I prayed she could, since I'd been unsuccessful.

"No one, aside from my teammates, is aware I came to you. And before you ask, yes, I trust them all with my life. Hell, with my wife's life." Jesse paused, probably waiting for my attention. "The only thing I can think of is someone was keeping tabs on the cleaner, and they picked up on the fact there was a breach. They'd have to be one paranoid SOB to do that. But still, why come after you? That'd only tip you off something is fucked up."

I surrendered my focus his way. "I considered that, too. And if the attack this morning is connected to the cleaner's list, that means the real killer is more than likely someone I know. And they're aware of what I'm capable of if I learn what happened to Bianca."

"Which is either stupid on their part to give you the heads-up shit is about to hit the fan, or they have an ulterior motive in wanting you to know."

Fuck if I know what to think right now. "In the meantime, I need the name. I don't care what Carter wants."

Jesse frowned. "Even once we track the cleaner down, there's no guarantee they know who hired them. They kept meticulous records of their jobs, and yet, no names."

"And why keep those records in the first place unless—"

"It's also his insurance policy against who hired him," Jesse finished for me.

Him? Well, I was getting somewhere. The cleaner was a man. Now if I could get a name, that'd be great. "If his clients have power and money, they wouldn't want any loose ends, and he'd be one of them. He must know that, so he has a way to protect himself from being eliminated as well."

"He knows someone is after him now, and if word gets out his files have been compromised, if it hasn't already, he's going to have a lot of people looking to put a cap in his ass before he can turn on them. Insurance policy or not, they'll take their chances."

Maria had given me until Sunday, but I doubted the cleaner had that long, which meant I had to do what I did best. Go hunting. And hopefully get to them before they came after me again. "So . . . his name?"

"It's not just about my team's concern that you'll go rogue and try and get to him yourself." Jesse's slight scowl didn't do wonders for my nerves. "Carter doesn't like your brother. He didn't tell me why, but he said there's beef there, and he doesn't want to work with him on this."

I know why. No time to discuss that now. "I can't keep my brother out of this, especially not after some *mafioso* showed up at my apartment this morning."

"But if I tell you this guy's name, it's my head, and—"

"And you knew that before you came to the restaurant last night," I reminded him. "You could've waited, but you didn't."

"Look, I want us to work together." He looked past me in the direction of Maria and Natalia. "Give me a few hours to convince my team to bring you into the fold." He held up a palm as if knowing I was seconds away from protesting. "If it's a no from them, then I'll go ahead and give you his name and deal with the consequences from Carter."

I considered the options. And beating the information from an old friend right now wasn't one of them. "You didn't invite me to the wedding," I said instead, knowing he'd understand my lack of arguing about the cleaner was an answer.

Jesse ran his hand across his mouth. "It wasn't exactly a normal situation. We had to fake the whole getting-married bit, but then we decided to turn in the paperwork later so it was legit."

"Fake marriage, huh?"

"That's a story for another day." He semismiled, putting eyes on Maria, her sister, and Ryan. "Do your brothers know she's coming?"

"Not yet."

"No chance your father's past has anything to do with what happened to Bianca? Your dad's old organization has had quite the shake-up lately."

"I don't think he's involved, but I'm not ruling anyone or anything out," I shared, thinking about the change in leadership in Sicily. A woman now ran things there, and from what I knew, she was solid and deserved the role. Married Irish, which turned a few heads and ruffled quite a lot of old-school Italian feathers.

"I really am sorry I had to drop this on you. But I won't leave you hanging." Jesse extended his hand, and his ring caught my eye. That circle of damn hope I'd never thought possible for me.

"Yeah, I trust you." I slapped his hand with mine; then we said our goodbyes before I started for the jet, anxious to take off, but not so eager to do so with two bodyguards on board. Constantine was paranoid and overprotective to think I'd need escorts while up in the sky.

I sent a quick text to my brothers about the change in plans.

Me: Let Mom know I'll have a plus-one at dinner tonight.

Alessandro was quick to respond, and I reread his punch-to-the-gut words.

Alessandro: Have you lost your mind? You want to put her in harm's way? Why?

He was right. I had lost my mind.

Constantine: We can keep her safe. If he wants her with him, then so be it.

I wasn't expecting that answer from Constantine, and part of me had hoped my eldest brother would knock some sense into me, because he was probably the only one I'd listen to. Well, aside from Maria, so it would seem.

Me: Can you have my car waiting for me at the airport? I want to swing by my place to grab some stuff before I head to Mom and Dad's.
Constantine: Yeah, but there's been a change in plans for this unexpected family reunion. We're going to stay at our place in Oyster Bay instead. It's more secure.
Me: You're making sure Izzy is coming, too, right?
Constantine: Of course. But she's bringing her boyfriend.
Alessandro: Boyfriend? She does realize we're all going to interrogate him, right?

Constantine: I promised we wouldn't. Only way I could get her to agree.

Alessandro: Fuck that. I didn't promise.

Constantine: Focus that anger elsewhere, like on finding Bianca's killer.

Alessandro: Yeah, sure. And hell, if this is turning into a party, I should bring a plus-one, too.

Constantine: Be serious.

Alessandro: You know me. Humor and copious amounts of sex are my coping mechanisms. Well, so the shrink says.

Since when did he see a therapist?

Constantine: We need to focus. Did Jesse give you the name?

Me: Not yet. I'll have it by this evening, though.

Constantine's slow reply meant he regretted not flying down to get the information from Jesse himself.

Constantine: I'll find Carter and get it from him if I have to.

From the sound of it, that wasn't a fight I was eager to see. And we needed to be on the same side. Jesse was right.

I looked over at Maria, and her eyes met mine. That sinking feeling in my stomach came back.

Me: Tell me one more time I'm not crazy for bringing her with me.

Alessandro: I can't do that. You are.

Constantine: Just do what you think is right. You always do.

What I always do? That would be the opposite of bringing Maria with me today. I pocketed my phone, unsure if I really knew what was the right decision. But Maria somehow had me breaking my own rules at every turn. And after that kiss this morning—

"You're sure about this?" Ryan asked, cutting off my thoughts.

"No, I'm not," I honestly shared, which had Maria shooting me a death stare. "But she's a pain in the ass, so I guess she's coming whether I want her to or not." And I wanted to spank that woman's ass for this, too.

"If anything happens to her," was all Ryan said, and it was all he needed to say. There'd be hell to pay across the board if so much as a hair was touched on her head.

"I don't think you should go, but I know I can't stop you." Natalia pulled Maria in for a hug, careful not to smash her pregnant belly, and then Ryan hugged her next. "A quick word alone, please?" Natalia tugged my arm.

"I'd expect nothing less," I said as I followed her away from the others.

"She's persuasive." Natalia cut to the point. "But you're not one to roll over for anyone. And all I know is that when I came over this morning, my sister was wearing only your T-shirt. Did you two sleep together last night?"

Shit. "No, we didn't have sex." I held my forehead for a moment, unprepared for that question. "You should talk to Maria about this stuff, though."

"Just keep her safe, okay?"

"That's a given." I smoothed my palm along my jawline.

"And don't break her heart." She gave me her signature stern look. "Promise?"

I swallowed, tense at the idea of ever hurting Maria in any way. Not knowing what to say, I kept my mouth shut, and I did my best to nod. Natalia gave me a quick hug, and we made our way back over to the group. We then said our goodbyes and boarded the jet.

The two bodyguards, who didn't look all too impressive, were strapped in near the cockpit, leaving a few rows of space between where

Maria and I sat. Thankfully, the jet didn't have a bedroom on board. If it did, I'd probably drag Maria in there and spend the flight distracting myself between her thighs, torturing her with my tongue . . .

Fuck, now I wanted to add "join the mile-high club" to that list of hers.

She buckled in across from me in the leather bucket seat and said, "The last time I was on a plane was six years ago heading home from New York. I guess I need to travel more."

And damn, I hoped one day I'd be able to take her all over the world. Show her every place she'd only read about in books to experience for herself.

"Everything will be okay," I said once we took off, my attention trailing along her outfit. She had on black jeans with a fitted thin red turtleneck.

She fidgeted with the neck of her top, pulling at it just enough that I could spot a bruise there.

Did I do that? Hell, I probably would've marked more of her body in my bedroom earlier had Natalia and Ryan not been in the living room.

Maria nervously combed her fingers through her thick, curly dark hair. Knowing we were having dinner with my parents later, she'd demanded the chance to shower and freshen up before we left for the airport.

Gripping the chair arms, she locked her eyes with mine, and her tongue swept along the line of her lips.

"If you keep looking at me like that, I'll need to throw those two men from the plane," I said. We'd only just taken off, maybe they'd survive the fall?

"Really? Why?"

Because I wanted to sink my teeth into her skin. Mark her again, which was a special kind of fucked up, and I didn't care. Her knees pinned together as her other hand clutched her leg, and I couldn't help but bite my lower lip. Oh, my girl knew why.

I leaned in closer, cocking an eyebrow. "Can't have other men looking at you while you come, now can I?"

She swallowed back a small moan, and damn if I didn't wish it was my mouth hiding the sound instead. I was trying to behave, since we weren't alone, and trying to not totally become the man I was before Charlotte. Because *that man* would've taken her how he wanted on the jet regardless of the eyes on us.

That man would've spread her out on the couch off to our left, fallen to his knees, and tossed her legs over his shoulders while sinking his mouth over her pussy.

But this was Maria, and like hell would I let any other man see her naked or hear her soft moans of pleasure while she came.

"I'm not kidding, sweetheart," I murmured in a low voice, my patience gone at this point. My control had snapped in half as of this morning.

The only question now was *when* I'd be taking her and where.

"Do not look at me like that. You need to stop tempting me. Because I want to punish you for doing this to me. For making me bring you along for this fucked-up ride that you should be as far away from as possible," I warned once we were at cruising altitude, but for whatever reason, I only seemed to provoke desire from her. Not fear.

She wet her lips as her dainty hand circled her throat. "Far away from the danger? Or away from you?"

"I am the danger," I bluntly said. "You know exactly why you shouldn't be on this plane. You're looking at the reason."

"What I'm looking at is a man who thinks he's not worthy of love. That he doesn't have a full heart to give because he lost his twin sister. Lost his other half," she softly said, and her words had my chest tightening. "But that man does deserve it. And your sister would want that for you." She unbuckled. "Now, excuse me while I use the restroom." Shit, were those tears in her eyes?

I snatched her wrist once she was in the aisle, and her gaze flashed to where I held her, but I reluctantly released her.

My eyes closed, and I sat back, trying to dismantle the intrusive thoughts that warred with each other. Like always. The good and the bad. The dark and the light. Without Bianca, I'd lost sight of the other side for so long.

I hadn't always been like this. After the first life I took in the army, it'd been Bianca there for me. Helping me get a handle on my guilt. We'd spent hours on the phone that night. And I'd had to convince myself the boy I'd killed had been eighteen, because if he'd been younger, I would've totally broken the fuck down.

Unsure how long I'd been lost in my thoughts of the past, I finally opened my eyes, discovering Maria back in her seat. There were questions she wanted to ask me, I could feel it. And why wouldn't there be? I'd kept so much of myself from her. I'd thought it was to protect her from the ugliness of my past, but maybe I was just scared she'd see me differently, and I'd lose her forever.

"Will you tell me the truth now?" Maria's soft request had me surrendering a deep breath. "Or you could give it to me in three acts," she suggested while I continued to contemplate what to do. "You know, like the beginning, middle, and end of a book. Tell me the first part now. Reveal the rest when you're ready?"

"Or when *you're* ready, you mean? Because maybe you're not prepared to hear how truly messed up I am."

She fidgeted with the seat belt, taking her time to respond. "The prologue for right now is fine," was all she said.

"You really want me to go *that* far back? All the way to Italy?" After her hesitant nod, I crossed my ankle over my knee, holding it while looking toward the window. I thought back to the story my parents had told us when we were old enough to understand, not too long before

I'd given up my dream of culinary school at Dad's insistence to join the army. "It all starts with my father."

"And?" That tentative little word drew my eyes back to her.

"An organization was created in Europe to fight crime. Off-the-books stuff. My father was part of the Italian division, which is how he met my mom." I didn't need to get into the details, but she'd get the idea. "And her father was in the mafia. Well, not just in it. The head of the crime family."

"Oh, so a *Romeo and Juliet* thing?"

"I guess you could say that, and this kind of love story between rivals is more common than anyone cares to admit." Well, so my parents always told us. "When my mom was only twenty, a criminal organization kidnapped her. And before her family could pay the ransom to get her back, my dad rescued her. Her family didn't know they'd been secretly dating for months."

"I take it that her family wasn't a fan of him."

"No, they didn't make it easy for her to walk away, but my father and the organization he worked for didn't give them a choice once my parents announced their marriage."

"What happened after that?" she softly asked.

"The mafia feared my father and his organization, and with good reason. My dad had earned a reputation. He was known as *Il Santo*, the Saint."

"A savior?"

"Not exactly," I admitted. "More like a man prepared to take your soul to hell if you crossed the line."

"So why'd your parents leave Italy?"

"Mom had four kids. Was pregnant with her fifth. She told my father it was time to change. Start over. And then Izzy was born once they were in New York, and my dad worked on building his business empire, saying goodbye to his old life."

"He did it for love," she whispered.

A surprising smile met my lips, and it softened her full mouth into one as well. "And then my mother's cousin, Giovanni, moved to New York to run the Sicilian division of the Italian mafia." Based on her confused look, I figured I'd better elaborate a bit more. "Things have changed over the years, but usually there are about five main families within the Italian American mafia."

"Like a gangs-of-New-York-type thing? And no, I don't mean like the movie. Although, I did watch a few episodes of *The Sopranos*. I want to say I vaguely remember something about mafia families being mentioned. But overall, my knowledge is limited."

I smothered a smile with my hand at her rambling, which I found adorable. I wished we weren't talking about reality. *My fucking reality.* "The families all have much less control now than they did in the old days, but I suppose all you need to know is when my mother's cousin came to New York, my father threatened him. If he wanted to stay stateside, he'd have to run his crime syndicate differently than the other mafia families. No trafficking of any kind. Drugs, people, animals. No murdering or hurting innocents."

"And he behaved?" she asked in shock.

"As far as I know. Giovanni claims his organization is more like a company, and their insignia a business logo." My gaze fell to my arm where good and evil warred there, the same as it did internally. "But I guess you could say all this shit is in my blood. It's who I was destined to be."

"No." She leaned forward and set her hand on my knee, and my gaze lingered there for a quiet moment before returning to her face as she added, "You're your own person. You can *do* and *be* whatever you want."

I wanted to believe that, but she only knew the beginning act, the start to my story, and I wasn't sure if she'd still believe that once I gave her all the hideous details from the middle.

The other issue was the end had yet to be written, and I didn't have a damn clue the direction my story would go.

"I won't back down from the threat I made to Giovanni." If she was suggesting that, she needed to know where I stood. "There will be no mercy if he doesn't give me a name."

"But Giovanni didn't know that his guys were sent to attack you." She pulled her hand back and settled in her seat, clearly unhappy with my words. "And you just said they're basically businessmen now."

Was she trying to walk me off the cliff of crazy? Did she forget a man had had a bat to her throat and a hand on her thigh? Did she not know what vile things that man-child had been thinking about while straddling her?

I shrugged. "I don't care."

"Enzo, there's a difference between going after whoever murdered Bianca and taking out some young punk who was looking for a fight at your apartment." She fidgeted with the sleeves of her top, and it was clear she was growing uncomfortable.

"And those young punks turn into the kind of men who hurt innocent women," I shot back, hating that ugly truth. But after everything I'd witnessed in my life, I knew I was right. I unbuckled, stood, and set my hand to the ceiling, peering down at her as I remarked in a rough voice, "I guess this means I know how you'll react when you hear the middle of my story. And maybe you were wrong about what you said last night. Maybe you will run."

FOURTEEN

Maria

"How are we fitting everything in there?" I asked as Enzo loaded only his weapons-case thing into a Porsche at JFK. The trunk was located under the car's hood at the front, which I already knew because Enzo had owned one back in Charlotte.

"We're not." Enzo closed the hood-trunk and swiveled around with his sunglasses hiding his eyes. "There's space behind the seats, but I need that for something else." He tossed a look toward the two security details and pointed to our suitcases by the car. "These will need to ride with you two," he instructed, and one of them quietly grabbed our suitcases and loaded them in the Suburban parked behind us.

"How'd you manage to get a case of weapons through security anyway? Didn't it have to go through a scanner or something?" I asked.

"I know a guy who knows a guy." He shrugged, and was that sarcasm or was he being serious? Right now, I couldn't tell.

I folded my arms, not ready to get into such a tight space with him, worried his bad mood would suck all the oxygen from it. "Are you mad at me?"

"Why would I be mad at you?" He walked past me and pointed to the passenger door, a silent command to get in.

"Oh, I don't know, because I'm here. You haven't talked to me in more than an hour, and you've altered between scowling, brooding, and just looking overall moody."

Turning to face me, he set a hand on the roof of the car. Leaning toward me, his lips twitched, a near smile. Was he laughing at me? "Pretty sure those are all the same thing, *bellissima*. Now, will you please get in?" He opened the door for me.

"Deflection, nice." I maneuvered around him to get in the fancy car as he said something in Italian before shutting the door, then walked to the driver's side.

He slid behind the wheel onto the burgundy-colored leather. "Buckle up."

I couldn't help but roll my eyes. Moody *and* bossy. *Great.*

I hated to admit the luxury car suited him. It was a metallic-gray Porsche 911 Turbo something or other. I knew he missed the Porsche he'd sold in Charlotte, but I had no clue he had another one in New York. Well, I was assuming this was his and not a rental. "So where are we staying while here? A hotel?"

"No. Constantine thinks we should all stay together at my parents' place in Long Island, but I need to stop by my place in Chelsea first and pick up a few things."

A curtain of shock had my eyes dropping closed at that revelation. "You kept your house? I thought you gave up your life here when you moved." I wasn't sure why that hurt so much, but it made me think back to my mother's irritating warning on my birthday that Enzo might leave me one day.

"I feel like we're about to fight, and I don't know why." Enzo sighed, and I opened my eyes to see his sunglasses up as he pinched the bridge of his nose. "I just like having my own place and car when I visit, that's it, Maria."

When I didn't respond, Enzo flashed me an uneasy look and returned his Ray-Bans into place.

I knew why *I* was mad at him. It was those last words he'd said to me on the jet before we both had gone radio silent for the remainder of the flight. He was trying to push me away again. His words were meant to scare me, and when would he learn I wasn't going anywhere?

I let several minutes of silence swallow the space between us as we left the airport before finally mustering up a conversation starter. "Won't it be weird to stay at your parents'?"

I'd been to his parents' home before, but the one that overlooked Central Park. I'd almost forgotten they had another place outside the city in Oyster Bay Cove, Long Island.

"This entire situation will be awkward. But Izzy will be there, too, and I'm sure she'll love seeing you again." His tone was a bit less edgy this time.

I hadn't seen Isabella since the funeral, and she had to be thirty now, or maybe already thirty-one. When I visited for my birthday six years ago, she'd been working overseas for a company in London.

She was living back in the States now, managing billion-dollar brands from what I'd last heard.

"Izzy's bringing her boyfriend." He revved the engine a touch.

"You don't like him?"

"I don't know him. None of us do. The fact she kept him hidden means she doesn't think we'll approve." He glanced at me while saying, "Bringing him to Long Island for the rest of the week can only mean one thing."

"And that is?"

"She's marrying him." He looked back while spinning the wheel with the heel of his hand, reversing the Porsche to avoid a roadblock in our way.

Why was it always so sexy when a guy did that instead of using the cameras? Of course, everything Enzo did seemed to turn me on. "What is it you need at your house?" I decided to drop the subject of his sister's boyfriend, worried his foul mood would return, and I needed a break from Mr. Moody.

"I have some of Bianca's things there that I want to bring with me," he answered without much emotion in his voice, which meant he'd probably worked hard to do that.

And at that, I realized maybe we shouldn't talk at all. To fill the uncomfortable silence, I turned on the radio and flipped through the stations until I found a song I liked. *Can't go wrong with Sam Smith.*

The grumbles from Enzo had me changing the station. Maybe it was too sexual?

Landing on a country station next, which made my heart happy, I hummed to Chase Rice's song, and either I sucked at humming or he hated the song, because when I glanced his way, his bladed jawline was tight. Not to mention his forearms were flexed. One hand on the wheel and the other on the stick shift thing.

"Can you change that, please?" he asked, and I hurried to do so, but I had the feeling he wouldn't exactly love the next song.

"You've got to be kidding. Someone is fucking with me, I swear," Enzo said as "Bad Decisions" played. He reached over and shut off the radio. "How about the sound of silence instead?"

I slumped back in my seat. Feeling restless, I grabbed my phone from my purse and opened my photo album to look at pictures of Chiara.

"Have you talked to him today?" Enzo's deep voice rumbled through the space a few minutes later.

"No, we haven't spoken since last night. And I've been dodging his calls today. If he knows I'm traveling with you, he'll flip out."

"He has no business dictating what you do. None." He faced the road again, and I honestly had no clue where we were now or what part of the city we were in, but it was bustling and alive. Exploding with energy. And so different from where I grew up.

He switched lanes and stopped at a red light before looking at me. But then his attention shifted over my shoulder, and his entire body seemed to go lax, including his mouth.

I pivoted to follow his eyes, unsure why a Catholic church, which looked like it belonged in the Renaissance era based on its architecture, had produced such a reaction from him. "What's wrong?" I faced him again, but he was already looking toward the road, pulling through the light, accelerating a bit more than necessary.

"Nothing," he whispered.

"Don't lie. Please." I reached over and set my hand atop his forearm and gave him a gentle squeeze.

"It's just . . ." He cleared his throat. "That was Bianca's church where she went to mass. And it was also where I was arrested for murdering her killer."

FIFTEEN

Maria

"I was upset. Drunk. Out-of-my-mind angry," Enzo shared, his voice distant and detached as if it weren't his story. "And I don't know what possessed me to go to the church that night, but I stumbled in there like some crazy person, and someone called the cops. Turns out, the police were already looking for me.

"I guess I went there hoping I'd hear her voice. Have her tell me that what I did was okay because it was for her," he went on, his tone rough with emotion. "We would've all gone to prison for years, but we were offered an unusual arrangement instead. And that included a cover-up story as to how he really died. And no, it wasn't from a car accident."

When he eased his arm free from my touch and changed lanes, I had a feeling he was done with sharing, and for once, I didn't press him for more. I wasn't quite ready to hear how he actually killed the man. And maybe I never needed to know those details.

I stowed my phone in my purse and kept my eyes on the window the remainder of the drive until we parked in front of his place.

I'd expected some fancy penthouse in the sky, not a stately brick town house with hints of Greek revivalism in the design. I'd dabbled in art and architecture in college, though quickly realized I lacked an important skill: drawing. But I'd always admired the beauty of certain buildings from my studies. And this was definitely a stunning home.

"Come on. We won't be long." He hopped out, then rounded the car to open the door for me before heading to the Suburban behind us. He exchanged a few words with the driver while I waited at his doorstep.

His eyes held mine when he climbed the few steps to get to me, and then he cleared his throat and wordlessly let us in. He stopped the wailing alarm with a code inside the foyer as I asked, "How many stories?" *Yeah, I suck at small talk.*

"Including the cellar and the roof deck," he began while discarding his sunglasses on a table in the foyer, "six. This is the parlor floor. The pool is at the garden level right below us."

"You have a pool inside your house?" I tried to mask my shock, but I knew I was failing as I did a slow three-sixty, taking in the modern and opulent interior. "This is what money looks like, huh?"

"I guess so. I, uh, didn't design it. This place isn't me." He pocketed his hands, an uneasy look crossing his face, and I couldn't quite place why. "I'm going to my office. You're welcome to wait here or look around. Up to you." And with that, he went toward the stairs and disappeared.

I found myself meandering around the "parlor" level, which sounded too fancy for me, then made my way downstairs to check out the pool. My jaw dropped at the sight of a wet bar extending the length of the long, narrow pool with cozy-looking gray couches on the other side. "A waterfall?" I mumbled when spying the cascading water going into the pool, unsure why it was even running if he didn't live there. And for that matter, why did such an unlived-in space look so clean?

I swiped my hand along the bar top as I passed by. No dust.

I circled the pool, and my heart stopped at the sight of a flash of red exposed beneath one of the couches. I snatched the material, and my shoulders fell at the realization it was a small pair of red bikini bottoms. Well, more like a string bikini.

Did he have women over when he visited home? With the bikini bottoms still dangling from my finger, I tried to remember the last time he'd been to New York, deciding I wanted to damage my heart a bit more at the fact it'd been this year after my split with Thomas.

So you chose to screw someone here instead of me?

"They're not mine." The deep voice had me flinching and letting go of the bottoms. Enzo rounded the pool, slowly walking my way.

"Obviously." I had no right to be jealous, and yet, I was consumed by that feeling right now.

Enzo stopped before me, leaving only a touch of space between us. "You're upset?"

I looked over at the pool, realizing he had me trapped there unless I managed to maneuver around him or swim to the other side. "Is this another reason you keep this place? So you can have women over when you visit?"

I will not cry. I will not cry. The mantra ran through my head, but along with it were images of a bunch of hot bikini-clad women in his pool all vying for his attention. Maybe they even swam in the nude? *I'm a grown woman. A mother. I don't get jealous.*

"Maria." Enzo reached for my chin, forcing my eyes on him. "You're jealous?" His faint accent I rarely heard anymore was there that time.

"I'm not."

"You know it's pointless to lie to me, right?" He arched a brow, continuing to hold my face.

"It's fine. You're a man. You have needs, and I wasn't meeting them." I lifted a hand between us, attempting to shove at his forearm so he'd let go of me. I didn't need him to see the wobble in my chin and the stupid jealousy as it leaked from my eyes, betraying my words.

Frustrated, more so with myself and my reaction to a pair of bikini bottoms, I did my best to turn and escape him. His hand left my chin but only to snatch my cheeks with both palms. "I do have needs, *cara mia*," he rasped. "And I told you I've been jerking off like it's my second job because of *you*." And then he stepped forward and back we both went. Right into the pool.

I shot up from the water and whipped back my hair, gasping from the shock of what had happened. We were in the shallow end, so I could stand. And when my eyes landed on Enzo, he was shoving his hair back, nostrils flaring. His shirt clung to his frame, molding to every muscular, hard line of his body.

He patted the water at his side. "Alessandro uses this place when he doesn't want a woman to know where he lives. Hell, he probably spends more time here than his own home, which must be why the waterfall is running. He was probably just here."

Alessandro? I didn't want my shoulders to fall with such obvious relief, but there they went. "So you don't . . ."

He shook his head and stared into my eyes. "No," he firmly said, "I don't." And then his lips slanted over mine, effortlessly guiding my legs around his hips so my ankles locked behind him. He deepened the kiss, his tongue finding mine.

I melded into him, but my soaked, clingy turtleneck felt like a barrier between us I wanted to be free of so I could feel his lips trail down my neck as he'd done in his bedroom earlier. "I need this off. Now," I begged.

He let go of me only long enough to peel off the top, then flung it into the water.

My breasts heaved up and down as he studied me, and I reached behind my back and unclipped my bra. I slowly slid the straps down and tossed it next. The water may have been warm, but goose bumps covered my skin and had my nipples erect.

He cupped his jaw, meeting my eyes. "You really are a distraction," he murmured. "I didn't think anything or anyone could get me to . . ." He snatched my wrist and pulled me back to him, and in one fast movement, he had me sitting on the ledge of the pool. "You're making me forget."

"Forget why we're here?" I panted, a pinch of guilt hitting me.

"Forget the pain," he gruffly said, and before I could respond, he brought both hands alongside my body and leaned in, circling his tongue around my belly button. He slid his lips a little higher, then tipped his chin to locate my gaze. "I want you, Maria. So damn much," he admitted, "but I do need to focus. There's a lot at stake."

I nodded in understanding, but then why wasn't he moving? Why was he still staring at me with heat in his eyes as if I were his everything?

"I need to remember the pain. Live in it. Exist with it," he went on. "Or I won't be able to do what I need to."

Ohhh. Now I understood the dark, conflicted look in his eyes. "So you can kill?" I whispered, and he quietly nodded. "But I'm here so I don't lose you," I reminded him, keeping my voice gentle, but the need between us was still so strong. It was like a vibration between our bodies. Pounding. Relentless. Determined.

When he unexpectedly dragged his hands down my body and unbuttoned my jeans, my heartbeat slipped all the way between my legs. "But just because I need to feel pain to press forward doesn't mean I want you to be in any."

What are you saying?

He palmed my sex over my jeans, freeing a trapped moan from my lips. "You need relief, and I want to give it to you before we go."

"No." I shook my head. "You don't need to worry about me. Not like that."

I wanted to keep him from going dark, but I also didn't want to stop him from finding Bianca's killer. He'd never forgive himself if her killer got away, and if I'd been to blame, I'd never forgive myself.

So no, he didn't need to get me off right now. Because he was right. There was a lot at stake.

"I'll always worry about you." He effortlessly hoisted himself up from the pool next to me, then bent down and reached for my hands, guiding me to my feet. "And I don't want you hurting for any reason."

"No, really." My face was on fire. Probably every inch of me when he pulled me tight to his body, and I felt his dick twitch against the fabric of his wet pants.

He ignored my words and snatched my forearms, resting them over his shoulders as if we were about to slow dance, but then he lifted me, tossing my legs over his arms as he held me tight like I was his to keep.

Without ever losing hold of me, he slipped off his wet shoes and carried me around the pool and to the stairs.

"Where are we going?"

"My room." He paused on the first step and peered into my eyes. "Alessandro wouldn't have used it, don't worry."

"I, um, wasn't thinking about him. Trust me," I said as he swallowed my last word with a soft kiss, and then he finished the climb. Two more levels after that, never letting go of me. And I was certain he could carry me up a hundred flights of stairs without losing his breath.

He nudged the door to his room open with his shoulder, and I looked around the space. All cold, clean lines. No pops of color. Well, unless gray counted.

The blinds were only partially drawn closed, allowing the space to be dimly lit. Walking me over to a bed that could easily fit five, he sat me down and knelt before me.

My hands went to his shoulders as he removed each ankle boot. Socks next. Then he looked up at me, his wet lashes only making his eyes appear even sexier as he stared at me. "It's time I get you off with my mouth."

Was this happening? Here? Now? And why was I so freaking nervous?

His gaze roamed over my breasts and up to my lips, which were now a match to my nipples again, since he'd surely kissed the lipstick free.

"You know enough of the truth now, so if you don't want me to . . ."

I reached for his head and slipped my fingers through his hair as I gently pulled him closer, letting him know I had no plans to leave.

"I need this right now more than I need anything else." His Adam's apple bobbed as if he was trying to wrap his head around what that meant. He needed me more than justice?

"Okay." I chewed on my lip, the nerves still getting to me. It'd been so long since anyone had been between my legs like that. Thomas had rarely gone down on me. But more than that, Enzo was . . . Enzo. The man I'd been picturing all year, and now here he was, about to fulfill those fantasies. And for the love of God, could I get out of my head and back into the moment? *For Pete's sake.*

"Maria?" A surprising grin flashed across his lips. "You back with me?"

I released his hair and rested onto my forearms to find his eyes. "I'm back."

"Good." He smiled. "I like you here with me." There was something so honest and sweet in how he'd said those words that it had my heart squeezing. His gaze traveled down the length of my body to what would be mission impossible: removing wet skinny jeans.

Apparently, not so hard for him. Because he had me on my feet and the jeans off within seconds. The man was good. *Damn.* And now I stood before him in only a pair of black satin panties.

"You're beautiful," he said before dropping his mouth over mine, kissing me as if I were his lifeline, and I was able to offer him oxygen and a second chance.

His mouth trailed a hot line from my lips to my neck while his palms went to my ass, and he squeezed.

As he gently sucked and nipped at my neck, my eyes fell shut at the sensations burning through me. Heating every part of my body with need.

"I'm fucked up," he said against my neck. "Wanting to leave my mark on you. All over your perfect body."

But I loved it. I buried my fingertips in his back, drawing myself closer to him. My breasts smashed against his wet shirt. "Please, take this off. Be naked with me."

He freed us of our entangled state and a look of hesitation washed over his handsome features, but then he tugged the dress shirt free from his pants and worked at the buttons. My knees buckled when he removed his pants next.

Standing before me in only black boxer briefs now, the beautiful, inked man before me demanded to be studied. God, I wanted him.

I swallowed the fraction of space between us and skated my palm down his sternum, and he didn't stop me when I slid my hand into the opening of his briefs to hold his cock.

He was breathing hard.

Restraint seconds from snapping.

His jaw was strained as he stared at me while I swirled a finger around the crown of his shaft; then I eased my palm up and down the length of him.

"No more," he growled out, giving me only a handful of seconds to touch him. "I'll lose my control, *Tesoro*. And that's one thing I can't afford to do right now."

I relented, even though I didn't want to, and stepped back, bumping into the bed. I would've fallen, but he snatched my wrist and hauled me against him.

His lips crashed over mine. Hands on my cheeks. Then in my hair. He was touching. Tasting. As much of me as possible.

He slid my panties down to my ankles a moment later and raked his gaze over me, his eyes settling at my swollen clit. "Fucking beautiful," he hissed before reaching between my legs to cup my sex.

He fisted my hair with his other hand, tipping my head back. He slanted his mouth back over mine, taking my tongue. And every coherent thought, too.

And before I knew it, he had me back on the bed, but he didn't join me. He remained at the edge, shoved down his boxer briefs, then fisted his cock a few times, simply staring at me.

"On all fours." The rough demand had chills chasing down my spine.

Shyness took over, and I bent my knees to my chest, hiding my body. "Why?"

He angled his head and wet his lips. "Because I'm going to eat your pussy from that angle. Not just because I want that gorgeous ass in my face but because I'll just miss that spot of yours you love me touching so much, and it'll make you slightly delirious."

My knees parted a little at the promise of what was to come, but I didn't fully surrender. "And do I want to be delirious?" *I mean, do I?* This was all new for me. My life had been vanilla with a side of vanilla before this man.

"You do, trust me." He pointed to my legs with his free hand, continuing to stroke his cock while his abdominal wall flexed and tightened. "Now, show me that greedy cunt of yours. I know you want me to see it. Show me how fucking wet you are."

God, he was right. I slowly spread open my legs and touched myself. "What happens next, after you, um, kiss . . . um . . ." I read books, sure. But dirty talk in real life? Could I do it?

A devilish smirk passed across his lips. "After I eat your pussy, just missing that sweet spot, I'll flip you over and give you what you need."

He let go of himself and climbed onto the bed. He reached for my leg and set a kiss on the top of my foot, then my knee. He worked his mouth all the way up, kissing my inner thighs without touching my sex, which was slightly agonizing.

"On your hands and knees," he demanded in a rough voice as he shifted to my side to allow me to obey.

Once in position, his hand skated down my spine, and I arched like a cat with my ass in the air. When he set his lips to my wet sex,

I cried out his name and bunched the bedding, fisting the fabric. He stroked, sucked, and feverishly licked. But as promised, he just missed that tender area, which had me borderline crazy.

I bucked and moved. Shifted. Even did some freaking Pilates thing to try and get my ass higher in the air, desperate for his mouth to hit that one spot, but he didn't give it to me. Instead, he kept bringing me to the edge, and the anticipation of what was to come had me dizzy.

"Enzo," I begged between pants as he flicked his tongue against that spot for one torturous second.

His fingertips bit into the sides of my ass as he kept me locked in place. I cried and pleaded for relief, never having experienced anything like this in my life.

Delirious? Yeah, he was right.

I wasn't sure how long he'd feasted on me, but then he swatted my ass so hard, it stung. I didn't have time to react to the delicious sensations coursing through me at the contact, because he flipped me over and pinned my body beneath his.

My legs went over his shoulders while he sank his mouth over my pussy, and I may have died for a second when he set his mouth over the sensitive area and licked.

He was right. I'd never felt like this before. Never knew I could even feel like this.

I was panting, gasping for breath as every part of my body tensed, and the muscles in my legs went tight, and then I exploded. And screamed. Cried and melded into the mattress with relief.

That wasn't an orgasm. It was an out-of-body experience. I'd seen the other side. And it'd been beautiful. Because he'd been with me. He didn't take my virginity, but he took my soul. I was certain of that.

"Enzo." My whole body collapsed as I came down, breathing hard.

He worked his mouth over my stomach before climbing on top of me, and he locked our hands together over my shoulders.

"You taste amazing, *Tesoro*."

Tesoro. I loved my nickname from him so damn much. "I wouldn't know," I teased, trying to smile, but every part of me was spent, even my lips. And yet, I'd give anything for him to be inside me.

"Be with me," I whispered, my eyes watering a little. "Please."

A rough sound left his mouth as he rotated his hips, allowing his thick cock to slide over my soaked sex, and he tightened his hold on my hands.

He closed his eyes, and I could see the battle. The indecision in the lines of his face and the tight draw of his lips.

"I'm yours. I'll always be yours," I reminded him. "Take me, please."

"Are you on the pill?" he gritted out, and heaven help me, was he finally going to give in?

"No, I'm not," I admitted. "Why torture myself when I'm not even having sex, you know?" But then my stomach dropped when I caught a shadow from the doorway. "Enzo," I cried in shock.

He was off me in a second and standing at the realization one of our security guys was there.

Enzo snatched the comforter at the side of the bed and covered me with it before facing the man even though he was still naked and rock-hard.

"I'm so sorry." The guard had a hand in the air, but he didn't bother to close his eyes or shield his face from the view of the sexy Italian before him. "You were gone a long time. No answer on your phone. The door was unlocked. I heard her screaming."

Enzo's hands snapped to his sides. "And you were standing in my door long enough to get fucking hard?"

"It was a second," the man mumbled. "I'm so sorry, sir."

"And yet, you're still here," Enzo roared, his shoulder blades drawing together.

"It was a mistake," I spoke up, trying to be Enzo's voice of reason, worried he'd burn the man's retinas because he'd seen me sprawled out naked and sated from an orgasm.

At this point, I no longer questioned the lengths Enzo would go to keep me safe or to protect my dignity.

The security guard nervously shoved both hands through his sandy-blond hair, his eyes now apologetically on the floor.

"You're fired," Enzo remarked while going to his dresser, and he snatched a pair of gray sweats and put them on. "I'm going to walk you out to make sure you don't lose your way."

"Enzo, don't . . ." *Don't what? Hurt him? Push him down the stairs?*

Enzo shot me a grave look from over his shoulder. "I'll grab our suitcases from his SUV. Stay here." And then he left with the guy, and I waited until I could no longer hear their steps to get up.

I didn't want to face his parents smelling like sex, and I knew our untimely interruption would prevent Enzo from resuming where we'd left off.

So I went into his adjoining bathroom. Luxury at its finest, that was for sure. But the man had a pool and waterfall in his house, so what did I expect?

I turned on his shower. Well, the *four* showerheads, and it took only a handful of seconds to warm up, unlike my place back home that took an eternity.

This home wasn't what Enzo really liked, though. He didn't give a shit about this stuff, right? He was happy with his life in Charlotte, wasn't he?

Or was it crazy for me to think cooking in a kitchen to make a modest paycheck was enough for a man who grew up in a fancy city with all the finest of things?

He chose Charlotte. He chose to leave this place, I reminded myself as the warm water ran over the contours of my body. But chills pricked my skin as the nagging thoughts penetrated my mind. *But he kept this place. Maybe he always planned to come back, and for good?*

SIXTEEN

Maria

With a towel wrapped around my body and my hair a wet, tangled mess over my shoulders, I went into the bedroom, startling at the sight of Enzo sitting on his bed. "I was sort of expecting you to join me after you, um, walked that man out."

Enzo had changed while I'd showered. New black dress pants that were tailored to perfection to fit his strong legs. And another crisp black dress shirt. Top two buttons undone to show a hint of the guardian-angel ink on his chest. Sleeves cuffed at the wrists, hiding the tattoos on his arms. His hair was dry now, but it was still a bit messy, as if he'd used his fingers to brush it back, and somehow, it looked even sexier that way.

"If I joined you in there, we'd never leave."

"The bodyguard still alive?"

He stood as his gaze flicked to where I clutched the towel at my breasts. "His limbs are intact."

Hopefully he hadn't hurt him. It wasn't his fault he'd walked in on us. Not entirely. "I guess we should get going?" He had my suitcase by the bed, waiting for me.

"Yeah, I need to get another phone, though. Mine was in my pocket when we fell into the pool."

"No secret room here like back in Charlotte with phones ready to go?"

A dark smirk played across his lips. "There's a room. Only burner phones. Nothing I want to use on a regular basis."

"Burner phones. Mm-hmm. Makes sense." I felt so completely lost in this world. Whatever world he'd once lived in and, well, was now back in.

"I called the store out by my parents' place to let them know to have one ready for me. I'll pick it up on the way."

"Wait, how'd you call them, since your phone is wet?"

"Your phone was in the car." He took three strides my way, swallowing the distance between us. "Yes, I bypassed the password to use it. Are you mad?"

"More curious how you did it, but I don't need a hacking lesson, just a change of clothes." I blew at a wayward strand of hair in my face. "And a brush."

He gently held my shoulder, then slid his warm palm down to my biceps. "Natalia has been texting. You might want to message her back. She's worried." I looked down to see my iPhone in his other hand. "And there are a few missed calls and texts from Thomas."

"Um, okay." My pulse was fluttering hardcore at my throat, and he brought his hand there, brushing the pad of his thumb over the beats.

"Do we need to talk about what happened?"

"I don't know. Do we?" I took my phone from him and peered into his brown eyes.

He only lifted his brows as if waiting for my next move.

"You spanked me." The memory of his palm on my ass had me tightening my legs, wanting more of him already.

"And I plan to do it again," he casually remarked.

Holy shit. The thought of Enzo spanking me again . . . did things to me. I squirmed under his gaze, then swallowed down my nerves, because *hell yes.* "Good," I whispered, watching his nostrils flare slightly.

"I'm going to leave so you can get ready."

"Because we won't leave otherwise?" I asked, taken aback by the husky tone of my own voice. *That's what a top-tier, best-in-your-life orgasm will do to you, though.* Make someone feel like a sex goddess who can read the phone book and make it sound good. Well, that was my working theory. I'd need a few more orgasms from this man just to be sure.

Enzo's gaze went to my cleavage. "Because I'll put a child in your womb if we stay, I can promise you that."

Ohhh. Well then. I mean . . .

He lifted his chin, eyes moving to the ceiling. "God help me, woman, I don't know how I'm going to survive this week at my parents' without touching you."

"Who says you can't?"

His attention returned to my face, and he captured the edge of his lip between his teeth. He didn't answer and only stared at me with a touch of uncertainty in his eyes.

"So, don't wear the red dress to dinner?" I teased.

"Fire," he rasped.

Fire, huh? Was he inviting me to play with fire or warning me not to? I didn't always know when it came to him.

He reached out and yanked the fluffy white cotton free from my body in one fast movement, then flung it to the floor.

A fleet of goose bumps set course, traveling over every inch of my skin as I stood there naked with only my phone in my hand.

"Cold?" His hand smoothed along his hard jawline.

"Yes."

"Wet?" His gaze fell between my legs, and I was still pink and swollen.

"Very," I murmured, then caught a whiff of his cologne. He always smelled so damn good. I had no clue how to identify scents, though. *Sandalwood? Cedar? Juniper berry?* I mean, what in the hell did juniper even smell like? The best I could do was maybe identify lavender and vanilla.

My shoulders slumped. Vanilla had been my life up until Enzo, too. And I didn't want that. I wanted something dark and spicy. Bold and seductive.

Enzo.

I just wanted Enzo.

"I lost you." Enzo cupped my chin, reminding me I was still naked and cold. And a bit speechless even though my brain was nonstop all the time.

"I was saying you, uh, smell good, right?"

He smiled. "Maybe you were thinking it."

"Oh." My embarrassment came out as a grin, and I probably looked ridiculous. "And what is the cologne you're wearing?"

He closed one eye as if not sure. "I forgot the name. But it smells like black orchids and notes of truffle, and maybe—"

"Of course, a chef would describe his cologne like it's food, making me both hungry and . . ." *Wanting sex.*

I jolted at the sudden rumble of thunder. Had the clouds rolled in while we'd been inside? And why did an impending storm and ominous gray sky feel fitting for today?

He released me. "I should let you get ready."

"Mm. Yes, please leave me alone while I'm wet and naked." The taunt tumbled from my lips at the same time the sky groaned, threatening to unleash hell.

And the way Enzo peered at me right now, it was as if he wanted to unleash something as well. But that tight lock of his jaw meant he was going to restrain himself. One of us needed to behave, I supposed. "Maria."

My hand lifted between us as I said, "I know, I know. Fire. And you need a phone because you probably have a ton of important calls you can't miss, and I'm a distracting pain in the ass."

He snatched my hips, his hands cut around to my backside, and he squeezed my flesh to that torture-pleasure point he seemed to know so well. "You are distracting. And a pain in my ass. But I . . ."

You what?

His eyes closed, and there was that battle. The war. Didn't he ever get tired of fighting it? I was exhausted for him, and I was only on the outside looking in, catching a glimmer here and there.

He freed me from his strong hands and turned. But he stopped just outside the doorway, and his hands went to the frame. They turned to fists as he bowed his head. "Wear the red dress. No panties," he ordered, and with that, he left.

Frustrated by the fact he was leaving but also turned on by his order, I hurriedly grabbed what I needed and went into the bathroom.

Maybe he was right to walk away, though. We were in New York to find his sister's killer, not to check off my sexual fantasy list. Enzo going down on me had been on the list, but I'd never pictured it happening in that hotter-than-sin way.

I unceremoniously dropped my things onto the vanity and combed my wild hair. I was a mess. On the inside and out, so it would seem.

Once I managed to tame my wet hair, I wrangled it into a side braid so I wouldn't have to dry it and slipped on the bra and modest but slightly sexy red wrap dress.

I finally unlocked the phone, and all of Natalia's messages were still unread, which meant Enzo had only seen the notifications and hadn't invaded my privacy.

Natalia: I've called five times. No answer. I'm worried.

Natalia: Okay, Enzo's not answering his phone either. Do I need to call Constantine?

Great, if she called Constantine and then he tried to get ahold of his brother, why'd I get the feeling he'd send the cavalry?

Me: Sorry. I was distracted.

Natalia: Oh, thank God. I was two seconds away from phoning every Costa I know.

Me: We had to stop at Enzo's, and I left my phone in the car, and his wound up getting wet.

Natalia: How'd that happen?

Me: His pool.

Surely my sister had been to his place before when she lived in New York, but she'd never told me how crazy-over-the-top his home was.

Natalia: ???

Me: We fell in.

Natalia: ???

Me: It's a long story.

Natalia: So, give me the bullet points.

Me: Well, Enzo kissed me six years ago at that bar. And then he got me off with his hand twice this past week. I saw him naked last night. And then we kissed for the first time in six years this morning. Somehow, we fell into his pool today. And well, you know, stuff happened after that. See, long story.

Natalia: I knew something happened back then. I can't believe you just breezed past that in a bullet point. Can you call me?!

Me: I have to go. Can you just trust that I'm okay? We didn't "go all the way" . . . Almost. And my head is a bit all over the place. Only ever been with Thomas. But Enzo is, well, a whole other level of everything. I don't know how to explain it.

Natalia: But are you okay?

Me: I mean, I think so.

Natalia: Liar.

Me: I'm . . . I don't know what I am. Confused. Worried. Scared. In over my head.

Natalia: I'm gonna kick his ass.

Me: It's not his fault. I pushed and pushed. He was trying to behave. I'm stubborn.

Natalia: So, what you're saying is his control finally snapped? I guess I can relate. I kind of made Ryan crazy back in the day, too. You sure you can't talk? I want to be there for you.

Me: I'll call tonight, okay? We're heading to his parents' house and staying there all week. Should be . . . interesting.

Natalia: I guess that makes me feel better. Just don't forget to call. I love you.

Me: Love you, too.

I set the phone down, determined to erase the nervous blushed color from my cheeks before facing Enzo, but then my phone lit up with another message. Ugh, Thomas.

A-Hole Ex: I heard what happened this morning. Did you get hurt? Talk to me. Are you okay?

How in the hell did he find out what happened?

Me: What are you talking about?

A-Hole Ex: I knew he was a danger to you. You should never have been at his place.

Me: How'd you find out? You're out of town. Are you having someone spy on me?

And why was I getting the weird Peeping Tom creepy feeling from him? *And you are a Tom. Shit.*

A-Hole Ex: Why in the hell would I spy on you?

I highly doubted Natalia or Ryan would've told anyone what went down that morning. No, it didn't make sense.

A-Hole Ex: And if you ever answered your phone, you'd know I just got back to Charlotte. Work emergency. I have to fly out tonight. Be back Sunday or Monday. Where the hell are you?
Me: Wait, what? You're home?

My phone buzzed as he tried to call, but I sent it to voice mail, knowing he'd hear the lie in my voice when I gave him a BS excuse.

Me: I had to leave town. I'm in New York. We're thinking of opening a second location here. I didn't tell you because I didn't want you getting pissed. I'll call my parents and have them meet you to get Chiara, and they can watch her until I get back.

I'd much rather Chiara be with my parents than with Thomas during this mess anyway. But now that she was back home, it made being away from her that much harder.

A-Hole Ex: You're in New York?! Are you fucking with me right now? You can't just leave without telling me, damn it.
Me: I need to call my parents. You can yell at me in person when I get home.
A-Hole Ex: Oh yeah, and when will that be? Don't even tell me you're with the chef.

Fine. I won't tell you. I called my mom, ignoring the flood of messages from him that followed.

I managed to get off the call in less than a minute, dodging as many of her questions as possible, promising to fill her in tonight. I needed a cover story first that made sense.

When I finally made my way back into the bedroom, I found Enzo waiting for me, and my cheeks were fire-hot from dealing with Thomas.

"Thomas is back in Charlotte. He had a work thing, so my parents are going to get Chiara. She'll stay with them until I'm back."

"Then I'm taking you home. You need to be with her," he said without missing a beat.

I folded my arms. "I'm here until Sunday. That's the deal. Don't argue with me. She's in good hands." I gave him a stubborn lift of my chin before my gaze fell to my suitcase. "So, how are we supposed to fit everything into the Porsche?"

He stroked his jawline, clearly contemplating an argument. He shook his head, grunted, and my shoulders fell with relief when he didn't push back on sending me home. "Fine. I'll send Alessandro to come back for the boxes tonight or tomorrow."

"So we came here for no reason?"

He surprised me with a smile and brushed his knuckles over my cheek. "I don't know, I feel like it worked out, don't you?"

My body shivered in response, but after he stepped away and took my suitcase, my arms fell to my sides at the memory of the first part of my conversation with Thomas in the bathroom.

Enzo's brows slanted. Had he read my thoughts? "What is it?"

"I'm just . . ."

His gaze dipped to the vee of my red dress, which showed a hint of cleavage, and I had to admit my breasts looked pretty damn good in this thing. The way his tongue traced the seam of his mouth like he was dying to taste me had me wondering if he even realized what he was doing.

"Maria." He shook his head as if trying to focus. "What's wrong?" His attention landed on my phone in my other hand. "Did Thomas say or do something that upset you?"

"He said he heard about the attack, but I don't see how he could've found out."

His gaze narrowed as if he'd just put together some puzzle in his mind.

"What is it?"

"It was him," Enzo hissed. "*He's* the one who sent those men to try and rough me up this morning. The attack had nothing to do with Bianca." He let his words sink in before adding, "Only it was his bad luck he sent the Sicilian fucking mafia to my house."

SEVENTEEN

Enzo

"Before you jump to conclusions and call Ryan, because you know he'll lose his mind, why don't we wait until you talk to your mom's cousin."

From behind the driver's wheel, I looked over at the woman attempting to be my voice of reason amid my chaotic thoughts, all ending in savagely destroying the man responsible for endangering Maria and Natalia this morning. "Yeah? Then text your sister and ask her if she or Ryan told anyone what went down. That's the only way anything could get back to Thomas, especially with him being out of town this morning. If their answer is no, then case closed."

"Maybe he stopped by my building when he came home and someone there told him about what happened?"

"We didn't report it to the police. No one else lives on our floor. No one else would know," I quickly reminded her.

"Fine, I'll message Natalia," she shot back like a challenge and quickly worked her fingers over her phone. And her shoulders fell when a response came back.

I didn't need to see the message to know the answer. "I should've considered this sooner." I slammed the heel of my hand against the wheel before making a sharp turn. Sheets of rain hammered the streets, and the storm hadn't been in the mood to let up as I'd driven to Long Island.

I'd already grabbed my new phone from the store, and we were only a few minutes away from my parents' place in Oyster Bay Cove.

"Thomas was pissed at our exchange yesterday," I went on, "and he knew I'd be home at that hour. With Chiara safely away with him, he chose today for his payback. He wanted my hands broken so I couldn't cook. Couldn't touch you."

"We still don't know for certain." Her soothing tone failed to relieve the tension coiling tight in my body. "How would Thomas know anyone in the mafia? He manages people's money."

"He has shady clients who have connections. I can see him reaching out to some fucker he golfs with for a recommendation."

"How do you know about his clients? Who says they're shady?" She let go of her phone to slam her arms over her chest, and was she defending that asshole? Or just trying to keep me from losing the last bit of sanity I had left?

I was so angry right now, all I wanted to do was pull over and shove her dress up to see if she wasn't wearing panties as I'd ordered and fuck her right there. But fucking the anger out of the both of us would accomplish nothing. I'd still be pissed because I hated her ex, and the fact she could've been hurt because of him only had my veins burning. And secondly, Maria deserved better than our first time in a car because I'd become unhinged.

I stopped at the red light and twisted in my seat to better face my fireball. Her cheeks were flushed, and her lips taunted me, begging to be kissed.

"You do realize there's no chance in hell I wouldn't run a thorough background check on Thomas while you were married, right?" I finally spoke, willing my dick to go down and with Thomas's name on my tongue, I assumed it'd help ease the pressure there. "Do you think I'd let you stay with a man I didn't deem safe?"

Her lips parted, but she didn't gift me with her soft words or her sass.

"So yes, based on the fact he knew what happened this morning, it has to be Thomas who sent the wrong fucking people to my apartment and not someone connected to Bianca's murder." I'd been so angry about Bianca's death and the fact Maria had been in danger I could barely see straight. And this woman distracted me to no end, that was abundantly clear.

"I just can't imagine Thomas would do this. It's so out of character for him."

"Men do crazy things for the women they love. And he messed up and lost the best thing to ever happen to him. Hell, he lost his mind when he saw me at your place," I explained as calmly as possible, needing to dial down my pulse before we faced my parents.

"That doesn't mean he loves me." Her shoulders slumped, and the honking behind me had me pulling through the green light.

"And if he does? Does it matter?" I had no clue why I asked that. Jealousy again? What the fuck? My heart and brain were rarely in sync, but they were on the same page when it came to her.

"You of all people know the answer to that already."

I didn't look her way, but I knew she was rolling her eyes at my stupid question, and I deserved it.

"But by checking on me, he just made himself look guilty. Why would he do that?"

Fair point. But I had my theories. "He hoped you wouldn't be at my place at seven in the morning when they attacked. And when he heard you were, he was more than likely worried he nearly got you killed. That's probably why he really came home early. He wants you back, Maria. He never wanted the divorce."

"Even if he didn't cheat, our marriage wouldn't have survived, not with . . ."

With me in your life?

"I don't know. I guess it's all possible," she said in a flat tone that time. "Shady clients. Cheating. I guess you never really know a person."

Why'd that last part sting so much?

Before I could smother her with more reasons why I believed Thomas was a world-class dick, she continued. "*If* Thomas is responsible, it's obviously bad, but it also means we're not in danger."

We were potentially still in danger with the cleaner on the loose, but I didn't want to scare her about that right now. One issue at a time.

"There's no 'if' it was Thomas. I know you don't want to think that about him because he's still the father of your child, and you're worried what this means I'll do to him, but—"

"Or Ryan," she whispered, concerned how her brother-in-law would react to the news as well, and I knew he'd be out for blood.

"Listen," I said on a sigh, trying to be gentle with her when my every instinct wanted to unleash the monster inside me and torture Thomas for what he was putting her through with such a stupid move as to come after me. "This was my mother's cousin's way of smoking out the name. He made sure the message was sent out that the job went sideways. And now Giovanni can follow that text trail. It'll probably lead to a middleman, Thomas's client, and then it'll lead to Thomas."

She unlocked her arms and went for her phone. "Then I should tell Natalia she's safe," she said, finally accepting the truth. "I don't want her unnecessarily worrying."

"Call them. Speakerphone, though. I need to talk to Ryan to prevent him from going to jail."

"And leaving Chiara with only one parent."

I bit back my desire to say, *I'll be her father*, and remained quiet as she phoned Natalia.

"Hey, I assume Ryan's attached to your hip since this morning. Can you put me on speaker?" Maria asked once Natalia answered. "You're on speaker as well," she added, and I knew that was to ensure Natalia didn't say anything she wouldn't want me to hear.

"What's going on?" Natalia asked, and Maria looked to me, a silent plea to share the ugly truth for her.

"You may not need to call for backup, Ryan," I shared as I turned down my parents' street, catching sight of their waterfront property at the edge of the dead-end road.

"Because this morning was probably about me," Maria decided to finish for me, guilt in her tone. "We think Thomas was jealous and hired those guys to go after Enzo."

"What?" both Natalia and Ryan snapped at the same time.

I shot a quick look at Maria, slowing my speed, since we were driving by houses now. At least the rain had finally let up.

"Thomas knew what happened this morning. There's no way he could've known, since we didn't tell anyone," I explained. "My guess is he asked one of his less-than-reputable clients for a contact outside the state he thought would never connect to him."

"And he wound up the unluckiest son of a bitch on the planet anyway," Ryan hissed. "Where is he right now?"

"He came home early, and my parents are meeting him to pick up Chiara and babysit. He's got a work emergency, so he's about to leave town. But please, don't go after him. Not yet, at least. Just don't do anything until I'm back. We'll handle this together." That was the best I could do for now. Delay his need for justice, because there wasn't a chance in hell Thomas would walk away from this unscathed.

"Fine," Ryan slowly remarked, but I knew his wheels were spinning, and he'd be pacing the floor with anger the second we hung up.

"Does that mean you're coming back home, Maria?" Natalia asked as I punched in the gate code to my parents' home.

"No, I'm not. I'll just be gone for a few days. But I need to be here. Can you help Mom and Dad with Chiara? Keep everyone blissfully ignorant as to why I'm here?" she answered before I had a chance to summon a response.

"Yeah, uh, okay," Natalia hesitantly agreed.

"We're at his parents' now, so I need to go. I'm just so sorry my stupid ex did this. We'll talk later." Maria ended the call before anyone could protest, and she shoved her phone into her purse in a hurry.

"You really want to be here? You're ready for this?" I asked while parking.

"Put on a smile and act like the world's not on fire? Sure, I took a theater class in college. Totally sucked at it, but you know . . . here's my chance for a do-over."

"Theater, huh?"

"Yeah, don't ask. Like I said, I suckity-sucked at it."

How did she have me wanting to smile right now?

"And wow. I mean, wow." She sat taller when setting her eyes upon the home. While unbuckling, her purse fell to the floor. "This place looks like the midcentury had a baby with the contemporary." She was talking with her hands, and when her gaze caught mine for a moment, I loved the way her eyes lit up.

"You have an eye for architectural design."

"I suck at graphic design. And I can't draw, you know that. Give me a ruler, and I'll draw you a crooked line."

"That doesn't mean you can't appreciate art," I reminded her.

Also, why hadn't we ever had that conversation before? We'd spent almost every day together this past year. Of course, we'd mostly been at work, because I usually did my best to avoid being alone in her apartment with her; otherwise, I'd have slipped my hand down her panties long ago. Clearly, my control around her was as flimsy as a piece of notebook paper floating in the wind. It'd be gone-gone-fucking-gone.

"True," she finally answered as her smile met her eyes. "When I see a good thing in front of me, it's hard not to notice."

"Yeah, I can relate." My gaze fell to her thighs, and I couldn't help but wonder if she was without her panties. *What is wrong with me?*

When her legs pinned together, it felt like she was blinking a yellow caution light. A reminder to behave and focus, and apparently I needed that. She truly was a distraction.

I scratched my chin, my facial hair in that irritating not-yet-a-beard stage.

"How, um, big is this place?" Her nerves stretched her words out, somehow making every innocent thing she said sexy.

"I think it's about fifteen thousand square feet. Only seven bed-rooms, though. Either you'll bunk with Izzy, or Mom will let her stay with her boyfriend and you'll have your own room." But knowing my mom, she'd never let Izzy share a bed while unmarried. "Mom won't let anyone stay in Bianca's old room."

Maria visibly shivered, her gaze going back to the driveway full of cars. "Looks like a luxury car dealership," she said, clearly opting for a subject change, and I didn't blame her. "The Lamborghini is Alessandro's, right?" I didn't follow her eyes and instead, slung my fore-arm over the wheel and studied her. A shy sweep of red climbed up her throat, nearly hiding the slight bruises I'd given her from kissing her a bit too roughly. "And the Maserati is classy and sophisticated. Constantine's?" Without waiting for my answer, she went on. "The Tesla has to be Izzy's. She probably cares about the environment." She frowned and tugged at the long sleeves of her red dress. "Not saying the rest of you don't, but Izzy—"

"Izzy is Izzy," I finished with a smile. "Yeah."

"But the truck? That's a curveball. I mean, it's a nice one. But doesn't feel like something a Costa would drive."

A Costa, huh? I looked over at the truck on the other side of the curved brick driveway, which had one of Italy's iconic pine trees at the center. Bianca had said that tree always reminded her of something from a Dr. Seuss book, tall and skinny with a thick canopy of needles high up.

And there went my heart. Hammering. Hard. Heavy. Fast.

"That's Hudson's. Constantine must've invited him to dinner," I shared, knowing she was about to ask some follow-up questions to that.

"Why does that name sound familiar?"

I arched a brow. "Our first kiss was in his office."

Her mouth rounded in surprise. "The bar. Right." She looked back to the house when asking, "And why would Constantine ask him to come when you need to tell your parents about Bianca?"

"Because Hudson was with us the day we murdered her killer." I closed my eyes. "Well, who we *thought* was her killer."

EIGHTEEN

Enzo

"Really? I mean, I knew you were friends, but I didn't realize you were that close."

She looked slightly panicky. Frantic even. Because deep down, she was pure and innocent. And as much as she wanted to be here, she would never be the type to light the match for me if I needed to burn down someone's world. Not that I wanted that to change about her. No, she was the type who saved spiders and let them outside. She didn't revenge kill or seek payback against her enemies. Not that she had any, thank God. She was the light that I desperately wished I could stay in, but as much as I tried, the darkness always seemed to find me.

I tossed my hands through my hair, deciding how much to share, when my mom appeared on the front porch just beneath the overhang.

"Hudson was in the navy like Constantine," I began. "But then his mom got sick, so he left after his eighth year. He took care of her until she died a few months later, and then he decided to join the FBI. He went to Quantico. Landed a position at the New York field office, too." I rattled off the facts as quickly as possible, and her eyes widened with every detail.

Yeah, fun fact, an FBI agent had been with us when we committed a crime.

"Is that how you knew so many details about her case? Well, what you thought were details, I guess."

I shook my head. "Feds don't usually get called in to murders unless they happen on federal land or are somehow connected to . . . well, FBI things." I wasn't too privy to the inner workings of the Bureau, and I didn't care to know. The feds weren't cool with people like me who took justice into their own hands. "So no, Hudson couldn't help in that department. He just wanted justice for Bianca. And he believed the court trial was bullshit, too."

"But he's not in the FBI anymore, right? I mean, I don't think an agent would own a bar." She shrugged. "But what do I know?"

"No, he, uh, quit shortly after we killed that man. He was pretty messed up about it."

"But you said you and your brothers were arrested. Not him?"

I looked back at the front porch, and my mom waved us over as Izzy appeared at her side. And God, she resembled Bianca more and more. It fucking hurt to look at her sometimes.

"No," I said, clearing my throat, "he wasn't identified as being part of it, and we sure as hell didn't give up his name. Probably part of the reason he felt guilty and quit the Bureau." I didn't know all the details because he'd always been much closer to Constantine. "We should go in. They're waiting." And with that, I shut off the engine and grabbed our suitcases that I'd crammed behind our seats since sending those guards home.

Once outside, it dawned on me Maria was still hesitant to go in. She was a horrible liar, which was an admirable trait in my opinion, so she was clearly worried about how to answer any questions she knew would be waiting for her.

She spun around, knocking into me, and I let go of the bags to catch her forearms, forgetting we had eyes on us. "What story did you give them as to why *I'm* here?"

"I gave them the partial truth. I explained your ex has Chiara until Sunday, and it's hard on you, so you asked if you could join me on my trip. I guess they don't need to know that Thomas is a psycho and his plans changed, and you're here just to be a stubborn pain in my ass now."

"I detect no sarcasm where there should be at the end of that sentence, mister."

I couldn't help but smile at that, damn her.

"And if I'm a pain, then good. Maybe you deserve it." Worry lines cut across her forehead as she asked, "You didn't tell them that we're . . . well, you know?" That innocent tilt of her head as she searched for the words had my heart beating harder yet again.

"That we're friends, colleagues, neighbors?" I arched a brow. "My mom is old-school, sweetheart. If I tell her I've had my hand and mouth between your thighs, she'll have a heart attack."

She pulled her arm back and playfully whacked my chest, and I deserved that. But it was worth the smile on her lips and the fact she appeared to shed some of her nervousness.

Her eyes narrowed, and she surprised me by saying, "There you are."

"Huh?"

"This you. This you is the one I know and love. The one Chiara adores. I can see you now. Lost you here and there since last night, but I . . ."

My world basically flipped off its fucking axis and I stopped hearing anything she'd said after *love*. She probably meant it as a friend kind of thing, but I didn't care. It was the first time she'd tossed that word my way, and I'd latch on to it and save it for when I started to lose myself all over again and needed to find my way back to her.

But hell, she was right. Standing there with her on my parents' driveway, the ground wet, gray skies and all, I could be whoever she needed me to be. And for a few seconds, I nearly considered letting the police handle Bianca's case.

"Can you do me a favor?" I reached for her hand, forgetting our audience again, because maybe there was hope for me after all. Maybe she was right, and she had the power to ground me. Keep me from falling too far. Too dark.

"Anything," she murmured.

"Remind me of who I am from time to time." I squeezed her hand. "The man you see. The one you think I am, at least."

Her eyes became slits, as if somehow my words nearly drew tears from her. "I'd happily remind you every hour of every day."

"Are you two coming or what?" Izzy called out, breaking us from the moment, and she waved as if we didn't see them waiting for us. And for whatever reason, they both seemed to sense it was better not to come to us.

"You ready?" I let go of her.

"I can do this," Maria said under her breath.

"I got you," I promised. "Always."

"And here I thought I came to New York to have your back." Only half her mouth smiled that time. An awkward but adorable one.

"Maybe it can go both ways?"

"Only a 'maybe'?"

I grabbed our bags and tipped my head, motioning for her to walk. "I'm a work in progress," I admitted. "I'm trying." And I really was.

"Finally!" My mom tossed her hands in the air as we approached, and then she eagerly pulled Maria in and squeezed her.

I set down the bags inside the foyer. "Come here, you," I said to Izzy and gave her a big bear hug, because it'd been too damn long since I saw my little sister. I swallowed. My *only* sister now.

Izzy squeezed me right back, holding on longer than I expected. I spied Maria doing her best to answer questions my mom was rapidly firing her way.

"Where's everyone?" I asked, rescuing Maria from my mother's inquisition. Giving one last squeeze, I released my sister, who immediately walked over to Maria and embraced her.

"The boys are in the study downstairs. Your father got tied up with something in the city. He promised he'd be home before dinner, though." Mom grabbed hold of my forearm and pulled me tight to her side while patting my arm like I was five. "What's up with the extra security Constantine hired? We expecting trouble?"

I knew my brother already gave her a reason why he had the extra security detail at the estate, but Mom was trying to entrap me. Ensuring Constantine had told her the truth. Knowing our history, I didn't blame her.

I looked back and forth between her and Izzy, trying to remember what Constantine had told me over the phone. "Homeland Security," I sputtered at the memory, finally jarring it loose from my brain. "DHS said there's been an increase in threats against some of New York's wealthiest families, and he's overly cautious. I'm sure there's nothing to worry about, Ma."

Her brows slanted. Nope, she wasn't buying our bullshit, but she wouldn't want to worry Izzy, and with Maria in her presence, she wouldn't press. "Well," she said, eyes on Maria, "I'm putting you in Enzo's old bedroom."

"Maria and I are sharing a room, huh?" I pulled my arm free from Mom's so she could swat me like I knew she was about to, and yup, right on the arm like my teacher used to do at Catholic school with the ruler. What could I say? I had a mouth on me back then.

"No, she's a Romano, silly. She's staying alone." Mom dragged out her last word for extra emphasis. "You're staying in the guest room with Alessandro."

"Like hell I am," I grumbled, feeling like a teenager again being back in this house.

"I put bunk beds in there, you know, in case anyone ever gives me grandkids one day." For whatever reason, Mom's Italian accent always became ten times thicker whenever talking about babies.

"Good luck with that, Ma." Izzy suppressed a chuckle with the back of her hand, and Mom elbowed her in the side.

"Well, there will certainly be no baby making happening while we're all in this house the next few days, which is why Pablo, whenever he gets here, is staying out in the pool house," Mom went on, pointing a finger Izzy's way while closing an eye.

"Pablo?" I held up a hand, shooting my sister a confused look. "Like, as in Picasso?" I couldn't help but tease.

Izzy rolled her eyes. "Don't start. Alessandro has already spent an hour giving me hell, and Constantine's been abnormally silent, even for him, which speaks volumes. So not you, too." She looked at Maria as if she'd assist her in the boyfriend department. "He is an artist, though."

"Oh, fuck me. This is too good." I slapped a hand to my chest, not realizing how much I needed the comic relief with so much shit going on.

"Watch your mouth. I'll still wash it out with soap," Mom warned, holding her finger in front of my face, brows stitched together, but there was humor in her eyes and a tremble of laughter she fought back.

"Yeah," Izzy said, eyes on Maria. "She totally did that. And God help us if we took the Lord's name in vain as kids."

Mom snatched Maria's bag from the floor. "Why don't I show you to your room now. Give you a chance to freshen up. Although, I have to say, you look rosy and quite fresh already."

I snuck a look at Maria, my tongue peeking between my lips at why this woman was probably so "fresh." *My tongue and the orgasm I gave her.*

Maria blushed, reading my thoughts, then gave my mom her attention. "Thank you again for having me. I needed to get away, and I guess Enzo did, too." Ah, her voice faltered there a bit, and her "I guess" had Mom peering at me.

I surrendered my palms in the air, doing my best to give her my puppy dog eyes, since I was her youngest son and Alessandro claimed she always had a soft spot for me.

"And you're just friends?" Mom asked, eyes sharp on me as she attempted to channel my thoughts.

I wished more than anything we were in New York for any other reason than we were, but facts were facts.

"Of course," I lied before Maria could, because I was much better at it than she was.

Mom had her back to Maria as she mouthed, "Romano," to me, as if I needed the reminder that my parents made some sort of "protection" and "no breaking hearts" deal with Maria's parents that included none of us Costas going near Maria or Natalia.

"Oh, one more thing you should know before I walk Maria to her room," Mom said, her eyes narrowing on me as if she were about to level me with something heavy. "I finally redid Bianca's bedroom. I turned it into a library. Wall-to-wall books. The french doors open to the water. She'd love it." She half smiled. "They're all of her books, too."

Maria's hand went to her heart, and her eyes fell to the marble floors beneath us. Yeah, I was on the same agonizing page.

And for some reason, I only just now realized Izzy was wearing a shirt Bianca would've loved that said: BOOKMARKS ARE FOR QUITTERS in glittery metallic lettering. Izzy lowered her gaze to her shirt and, based on the hint of red on her bronzed cheeks, I had to wonder if it'd been Bianca's top. It looked like it'd been washed a hundred times already. But given my sister's ripped high-waisted jeans, hair in a messy bun, and unlaced Doc Martens, maybe "messy" was trendy? Hell if I knew what was in style.

"Well, how about we go to your room now," Mom suggested to Maria, as if realizing Izzy and I needed a second to catch up alone. "Shall we?"

Unsure how to process pretty much anything, I gave Maria a stupid wave before shoving my hands into my slacks' pockets.

"How long have you two been sleeping together?" Izzy asked once it was just us, and she folded her arms and scrutinized me with a hard look. "She's too young for you."

I frowned. "We're not." *Not technically.* "And she's not that much younger than you."

"But eight years younger than you," she reminded me before fake-zipping her lips and tossing the key into the metaphorical water. "I should shut my mouth, since Pablo is a decade older."

"A decade?" I scoffed.

"Mm-hmm." She nudged my suitcase with the tip of her boot. "You failed my test, you hypocrite. He's only three years older. But what he lacks in age difference he more than makes up for in the bedroom."

Payback was a bitch. "Yeah, I don't need that mental image. Because Pablo will have his ears removed if I think—"

"That was Van Gogh. He's the one who cut off his ear," she interrupted as I grabbed my suitcase.

"Yeah, okay, well, I'll chop something else off, then." I winked, and she nudged me in the side as we started down the long hall toward the guest room, which happened to be on the other side of the house from my old bedroom. *Well played, Mom.* But my room had a balcony overlooking the water, which meant I could easily access the room at night.

"Sure, sure. I'd say your bark is bigger than your bite, but I know you. And both are equally scary." She elbowed me again. "Jeez, you're still made of rock."

"I was going to say you must be hitting the gym yourself at how hard you poked me," I joked, faking arm pain with a dramatic moan.

We stopped outside the guest room, and I saw Alessandro had already claimed the bottom bunk with his bag.

"Why can't Constantine share with him?" I grunted like I was that teenage boy again. But at least that me was still innocent. Had yet to take a life.

"Constantine share?" She snorted. "Sure." With her arms folded now, she set her back to the hall wall outside the bedroom.

"And where is your artist who isn't Van Gogh? Why didn't he come with you?"

"He had to wrap up a project at his studio first. He has an exhibit next week, so it's a big deal he's even coming here for a few days." She checked her watch. "Should be here any minute, though."

"Wow. I really look forward to meeting him," I dryly said, rolling my eyes. "But if you're introducing him to the family, it must be serious."

She held up her ring finger, and thank God, there was no ring. "He's planning to ask you all for my hand in marriage. I figured if we're all here, it made sense to do."

"What?"

She followed me into the room. "He proposed already, and I helped him stand back up and kindly told him to try again after he talks to you guys and Dad. Because you know—"

"He'd lose a limb if not?" I smiled, but fuck, it wasn't funny. I didn't want her marrying some guy I'd never met and already had a bad feeling about.

"So." She pointed at my suitcase as if the answers were there. If only. "Why are you really here? You don't think any of us are buying the Homeland Security BS, do you?" she asked as I peered at the couch opposite the bunk beds. It was loaded with stuffed animals for the grandbabies Mom hoped to have one day.

Shit. "We'll tell you tonight. I promise." I dropped my bag and flipped open the blinds, catching only a partial view of the water from this side of the house.

"It's not good, is it?"

I let go of the wooden blinds and slowly faced her.

"Tell me now. Don't make me wait. Hell, clearly Hudson knows what's going on or he wouldn't be here." Izzy was leaning into the interior frame of the door now, her humor and happiness absent from her face. All hard, sad lines now. "Please."

I gathered in a deep breath and scratched my jawline, contemplating what to do. Before I could decide whether to confess the truth, my phone began vibrating in my pocket.

It was my mother's cousin. "One second. I need to answer this message," I told her.

Giovanni: I have the name. I'd rather share it in person. Offer my apologies to your family face-to-face. I heard you were back in New York.

The fact that news had traveled fast that I was in town didn't shock me. There were always eyes on me when I was here.

Me: You need my parents' blessing for an impromptu visit. Call them. And just give me the name now.

"What is it?" Izzy asked, coming closer, and I looked up to see her worried expression.

"Just Maria's ex causing problems," I said once reading the information he'd texted. As I'd suspected, he provided Thomas's name.

Giovanni: Are we good now?
Me: Did you shut down their side operation?
Giovanni: They work for Nico since he's slowly taking over for me. I already spoke with him. He'd like to come to your home as well. Apologize in person.

I didn't know Nico that well, which only meant the man hadn't done anything to piss my brothers and me off yet.

Giovanni's wife had only given him a daughter, and he'd always wanted a son to take over for him. From what I knew, he'd arranged for his daughter to marry a Sicilian when she was barely even out of high school. And Giovanni had been grooming Nico for twenty years to become the head of the family "business."

When I didn't answer, Giovanni texted again.

Giovanni: If your family agrees, we'll all come tomorrow. Make amends.

I didn't bother to respond, too damn angry. I shoved my phone back in my pocket, still unsure how to handle the Thomas situation. But I'd need to shelve that problem for later. I had to catch Bianca's killer first.

I fixed my attention on Izzy, wishing it'd been Jesse who'd texted instead. No messages or voice mails from him while I'd been out of contact, since my phone had gone for a swim.

"Who was that?" Izzy asked, but then I was saved by the bell. Well, the doorbell. "That must be Pablo." She nervously slapped her hands to the sides of her legs as if trying to discard sweat from her palms.

I set my hand to her back and motioned for her to walk. She remained quiet as we made our way back to the foyer, but Alessandro beat us to the door. He was busy talking to Izzy's boyfriend, so he didn't notice we were there yet.

"Your last name, what is it?" Alessandro had his hands in his gray slacks' pockets, eyes steady on his target.

Pablo-not-Picasso had his blond hair up in a man bun, and he had ripped jeans like my sister's but with paint on them and a tattered tee with . . . flip-fucking-flops.

Were we being Punk'd?

"Why do you need to know?" Pablo asked, eyes moving to Izzy as if searching for a save, and she quickly went to his side and hooked an arm around his back to protect him from the scrutiny of my brother. Good luck with that. I was next in line, too.

"I need a name to run a background check," Alessandro plainly said. "I can snap your photo and upload that, but that's a time suck."

"He's funny." Pablo pointed to him before his eyes landed on me, and he took an uncomfortable step back.

What, did I look threatening? *Good.*

Alessandro faced me, and his expression changed from menacing to warm. "Hey." He pulled me in for a one-arm hug, patted my back twice; then we both became laser-focused on the man I sure as hell didn't like.

"He doesn't have a last name." Izzy spoke for her boyfriend that time. "He changed it to just Pablo."

"Like Cher. Prince. Madonna. Elvis." Pablo smiled. "Just Pablo."

"Well, *Just* Pablo," my brother drawled. "Elvis had a last name. Presley. God help *you* if you don't know that." He *tsk*ed and raked a hand through his brown hair.

Izzy leaned into her boyfriend, setting a palm to his chest, and lightly patted. "He's teasing. Don't worry."

"But I'm not actually," Alessandro said, using his flat tone of voice again, not laying on any of his typical charm.

I looked up to see Constantine on approach, and the grim look on my brother's face meant he knew I didn't have the cleaner's name yet. "We need to talk. Alone." Constantine's gaze flicked to Pablo, and he looked away as if the man were but a shadow there and nothing to worry about. Hell, not even a hello. He angled his head down the hall where he'd come from, a request to follow.

"I'm sorry they're being so rude," Izzy apologized. "But that's Enzo. The comedian with the questions is Alessandro." She let go of Pablo to block my path to try and stop me from following Constantine's request to leave. "My eldest brother with clearly no manners is Constantine."

"Nice to meet you all?" Pablo said it like a question.

"I guess if Mom isn't running here to see him, she's already met Pablo-not-Picasso?" I asked. "And she didn't tell us for obvious reasons."

Pablo frowned. "He knows I can hear him, right?"

"Yeah, you still have both your ears." Alessandro chuckled.

"That was Van Gogh," Izzy said with frustration. "I swear, you two."

But come on, she had to know we wouldn't like the guy, and how could we?

"I guess I'll take you to the pool house." Izzy scowled at me, then rolled her eyes at Alessandro before snatching Pablo's hand.

Pablo grabbed his bag, and the two of them went down the other hall, avoiding Constantine.

"I don't like him," Alessandro said once the three of us were alone. "Pretty sure Constantine will kill him before night falls."

"That's being generous," Constantine rasped before turning away.

Before I had a chance to follow him, Mom called out my name, and I pivoted to see her approaching. "Maria seems nervous. Maybe you should go talk to her?" She came before me and opened her palms. "I was hoping Izzy and Maria would cook dinner with me tonight. I'd ask you, but you need a break, I'm sure."

I wouldn't mind cooking. It was an outlet, my way to destress. Using my hands for something that brought pleasure instead of pain.

But tonight wouldn't be the night, not with why I was there.

I looked at Alessandro and Constantine waiting for me and then back toward the hall where my old room was, and why did it feel like I was being asked to make a choice right now? Justice or love?

NINETEEN

Maria

"Stuffy will be back soon. He's just on vacation. Like Mommy is," I said over FaceTime to Chiara, trying not to cry at the sight of my daughter on the small screen. I missed her so damn much.

Ten minutes after Thomas had met up with my parents at the halfway point between Charlotte and their small town of Waxhaw, they realized Stuffy had been left in the back seat of Thomas's car. They'd called him, but the jerk had refused to turn around. He'd said he had a plane to catch and didn't have time.

"That's okay, baby girl. Nanna's got some fun toys for you," I went on, hoping to calm Chiara down as my mom held her inside her living room. "I love you so, so much." I blew her an air kiss, which had her smiling, thank God, and she blew one back to me.

"Hon, can you take her while I have a word with our daughter?" my mom asked my dad, and he popped his head into view to wave, then took Chiara from her. No lecture from him, but I knew one was coming from Mom. "I just don't understand what you're doing at the Costas' in New York." Mom cut straight to it.

"I needed a vacation," I said on a sigh.

I peered at the massive yacht with the Costa name scrolled on it, which sat regally in the water, as Mom said, "You didn't even tell me you were getting on a plane. The fact I had to hear from Enzo's mother that you're at their house just screams something is wrong."

At her words, I started to pace. Enzo's mother must've redecorated his old bedroom, since it looked more like a guest room staged for a furniture store. A sailing theme to go with the bay.

"I assume Thomas doesn't know you're there? I'm surprised he didn't grill us with questions when we picked up Chiara."

"Yeah, well, Thomas can kiss my ass," I snapped just as there was a knock at the door. *Shit.* "I have to go. Talk later." I chucked the phone on the bed as the door opened.

"I'd prefer Thomas to go nowhere near your ass." Enzo casually walked in, then shut and *locked* the door, barely giving me time to process he'd overheard what I'd said to my mom.

I dropped onto the bed and tugged at the soft fabric of my dress, feeling a draft, since I was without panties. The dress went to my knees when standing but only brushed my thighs whenever I sat. "I thought you'd be with your brothers."

He sat next to me and rested his palm on my knee. "Yeah, but they can wait." He looked at me, and I let go of a ragged breath. "Are you okay?"

"I think so?" My brows slanted, giving me away.

"You really aren't a great actress." His lips teased into a semismile before he shifted to the side a bit to better face me and walked his palm up my thigh like a slow, sensual caress. "Did you do as I asked?"

I swallowed, setting my hands on each side of me on the bed as my nipples pebbled at his unexpected touch. I barely managed a nod with his hand on me.

He shifted the fabric aside and traced the seam of my sex with his finger. "I don't know if I can handle you being bare at the dinner table. There will be other men there, and maybe I wasn't thinking straight when I asked you." That deep, husky rasp as he thumbed the sensitive spot of my clit had my eyes falling shut, and I barely heard anything he'd said. The man knew how to relax me, that was for sure. I forgot all about my nerves.

I rested back on my forearms as he continued to softly stroke that bundle of nerves. "You should be with . . . your . . . brothers. Not worrying about me. I'm . . . fine." *Just breathless and panting with your hand and eyes on me.*

"I told you earlier, I'll always worry about you." His other hand slid down the front of my dress, and he palmed my breast beneath the bra. "And you don't really want me to stop, do you?"

"No." My eyes flashed open at the loss of his touch.

"Good." He stood and twirled a finger. "Center of the bed on your back this time," he commanded while fixing the cuffs of his shirt as if about to go to a meeting, not get me off. Was he serious?

I stared up at him, unsure what to do. Give in to desire and let him relax me or demand he go to his brothers and do what he came to New York to do. Could he really afford to be distracted another time?

"I won't ask again." His voice was rough as he let go of his sleeve.

"And what will you do if I don't behave?" Oh jeez, what was with my new obsession of playing with fire? Then again, I was single now, and there'd been months of hot back-and-forth between us. Sexual innuendos buried within our words. A bit of cat and mouse. Foreplay without the actual "play" up until recently.

"I'll show you, sweetheart." Without giving me a chance to follow his order, he hoisted me to my feet and tossed me over his shoulder.

My dress went up, and he spanked my ass with one hard smack while carrying me to the fancy chaise longue by the french doors.

He let me go only long enough so he could sit. Snatching my wrist, he pulled me onto his lap, and I found myself facedown, my side braid hanging in my face and my dress bunched at my waist with his hard cock near my center.

My nails bit into the suede fabric of the seat when he began to smooth his hand in small circles over the area he'd spanked.

And then his fingers slid inside me as his thumb pushed against my other hole, and I squirmed, but he held me firm in place.

"Relax, *Tesoro*." But his dick was rock-solid, and I couldn't help but rotate my pelvis, dry humping him like I was a decade younger and still a virgin.

"You're touching me . . . there," I whispered in embarrassment, but whatever he was doing, touching me from both angles was like sensory overload but in an amazing way.

"Mmmm. We have a list of yours to check off," he reminded me, and he was right, I was pretty sure being "punished" was on the list.

And that husky tone of voice of his, as if he were being throttled by his own desire to fill me with his cock instead, was going to set me off.

"You need to come so you're not so wound up when you go cook."

Cook, right. Sure. That's what I was thinking about right now with his hands touching me from both angles and my ass in the air on his lap, and I'd probably be wearing the mark of his handprint for a few hours. And I fucking loved it.

"What about you?" I clawed at the fabric as he brought me to the edge, drawing the breath from my lungs faster and faster with each stroke of his hand over my sensitive flesh.

"Later, I promise. I don't think it's a good idea to be this tense anymore. Because I'll lose my mind in front of my family otherwise."

At least he was finally coming to his—

My thoughts died as he managed to free the orgasm from somewhere deep inside me and had me coming hard, coating his fingers in my arousal.

I nearly sank my mouth into the fabric to try and bury my scream but instead accidentally bit the inside of my cheek as I came undone, my stomach muscles getting a great workout.

"Wow." I think I panted the word as he helped me stand. I adjusted my dress, my face probably as red as that one spot on my ass. I was hot all over.

He smirked, then went into the connecting en suite and washed his hands as I slipped on the panties I'd grabbed from my luggage.

I looked over and found him in the doorway, leaning against it with folded arms. "Is this how you'll be relieving my tension from now on?"

"I told you orgasms help you live longer." He winked. "Want you living forever, *bellissima*."

Wellll. "Ditto." My gaze flirted with the bulge in his pants as he shoved away from the door. "So let me help you." I went for my side braid and freed my now-dry hair, allowing the soft waves to fall over my shoulders.

He ate up the space between us and brushed the pad of his thumb along the line of my lips. "This mouth was made for fucking."

My eyes fell between us, wondering if he'd finally let me taste him.

He held my cheeks before bowing his head to mine. "But not now. I need to tell my brothers what I just learned. My mother's cousin confirmed Thomas was the one who hired those *idiotas*."

"And you're only just now telling me that?" I stepped back in surprise, and he released his hold on me.

"Thought it'd ruin the moment," he answered, and yeah, he was right about that. Thomas losing his marbles and hiring some "third party" to attack Enzo was for sure a mood killer.

"I'm so sorry he did that." I turned, feeling red all over again, but he snatched my wrist, drawing me back to him.

"Never apologize for that man." His eyes thinned as he studied me, and there were more words he wanted to say, I could feel it, but he chose to keep them trapped behind his lips.

"So glad Chiara is away from him and with my parents."

"I would've devised an extraction plan to get her if things hadn't worked out the way they did." There wasn't any humor in his tone, and that actually made me feel better.

"Does this mean we can lose the extra security here?"

"We're still not out of the woods, not with the cleaner out there and his clients more than likely knowing their names are at risk." He admitted what I'd been worried he'd say.

"Then you should go to your brothers." I nodded, noting the time on the wall clock. It was six, and surely he wanted to talk to his brothers before his father arrived for dinner.

He laced our fingers together. "Will you be okay?"

"Much better now." I smiled, but he shook his head.

"You need to stop lying to me." He tightened his hold of my hand.

"And you're Mr. Honest, are you?" I challenged.

He let go of me and murmured, "Work in progress, remember?"

TWENTY

Maria

"Hey." I stopped outside the open doorway at the sight of Isabella in the room. And then my stomach dropped when I realized it was their new library, which meant it'd been Bianca's old bedroom.

"Can you believe it's my first time coming in here since Mom changed it?" Isabella reached for one of the books on the shelves. *Great Expectations*.

"Your parents mostly stay at their place near Central Park, right?" I nervously entered the room, unsure if I belonged there and a bit worried if I'd be able to handle being surrounded by what felt like Bianca's presence and not cry.

"Yeah, Dad still works nonstop at the office even though he should retire and let Constantine take over." She slid the book back in place and faced me.

"And you never wanted to work at the office?"

"Mergers and all that jazz doesn't exactly excite me." She freed her hair from the bun, only to pile her dark locks back up again, reining her hair in with a pink scrunchie. "Can I ask you how Enzo's doing? He looks off. Like he was trying to act normal and joke around, but it felt like he was doing it to hide something. Trying too hard."

Shit. I'd already been peppered with questions by her mom, and I'd nearly failed. I didn't want to fumble my way through another conversation full of lies.

She held up a hand and shook her head. "Don't worry. You don't need to betray him and spill whatever secrets he's carrying around. I wouldn't ask you to do that." She went over to the french doors and pushed them open, and I joined her on the balcony.

It was breezy out, and the sky was still overcast, but no rain, at least. "Where's Pablo? I'd love to meet him."

"Pablo is meditating in the pool house. He says he needs some space to remove the toxic energy he felt from my brothers." She faced me, setting her back to the railing. She was the only sibling who lacked any kind of accent, since she was born in New York. But her tone of voice still had this beautiful quality to it I admired. She'd make a great audiobook narrator. "They really hate him."

"I don't think they'll like any guy their sister brings home." I stood alongside her, peering out at the choppy water. "A brother thing, I imagine."

"My therapist says I always pick men I know my family won't approve of because I want my brothers to love me as much as they loved Bianca, and dating the wrong men will get their attention and—" She cupped her mouth, and I had to replay the words she'd confessed to ensure I'd heard them right. "I'm so sorry, I didn't mean to say that," she added once she'd lowered her hand.

"No, it's, um, okay." *I lack a filter, too.*

She fidgeted with the hem of her tee, and I eyed the writing there. "I'm trying to get into reading. I was hoping it'd make me feel closer to Bianca, since she was a writer."

"And does it?"

"She's dead," she whispered. "The best I can do is be close to a ghost." Her eyes slowly met mine. "And that's another thing my therapist likes to remind me of. I'll never see her again."

Damn. "Maybe you need a new therapist? I mean, I'm sorry, it's just, I'm not a fan of her advice, I guess. But who am I to know what's best? I probably should've seen someone after my daughter was born." I'd blamed hormones for my unhappiness, and maybe for a few weeks they were responsible, but in truth, I hadn't been happy in my marriage for a long time.

"And I probably should've seen one after I found my sister dead in her apartment." Her eyes fell closed, as if regretting her words again.

How'd I not know she was the one to discover her sister murdered? I banded my arm across my midsection, sick to my stomach for her. I couldn't comprehend the idea of ever finding Natalia like that. "I didn't know."

She opened her eyes and shared, "We were supposed to have breakfast, and it wasn't like her to not show up. After she didn't answer her phone, I used the key she'd given me and let myself in." Her eyes slowly worked up to meet mine. "When we told Enzo what happened while he was deployed, it was as if he already knew what we were going to say. Growing up, we used to joke that they shared a brain."

And a heart. I sniffled, realizing tears threatened.

"But yeah, he felt her absence before we told him what had happened." She let go of her shirt. "You probably don't need to know this. I'm sorry. I tend to overshare."

"It's okay. I happen to appreciate honesty."

"And yet, you're friends with Enzo, and he's not so great at talking. How does that work?" Then she whispered a quick apology. "No filter." She opened her palms. "See?"

"No, it's a fair question. He's trying to open up." *A work in progress.*

She reached for my arm and her brows slanted. "Just be careful with him. I don't know if he's capable of love after Bianca died. I mean, he doesn't even know how to love me." She let go of my arm and angled her head toward the door. Between her words and the sad look in her eyes, I wanted to both hug her and cry.

"Isabella, of course he loves you. He may not be good at showing it, but he adores you."

She quietly looked at me for a long moment. And staring back at me were the eyes of an eighteen-year-old girl instead. A hurt, lonely kid who lost her big sister.

"Well," she said, blinking back tears, "Mom's waiting for us." And then she made a beeline for the door before I could stop her.

I took a second to collect my thoughts and went out into the hall, but she was already gone by that point.

My shoulders slumped, and a weird feeling struck me. I stopped walking, doing a three-sixty, feeling as though I had eyes on me. But the hallway was empty. *Pull it together, Maria.*

I shook it off and managed to find my way to the kitchen inside the house. Or did a fifteen-thousand-square-foot home qualify as a mansion?

I spotted Isabella sitting on the counter talking to her mom.

"There you are," Mrs. Costa said, and she quickly poured a generous glass of Chianti and started my way. And why did I feel like this was also meant as truth serum? I nearly choked on my first sip when she looked me dead in the eyes and asked, "So, are you in danger? Is my son protecting you and that's why all those extra security guards are roaming my estate, making this place look like a war compound?"

TWENTY-ONE

Enzo

"Just be careful with him. I don't know if he's capable of love after Bianca died. I mean, he doesn't even know how to love me." I replayed Izzy's words in my head as I went to the study to join my brothers and Hudson.

After I left Maria, my mother had trapped me en route to get to them and asked a few more uncomfortable questions about why I was there, and then I'd decided to head back to clue Maria in so we were on the same page. But I'd paused outside Bianca's old room as Izzy had leveled Maria with her warning.

Realizing my sister was about to make a quick exit, I stupidly ducked into the bathroom in the hall and waited until they were both gone.

I understood my sister was only looking out for Maria, but it crushed me that Izzy didn't think I loved her. How had I fucked up that badly to let her think that?

"What took you so long?" Alessandro asked once I met up with them in Dad's study.

"I got sidetracked," I said in a bit of a daze while shutting the door behind me.

"Looks like you need this." Alessandro handed me a glass of bourbon and settled onto the couch by Hudson.

"I guess I'm not surprised to see you here," I said to Hudson, unsure why Constantine hadn't given me the heads-up he was coming.

"What'd you think I'd do when I found out Bianca's killer's still out there?" Hudson rasped as I swiveled my focus Constantine's way.

He was at Dad's desk, working on a laptop, but he closed it as our eyes met. "I take it you don't have a name." He stood and went to the bar cart. He snatched a glass, filling the tumbler with bourbon.

I took an uncomfortable sip of the drink, allowing it to burn my chest before sharing, "Not yet. But I did talk to Giovanni, and it turns out the attack this morning was unrelated to Bianca." That had Constantine whirling back around, his glass only half-full. What a fucking metaphor, too. "Maria's ex. I struck a nerve, I guess."

"Her ex sent those men after you?" Alessandro scoffed. "And he had that bad of luck to go to—"

"Yup." I took another healthy swallow of bourbon, hoping that news was why I felt so unsettled and it wasn't because I was missing something important.

"And what brought on the beating?" Hudson asked.

"Could've been the fact I threatened him to confess to cheating to the judge so Maria could be free of him sooner. But he also came over yesterday morning and wasn't happy to see me there." I shook my head at the memory, the anger toward that prick washing over me again, reigniting my hate for him. "With his daughter out of town, he decided to come after me."

"Clearly doesn't know you," Hudson responded, eyes on me.

"And I'll deal with that asshole, trust me." I just didn't know how to yet, because he was still Chiara's father. "For now, I'm here to focus on the case. Find Bianca's killer."

Constantine set down his glass. "Once we track down the cleaner, I'll get him to talk."

And I didn't doubt that. Among the four of us, we were well versed in getting assholes to talk and share their deepest, darkest secrets.

"I can't wrap my head around who would've wanted to hurt Bianca." Alessandro echoed what Constantine and I had discussed on the phone that morning. "But statistically speaking, this stuff usually happens by someone you know, right? We thought it was random, but that was because the cleaner planted evidence and made it look that way. And now we're back to square fucking one."

"Which is why we need his name," Constantine hissed, deciding to direct his anger at me, since his options were limited right now, and he saw Jesse as the gatekeeper to the answers.

At his words, I swapped my glass for my phone and called Jesse, but it went straight to voice mail. Two more times. The same.

"I should've come down there." Constantine removed his suit jacket and tossed it, then began working the sleeve of his shirt to the elbow. Unlike me, he didn't have any ink, but there were jagged scars on his right arm, which brought back painful memories of a botched job four and a half years ago that led to him being held captive, and he'd nearly died.

"Jesse will come through for us," I finally said. "But in the meantime, to Alessandro's point, a stabbing does feel personal. What if it's someone we all knew who killed Bianca?" I looked to Hudson for his thoughts, since he'd been FBI, even though his time at the Bureau had been brief.

"The knife could've also been a convenient weapon of choice. We can't jump to conclusions," Hudson said, as if regretting that was all he could contribute.

"We were going by the evidence the cleaner planted thirteen years ago, and we assumed the asshole followed her home and forced his way inside," Constantine went on. "But it's possible she let her killer in."

"Which means we need to figure out who Bianca would've trusted enough to let in and who'd also have the motive to . . ." Alessandro let his words trail off, clearly not having the stomach to finish his thoughts.

"We can't rule anyone out when putting together our potential suspect list. Someone Dad pissed off. Hell, even Giovanni," Constantine began. "I was trying to find a way to get my hands on untainted footage from the night of her murder, but the club's out of business now."

"Right," I remembered. "The nightclub cameras were manipulated, which was mentioned in court. And multiple vantage points were erased, so the prosecution believed the killer hid the fact he was there with Bianca that night."

"But the cleaner may have done that on purpose during his frame job. The story of the guy following Bianca home from the club would fall apart in court if he was never there in the first place," Constantine pointed out. "But that doesn't mean the real killer wasn't there."

"And the security footage near Bianca's was also manipulated, which is why the police never saw her killer come and go from her place back then," Hudson noted. "No chance you can unfuck that footage to see the real picture?"

"Unfortunately not," Constantine said. "But I had another idea."

Thank God for him. My brother had turned into a tech-savvy genius in the last decade, which had saved our asses time and time again on ops. And when he couldn't hack his way into a facility, Alessandro would charm his way in for us.

"I'm in the process of creating a program to tap into any available CCTV footage from that night within a block of the club," Constantine explained.

"So you think the cleaner didn't tamper with all the cameras in the area?" I asked.

"Only the ones at the bank across the street, which faced the entrance to the club, appear to have been altered," Constantine said. "Which is why I'm expanding the search farther. If we see anyone near the club that night who Bianca would've known, they get moved up to the top of the suspect list."

"But this is all a long shot, right?" Alessandro mumbled, frustrated, but I'd take a long shot over no shot at all, especially with Constantine at the helm trying to figure it out.

Before I could say more, my phone vibrated in my pocket. "It's Jesse." Constantine motioned for me to put him on speakerphone, and the guys crowded around me. "Hey, tell me Carter is ready to work together."

"Sorry for the delay. We were in the air. Just landed," Jesse answered. "We're in New York but not near you."

"Where?" And why'd it feel like he was about to hit me with shitty news?

"We're in Syracuse. The cleaner was captured just over the Canadian border, and a few spies swooped in and grabbed him from border control," Jesse explained. "Carter was able to figure out where he was taken. The CIA officers brought him to a remote location outside Syracuse."

"The CIA brought him stateside?" I asked, because the international field was normally the Agency's playground. "And why the hell to Syracuse?"

"Yeah, something is suspect," Jesse said. "But if you'd like to help us extract him, and you're willing to use rubber bullets and Tasers, then—"

"What time?" I interrupted.

"We can't afford to wait too long after dark. We're going to hit the cabin around twenty-three hundred hours. Can you get here by then?"

"Yeah." It was a quick flight to Syracuse, since we had our own jet, thankfully. "Send us your location."

There was noise in the background and then static popped over the line before a deep, unrecognizable voice said, "Constantine?"

My brother snatched the phone. "Carter."

"You're only joining because I'm working with half my team on this op and need the extra bodies," Carter hissed. "But if you get captured, I don't fucking know you. You're on your own, understood?"

"Yeah." My brother's lack of an aggressive response to Carter's determined tone was almost surprising.

"And one more thing," Carter started. "The cleaner never leaves our custody. You're not to kill him. You get the name, and then you go on your way."

Constantine closed his eyes, and I knew he was struggling that time. Same as me. I wanted to kill the bastard for being complicit in Bianca's murder, but he hid other crimes as well, and everyone deserved justice, not just us.

"Fine," I said, speaking for everyone. "Thank you for allowing us to join you."

"Sorry about him," Jesse said after a few quiet moments had passed, and Carter must've handed him the phone and left. "He's upset the Agency got to him before we did."

"Why are you working with only half a team?" I asked.

"We had to divide and conquer for our current op, which we hate doing, but we have another lead for our case, so my other team leader is handling that with some of our crew," he explained.

I looked at my brothers and Hudson, and they were now discussing something out of earshot. "We've got you covered," I promised, and then I shared with Jesse the news that the hit that morning had been tied to Maria's ex.

I ended the call after exchanging a few more words, my stomach turning at the idea I'd be infiltrating a CIA safe house and leaving Maria tonight. What if something went wrong? The CIA officers sure as hell wouldn't use rubber bullets.

"We'll leave after dinner," Constantine said, facing me now. "Let's not tell Mom and Izzy. They don't need to know about this. Not yet anyway."

Izzy. Guilt burned down my throat at the memory of her words. "Yeah, I guess," I hesitantly agreed, unsure if leaving my sister in the dark again would only make things worse for our relationship, but at the same time, why would I want to burden her with the painful truth if I could avoid it a bit longer?

"I guess this means Pablo lives to see another day," Hudson remarked in a gravelly tone.

"We'll deal with *that* problem when we get back," Constantine bit out, then motioned for the door.

Instead of following them out, I went over to the window and set a palm to the glass, my thoughts racing. I still couldn't grasp the idea someone Bianca knew would want to hurt her. But I'd never thought Thomas would come after me, either, and . . .

"People in love do crazy things," I said at the memory of my words earlier to Maria about her ex. "Did you love someone, Bianca?" *And if so, why'd they want to kill you?*

TWENTY-TWO

Maria

The dining room table was covered in platters and dishes, and everything smelled amazing. Not that I could take credit for anything other than the salad. I was pretty sure Mrs. Costa didn't trust my culinary skills.

At the feel of a warm body behind me, I closed my eyes, knowing it was Enzo. He wrapped his arms around my waist and pulled me tight to his frame, setting his chin on top of my head. "You okay?"

I wasn't sure how much time we had alone before everyone joined us, so I shared my wine-induced thoughts. "Your mom hates me."

"No way. She loves you." He was quick to respond, but he wasn't in the kitchen while his mom had given me the third degree, and I'd nearly caved to the pressure and shared the real reason we were in New York.

"All I know is that she doesn't want me with you." Not that she said that, but that'd been the vibe.

He turned me around and snatched my cheeks. "She doesn't want *me* with you, that's the issue. You're a Romano, remember? My parents promised to protect you and Natalia. That's all. And she thinks I'll break your heart." Worry lines cut across his forehead, and then he frowned. "My sister thinks the same."

Brittney Sahin

"She told you that?" I lifted my brows in surprise.

He let go of me and backed away, his eyes going to the entranceway as if checking to ensure we were still alone. "I came to see you earlier, and I overheard her talking to you. She doesn't think I love her."

Before I could respond, Isabella and her boyfriend came into the room, along with Mrs. Costa. "Looks like your dad will be late. He said to eat without him."

Enzo let go of a deep, gruff breath. He must've been eager to talk to his father and let him know what was going on. Given his father's past, maybe he could help.

"This is Pablo," Isabella introduced him, and Pablo stepped forward, taking a bit too long in admiring my dress, and before I knew it, Enzo stepped around me, blocking my view of Isabella's boyfriend.

"Your ears aren't the only thing you're in danger of losing," Enzo sharply warned, and Isabella grabbed Pablo's arm.

"He's an artist. He's just admiring beauty, and Maria is stunning." Isabella's excuse didn't seem to do anything for Enzo, so I came by his side and gave Enzo a gentle nudge, hoping to redirect his focus.

"My girl is right." Pablo smiled. "She's an understanding woman. I paint women in the nude all the time. It's just art." He held open his palms as his gaze took a slow journey over my body again. "I'd love to—"

"If you say you want to paint Maria, I'll fucking kill you," Enzo remarked in a low, cutting voice.

"Enzo," Isabella snapped. "Seriously? Why do you have to be such a dick?" She released Pablo's arm and left the dining room, and their mom held up her hand, probably a directive to Enzo not to follow her. Not that Enzo would leave me alone with Pablo.

Isabella's mom went after her, and Pablo's shoulders shrank without his girlfriend there to protect him, and he stepped back—right into a wall of three other intimidating men.

Startled, Pablo turned to see Constantine, Alessandro, and Hudson there.

"What's wrong?" Hudson was the first to ask, and he turned to the side, his attention lingering in the direction Isabella had run.

I walked my fingers up and down Enzo's spine, hoping to calm him. He was wound tight for so many reasons, and the artist was about to get the brunt of all his anger.

"He wants to paint Maria naked," Enzo said as Pablo twisted back around to face him.

"I'll paint you both. I don't care. A beautiful body is a beautiful body." Pablo's tone was borderline panic now. "Your sister lacks curves. Not much up top, either, if you know what I mean." He held open his palms, eyes set on my chest as if he were considering touching me. Was the man insane?

And that had Enzo snapping. He reached out and circled Pablo's throat with his hand.

"Let him go," Constantine abruptly ordered, and it took Alessandro and Hudson prying Enzo away from Pablo to get Enzo to listen.

"You can't choke every man who looks at me," I reminded Enzo, then peered at Pablo as he held his throat. "But *you* are kind of an asshole. And Isabella deserves better." I stepped forward. "So," I began, nearly snarling, and my protective instincts kicked in, "if you don't want these guys killing you in your sleep tonight, I suggest you apologize to Isabella and then leave."

Pablo backed up, bumping into Alessandro, who did some ridiculous but cute kind of growl, and then Pablo took off after Isabella.

Enzo spun me around, clearly not giving a damn we weren't alone, pinning me against his chest. His brows slanted as he held the sides of my arms. "What you said . . . that was hot as fuck." Then he bent forward and captured my lips with a searing kiss.

But seconds later, his mother interrupted our moment. "Lorenzo Costa, what do you think you're doing?"

Enzo took his sweet time peeling his mouth away from mine, and then he released my arms to face her. "Is Izzy okay?" he asked instead of acknowledging his mother's question, and I knew my cheeks had to match my dress.

"I highly doubt it, since from the sounds of it, Pablo is threatening to break up with her because of her crazy family." She cut her hands in the air and began yelling at him in Italian.

Hudson looked at me and shrugged, and oh . . . *Hudson.* It just dawned on me we'd yet to say hi, and the last time I saw him was in his office where we'd been exchanging banter six years ago before Enzo had kicked him out.

He nodded a small hello as if registering the same thought himself, and then he tipped his head to the side, suggesting we leave since this seemed to be a family fight.

We stepped out onto a balcony just off the dining room, and I spied two guards down below, walking the perimeter of the property near the water.

"You remember me?" I asked Hudson as he grabbed hold of the railing, and his eyes went to the cloudy sky that hid the last bit of sunlight as night loomed in the distance.

"I do." He looked at me from over his shoulder. "I also know you're the woman who's been driving Enzo nuts the last two years in Charlotte."

"Have I now?" I chuckled. "Why do I feel like that's a guess? I doubt Enzo would tell anyone that." Well, would he?

"They're Constantine's words. But Enzo talks to his brothers regularly."

Oh. I wasn't sure why I was surprised by that. Maybe it was the fact he never told me they had heart-to-heart talks like I did with Natalia.

"Sorry about your ex. I heard he was the cause for this morning's scare." He let go of the railing, fully facing me.

"Yeah, I'm still not sure how to wrap my head around that. He's my daughter's father, but you saw Enzo with Pablo just now . . . I don't know what he'll do to—"

"He won't. I'm sure he wants to, though," he cut me off. "But hurting your daughter's father would hurt your daughter. And from what Constantine's said, Enzo loves that little girl like she's his own. He'd never do anything to hurt her. Or you."

I wanted to believe him. But did he not see just how quickly Enzo had gone overboard in choking Pablo?

"Pablo deserved that," Hudson said, and I was beginning to wonder if I was truly that easy to read. Did I have a thought bubble over my head? "Pablo's on something. High as a kite."

"Wait, really? How could you tell?"

"Pupils blown and stupidly honest."

Right. Wow. "Well, I suppose he did more than meditate in the pool house."

"Bella has horrible taste in men."

"Bella, huh?" I stared at him with curiosity. "I've never heard anyone call her that."

The side of his lip hitched as if fighting a smile, but instead, he shrugged.

"You know," I began, unable to stop myself, "my brother-in-law was the only one to call my sister Talia. And now they're married. Maybe—"

"That's a bit of a stretch," he interrupted, smiling now. "And no, she's too young for me." He slid a finger beneath his chin. "Don't have a death wish, either."

"Fair enough." I peeked back through the french doors into the dining room, but it was empty now. Maybe the guys had gone after Isabella to apologize? I doubted it was to stop Pablo from leaving. "How'd you meet the Costa family?"

"I moved from Texas to New York when I was sixteen. I met Constantine in high school, and we became friends."

"You're the same age?" It was hard for me to imagine Hudson over forty, but then I remembered the brief timeline Enzo had provided, so I supposed it made sense.

"Yeah. Over-the-hill. Officially," he said with an easygoing smile.

"And you were close to Bianca, too?" I regretted the question immediately, since his lips flatlined, and he faced the water and white-knuckled the railing.

"Yeah, we were friends. The last memory I have of her was trying to get me to come to her monthly book club meeting. Pretty sure she was really trying to set me up with someone there."

I thought back to Hudson's bar, remembering all the books in his office. "Right, you're a reader, too."

He nodded without looking at me. "I should've just gone to her book club. Made her happy, you know? Instead, I now have to remember disappointing her as my last memory. How fucking depressing is that?"

I wasn't sure what to do right now, but it didn't seem appropriate to pat his back or hug him. So I whispered, "Try and focus on the good memories instead." Wow, was that the best I could do?

My list of things I sucked at was growing. Couldn't draw. Write. Act. Or talk poignantly.

I'm a good mom, I tried to remind myself. But was I a failure at that, too?

"Yeah, sure. Good memories. I'll think about those," he remarked flatly.

And damn, I knew that tone of voice. Cold and detached. Friendly Hudson was now gone, and I had the feeling the man Enzo had warned me to stay away from six years ago because he could only "fuck just to fuck" was about to show his face.

"I better check on them." He gave me a tight nod, then bailed, leaving me alone on the balcony, and I rolled my eyes at how not-smooth I could be in conversations.

I shivered as the mild September breeze blew my hair in front of my face, and I swiped my palms up and down my arms over my sleeves to warm up.

"I'm sorry about that." I flinched at the deep voice behind me, then slowly turned to face Enzo. He skimmed my cheek with the back of his hand.

"How's Isabella?"

"Pablo left. He broke up with her, and now Izzy's in her room refusing to speak to any of us." He shook his head. "I can't be sorry about it, though. He was a fucking idiot."

"She just needs time and space. She'll be okay."

"Hope so." He set his other hand at my hip. "Are you mad at me?"

"For going caveman on the guy?"

A slight smile tugged at his lips. "Is that what it's called?" He grabbed my ass and squeezed. "I think I'm just a bit tense."

"Oh, you don't say?" I slipped my hands between us and set them on his chest. "I'm guessing dinner is canceled?"

"Unless you're hungry, I was thinking we could talk before I go."

I blinked in confusion, pulling away at his words. "Where are you going?"

"Let's go to my old room." He offered his hand, and I hesitantly accepted it, allowing the heat from his body to warm me up as we walked the length of the balcony to get to the bedroom.

Once there, he locked the french doors and closed the floor-to-ceiling curtains. *Annnd* we probably should've done that earlier when I was on his lap having him finger me into orgasming.

"Where are you going?" I asked again, hoping for an answer this time as I sat at the edge of his bed, willing my nerves to dial down. But it'd been a long day. The two glasses of Chianti were doing nothing to extinguish the anxiety coiled tight in my stomach, chest, and pretty much every part of my body.

He locked the bedroom door next, then stood before me. "Jesse located the man who should know who really killed Bianca. And we need to go to Syracuse tonight," he finally shared, and that was a good thing, right? "The thing is, he's in the CIA's custody, which means we have to break him out. We won't hurt anyone. Rubber bullets."

I would've fallen onto my ass had I not already been seated. "But you could get hurt? Arrested?" A million other horrific things, too. And now my heart was racing ten times faster, and I could feel my pulse pumping all the way into my ears.

"I won't. This isn't my first time doing something like this."

"First time breaking someone out of a secure location, or first time going up against the Central freaking Intelligence Agency?" My voice squeaked. High-pitched panic that I was incapable of hiding had my hands turning to nervous balls at my sides. I was going to visit this man in a morgue or prison, wasn't I?

"Hey, it's okay." Enzo dropped to his knees before me. He snatched my fists as if they were fragile pieces of glass and covered them with his hands.

"Nothing about this is okay," I cried, the shudder in my chest escaping through my voice. "Please don't go."

"Maria, I promise I'll be fine, and I won't hurt anyone."

"But you plan to torture this man you're kidnapping from the CIA, right?" I couldn't even swipe at the tears because he had such a hold on my hands, and I didn't have the energy to pull away.

His quiet nod had my stomach turning. "You're not just good with a knife in the kitchen," I blurted, my irrational fears washing over me and coming true before my eyes.

He lowered his gaze to my lap, where he kept hold of my hands. "I'm good with my hands in multiple ways, I guess," he said in a solemn tone. "I'd rather cook, though."

Then slice and dice a man? Oh jeez. There went my stomach again. Tip-tilt-twirling around. "The middle of your story. Just tell me now. Please. Rip off the Band-Aid and get it over with, because I'm pretty sure I've already filled in the blanks myself anyway." My gaze climbed up the ink on his exposed forearm, the one with the rosary inked there.

"How detailed do you want it?" he asked, an uneasy expression crossing his face.

"I, um, don't need to know exactly how you killed that man. I'm guessing you made him suffer, though." At his nod, my pulse climbed. "Just tell me what you think I need to know."

"I can do that." He looked up for a moment, as if searching for the courage to reveal his past.

I could feel his fear that I'd hate him afterward in the squeeze of my hands. See the guilt vividly in the lines of his face when our eyes once again met.

"The deal my brothers and I were offered to avoid prison time was with the US government," he finally began. "I don't even know the name of the group we worked for, but they weren't CIA or FBI. Not the NSA or Homeland Security. And it doesn't matter anymore, they were disbanded three years ago, and our contract was voided early." He paused for a breath. "Those years after Bianca's death, my brothers and I were basically unpaid mercenaries for the government. We were sent on ops around the world a few times a year but without backup or support. We were on our own if caught. My path also crossed with Jesse's on occasion during that time."

Well, that didn't sound horrible. I could handle that.

"The thing is, we were really good at what we did. Really fucking good. And it was hard for us to look away when we saw injustices happening all around us. People going unpunished for crimes they committed because of legal bullshit. And as long as we did what we were told by the government, they didn't seem to care if we went off on our own from time to time."

"What do you mean? Like what your dad did in Italy?"

He offered only a tight nod, letting me know there were details I didn't need to hear, and I wouldn't want to, either.

"So when Natalia offered you the job at the restaurant, you took it because you were done with your government contract and . . . what? You decided to quit being a vigilante, too?"

"I didn't like the person I was, Maria. The path I was on was a dark one. And I knew Bianca wouldn't approve, so yeah, I decided to quit and leave New York. My brothers agreed to quit as well." He let go of my hands and shifted back, sinking onto his heels, remaining looking up at me like a man searching for forgiveness. "It's not like we went around killing everyone we deemed a bad guy, if that's what you're thinking."

"Well, I wasn't, but I can't get that horrific image out of my head now."

Sure, I loved the morally gray men in romance novels who'd burn down the world for the woman they loved. But that was fiction. Could I handle it in the real world?

"I'm sorry." He set a fist at his side and pushed up off the floor to stand. "I can tell this is too much for you, and that's why I didn't want to make love before you knew the truth. I knew that you—"

"Stop." I rose to stand before him. "It is a lot, you're right. And I'm processing, sure. But don't put words in my mouth." I grabbed hold of his shirt, and his jaw clenched as he lowered his eyes to my hand. "But I need to know if there's more to your story. Or any other half-truths. Lies?"

"Maria." His hand tangled in my hair, cupping the back of my head, demanding my attention. "I've only truly lied to you once."

"What was it?"

Bending in, drawing his lips closer, he exhaled a jagged breath over my skin. "That I could only be your friend."

He wound my hair around his fist and tugged, drawing my lips up like an offering, and he waited to see if I'd take it or refuse him.

His focus ran down between us, blazing a trail of heat over my skin as he looked at me. Finding my eyes again, he rasped, "I told you before, you hold the power over me, so tell me what you want, *Tesoro*. Am I letting go of you, or are we making love?"

TWENTY-THREE

Maria

"You know what I want."

"What are you saying?" I felt the dark murmur of intent in Enzo's tone all the way down to my toes as he let go of my hair.

"That I accept you for you. I'm not running." My palm flattened on his chest, his heart beating as wildly as mine. "Be dark. Be the light. Be anything or anyone you need to be," I rattled on crazily, but it was the truth. "Just be mine." I innocently shrugged. "That was corny, right? I'm replaying it back in my head, and it was—"

His mouth closed over mine, stealing my words, breath, and, well, he already had my heart, so . . .

His kiss was soft. Delicate. No tongue. A bit unsure, even. Was he still nervous? Worried this wasn't real?

"Maria," he whispered against my mouth. "You know the truth, and you still want—"

"Yes, how many times do I have to tell you that? How else can I prove to you that you're who I want no matter what?" I pleaded. "You have to let go of this guilt. It's crushing you. Instead, see yourself the way I do. The way I know Bianca would if she were here. Please."

His brows snapped together, his gaze softening as he considered my words. Then his lips crashed over mine. His tongue plunged into my mouth as the last bit of fight in him to stay away died.

Hoisting my legs around his hips without severing our kiss, I anxiously tugged his dress shirt free from his pants.

"Enzo," I cried a heartbeat later. "I need to feel you inside me."

Still holding me, he nuzzled his nose against mine. "You taste like wine, sweetheart. Have you been drinking?"

I wrinkled my nose. "Don't you dare say you won't make love to me because I had some wine. I might just lose my mind. Officially."

"We wouldn't want that." His devilish smile had my brain turning to mush as he eased his mouth over mine.

"We do have a problem," he remarked a beat later while gently placing me on the bed to peel off his shirt. "You're not on the pill, and I didn't bring condoms." Unbuttoning his pants, he let them hang lower on his hips, showing the ridiculously amazing vee lines that I wanted to run my tongue over.

"I have them." I smiled, focused on the tent he was pitching in his pants.

"Really?"

"Yup. When I went to get M&M's at the airport, I spotted a package of condoms and on a whim bought 'em."

"On a whim, hmm?" Kicking off his loafers, he unzipped his pants and allowed them and his boxer briefs to fall to the floor.

I gulped as he took his cock in his hand and began lazily stroking himself. *Damn, this is hot.*

"Mm-hmm." I was going to chew a hole in my lip if he didn't come closer, though. I needed to touch him and soon. "In my purse." I lifted my chin, directing him to where I'd tossed it.

I was about to rise, but he lifted his free hand, instantly halting my movement.

"Do you want me naked on my back or on my hands and knees?" I licked my lips, proud of the fact that the timid tone was absent from my voice this time.

"Every position sounds perfect to me." He cocked his head, eyes holding mine. "But right now, I want you naked at the center of the bed like you're about to pray, ass on your heels, Maria." The dark edge of desire slicing through his words had my sex pulsing. "Because you'll be calling out God's name soon, *Tesoro*."

Holy. Shit.

"Strip," he ordered while stroking his cock.

"Is it wrong that I kind of like to disobey you in the bedroom?" I shared the dark thoughts circling my mind as I remained seated. "I like this feeling of being 'bad' when we're together." I swallowed. "I feel like I have to be perfect all the time, and with you, I . . ." The way he was staring at me, hand still on his cock, had me biting the inside of my cheek with anticipation.

"Sweetheart." He angled his head. "You can always be whoever and whatever you want with me." Then his lips curved at the edges, a delicious promise there. "But if you're going to be bad, it'd better *just* be with me."

My breath caught as my body reacted to his words that were sweet but also delivered a warning. A hint of what might happen if I did "misbehave." Knowing our time was limited, I wanted to surrender to him and cherish every second before he left. "But I think tonight, I'm going to be your—"

"My good girl," he remarked in a dark, seductive voice that coated my body in chills and pebbled my nipples.

"Yes," I whispered, rising to my feet to untie my wrap dress, and he resumed running his hand up and down the length of his shaft.

Slipping my hands to my shoulders, I slowly lowered the top and worked my arms loose from the long sleeves before letting it fall to the ground.

He watched every movement. Every reveal of my soft, tan skin.

The fling of my bra to the floor. Heels and panties a memory off to the side. When I lifted my hair in a mock ponytail, he twirled his finger, demanding a full three-sixty show, and it was one I'd happily give him.

I slowly turned, allowing his heated gaze to devour every inch of my hot skin, offering a view of my heart-shaped ass he seemed to love.

When I faced him again, the look in his eyes was borderline feral. Primitive.

"Want me on the bed now?" I snatched my lip between my teeth, unsure how to be provocative and sexy, but I was doing my best. Based on the glint in his eyes and the rise and fall of his chest, it was working for him.

He quietly nodded his answer, and I crawled, wiggling my ass intentionally as I made my way to the center of the full-size bed.

Sitting back on my heels, I set my hands on my thighs, doing my best not to judge my naked body.

Prowling with slow, deliberate movements, he studied me, desire in his eyes. "I have no fucking clue how I resisted you for so long." He set a hand on the bed before me and crooked my chin up with his finger so I was looking at him.

With his other hand, he swept my messy hair to my back, and his teeth grazed my skin before his mouth worked up from shoulder to neck. As his lips raced over my heated body, he palmed my breast and pinched my nipple, causing a slight whimper to escape my lips.

I reached out and gripped his thick length, pleading, "Please, I need to taste you."

He dipped his head, eyes meeting mine. "It's been a long fucking time for me, Maria. That sinful mouth of yours wrapped around my cock will be my undoing." The deep timbre of his tone barely had me registering the fact he was letting me know he hadn't been with another woman in a while, and it made my heart do a stupid little dance.

"Just a taste? I'm in the perfect position." I let go of him and pushed upright a bit more, so I was a touch taller, readying myself. Anxious to make him feel as good as he'd made me with his mouth.

His nostrils flared, a war in his eyes. "I have rules, and I always get a taste first."

"That's a little rude, Chef," I teased as his hand lay flat on my breastbone, and he pushed me back on my heels, awakening a shuddering cry from my chest when he cupped my sex like he owned it, then pushed two thick fingers inside me.

"I love you like this. Confident and naked for me to look at." He traced each nipple with the pad of his thumb. "Tits out." His thumb went to my mouth, and he slid it between my teeth. I lightly bit as he worked his fingers in and out of me rhythmically like a dance he was teaching me the moves to. "Lips swollen," he said before pressing a quick kiss to my mouth. "These lips puckered and ready, too," he added when swiping his fingers over the sensitive part of my sex.

God, he was touching me in so many places, I couldn't keep track.

Before I knew it, he was stretched out on his back, guiding me on top of him. "Sit on my face, sweetheart. Let me get that taste."

I grabbed hold of the headboard with one hand as he cupped my ass cheeks, urging me to kneel over his mouth. Was I really doing this?

That shy heat of embarrassment flushed my body, raking like hot coals over my skin.

"Maria, if you don't fuck my mouth, my cock won't fuck yours."

"You're playing dirty." I looked down at him and mock-pouted.

"You don't need to be shy." He squeezed my ass harder, and I whimpered, situating myself on top of this freaking gorgeous man, and my nerves and insecurities melted away the second his tongue flicked my clit and he began feasting on me.

He growled and moaned and made other hot, sexy sounds that had my head spinning. My thoughts became a chaotic, undecipherable mess.

"I don't want to get off yet, Enzo. I want you inside me for that," I begged, realizing he was taking me to the cusp of an orgasm, and I was about to cry for God in a second. "Let me . . . taste you," I said. Well, panted.

The word "fiiine" slid over my sex as he said it, and then he had me back on my knees with him standing on the bed before me all in a matter of seconds.

I grabbed hold of his muscular leg and tipped my chin to look up at him. I circled his cock with my other hand and wet my lips as I brought myself closer to him.

I sank my mouth over his head and swirled my tongue as he gripped my hair, guiding my eyes up to peer at him.

My cheeks hollowed out, and I took him inch by inch, as far back as I could get. Maybe it was too far, because I gagged a little, and that had his dick twitching in my mouth. I eased back up some and used my hand to glide up and down in time with my mouth, adding a little pressure.

"Fuuuck," he hissed, nearly snarling at me as if he were trying to maintain his control and angry I was about to crack it in half. He began cursing, this time in Italian, while guiding my head with my hair, helping me out, and then he shoved back a minute later, nearly pushing me free from him. "Fire," he remarked in a grave tone, reminding me to behave. Not to get him off, and I had a feeling there'd be consequences if I did.

And why'd I feel giddy at the idea of this man punishing me for being bad?

He stepped off the bed a moment later to grab the condoms. I watched his firm ass muscles and legs flex as he walked. Every inch of him rigid as he came back to me. The fire I wasn't supposed to play with lit a path straight to me, and I felt the singe creep up on my skin, warming me. Igniting my every nerve ending with expectation of what was to come.

Finally.

"My Maria," he said with brows slanted as he rolled the rubber over himself, shielding us from the possibility of a baby I hoped he'd give me one day. The idea of Chiara having a brother or sister had my heart leaping.

Armed with protection now, he stood at the edge of the bed and simply looked at me, like he was seeing me for the first time. Soaking in the sight of me.

God, did I feel stunning and beautiful whenever his eyes were on me.

"You," he half grunted. "You make me feel again." His hand went over his heart as his tone changed to a more tender one. "I didn't think it was possible."

His words had my chest going tight as every emotion flooded my system.

"Thank you," he whispered before joining me on the bed. With a hand to my chest, he gently guided me to my back and climbed on top of me.

"You make me feel, too," I said, letting him know we were on the same page, and he nodded before nudging my thighs apart.

"It's going to hurt," he warned while dragging his tip over my center. "But only for a second. Because your body was made for me, *Tesoro*. Mine for you," he hoarsely added, and as I grabbed hold of his biceps in anticipation, he plunged deep inside me with zero hesitation.

He was buried to the hilt, and I moaned while arching into him. His forehead dropped to mine as I sucked in a ragged breath. *Holy shit.*

Pulling his head back, Enzo gritted out a string of Italian words I didn't recognize. As he gazed deep into my eyes, a fluttery sensation overwhelmed me, and I felt . . . whole.

I couldn't hold back the tears burning my eyes as he started to move again, slowly stretching me, filling me to perfection. "You're my forever," I breathlessly confessed.

He studied me, and an unexpected sheen covered his eyes. "Mine, too," he whispered, leaning in to softly kiss me. And then . . . holy shit . . . he let me have it.

Harder. Faster. Pistoning in and out.

Meeting him thrust for thrust, I ground my hips against his as he hit my sensitive bundle of nerves. Every. Single. Time. "Oh God," I cried and began a slow murmur of chants in between breathless moans as I climbed the mountain of ecstasy.

"Come for me, *Tesoro*," he said a few minutes later, straining like he was doing his best not to lose himself first.

My body tightened, toes curled, and every part of me was on fire as I fought back the urge to scream so loud that everyone in the house-mansion would hear me.

Slapping a hand over my mouth while maintaining hold of his other arm, I cried against my palm as my release tore through me.

Studying me, Enzo's jaw tightened, and I felt his cock jerk and thrum as he reached his release. He groaned, and when my tired arm fell to my side, my hand leaving my mouth, he bent in and set his lips to mine. He kissed me softly as he rode the rest of his orgasm, and I surrendered to the rest of mine.

I knew after this, I'd never be the same again. I'd never accept anything other than what I deserved. And this man made me feel like I deserved the entire world, and God willing, he'd stay with me in that world forever.

"Enzo!" Constantine's deep voice, and the harsh rap at the door, throttled me free from the moment. I shivered at the realization of what was about to happen, that Enzo would be leaving me. "Dad's home. We need to talk to him, and then it's wheels up."

TWENTY-FOUR

Enzo

"This is un-fucking-acceptable!" Dad bellowed, chucking his glass of scotch into the fireplace before pacing his office. My brothers and I remained quiet, waiting for him to continue.

"The evidence was stacked against him," Dad continued, struggling to grapple with everything we'd shared. "You're telling me for thirteen fucking years my daughter's murderer has been walking the streets?"

Dad's attention landed on Constantine. As the eldest son, he would have inevitably taken the brunt of Dad's anger. "This is my fault. I should've looked deeper." He stepped forward, his apology doing nothing to alter Dad's vicious stare.

Facing the fireplace again, Dad's shoulders broke forward, a touch of that vitriol pointed at my brother waning. "What's your plan?"

Taking the lead, Constantine explained how we planned to meet up with Carter's team in Syracuse to take the cleaner in for questioning. "We'll figure this out, you have my word." He glanced at Alessandro, then over at me. "I know Mom never wanted us to follow in your footsteps after you left Italy, but I suppose it was fate that we did. We may have let you down, but we—"

"It wasn't fate." Dad sighed and went over to his desk. He dropped onto the leather swivel chair, his eyes coasting back to the raging fire.

"I didn't mean about Bianca's death," Constantine quickly stated, his tone harsh with regret.

Dad waved a hand in the air, an apologetic frown on his face. "What I meant is you followed in my footsteps because I put you on that path."

My arms fell to my sides as I stepped forward, Alessandro mirroring my actions. Did we just hear him right?

"It was my idea." He reached for a new glass on his desk and poured himself another drink. "I called in a favor in Washington. A big fucking favor, borderline blackmail."

"You're telling me *you* arranged our 'get out of prison' deal? You're why we became mercenaries for the government? Taking kill-or-be-killed-type orders on missions from that shadowy group that made the CIA look like the Boy Scouts?" I hadn't realized I'd walked all the way to his desk and planted my hands on it, but there I was, ready to square off with my old man.

"I wasn't about to let my sons rot in prison for doing the right thing." He sipped his drink, eyes falling to the amber-colored liquid, and he swirled it around. "I didn't expect you all to become like me in other ways. Seeking justice in our own city."

"How could you not expect that?" Alessandro snapped, and I looked back to see him throwing his hands in the air. "We're your sons. It's in our blood. Of course we're going to wind up like you, especially when you put us on the same damn path." He turned and dragged his hands through his hair. "I'm an addict, Dad. A fucking addict." He whirled back around. "I'm addicted to the hunt. To the chase. Nothing satiates it. Not women. Jumping from planes. Fast cars. Nothing." He pointed to his skull, appearing to be on the verge of some type of break-down. "I'm fucked up, Dad, don't you get it?" He pointed at me, then Constantine. "Fuck, all of us are. You should've let us do our time in prison!" And then he stormed from the room and slammed the door shut behind us.

Holy shit. I knew my brother missed that life, but . . . damn.

"Is it possible you pissed off the wrong people and they killed Bianca as retribution?" Constantine finally asked, interrupting the silence that had hung in the air since Alessandro left.

His question had my father on his feet and throwing his second drink into the fire, just missing Constantine's head.

"Absolutely not." Dad circled the desk and set a hand to Constantine's chest, and although Dad was shorter than him, he stared at Constantine as if letting him know he was still the man of the house. The one in charge. But was he really? I wasn't so sure.

My father didn't intimidate or scare me, not anymore. He may have chosen our destiny thirteen years ago, but I wouldn't let him dictate my future.

"I need air. And we should go soon," was all I said before leaving Constantine to face off with our father.

I went to the guest room to change into what I'd wear tonight, then sought out Maria, the only one capable of calming the storm inside me.

She was on the phone with Chiara when I found her, and I quietly shut the bedroom door. She had on a fluffy white robe she'd probably found hung up in the bathroom, thanks to my mom's attention to detail. The thing practically swallowed her up in the heavy fabric, and fuck if I didn't just want to take it off her and walk my mouth over her naked body, sucking and kissing every inch of her.

That's what I *wanted* to do. But what I *needed* to do was go infil a CIA safe house and interrogate a man, taking him to near death to find out who really killed my sister.

Maria ended the call and set the phone on the bed. She slowly took inventory of my current look of head-to-toe black. Combat boots, cargo pants, a dark tee and backward ball cap. It wasn't exactly a look she was used to seeing me wear, and yet, aside from my chef's coat, I preferred it to a suit.

"You're . . ." She blinked. "You look ready for war minus the face paint."

I closed the space between us, taking cautious steps for whatever reason, as if worried she might see me as a predator and take off. "Face painting is later," I said with a wink, trying to ease her distressed look.

I wrapped my hands around her waist, the bulky fabric an inconvenience when I wanted to feel the silhouette of her beautiful body. God, I loved her curves. And Thomas, who still needed to be dealt with, was an asshole for making her feel anything less than a goddess.

"You're leaving?" she whispered, her tone fragile, and that sad look in her eyes cut deep.

I nodded, but then her brows slanted, and she cocked her head to the side. "What is it?" Damn, was I that easy to read? No, she had been breaking down my walls, and I was letting her. Letting her get to know the real me.

"My father," I finally shared, releasing her to sit. She sat on the bed next to me, and I took her delicate hand between my palms and held it captive. "He made the deal with the government. He's why I became a mercenary, ultimately leading me down the other path as well . . ." *Taking justice into my own hands.*

I wasn't sure if prison would've been a better option, but at least I wouldn't have as much blood on my hands. Even if I'd only ever gone after bad guys, no amount of cooking and repenting could unwind everything I'd done over the years.

But then . . . what would've happened had my brothers not stopped that terrorist and killed him? Or if we didn't intervene and save that woman from her abusive ex? And more and more stories flooded my mind. For whatever reason, good couldn't seem to exist without evil and vice versa. Balance seemed to be needed for the universe to survive. And my brothers and I, in our own way, somehow kept that balance. Right or wrong, though? Fuck if I knew.

Maria flipped my forearm over, tracing the rosary with her finger. Then she skated a path along the words *no mercy*.

"Not everyone deserves mercy," I said, thinking about the evil I'd encountered.

"But do some?" she whispered. "Does Thomas?"

"I don't know," I hoarsely responded, and I really didn't know, that was the problem. "I, uh, should go." Emotion caught in my throat as I freed us from our entangled state and we both stood.

I seized her cheeks, holding her face with a bit of terror fastening around my heart that I might not make it home alive, a thought that hadn't crossed my mind in thirteen years. I'd had no one to come home to after those missions, so I'd always felt invincible. It was harder to hurt a man who didn't fear death, and it was much easier to attack someone who had everything in the world to live for, and now . . .

"Get the bad guy. Stay safe. And come back to me, okay?" Her voice was so tender, I could nearly hold it in my hands as if it were a tangible thing.

"Yes, ma'am," I whispered, hoping I could follow her orders. All three of them.

"But, Enzo," she began while pressing up on her toes, her mouth seeking mine, "you don't need to show mercy to the asshole who killed your sister." She shook her head, her eyes narrowing. "Not a drop."

TWENTY-FIVE

Enzo

"You got laid, didn't you? About damn time."

I winced at Alessandro's comment; then memories of my time with Maria a little over an hour ago tore through my mind. And I'd give anything for us to be together, her safe in my arms. Chiara asleep in her crib. No worries in the world.

Instead, I was on a jet heading to Syracuse to steal a man from CIA custody, and Maria was left alone to handle my parents and sister.

"You're really asking me that?" I wasn't in the mood to discuss my sex life with a man who'd been using my home to get laid so women didn't find out where he lived.

Alessandro casually leaned back in the leather seat aboard our private jet. We'd been in the air for twenty minutes, and it was his first time talking since he left the office.

I looked over at Hudson as he busied himself with prepping his MK 13 sniper rifle. Not made for rubber bullets, clearly. More like .300 Winchester Magnum caliber. The rifle was a bit more compact but had greater accuracy. One of my preferences as well.

We really did owe some hefty Christmas bonuses this year to our people at the airport who helped ensure our gear and weapons safely made it to our jet without getting flagged. We weren't flying commercially, but it helped to have an inside man, or woman in this case, to get our shit into the hangar.

"I need a distraction from the fact our father ruined our lives." Alessandro wasn't going to let this go, was he? The man had been an impossible thorn in my side ever since I moved to Charlotte and he realized how I felt about Maria. For a man who claimed he had no heart, he'd spent a year pressing me to follow mine.

"What are you thinking about?" Alessandro glanced at Constantine, who was putting away his Ruger Precision Rifle, his preferred long-range shooter.

Constantine positioned his hand on the ceiling overhead. "Dad did what he did for Mom. She wouldn't have survived the death of her daughter and her three sons in prison. Everything he does is always for her, you know that."

"He told you that?" I asked in surprise.

"He didn't have to. That woman is his world. He'd do anything for her." Constantine's neutral expression softened a bit, a message to me: *You'd do anything for Maria.* And I would. "In Dad's mind, he did what he believed needed to be done, even if it meant betraying his word to her in never letting us live the same life as he had in Italy."

Alessandro stood and went over to the scattered gear, moving aside the case that held our M4 carbine, a short-barrel rifle meant for close-quarter combat.

"None of us had a chance anyway. You realize that, right?" Constantine reached for Alessandro's arm, urging him to look at him. My brother slowly turned to face Constantine, his shoulders still squared back, body taut. Ready for a fight. But he couldn't shoot his way out of this problem. Our past. "We were all fucked long before Bianca died." Constantine drilled in the point. "Just look at our family's background."

"I don't buy it. We could have done something else with our lives." And yet, defeat penetrated Alessandro's tone.

Constantine let go of Alessandro, his gaze moving to Hudson, who'd remained quiet during our family discussion.

"What if I told you I'm so messed up that I never actually quit, then what?" Alessandro looked over at me, an apology in his gray eyes. "Like I said, I'm addicted."

Sitting taller with shock, it took me a moment to register his words. "So all that talk the other day about missing the hunt, and you're never satisfied by anything, was bullshit?"

And why didn't Constantine look pissed? Or Hudson, for that matter?

"I can't look the other way when bad shit happens. Can you blame me?" Alessandro asked, trying to downplay whatever he'd been doing in the two years since our supposed retirement. "But I miss when we were a team. Nothing in the civilian world can compare to that."

"Ain't that the truth," Hudson mumbled under his breath, breaking his silence.

"I get it." Constantine coughed into a closed fist, his gaze shooting uncomfortably to me. "I didn't stop, either."

"You're kidding me? All that talk about . . ." Alessandro let go of his words, realizing he was about to parrot what I'd just said about him. "So we've been riding solo when we could've been united? Well, that sucks." He peered at me as if double-checking the sincerity of my surprise.

"I stopped when I moved to Charlotte," I confirmed, then checked with Hudson.

Hudson palmed his bearded jawline, eyes falling to the floor.

Alessandro peered at Hudson. "Fuuuck. You too?"

"I haven't taken a life in years, though, if that makes it better?" Hudson shrugged.

Hudson had never been part of the deal with the government, but that was because we'd never offered his name when arrested. But he'd been at our sides every step of the messy way as we handled injustices as we saw fit.

"Looks like you're the only one who really retired and changed, brother. Guess you do have a shot at a normal life," Alessandro said to me.

Changed. The word pummeled its way through my mind as I processed the truth I'd struggled to acknowledge out of fear it couldn't be true.

I'd walked away from that life, but I'd had Maria and Natalia to help "tame" me. Keep me under control. And I supposed working with my hands in the kitchen had been another way for me to escape. Also, I never read or watched the news. Made sure all alerts were turned off on my phone. I wouldn't be able to handle hearing about some asshole hurting someone innocent and do nothing about it.

I did change, didn't I?

"We need to focus on tonight. We can figure everything else out later," Constantine declared. But what was there to figure out? They needed to stop, like we previously agreed, right?

Swallowing down the uncomfortable lump in my throat, I decided to switch gears and asked, "Can you really work with Carter?"

Constantine squeezed the back of his neck. "What choice do I have?"

"Good. Just don't start shit with him." I shook my head. "And maybe we'll all survive the night."

TWENTY-SIX

Enzo

"Get it over with. I'll even give you my good side to hit." Constantine turned his cheek and made a come-hither motion to a man who looked every bit as intimidating as my brother.

So much for not starting shit. I stepped around Constantine and spread open my arms, blocking him from Carter's path. "It'd be better for us if he has use of both eyes when we go break a few dozen laws tonight," I told Carter in case he was considering the offer.

"He's right," Jesse remarked, standing between Carter and his other teammate, Jack London. Jack had been army SF and after that worked for the CIA's Special Activities Division. All I knew was if Jesse trusted him, so did I. "We need to be united tonight," Jesse went on. "Put the past behind us."

Constantine elbowed his way around me to get to Carter. "Let me guess," he began, "that pistol you have at your side doesn't have rubber bullets. What are you planning later? Accidental crossfire?"

In all fairness, my Sig Sauer M17 wasn't exactly shooting blanks. Hopefully, I wouldn't need to use it tonight.

"If I wanted you dead, I'd look you in the face and do it, and you know that." Carter's words were a low hiss, a crackle in the night air.

We were outside Syracuse in Fayetteville, four miles away from Green Lakes State Park. The CIA's location for a safe house was a bit of a question mark, and although my opinion on the Agency was less jaded than Constantine's, I had some concerns about the officers who had the cleaner. Hence the pistol at my hip and the rifle I'd be taking with me tonight.

Jesse set a hand on Carter's shoulder, urging him to step back. "We need to roll out."

"Come on." I grabbed hold of Constantine's arm, mirroring Jesse's moves.

"I'm sorry," Constantine surprised me by saying. "I never said that to you back then. Only to her." He drew his hands to his hips and bowed his head. "You weren't just her friend in college. You were dating her, and I convinced Rebecca it was a bad idea to date a friend. I shouldn't have done that, and I'm sorry."

Ah shit. Well, I supposed the anger from Carter made a little more sense now.

"But you weren't really her second choice. She should never have been with me in the first place, and she did go back to you." Constantine spoke as if trying to reinforce his words with titanium so they'd deliver more of an impact. "I get it, you had to pick up the pieces after I left. And I'm sorry for that. I'm sorry she died."

Carter's shoulders relaxed for the first time since we'd arrived. "We were young," he said. "And I'm angry she died. I'll always be upset." He shook his head. "Like you'll always be upset about Bianca." He jerked a thumb toward our SUVs parked side by side, a motion to get a move on. "Let's just do what we came here to do." And then he turned, and Jack followed him to the back of their SUV.

Constantine joined Hudson and Alessandro, and they began strapping on their vests. Prepping for the mission.

Jesse looked back at his team leader, then focused on me. "That was close. Carter's not one to let go of a grudge."

"I can see that. You sure he's going to be fine to roll on this op?" I asked him.

"He's one of the best, so yeah, he's solid," Jesse remarked with a nod. "And we've called in for backup just in case we get any unexpected visitors showing up looking for the cleaner as well." He checked his watch. "But the schedule is tight. Not sure if they'll make it in time, and we can't afford to wait for them."

"Let's hope we're first to the cleaner, then," I said as Jesse reached out and patted me on the shoulder before joining his teammates.

I went over to our rental SUV and double-checked my Kevlar plate carrier vest. The ballistic vest came with chest plates for protection, a first aid kit, a grenade pouch of ten, twelve ammo mags, and more. And tonight, rubber bullets.

"I got a bad feeling. You?" Hudson asked as I adjusted my knee pads, then flexed my hands into fists, stretching out the tactical gloves.

"You feel like we're being watched?" I looked over at the bank of trees off to my right.

"I do, so heads on a swivel." Hudson patted my shoulder as Carter and his men joined us.

I clipped on my helmet and knocked my night-vision goggles up out of the way.

"Your comms." Jack handed out the earpieces. "We'll be in your ear the whole time. No need to tap them on or off."

Alessandro positioned it into his ear, and I did the same. "You ready?"

"Let's go over the plan one more time." Carter had an iPad, and we gathered around him, since he was Alpha One, team leader tonight. And thankfully, Constantine hadn't argued about that. "This is our insertion point." Carter zoomed in on the aerial view of the cabin. "Only four heat signatures inside. Pretty light for the CIA."

"Yeah, I'm thinking Uncle Sam didn't approve of their grab-the-cleaner-from-the-border-mission." Jack spoke up.

"It's possible the man we're hunting paid off those CIA officers," Carter said.

"And does that man have a name?" I asked.

"No, but we're hoping to find it out tonight," Carter answered, eyes on me. "But still, no killing any officers. We clear?"

"Roger that," we agreed in unison.

"We'll advance together until we're three hundred meters from the cabin," Carter went on. "We'll break off, and the assault force will move in, and snipers will head to overwatch."

The assault team consisted of Jesse, Jack, Alessandro, and myself. Carter, Hudson, and Constantine, the best shooters, would move to higher ground to get to a better field of vision with the widest coverage, and they'd have our sixes as we moved in. Well, that'd been the plan Jesse had shared with us on our drive to meet up with them from the airport. With any luck, it'd be a quick in and out.

But historically, luck was rarely on our side, and shit always went sideways. And with that "watched" feeling having my spine tingling, I readied my rifle and lowered my NVGs, and the green glow filled my line of sight.

"Let's do this," Jesse said after we did a comms check; then he fist-bumped us all, and we scattered into our positions.

I kept tabs on the rest of my crew on the assault team over comms, since I couldn't visually make them out anymore, our camo clothes blending us into the terrain. "Nearing target location," I shared, and a pop of static filled the line, followed by bursts of rounds being fired off in the distance. And then there it was. The bad feeling coming to life. "The cabin is under attack. A sharpshooter somewhere. Probably two."

"This is Alpha One," Carter said. "Get down until we can make out their positions. Stay low until the threats have been eliminated."

"The men inside won't have time." I low-crawled, trying to locate where the shots were coming from.

"This is Alpha Five, I have one scoped. Let's hit the snipers at the same time. Can anyone locate the second shooter?" Hudson asked.

"This is Alpha Seven. I have movement. Prepping the shot." I lined my sights on the man's chest. Dialed in my scope to two hundred meters. Then, letting go of a breath, I relaxed my body in anticipation of the shot.

"On my count," Hudson said. "Three, two, one."

I squeezed the trigger, and the recoil came back and into my shoulder. Contact made. "He's down."

"Mine as well," Hudson answered.

"Charlie Mike," Carter ordered. *Continue mission.*

"Fuck." I heard someone curse over the line not even a second later, certain it was Constantine. And then an order. "Shields the fuck up. We've got a swarm heading our way from behind. We were followed."

~

"I have movement. There's still someone alive inside," I said amid the gunfire. Screw rubber bullets. We'd been under attack for the last five minutes from every angle. I'd taken three lives so far tonight, and as I neared the cabin to check for life, I had a feeling there were more kills to come. "Permission to move inside and check?"

"This is Alpha One, I've got you covered. Move in," Carter answered. "Alpha Two, go in with him. We've got you."

Maybe it was something primal inside me, but as I maneuvered along the side of the cabin to access the room where I'd spied movement, my body hummed, and adrenaline propelled me forward. This was what I was good at. What I felt like I'd been made to do. Fight. Win wars. Be a fucking gladiator of modern times.

I caught a flash of movement from the side, ensured it wasn't someone from my team, and set my crosshairs on him. After a quick calculation, I adjusted and squeezed off a round. My fourth kill now.

"Keep your head down, Seven." Constantine's voice cut over the line, using my call sign, as I swapped my rifle for my pistol.

Jesse set a hand to my shoulder and tapped, letting me know he was there. I kept my head low and carefully opened the door. A bullet punched the door, almost hitting me.

"Fuck. Sorry," Constantine groaned. "You're clear."

"A little close there, brother," I hissed while moving inside.

The cabin was pitch-black, but with my night vision, I could make out two bodies not going anywhere, face down in the room. And another in a chair. Head hung. Probably cuffed to it. "Cleaner is down," I alerted the team in a low voice. "But we have movement. Looks like one officer is still alive." And he was crawling, trying to get cover.

"This is Alpha One. That's a good copy. See if he knows anything. Get him to talk. We've got your back out here."

War rumbled around us from outside and from every direction. And from the sounds of it, we'd be needing that backup and soon. By my guess, we had more than one team of bad guys out there trying to get inside the cabin, and we were all that stood in the way of them doing it.

A few more bursts of fire tapped at the exterior of the cabin, and I ducked out of view of the window and put eyes on Jesse, ensuring he was still good. He nodded and flicked his wrist and pointed to the guy crawling.

"We're friendlies," Jesse told him. "Here for a rescue."

The man on the floor went still, and I spied his hand curling into a fist. Did he have something he was trying to protect?

"How do I know I can trust you?" he asked, still flat on his belly. No weapon in hand from what I could tell, and whatever was in his palm was too small to be a grenade.

"And how do we know we can trust you?" I countered. "The government sent a small team for such a valuable man. It's almost like your boss didn't clear this mission." I took a knee, keeping my arm extended, pistol on him.

"Everyone wants the cleaner, but he's dead. If you get me out of here, I'll give you the client list he gave us just before the attack," the man said instead. "Do we have a deal?"

232

Fuck, that was good news. "Deal," I said without hesitation, but then a prickling sense of awareness washed over me as a red dot appeared on the guy's back.

"Move," I yelled to him, but it was too late, and he collapsed as the round made contact.

Jesse and I searched for cover as an unrecognizable voice came over comms. "This is Echo One. Sniper down."

Echo One? And was he British? "Tell me that's our backup," I mouthed to Jesse, and he nodded.

"Sorry we're late to the party, boys," the Brit went on, "but we're here now. And it looks like we have company. Two vehicles are en route, and they're armed to the teeth. I suggest you get cover now."

"Roger that," Jesse replied, then low-crawled to the downed officer, and he unfurled his palm. "We have jackpot," Jesse announced, letting the team know we weren't walking away empty-handed.

"Wait for my orders to leave the cabin," Carter said. "We need to get you and that package out of there, and there are too many threats out here."

A whooshing sound of static hit my ear from the comm, followed by rapid sounds of gunfire outside the cabin as we made our way back to the side door. I exchanged my pistol for my rifle while we waited for orders.

"This is Echo Two. You want any of these fuckers rolling up in armed vehicles alive, or do you prefer them extra crispy with a side of bacon?" A Southern accent rolled through the line, hard to miss even over comms.

Who the hell were these guys?

"This is Alpha One. Keep a few alive if you can."

"Roger that," the Southerner answered.

"Echo Two's my wife's brother," Jesse shared with me in a low voice. "So don't worry, he's highly motivated to get us out of here." He looked back at me, and a flash of his bright-white teeth from a smile was visible through the green hue of my night vision.

"So your wife will kill him if something happens to you?" I asked.

Another smirk from Jesse. "Let's just say you don't want to get on a Southern woman's bad side."

"That's the truth." Another unfamiliar voice, and I detected a Boston accent. I forgot the fancier-than-normal comms meant they could hear us whether we wanted them to or not.

"And that voice you just heard . . . my sister's husband," Jesse remarked.

"A family business, huh?" I was shocked we were smiling and joking in the middle of battle. But hell, it only brought me back to my days in the army. And it wasn't any different back then, only my dark sense of humor in my early twenties was a lot worse than now.

"You don't know the half of it," the Southerner, Echo Two, said in response. "And we're preparing to send a little gift basket in the form of a fuck-you-up-the-ass present to the men hot on your tail on the southside. Take cover," he warned.

"Roger that," Carter remarked, and then an explosion rattled the ground.

"I could use a gift like that," Alessandro said. "I've got two fuckers who just won't quit twenty meters from the east side of the cabin. Lassoing their location with the IR laser now."

"This is Echo Two. Target location confirmed," the Southerner said. "And you're welcome," he added before the ground rocked beneath our feet yet again.

"This is Echo One," the Brit said in my ear a minute later. "I can confirm from my vantage point there's no more movement. Targets all appear to be down. There's a chance one or two are alive, but they're for sure as hell not threats now."

"Roger that," Carter responded. "Alpha Two and Seven, you're clear to move," he told us, and we left the cabin.

I took a deep breath, trying my best to relax, but we weren't out of the woods yet. Literally and figuratively.

"This really your life now?" I asked Jesse as we moved, meeting up with Hudson and Alessandro on our trek to exfil.

Jesse tapped his ear, muting his comm this time, so I copied his move. We could still hear the others, but our conversation was now private. "Well, we prefer not to call in SEALs for an assist, because they'll give us army boys hell for it later, but we do what we have to do."

Alessandro motioned to Hudson and said, "SEAL too."

"Of course you are," Jesse laughingly commented.

"That wasn't what I meant," I told him, not referring to the fact they had SEALs for backup.

"I know." Jesse looked over at me, his night-vision goggles still blocking his eyes. "But yeah, this is my life. You looking for it to be yours, too? Or are you out for good?"

My stomach dropped at what felt like an offer. But I didn't have a chance to answer, because the thump of rotors overhead had me going still. I peered up at the sound of the *whup-whup-whup* chopping the sky and searched for a helo.

"A lot of people really want this list," Jesse said under his breath before unmuting his comm. "Looks like it's not game over yet. You ready?"

We all nodded before Alessandro said, "Yeah, let's go toast these fuckers, shall we?"

"And try not to start a forest fire, if you don't mind," the Brit said as figures overhead began to fast-rope down.

"This is Alpha Two, they're dropping in from the sky at our location," Jesse told the team.

"Like shooting fish in a barrel," Hudson remarked, shifting into position while readying his rifle.

"Oh, I like him," the Southerner answered over comms.

"You would," Jesse said. "He's apparently one of you. A Team Guy," he added before Hudson squeezed off a shot.

TWENTY-SEVEN

Maria

"Mmmm. That feels good." I let free a moan as a pair of strong arms swallowed me up into a warm embrace, but the fog of sleep had yet to be lifted.

"I'm back, *cara mia*," a husky voice whispered into my ear, and Enzo's words officially shocked me out of my dreamlike state.

He was there in bed with me, and I wasn't imagining it. Turning toward him, I felt him readjust his arm, settling it on my hip while drawing me closer, and my hands slid between us to cup his cheeks.

I wasn't sure what time it was, but morning had to be around the corner. Syracuse by plane was a short flight, but had he really gone and come back before the sun came up?

"You're here." Tears of relief filled my eyes, and I slid my palm in small circles along his jawline. He kept his eyes shut, leaning into my touch. "I didn't mean to fall asleep. I must've drifted off while waiting for you to call. But you're here instead."

"I'm here," he murmured in a groggy-sleepy tone. "And I'm glad you slept. You needed it."

"Sounds like you need it now."

"All I need is you," he returned in a low voice without opening his eyes.

I brushed my mouth over his and surrendered to the surprise of his tongue sliding between my lips for a soft but sultry kiss.

"Mmmm. I needed that," he said a moment later, opening his eyes. "Long night."

"I'm assuming if you're cuddling me, everyone is okay. Your brothers and the guys you worked with?" My heart did an unexpected little tap dance against my rib cage when I noticed the slight curl of his lips downward. There was enough light in the room to make out every detail of this handsome man's face, and I was glad to see it was unmarked by wounds.

"We're all okay, but things didn't go as planned."

I let go of his cheeks and slid one hand into his messy hair.

"A lot of people wanted the man we were after, and we didn't get to him in time. He was killed before we arrived. We were under heavy fire from more than one enemy. They converged on our location, and things got dicey."

I snaked my hand around the back of his neck to pull myself even closer, and his tired eyes kept falling shut, clearly fighting like hell to stay awake. "I'm just so glad you're okay," was all I managed. "You don't need to talk now," I said, noticing his breathing slowing down, his body slipping nearly into sleep. "Get some rest, babe."

"Babe?" His tone was warm and slid over my skin. "I like that." And then he went quiet, and I was pretty sure my exhausted man had fallen asleep.

I stayed awake for a little bit with his arm protectively over me and my hand behind his neck, playing out scenarios in my head of the "dicey" situation and what may have happened to him while he'd been gone.

I fell asleep at some point, and when I woke up, I patted the mattress in search of him, finding myself alone. Terror climbed into the walls of my chest at the idea it'd been a dream and he'd never come back.

Soft light filtered through a small opening in the curtains, and when I rolled over to check the clock, I couldn't believe it was already nine in the morning.

I forced myself to sit and checked my phone on the nightstand to see if Enzo had ever texted last night, still worried I'd made up his homecoming in my head. But there weren't any notifications.

Once out of bed, I changed into yoga pants, a sports bra, and one of my worn-out tees from my college days.

There was a knock at the door, followed by the question, "Are you decent?" a moment later. I opened up, realizing it was Angela, Enzo's mom.

We hadn't spoken since the Pablo fiasco in the dining room last night, and after Enzo had left with his brothers, I'd pretty much hidden in the bedroom.

"Is Enzo home?" *Please say yes and I wasn't dreaming.*

"He's in the study downstairs."

Thank God. My hand slammed to my chest with relief.

She leaned into the interior doorframe, her dark-brown eyes focused on me, concern still swirling there, and I wasn't sure why it felt pointed my way. "I know what happened last night."

About the operation or the fact we made love in the bed behind me? And now my cheeks were probably a shocking shade of red.

I wanted to make a beeline for the study and throw myself into Enzo's arms. Learn the details of what happened and decide if I was safe to exit panic mode or whether I needed to stay swimming there, fighting the tides, a bit longer.

"My daughter's killer is still out there, and that's why the extra security," she finally spoke, sharing the grave news, and now I understood her face, her posture, her overall everything.

"And I know my sons are trying to find out who did it, and I trust they'll get to the bottom of it." She reached for a crucifix atop her dressy black blouse and smoothed it between her fingers. "My husband also shared that my cousin's men nearly hurt you yesterday, and I'm so sorry for that. Giovanni and his family are coming over in a little bit to offer their apologies, if you're okay with that?"

Am I okay with meeting a crime boss? Not really. "As long as Enzo is good with that."

She nodded. "I know it must seem shocking that my family is mafia, but the Sicilians have a very small piece of the organized-crime pie over here in America. Back in Italy, things were different. And the fact your mother never told you—"

"Wait, my mom knows your family is mafia?"

She nodded. "Your mother got mixed up with a man who worked for my father early on in her life. But after she married your father, she ran into him again, and that's when my husband saved her from him. I felt horrible about it all, and, well, we became close friends."

Wow. So my mom was right. We did both have a "type." But unlike Mom's ex, Enzo was a good man.

"Enzo told me this morning why you're really here with him." Her tone was soft, a whisper of apology in her voice. "You're here to keep him from going off the deep end. And seeing the way he looks at you," she said while letting go of the crucifix, "makes me feel like there's still hope for all my boys. Hope they'll all settle down and fall in love one day."

Oh, wow. Um. What was I supposed to say to that? I was barely awake, and I didn't trust myself to not trip all over my words.

"From mother to mother, thank you for teaching my boy how to feel more than hate and anger. Teaching him how to love again." She reached out and squeezed my shoulder. "I'm sure he'd like to see you now." And then she left, as if she hadn't just tilted my world, shifting it off its axis for a moment.

It took me a few deep breaths before I could unglue myself from my position and search for him.

I found him with Constantine downstairs in the study. Constantine was focused on a laptop. Enzo was in black sweats and a black tee standing off to his side, a hand on the desk, studying whatever was on Constantine's screen.

I remained in the doorway, relieved to see him. He lifted his head, gaze shifting to me, and the harsh lines of stress disappeared. His face relaxed before his lips twitched into a slight smile.

"Hi." I tossed my hand in the air for the second nervous greeting that morning, and his smile broadened before he stood tall.

Enzo rounded the desk, and I couldn't stop myself—I ran to him and jumped into his arms, wrapping my legs around his hips, and he captured me and held me tight, his mouth working fast to find mine. *"Tesoro,"* he whispered against my lips between soft, reassuring kisses.

He was okay. My man was okay.

There was a deep throat clear a few moments later, but it came from behind me, which meant someone else had joined us in the room.

I slid free from Enzo's arms, and once my feet found the ground, I turned to see who was there. Enzo snatched my hips, holding my back to his chest as if unbothered by the fact his father had caught us kissing.

"Anything yet?" their father asked, eyes on Constantine.

"Should have the list downloaded in five minutes," Constantine spoke up. "I had to write a new program to decode the damn thing. This type of encryption is even a few levels above what the Agency uses."

"The list?" I asked, turning back to face Enzo, hoping he'd clue me in. I still had no idea what happened last night other than the man they were after died and things had been "dicey."

"Enzo, the less she knows the better." His father's warning coated my skin in chills, and Enzo never broke eye contact with me despite his words.

"She knows enough at this point that hearing the rest won't make a difference," Enzo remarked, and my shoulders relaxed at the fact he wasn't planning to keep me in the dark. He took my hand and tipped his head toward the door. "Come on, let's take a walk."

"Be back in five," Constantine said. "I'll have the answers then."

We faced Mr. Costa, and he hesitantly moved aside so we could leave, but the sharp, almost disappointed look he gave Enzo didn't exactly do wonders for my nerves.

"Is he mad at you?" I asked once we were in the hall.

"He can get over it." He tightened his hold on my hand, and we went into the room one door down. It was a movie theater. Rows of leather recliners in front of a massive screen.

He shut the door and set his back to it, one hand on my hip, his gaze on me. An exhausted, pained look in his eyes.

"Did you get any sleep?"

"Enough, don't worry." He brushed his knuckles over my cheek, his brows slanting.

"Hard not to worry about everything right now."

"I'm so sorry." His hand moved to my arm, and he gently squeezed. His eyes fell closed as if harsh memories from last night pulled at the edges of his mind, and he was probably worried how to share them.

I set my hand over his heart, finding it thudding hard and fast. "What happened?"

"The CIA officers who picked up the cleaner from border control were crooked. From what Jesse's team determined, they grabbed him to get the list and silence the cleaner before he could talk to anyone else," he finally shared. "They may have even killed the cleaner before the ambush."

Ambush?

"There was another team there when we arrived. Jesse and I managed to get inside the cabin before their team could, and we found a USB on one of the officers. The cleaner's client list."

I replayed his words in my head, thinking about the danger he'd been in. *Deep breaths,* I reminded myself.

"We were on our way out when we were attacked again. Based on what we could tell afterward, it was by a different crew. Thankfully, Carter called in backup, too. He hadn't been sure if they'd make it in time, though, which was probably the only reason he'd allowed us to join him in the first place." He shook his head. "So we were lucky we had that assist. We needed the extra numbers or we may not have . . ."

He let those harsh words remain hanging in the air, recognizing I didn't want to hear the fact he could have died last night.

He lightly squeezed my arm, reminding me he was alive and there with me. "Constantine convinced Jesse's boss to give us a copy of the USB before we came home. And we're hoping the answer to who was responsible for killing Bianca is on there."

"If so many dangerous people are after that list, is there a chance someone can connect the dots you were there? I mean, you flew there in your private jet, and—"

"We thought of that." He interrupted my frantic thoughts. "Fortunately, Carter's team has connections all the way up to the White House. People he trusts. And they erased the fact my brothers and I were ever in Syracuse. The flight records have been altered so there's no digital footprint we were even there."

"But?" I could feel the bad news coming.

"The second the cleaner went on the run after he realized he'd been compromised by Jesse's team . . . well, it's possible all of his clients went on high alert, realizing their identities and crimes might be revealed if the cleaner were to be captured." His gaze softened with regret. "And that's why we still have the extra security here."

"But the cleaner's dead, so won't the bad guys assume their secrets died with him?"

"That's what we're hoping. But if anyone found out about the list and that Carter and his men now have it . . ."

"They'll be targeted." I finished his trailed-off thought.

"They can handle that. They're okay with being bait, drawing the fuckers to them and right into a trap. It's what they do. And no one knows we have a copy or that my brothers and I were ever there," he reminded me, trying to keep me sane. "Our identities are safe."

"Do you need to help them?"

"They have plenty of additional reinforcements now. They don't need us. So we're focusing on Bianca's killer, and we'll hopefully have that name any minute."

"Why do I feel like there's something else? Something you haven't told me?"

"I just have a bad fucking feeling in my gut." His shoulders dropped as he shared with a slight tremble in his tone, "I'm worried that I missed something and I'll lose the only woman I've ever been in love with because I was distracted." He closed his eyes. "What if my love for you is what gets you killed?"

Love? I tensed, swallowing as my stomach flipped and my brain turned to mush. I was pretty much out of order at his words. "Enzo," was the best I could get to exit my lips before a call came through for him.

"It's Jesse. He must've decrypted the list faster than us, and he's letting us know." He brought the phone to his ear. "What do you know?" His gaze cut to the floor, and he let go of a heavy exhale. "No," he said a moment later, "I have no fucking clue why they'd want her dead. I need to talk to my family. Watch your back. Stay safe."

"What'd he say?" I asked after he ended the call.

"Remember when I told you there are five main families in the Italian American mafia?" I nodded at the memory from our plane ride to New York. "Well, one of those families, the Brambillas, who happen to have the most power now, hired the cleaner. The files directly tie them to her case."

"So the Italian mafia was responsible for her death, just not the Sicilian branch of the mafia?" I searched for clarification.

243

"Looks like it, but I don't understand why. We don't have any contact with them. As far as I know, my father never threatened them. Unlike Giovanni, the Brambillas are much more powerful, and it'd be a death wish if . . ." His words trailed off at that, and shivers darted up my spine. "I thought my sister may have been murdered because of someone she may have loved, and like Izzy, she didn't want me to know about him, knowing I wouldn't approve."

"But she wouldn't fall in love with someone in the mafia, would she?"

"No, like hell would my sister—" He dropped his words and his head. "No, it can't be."

"What?" I reached for his arm, urging him to look at me.

"The story she wrote just before she died, well, she told me it was based on a true story. But she said no one would ever know that."

I thought back to the story published in the magazine, trying to remember the details. "And you think it might be based on her own life, and she just wrote the ending she hoped she'd get?"

Love. A happily-ever-after. Who'd want anything less?

"I don't know what to think, because if that's not the case, that means only one thing."

"And that is?"

"That my father more than likely pissed someone off in the Brambilla crime family, and he's responsible for her death." He opened the door and shot a quick look back at me, and I could read his thoughts.

No mercy.

TWENTY-EIGHT

Maria

"You're asking me that again. In front of everyone here?" Enzo's father slid his hand down the column of his throat, his back to the bay window. The water was calm today. The sky clear. And yet, the storm was in the room.

"Well?" Constantine stood from behind the desk, his arms locking across his chest. Despite being in battle last night, he was in a three-piece suit.

Enzo reached for my hand and threaded our fingers together, sensing my unease, and maybe I shouldn't have been in the room, but I refused to leave his side when I knew he needed me.

"I told you last night I had nothing to do with her death, and I'm telling you the same now," Mr. Costa seethed, clearly upset at his sons for pressing him. "But now that we know someone in the Brambilla family hired the cleaner, I'll do everything in my power to find out who and why. And I'll kill them myself."

Enzo's grip on my hand tightened as he turned toward the door, and I followed his gaze to see Alessandro there in cargo pants and a black tee. "You have her things?"

Alessandro nodded. "The boxes are in the safe room in case we need them." He pocketed his hands, leaning against the wall by the door. He looked worn out, like a man who'd fought all night long. And, well, he had. "Where's Hudson?"

"He's working on a few contingency plans. Making calls," Constantine spoke up, and his cryptic words meant I'd be in the dark on that.

I'd never seen Constantine even slightly off-kilter, and he looked like he was ready to throw the laptop now. His facial muscles were locked tight, and his body screamed, *Fuck around and find out.*

"The Brambillas are ten times more powerful than they were thirteen years ago, and you know they'd love nothing more than a reason to come after us," Alessandro said, which meant Constantine must've given him the heads-up before he'd arrived that the list had been decrypted.

Decrypted? Yeah, not a word I'd ever thought would roll through my thoughts. I was still in *Mickey Mouse* and *Bubble Guppies* territory back home.

Enzo released my hand to go for his phone and then shared, "Looks like we gave them extra motivation to do exactly that last night. Jesse just texted they identified some of the downed bodies from our mission. They worked for the Brambillas."

"The Brambillas also appear to have been one of the cleaner's most frequent clients. And based on the fact they're responsible for half a dozen deaths on his list, I can see them wanting to get to the cleaner the second they heard he was on the run," Constantine noted. "But that still doesn't explain why someone in their organization wanted our sister to die."

"They identify anyone else from your op?" Mr. Costa remained standing by the window, eyes on Enzo, jaw moving with a tic. "Or just the Brambillas?"

"It was a clusterfuck of bad guys. Not just them." Enzo shoved his phone back in his pocket, eyes on me as he added, "Nothing we couldn't handle."

But without the backup, what would've happened? I shuddered to think about it, and why was I? They were okay, and I had to focus on that. Well, *okay* was a loose term. Okay for now, sure. But later?

"Without knowing who within the Brambilla crime family hired the cleaner, we'll need to do some more digging ourselves." Constantine turned on the flat-screen behind the desk and then synced his laptop with the screen. "Footage from outside the club that night thirteen years ago." He pressed "Play" and turned to the side. "I still think it was someone she knew and she let them into her home. I just don't know why she'd ever associate with someone from the Brambilla family."

Constantine paused the screen, and my heartbeat became hostage to my frozen thoughts. Every part of me rooted in place at the sight.

The camera angle wasn't great, and the screen wasn't in color, but I could tell it was Bianca.

Enzo walked over to stand by his brothers, so I sat in a nearby leather armchair.

"What if she fell in love with someone in the Brambilla family?" Enzo asked in a low voice, sharing the idea we'd discussed in the theater room.

That had his father's attention, and he snapped his focus around, his harsh gaze focused on Enzo. "Are you out of your damn mind? Your sister had a heart of gold. She'd never sleep with the enemy."

"No, I agree with Pops," Alessandro said. "She'd never." He looked at Enzo. "Maybe she was writing a nonfiction piece for the magazine, and her research led her somewhere dangerous? She might have notes in one of those boxes in the safe room. We didn't read over her work files back then because all the evidence had pointed to that guy."

"You were young," Mr. Costa said. "No excuse for me. I should've questioned things more."

"I don't think Bianca would write a Lois Lane–type exposé. It wasn't her style. She loved love," I said, sharing my thoughts. "But even if she did decide to write something dangerous, which led to her attack, the killer would've searched her place and taken any notes she had or evidence tied to them, right?"

Enzo nodded in agreement. "Play the footage," he suggested, facing the screen again.

The camera angles bounced around, never losing sight of Bianca as she walked. It was as if Constantine had designed a program to recognize her face and follow her every step.

"Her head is down. Shoulders forward. I can't see her face, but I can read her body language. She's sad. The kind of sadness that only happens when . . ." Enzo's gaze cut back to me. "When you feel like you can't be with the person you love."

My hand climbed to my chest at the anguished expression on his face as he studied me, and I couldn't help but replay his words to me in the theater room that we hadn't had a chance to discuss. His "I love you" had been buried among fear and worries, but it'd been there.

"Go back to the cameras by the club. Change the time to within thirty seconds of when she left. Let's see if we recognize anyone leaving the club after her," Alessandro suggested, and Enzo slowly faced the screen as I gripped the armchairs, nervously waiting, and it didn't take long before Alessandro hissed, "Stop."

"Is that who I think it is?" Constantine asked, and I stood to try and get a better view as he zoomed in on a man's face.

"*He* was at the club that night?" Enzo whispered in disbelief, and chills scattered over my body.

"Who?" I asked, my timid voice nearly just a squeak of sound.

Enzo slowly faced me. "Giovanni's son-in-law. His daughter's husband, Nico."

"Wait, the man outside the club that night is also the same guy in charge of the three men who came to your place yesterday. And now he's on his way here?" That felt a little . . . suspect. Even for me.

Enzo's palms went into prayer position, and he bowed his head against his hands and tapped twice. He cursed, this time in Italian, and dropped his palms. "Those three *idiotas* weren't stupid. It was an act. They didn't have a side operation. They knew who I was beforehand, and Nico sent them to me. I'd felt like I was being watched the night before when Jesse was talking to me, but he said he hadn't been followed." He shook his head. "That's because they were already in Charlotte. Watching *me*."

Wait, what?

"Now that we know the Brambilla family regularly used that cleaner, it makes sense they'd keep tabs on him. The moment they knew there was a breach, they'd started working on a game plan," Constantine said.

"For whatever reason, Nico must be in league with the Brambillas, and he clearly has been for a long time," Alessandro spoke up.

"They've been watching my every move since I arrived in town," Enzo said. "Must have followed us to the cabin last night. We led them right to the cleaner." He cut an angry hand through the air. "I was playing checkers while they were playing chess. I walked right into it because I was—"

"Distracted," I murmured in defeat, assuming that was the direction he was going, and bricks of guilt suffocated me at that fact. "What does this all mean?"

Enzo looked at me and let go of a ragged breath. "Nico's men saw me with you in the parking lot before Jesse showed up. They saw you show up at my place later that night. And maybe they were even outside the morning before when Thomas came."

"You're saying they framed Thomas?" I asked in shock.

"Nico gave me Thomas's name, because he wanted me to think it was Thomas. For me to think the attack yesterday was all a big coincidence. Nico planned everything. Even getting word to Thomas about the attack, which made him look guilty."

Thomas is innocent. My heart slapped my rib cage with a hard whack. "Why would they do that?"

"A Trojan horse," Constantine answered.

"I'm still not following." I wasn't dense, but this was still over my head.

Enzo swallowed the space between us and reached for me, guiding me to my feet. "Nico had those three men show up at my place yesterday not only as a distraction but to use it as a reason to get inside our home here. Open the gates for them, like we're about to do, so they could apologize for the attack."

Instead of a gift, the trap is an apology?

"Giovanni may not know Nico is working with the Brambillas," Mr. Costa pointed out. "But if he does, he'll do whatever is necessary to protect his family."

"And if the Brambillas have Nico by the balls," Constantine said, "they're more than likely behind everything that's happened in the last few days. The mastermind behind the plot."

I turned back to the screen that was paused on this Nico guy. "But why'd he want to hurt Bianca? His wife is family."

"We can't really think Bianca fell in love with not just the enemy but a married man, right?" Alessandro asked. "And then he killed her because . . . why?"

"I don't know," Enzo said, his tone softer that time, and he squeezed my hand and faced Alessandro. "But Nico was there that night, and he's about to be here now. And we know for certain the Brambillas hired the cleaner to cover for Bianca's murderer. This is the only thing that makes sense, even if it doesn't make sense now."

"Can you cancel the meeting?" I asked what felt like such a silly question, because of course they'd cancel now that they knew the truth.

"They've been two steps ahead of us," Constantine replied, "and if we cancel, they'll know for sure we figured things out. If we let them walk in, they'll assume we're still in the dark. And they'll believe the client list died with the cleaner last night."

"So they may not attack once here?" I asked, searching for clarification.

"No, they'll attack," Enzo said, no doubt in his tone. "But this way, they'll be the ones surprised. Because they won't be expecting us to be prepared for it."

"We need to get Mom, Izzy, and Maria out of here before they arrive," Constantine said, eyes on me, and my heart jumped into my throat.

"No, I don't want to leave. I'm safer with you."

Enzo gently hauled me into his arms, crushing me against his chest as if preparing for a goodbye I didn't want to hear. "War is about to happen here. You could be caught in the crossfire. I won't let that happen."

I listened to Constantine bark out orders, presumably to Alessandro. "You're taking the women out of here. Assemble a team. Take the armored SUV you used this morning."

"I'd rather join the fight. Hudson can take them," Alessandro responded as Enzo released me.

"Hudson's a better sniper. And Mom and Izzy need one of us with them," Constantine said in a low, steady voice, and Alessandro reluctantly nodded.

No. This was all happening too fast.

"We have a secure site on Long Island that's off-the-grid. You'll be safe there." Enzo cupped my cheeks, searching for my gaze, but I didn't want to look at him, not with him sending me away.

"If it's safer, then shouldn't we all go there?" I pleaded, finally giving him my eyes. "And isn't this still speculation? What if Thomas really was behind the attack and it was a coincidence? Maybe Nico just liked that club and left shortly after Bianca, and it was bad timing?" But as I said the words, I knew they were bullshit.

"We can't take any chances. We need to prepare for the worst and assume anyone walking into our house today is an enemy. Even Giovanni," Mr. Costa explained. "And if Nico really is working with the Brambilla family, they'll be coming, too, and it'll turn into a bloodbath."

Bloodbath? I was going to faint, but Enzo kept me upright and in his arms. He leaned in and brought his mouth to my ear. "I can't do this with you here. Please. I need to know you're safe."

Because I'd already distracted him enough, hadn't I? I battled back the tears, trying to keep my cool. But this whole situation was miles outside my wheelhouse. "Please come with me." I had to try one more time.

He only shook his head in apology, then peered at Constantine, who was giving Alessandro a few more instructions. "I'll have Maria waiting for you by the garage in three minutes," Enzo told him, breaking my heart; then he quickly walked me from the room, holding on to my arm like I might refuse him.

"Don't do this," I protested as we went upstairs, but he didn't talk again until we were in the guest room.

"I have to." He let go of my hand and knelt by his bag and unzipped it.

I fell to my knees on the other side of the bag, allowing the tears to glide down my cheeks. This was happening too fast. And there were still too many unknown variables. He needed more pieces of the puzzle. More clues. I was going to lose my mind. Officially. Choking out a sob, I barely registered what was in Enzo's hand.

"Bianca's rosary." He set the necklace in my palm and curled my fingers over it. "Keep it with you." He leaned over the bag and brushed his lips across mine, offering a tender kiss. "You can give it back to me when this is over."

My hand trembled as I held the rosary, trying to find the right words to convince this man not to go through with this.

"I wanted it to be Thomas. I really did. Because I hated him, and I wanted any reason to go after him, and for that, I'm so fucking sorry," he murmured, his hand still covering mine. "Plus, if he'd been responsible, that'd also mean it wasn't my fault you were in danger."

"Whoever murdered your sister is why I was in danger. Not you," I reminded him, because he didn't need any guilt eating at him. "You're not prepared, and you barely slept. Can you please try and, um, reschedule?" *Reschedule war? What the hell is wrong with me?*

"This is what I do," he whispered. "I'll be okay as long as you're not here."

"This isn't what you do. Not anymore," I pleaded. "You're a chef now. You're . . . you're mine. I—I can't lose you."

"You won't." He helped me to my feet and gathered me in his arms. "When this is over, I can finally be free of the past, Maria. I can be free of it once and for all." He held my cheeks and bowed his forehead to mine. "Don't you see? This is why I was never truly able to let go and move on, because justice was never really served."

I pulled back to find his eyes. "And she wouldn't want you dying to get it."

He brought his lips close to mine. "I won't." He kissed me. "We have a list to check off." Another kiss. "Memories to make." More kisses. "Babies to have." A softer, longer kiss this time that nearly distracted me from what he'd said.

And then, before I knew it, he had me in the garage.

Just outside the SUV, I listened to protests from his mother and sister as they argued with Alessandro.

Enzo held me tight and brought his mouth to my ear. "I love you, Maria. I won't die on you." He swiped the pads of his thumbs over my cheeks, catching my tears as I processed his words. "I promise I'll see you again, *Tesoro*," was the last thing he said before tucking me into the car and closing the door.

TWENTY-NINE

Enzo

"Are you sure I can't convince you to get to safety, too?" I strapped my chest and backplate on, then hid it beneath a black dress shirt and suit jacket. Not ideal for battle, but we couldn't greet Nico and his family wearing Kevlar vests and not tip them off that we knew what was going on.

"It's been a long time since I've fired one of these," Dad said while chambering a round in his rifle. "But I'm not going anywhere. I'll be by your side through all of this."

"I'd feel much better if you weren't, though." Constantine rounded the corner, joining us in the kitchen.

"You're stuck with me, son." Dad set down his rifle. "And there's something I need to say before this goes down."

Constantine held up his hand and lightly shook his head. "You don't need to do this."

Dad frowned. "I do, actually. I owe you all an apology for making a decision about your lives without so much as consulting you first." He faced my brother. "But I owe you a separate apology. I've been hard on you. Forcing you to make sacrifice after sacrifice." He gripped

Constantine's shoulder, his tone dropping an octave as he repeated his words in Italian.

"I'm good. I promise. You did what you thought was best," Constantine answered, keeping his voice level and serious, and then he looked my way.

"What he said," was all I could manage, not used to my father talking in such a manner, so it threw me for a loop. "We forgive you," I finally added, since Dad so clearly needed to hear the words, and I didn't want his head off for what we were about to do. And, I supposed, I truly did forgive him.

When Hudson walked into the kitchen a moment later, Dad cleared his throat and lowered his hand.

Hudson looked at the three of us as if realizing he'd interrupted a "moment," but Dad nodded, a silent request for an update on his part of the plan.

"They're on standby. Orders not to intervene until I give them the go-ahead," Hudson shared. "And if they don't hear from me by twelve hundred hours, they'll come in anyway."

"Not a fan of working with them," Dad began, his shoulders back and confidence returned, "but I understand this is the best option."

"The room ready?" Constantine asked as I tucked my Sig at my back beneath my suit jacket.

"Yeah, it's rigged, and Hudson will be able to set his crosshairs on them from the boat." I looked out the bay window at our family's yacht. We had to assume the Brambillas would hit us by air, land, and water. A full-on assault. And our security detail would be hidden from every vantage point, waiting to take them out guerrilla warfare–style. No front lines. Not any fucking lines today. Just surprise hits that we hoped no one would expect.

Hudson handed out the wireless comms Jesse's team had gifted us last night. "These are much better than our other ones," he told my father. "You don't need to tap anything to talk."

I checked the security camera in the kitchen. "Two SUVs are waiting outside the gate."

"They're going to be okay." Dad wrapped a reassuring hand over my shoulder, referring to Maria, my mom, and my sister.

I gave him a hesitant nod, hoping he was right. My hand hovered over the controls, waiting for the order to let in the vehicles.

"Now," Constantine said, and I opened the gates so the two black Suburbans could roll through.

After, I grabbed my rifle, knife, and a second pistol, and we went downstairs to the study and hid the weapons in easily accessible locations, and my dad and brother did the same. Then Constantine and I left him there and went to the foyer to greet our "guests."

I still had no idea if Giovanni was complicit in anything, but I'd consider everyone a threat until they proved otherwise.

"You think our theory's right?" Constantine asked while waiting by the double doors.

"I guess we're about to find out." The doorbell rang, and my mother's cousin was the first face I saw in the security camera by the door. I tensed at the sight of the others there. Nico and his wife, Alice, were just behind him. Giovanni's wife was MIA, not a surprise.

Constantine gave it another second, then slowly swung open the door and stepped back.

Giovanni was a few years older than my father. His black suit matched his hair, and I knew he'd have one or two pieces holstered beneath his jacket, regardless of the reason for our meeting.

"Constantine. Lorenzo." Giovanni offered his hand, and the three diamonds in his wedding band glinted as our palms met.

"Alice. Nico." I mimicked Giovanni's greeting when offering my hand to them next, trying not to forgo the plan and kill everyone right there.

Nico was a year or two older than me. Same dark hair and eyes. But his hair was a bit shorter, and his eyes were colder.

And then there was Alice, a spitting image of her mother, standing there with confidence in her red pantsuit. Her black hair was up in a tight bun, and her green eyes moved back and forth between us.

"My father's waiting for us in his study." Constantine walked ahead of them, and I hung back behind them all, ensuring they didn't make any preemptive moves.

From Hudson's vantage point on the yacht, he'd be able to zero in on our targets in the study. And *if* we gave him the signal, he'd be the one to take out Bianca's killer.

"Where's the rest of your family?" Giovanni asked once downstairs.

"They're somewhere around here," I answered as we entered the study.

Dad remained by his desk, not standing to greet them. His hello was a tip of the head, a harsh look in his eyes. "Sit." He motioned to the couch facing the bay window by the bookshelf. The men quietly sat as instructed, but Alice remained standing. "So you're here to apologize?" Dad asked as Constantine and I flanked his sides.

Nico sat taller, hands going to his thighs. "I was unaware my men were taking side jobs, and they've been dealt with, I can assure you of that."

"And that's the story you want to stick with?" Constantine asked, jumping a bit ahead of schedule.

"I'm sorry?" Nico unbuttoned his suit jacket and arched his shoulders back.

My gaze shot over to Alice as she tipped her head, assessing us. "You know," she murmured a few seconds later.

"What do they know?" Nico looked up at her, and he was either truly clueless or a stellar actor.

"That you were fucking Bianca," Alice said, her tone still absent of emotion.

"You were what?" Giovanni quickly stood, his back to the window now, eyes targeting his son-in-law, and I not so patiently waited to see how this would play out between them.

257

"He was having an affair with a Costa," Alice went on, confirming the theory I didn't want to be true.

Giovanni focused on Nico, a hand hovering near his hip, as if he were about to break leather and draw his sidearm.

Nico peered our way, recognizing we were the main threat in the room, not his wife or father-in-law. "He didn't really kill her, did he?" he asked, his tone softer than I'd expect. "The man you all murdered back then, he didn't do it?" Realization crossed over his face, and his hand at his side curled into a fist. Breathing hard, he turned his attention on Alice. Before we knew it, he had her pinned to the wall, a hand circling her throat. "What'd you do?" he hissed.

"Don't," my father barked out at the sight of Giovanni going for a gun, and he slowly lowered his hands, his eyes remaining laser-focused on his daughter.

A ghost of laughter fell from Alice's lips at her husband's attempt to strangle the answers from her. She didn't resist or fight back. It was some sick game to her, and it was taking all my restraint not to finish her off myself.

"Let her go, Nico," Dad ordered. "We can't get answers if she's dead."

Nico hesitantly released her, then took two steps back.

"If only you showed me this kind of passion in the bedroom, maybe things would be different." Alice smirked as if choking was a kink of hers.

"Explain," my father said, the word crisp from his tongue, before he beat it out in Italian repeatedly, his patience gone.

"Your perfect little daughter was fucking my husband is what happened." Alice eyed her husband.

"Watch yourself," my father snapped, and I did my best to remain quiet and allow Dad to take the lead as previously discussed.

"What did you do, Alice?" Giovanni asked her.

"You forced me to marry this spineless man." She pointed at Nico. "You chose him to take over for you instead of me. What'd you think would happen?" She shook her head, eyes back on Nico. "I didn't give a damn that you had an affair. But with her? With a fucking Costa? And then you wanted to leave me. Run away with her. No, no. I couldn't let that happen."

"She turned me down. If you were following me that night, well, you missed that part of our conversation," Nico slowly shared. "She wouldn't leave her family and run away."

My stomach twisted at his words, at the memory of her walking away from the club sad and with her head down. *That* was why she looked that way. And had we watched more of the video, we would've most likely seen Alice exiting the club shortly after Nico.

"And you wanted to run away because you were too much of a pussy to ask for a divorce. You didn't even seek vengeance when the woman you loved died." She lifted her chin our way. "At least the Costas have backbones. Not that they killed the right person."

I took a step forward without thinking, but my father shot out his arm, a reminder to keep my cool. To follow the plan.

A humorless laugh left Alice's lips as she focused on her father. "Did you really expect me to sit back and let him do what I was meant to?"

"Alice." Giovanni's tone softened that time. "What are you saying?"

"It's been me behind the scenes handling everything for years. And I'm done letting him take the credit." She brought her wrist to her mouth. "It's time," she said, presumably having someone on comms. And in one quick movement, she reached around to her back, revealing two pistols. One pointed at me. The other at her family.

I went for my Sig and, from the corner of my eye, spied my father and Constantine standing, armed as well.

Nico and Giovanni surrendered their palms as Hudson's voice came over my comm, and he shared, "There's a helo en route. And a boat at my nine o'clock that has military-age males on it heading my way."

"We can work this out," Giovanni went on, trying to walk her off the cliff of crazy, but that ship sailed thirteen years ago when she stabbed my sister seven times.

"Bianca let you into her apartment," I rasped, unable to stop myself from speaking that time. "And then you . . ."

"I confronted her that night. Told her I knew she was sleeping with my husband. She had the nerve to cry and apologize. She said some bullshit about not knowing he was married before she fell in love with him." The smirk from her nearly had me pulling the trigger. "I did what any respectable woman in the Sicilian mafia would do. Handled her myself."

Nico charged her again, not appearing to be as spineless as she claimed him to be. The man had loved my sister. Maybe still did. But his love for her got her killed. And the only reason I wouldn't end him for that was because she had loved him back.

"We have men fast-roping down from a helo and another team setting a breaching charge at the gate," Hudson warned over comms. "All teams, move into positions," he ordered our other men positioned outside who had one mission: keep the tangos from breaching the house. "I'll deal with the swarm of fuckers I've got out here in the water. But that means I don't have you in my sights now."

"Roger that," Constantine answered, giving away the fact we were on comms, right on cue as planned.

"I was wondering why I didn't see any guards when we came," she steadily said. "They were hiding and waiting. Your people won't be able to handle the Brambillas. There's too many of them."

"The Brambillas?" Giovanni asked in surprise.

"Who do you think I cut a deal with thirteen years ago to help me turn lemons into fucking lemonade?" Alice returned, and my father had to block my path to her yet again, which had the venomous woman smiling, thinking she was untouchable.

"I didn't know any of this," Giovanni quickly revealed.

"Of course you didn't. You've spent too much time golfing and traveling to know I've been the real reason we've survived so long. It's the deals *I've* been making with the Brambillas over the years that kept us afloat," she went on, but then she surrendered a small flinch when an explosion just outside rattled the room, and I looked over to see a speedboat on fire.

Hudson never missed his mark. Thank God.

"Another deal I made with them," Alice remarked, "is that you retire, Papa. I'm taking over. *Not* Nico. I'm done waiting. It's—"

"You set everything in motion." I cut off her solo act as realization struck me.

"It's been years of promises from the Brambillas that they'd help me push Dad out. I was done waiting."

"So you gave the Brambillas the motivation they needed," I said in disbelief. "You set up the cleaner. Revealed his location. Waited for the right time to make your move." *That's how Jesse's team found him in the first place. The cleaner was always the bait.* How long had she been keeping tabs on me? Preparing her plan? She'd used my career change, and the fact I'd stopped looking over my shoulder long ago, to her advantage.

She really had been playing chess. But like hell would I let her call checkmate.

Giovanni remained quiet, coming to terms with the fact he'd missed the signs when it came to his own flesh and blood going off the deep end. "You planning to kill me, Alice?" he asked her. "Because that's the only way you'll get rid of me." He grabbed hold of a weapon from beneath his suit jacket and pointed it at her, seemingly on our side in all of this.

Alice kept steady, not faltering even though she had us and her father to deal with. "You won't hurt me."

"Do you really think you're walking out of this room alive?" Constantine asked, breaking his silence.

"Absolutely. Because I'm seconds away from having what you want. Or I should say *who* you'll do anything for." The only real devil in the room was her, and I realized I didn't belong in hell, she did. And I'd be sending her there soon. "Nice trick with the two vehicles," she went on. "I knew you wouldn't let the women be here for our meeting, whether you were aware of the truth or not."

My turn for the surprise. The corners of my mouth lifted, and a smirk slid across my lips, which had Alice taking a step back, recognition dawning on her. "You didn't send them away," she said under her breath. "The vehicles are decoys."

I exchanged a quick look with Constantine and nodded, letting him know it was time for phase two of the plan. Our turn to join the battle. He reached into his pocket for the remote detonator.

"Alice?" I waited for her to look at me. "We knew it was you before you walked into the house." *Thanks to Maria's last-minute warning.* "We just didn't know if Nico and Giovanni were complicit," I revealed right before we dropped to our knees and ducked behind the desk, anticipating the blast that'd soon knock them off their feet.

THIRTY

Maria

Thirty Minutes Before

"What are you doing?" I whispered when Enzo opened the SUV door inside the garage and grabbed my free hand, pulling me out seconds after leaving me speechless with his "I love you."

"It's a mistake to send you away," Enzo rushed out. "My head was off. We're all . . . a bit off." He squeezed my hand. "You can't leave. You're right. You're safer near me."

Alessandro exited the front seat and Isabella and her mom joined us by the vehicle.

"They've been ahead of us this whole time," Enzo said. "What if they have eyes in the sky and follow the SUV and use them to get to us?"

"Use us to get to you? Who?" Isabella cried, turning to her mom for answers, but she remained quiet, only an apology in her eyes. Enzo's father must've only told Angela the details last night, and they'd chosen to keep her in the dark.

Alessandro gave us an uneasy look. "I don't like them being here, not with war coming our way."

"War?" Isabella asked as her mom pulled her to her side. "I thought you stopped. You're out. That life . . ."

"We'll explain later," Alessandro promised as I kept a tight hold of the rosary in my other hand, trying to keep myself calm. Images of my daughter tethered me to reality, though. Brought the fear up and into my chest and throat. The idea of never seeing her again wasn't something I could stand.

"The safe room is our best bet." Enzo peered at me as if reading my worried thoughts. "It's on the other side of the house, far away from the study. Not near any open land or water. It's fire- and bulletproof. It can withstand a blast."

A blast? The rosary nearly slipped from my hand. Maybe we'd be safe in there, but what about him and the others if they weren't with us?

"Dad won't like this, but I think you're right. It's the safest option," Alessandro agreed. "What about a decoy, though? If they're expecting we'll send the women away, why not redirect some of their men away from here, too?"

Enzo nodded, already on the move, guiding me back inside the house. "I'll have Hudson grab two of our guys. The armored SUV and another one. Two different directions."

Enzo stole a look at me from over his shoulder as we walked down the hall, slamming into his father in the process.

"What the hell are they still doing here?" Mr. Costa blocked our path.

Enzo explained his reasoning, then added, "The safe room here is a much better option than sending them away. We're not thinking clearly because of . . . because of Bianca."

And if they weren't thinking clearly, did that mean they'd be at an increased risk when "war" happened?

"Fine." His father grabbed hold of Angela's and Isabella's hands, and he led us to the safe room.

It was hidden inside a storage room. Well, behind a shelving unit inside the room was another door. After typing in a code, a door slid open, revealing a staircase.

We went downstairs and were greeted by a vault-like door. One more code. Then we were inside.

The lights flickered on to show a decent-size space, the size of my bedroom back home.

Enzo let go of my hand to face his brother. "Someone has to stay with them down here."

I set the rosary down on a nearby table and grabbed both his hands. "Can't it be you?"

"It needs to be Enzo up there," his father said before Enzo could answer me. "Alessandro won't be able to kill someone he knows."

"So you're saying Enzo can do that?" I asked in a soft voice.

"Yes, if I have to," Enzo murmured, never losing sight of my eyes. "I'm sorry, Maria. But I won't let anything happen to you."

I forced a nod, fighting back tears, then pressed up on my toes to kiss him.

He pulled back, his lips lingering near mine. "I'll get you back to Chiara, I promise," he whispered before letting me go.

His mom pulled him in for a hug. Isabella was next. Then he squeezed my arm before heading upstairs after his father said his good-byes as well.

Feeling alone even though I wasn't, I looked around the room. There was a daybed, a shelf of food, weapons, and two screens on one wall with a large control panel between them. Lastly, my attention fell to the three boxes near the door. *Bianca's things?*

"Is anyone going to tell me what's going on?" Isabella asked as Alessandro powered on the screens, which was a security system, offering a view of the exterior of the home.

"Can we see inside, too?" I asked as Angela sat on the daybed with Isabella and began sharing the details of our predicament.

"Yeah, but are you sure you want to? It might not be easy to watch," Alessandro said.

"Don't you need to know in case they need backup?" I stepped closer, wringing my hands.

"Yeah, but I didn't think you'd want to see Enzo killing anyone." He turned to look at his mom and sister, and I spied the gun tucked at the back of his jeans.

"We need to keep an eye on them." No way could I sit safely in that room and be clueless of what was happening.

Alessandro focused back on the screens and tapped at a few buttons on the control panel. One screen split in half, keeping the view of both the front and back of the home. The next screen lit up with an image of the kitchen, and I set a hand to my chest at the sight of Enzo there.

"How long until Giovanni and Nico are here?" I asked.

Alessandro checked his watch. "Soon," was all he said, which wasn't exactly illuminating.

"And if these people come here and start shooting, won't the neighbors hear? And what if they become casualties?" I thought back to the homes on the street that were fairly spread out, and I was pretty sure none was visible on either side of the Costa mansion, but . . .

"We called the two neighbors closest and told them to quietly leave their homes. And if anyone else happens to see anything and call the police, we have that covered," he explained.

I nodded, then focused back on Bianca's boxes. "Do you mind if I have a look?"

"Sure," Alessandro answered.

"Do you think something in there might help?" Isabella asked.

"They think Nico is responsible for her murder, but we still don't know why. And Enzo and I were considering that maybe the love story Bianca wrote for the magazine just before she, um . . . well, maybe it was about her and Nico," I told her, unsure how she'd react to that news.

"Oh." She frowned. "I was so young back then, but it's possible she was secretly seeing someone. She'd been acting a little off. Like her head was in the clouds whenever we talked." She knelt and removed the lid from one of the boxes.

"She printed all her stories out for her editor," Angela spoke up. "The drafts. Notes from her editor. I helped pack her desk. Everything should be in there." She gathered around us, and based on her lack of a definitive "no, she'd never love Nico," I had to believe Angela had a feeling Bianca loving someone in secret was a possibility.

"Here." Isabella offered her mother a folder, and Alessandro waved his hand, letting her know he didn't want one. I doubted it was only because he wanted to focus on the monitors. It would be hard to stomach reading Bianca's notes. To see her handwriting.

"I'll look," I offered, kneeling alongside her, accepting one.

I opened it up, realizing the one she'd given me appeared to be the first draft of her final story for the magazine.

There was a bunch of red ink crossing out entire paragraphs. Notes in the margins. Even a conversation on sticky notes going back and forth between Bianca and her editor.

I did my best not to cry as I read a note from her editor on the fourth page.

Editor: *No one likes the cheating trope. Don't have the hero be married.*

Bianca's response: *But it's not like that. She didn't know who he was or that he was married when they met. And it was an arranged marriage he never wanted to be in.*

Editor: *I don't care. Lose the wife or the story is scrapped. The wife always finds out. And then you'll have a murder mystery on your hands, not the sweet love story you promised me.*

"Oh, shit." I dropped the papers and scrambled to my feet, patting my back pocket for my phone, realizing it must've fallen out in our rush to get there. "Can they hear us? Is there a speakerphone thingy in here connected to the kitchen?" Alessandro shot me a puzzled look, then slammed his hand against a button, and I stood and rushed to his side and cried out, "Nico's wife. I think Nico's wife is the killer."

THIRTY-ONE

Maria

"They're okay," Alessandro calmly told me.

But it'd be hard to believe anyone in the study was okay until the tendrils of smoke from the blast had cleared out so I could visibly see Enzo and the others.

"Shit." Alessandro slammed his hand over a button on the panel. "She's getting away. Crawled into the hall," he rasped, letting his family know Alice was on the move amid the chaos.

With the fog of the explosion settling down, Enzo—thank God—appeared on camera. He was on his feet, weapon drawn. "Which way did she go?"

Alessandro flipped through the different camera views, searching for her. "She's heading upstairs. But you have incoming. The house has been breached. Three tangos by my count heading your way."

"Roger that," Enzo said while his brother and father rose.

I could see Nico and Giovanni now on the floor, surrounded by debris.

"You alive?" Constantine asked them.

"Yeah," I heard someone respond between coughs.

"Stay here. Barricade yourselves," Constantine ordered.

"You're clear to move out," Alessandro let them know as Angela turned away from the screens and Isabella walked her back to the daybed and sat with her.

"I'm switching to comms. I'll be your eyes." Alessandro positioned something into his ear; then he tapped it. "You copy?"

I couldn't hear Enzo anymore, but he was in the hall now with Constantine and his father, and seconds after Alessandro warned them, I stifled a gasp with my hand when a man appeared and Enzo shot him without hesitation.

"You have a tango at the top of the stairs," Alessandro alerted them next, and Constantine moved to the other side of the stairwell and ducked off to the side. The second a boot appeared, he reached between the banister and grabbed his ankle. The man stumbled, and Enzo, already waiting on one knee, threw a knife at him. It was like something from a movie. "You're clear to move up."

"Okay, maybe I can't watch," I admitted.

"What?" Alessandro quickly looked at me and shrugged while saying, "Chefs do that."

His joke, if that was what it was, did nothing to ease my nerves. "I'm just, um . . ." My attention landed on the outside view of the home, spotting even more bad guys there, all working hard to get inside, and their roadblock was the Costas' security team.

"Enzo told me to tell you not to worry and please don't watch." Alessandro gently grabbed my arm. "He can hear you," he mouthed.

I nodded in understanding; the last thing I wanted was to distract him. I went over to the daybed, and Angela and Isabella made room for me. Angela wrapped an arm around me like I was her daughter, too, which made me want to cry for whatever reason. Maybe it was because I was a mother, and I never wanted to suffer the kind of loss Angela had endured. God, I missed Chiara. But I was thankful she was far away from here.

Alessandro continued to guide and give directions to his family, but I couldn't peel my eyes away from the screen, even from a distance.

The exterior camera had a view of the front of the house, and black Tahoes appeared, rolling over the gate that'd already been blown up by the Brambillas while Enzo had faced off with Alice in the study.

"Oh God. More of them?" I lurched to my feet, losing the battle to my anxiety, unable to keep calm.

Alessandro tapped his ear but didn't look our way. "They're FBI. We needed help. Hudson called in a favor earlier and then told them to wait for his call before they arrived."

I nearly collapsed, shuddering from relief at their contingency plan.

Alessandro tapped his ear again. "I think Nico and Giovanni's location has been compromised. I lost visual of the room. Camera is out. I don't know what happened."

"Are they dead?" Angela asked, and he looked back at her with apologetic eyes.

"I don't know, Mom," was all he said.

I forced myself to stand at his side again, watching as the Federal agents swarmed the house, dealing with the bad guys alongside the Costas' security team.

"The Feds are converging on the house. If you want to kill her, you better do it before they stop you," Alessandro quickly told Enzo and the others, continuing to flip through screens to try and find the woman responsible for murdering his sister.

"There!" I cried out at the sight of a flash of red from her suit on-screen. "Bianca's room."

Alessandro toggled the controls, shifting the camera angle around, and there she was. But she wasn't alone.

"She's in Bianca's bedroom. And she has a gun to Nico's temple," Alessandro said. "She must've been the reason the cameras went out. She circled back downstairs to get a hostage."

I watched the screen as Enzo and Constantine approached the room a few seconds later, their weapons drawn, stealthily and cautiously moving.

"The Feds are on your ass," Alessandro warned as Enzo and Constantine went into Bianca's old room to face off with the woman who had forever altered their lives.

Nico was on his knees by Alice's side, his hands behind his head.

Alessandro shot the three of us a look, letting us know to remain quiet; then he hit a button on the panel so we could all hear what was being said in the room.

"Let me out of here or the man your sister loved dies," Alice warned, but she had to know she'd already lost, right? How could she not?

Enzo was hesitating. Constantine too. I could see it in their body language. The expressions on their faces. They didn't want to watch the man their sister loved die.

I ran my hands up and down my arms, trying to erase the chills beneath my top, but it was pointless. Even my teeth were clicking from nerves.

Alessandro pressed a button to mute the sound in the room and said over his comm, "Twenty seconds until you have company from the Feds." He pressed the button again, and I missed whatever conversation happened in that time, but on the second screen, I saw the Federal agents gaining ground, nearing their location.

"Just shoot her," Nico urged. "I should've figured this out long ago. This is my fault. Just kill her, and—"

"Weapons down!" armed agents yelled from the doorway, rifles in hand.

And during the distraction, Alice's focus shifted, and I knew what was coming. Because I knew Enzo.

He lifted his weapon despite the Feds' orders, and Nico shifted to the side, falling to the ground to give Enzo space to shoot her.

Alice went down. Almost in slow motion. Or maybe my brain had glitched. I wasn't sure. But the gun had fallen from her hand, never discharged, and she'd landed facedown.

Agents barked out orders for Enzo to lower his weapon, and he slowly set down his rifle and went to his knees, hands behind his head.

His gaze lifted to the camera as he was cuffed, and he mouthed words I knew he'd meant for me to see: "I'm so sorry."

~

"Alice had a gun, and he had no choice. The Feds saw that, right?" I sputtered, pretty much talking to myself in the safe room. My head and heart weren't on the same page right now. Both were pulling me in two different directions. Confused. Scared. The fog of shock hadn't been lifted.

All I could focus on right now was that Enzo was in cuffs and in the back of an unmarked vehicle in the driveway. Constantine and his father had yet to be cuffed, but Hudson was outside talking to someone from the FBI task force.

"Can't we go out there?" Isabella asked her brother, and he shook his head.

"Not until Hudson lets us know it's safe. I don't want them taking you all in for questioning if I can help it," Alessandro explained, and the idea of being in an FBI interrogation room with my below-par acting skills wasn't the best idea.

Angela's eyes fixed to the screen as the Feds escorted Giovanni from the property alongside Nico. "Alice didn't kill her dad." Her tone was soft, a bit unsure. "It's over, though. It's all finally over." She faced me and grabbed my hand. "I'm so sorry you were dragged into our mess. I broke my promise to your parents to protect you."

"But I'm okay," I reminded her. "It's Enzo I'm worried about. If Hudson was able to pull off a miracle and get the Feds to show up so fast, then—"

"Hudson *will* get him out. The Feds have to follow protocol, though, and Enzo killed someone right in front of them," Alessandro cut me off, his gaze going to his mother, and she let go of me. "I need you to try and keep calm. I know with everything that's happened, that's a big ask, but please. Enzo's feeling pretty fucked up right now, knowing you had to watch all of that, trust me, I know him. And then he killed a woman for the first time in his life. And—"

"For a notorious charmer, you're failing to calm anyone down," his mom interrupted him.

Alessandro frowned, then in a softer tone shared, "Hudson called in a favor to the governor minutes before everything went down. He offered the Brambillas on a silver platter if the governor could ask the Feds to assist us this morning and ensure all 911 calls were intercepted," he went on, searching my gaze. "This way, the governor and ADIC get credit for taking down the most powerful Italian *mafioso* family on the East Coast. Shit like this helps win elections, I guess."

"The ADIC?" My voice was so freaking small right now. *And the* governor *governor? Like of New York?*

"The assistant director in charge at the field office in New York," Alessandro clarified. "He's been building a case against the Brambillas for years, so Hudson had a feeling it'd only take a nudge from the governor to finally close in on them today."

I had so many questions, I didn't know where to start. "But was the crime boss even here?"

"No, but the Feds can use the cleaner's files Hudson shared with them as a means to arrest him and search his properties," Alessandro went on, and Angela reached for my hand and gave it a reassuring squeeze. "And since Giovanni and Nico are alive, I'm sure they can offer additional intel to take down the Brambillas in exchange for immunity."

"Hudson couldn't help my brothers thirteen years ago," Isabella spoke up, "but you can trust us when we say he'll be able to help Enzo this time."

"Because of the Brambilla deal?" I needed this all spelled out for me, and I was still shaken up and in disbelief at what had happened this morning. I'd yet to process the danger. Or the lives I'd witnessed Enzo take before my eyes.

Isabella exchanged a quick look with her brother. "Well, yes, but also because Hudson's dad is the governor."

What? "Didn't Hudson leave the navy to take care of his mom? Why didn't his father help, too?" Not relevant, and yet, the questions popped free from my mouth anyway.

"His parents divorced when he was young. His mom raised him. His dad wasn't home much. Military," Alessandro quickly answered as a buzzing sound greeted us. "Hudson's outside the safe room. Looks like we can go out."

Alessandro punched in a code, and the door slid open. Hudson stepped into the room, and Isabella rushed his way. Hudson flinched when she wrapped her arms around him for a hug.

From over her head, Hudson looked at us, a nervous expression on his face; then he gave in and hugged Isabella back. "It's okay," he told her.

"Alice died in Bianca's room," Isabella whispered, barely loud enough for me to hear.

"I know," he murmured, "but I promise everything will be okay."

Alessandro faced me and added, "The Brambillas are small fish compared to the marks we've gone after in the past. We can handle them. You can trust us."

Isabella didn't seem to have any plans to free herself from Hudson's muscular arms as he softly reassured her, "It's over." He stroked her back. "We'll make sure no one is ever a threat to any of you ever again. You have my word."

THIRTY-TWO

Enzo

I'd promised Maria I'd get her home to her daughter by today, and I was still in FBI custody. No charges had been drawn up, but I'd been in holding since Thursday with frequent interviews from the top down to the rookie sitting across from me now.

But we were nearing the seventy-two-hour mark, and I was confident I'd be released any minute.

I trusted my family to keep Maria safe while I was here, but I was losing my mind every hour away from her. I needed to apologize in person for what she witnessed three days ago.

"I didn't think people like you existed outside of film."

I looked up from my hands cuffed to the table at the agent, not sure where he was about to go with that statement.

"Yeah, we have a file on you. I did a little light reading this weekend." He fingered his butter-blond hair, swiping it away from his forehead. I wasn't sure if he was trying to bait me into a conversation to get me to talk about my past, but that wouldn't be happening.

"Where's Special Agent Lee?" I asked, my way of letting him know I had no plans to discuss my past.

The fresh-out-of-Quantico agent—and yeah, I could read him that well—checked his watch. "He'll be here any minute."

Agent Lee was a friend of Hudson's, and he'd been keeping me abreast of all details since I'd been in custody per the ADIC's orders.

I'd asked him for a report about our security team and had requested to see photos of every person who'd come up against us on Thursday, and he'd secretly followed through with my request.

My team hadn't suffered any losses. Many wounded, but they'd all be okay. Alice's people and the Brambillas . . . not nearly as lucky, though.

And I wouldn't cry over the fact the asshole who'd straddled Maria on Wednesday died on Thursday. He'd been on one of the boats, trying to kill Hudson. And the other two *idiotas* from the failed attack were in the ICU. One in a coma. And Jensen, Giovanni's nephew on his wife's side, would be on a liquid diet for weeks. A broken jaw the least of his worries.

I was pretty sure Agent Lee also felt indebted to my family, considering he'd been after the Brambillas for years. Between the cleaner's files and Nico's and Giovanni's statements, he could finally close his case.

Of course, Constantine offered the FBI evidence from the cleaner's files only related to the Brambillas for now. We didn't want to screw up whatever work Carter and Jesse were doing and have the FBI blow their covert op.

The door cracked open a moment later, and Agent Lee was there with another guard. I hadn't seen him since last night, and I'd never thought I'd be so happy to see a Fed.

"Uncuff him. He's free to go," Agent Lee requested. "No charges are being filed."

The rookie stood and looked at Lee as if he might protest but then smartly shut the fuck up and left.

"I'm sorry this took so long," Agent Lee apologized once I was uncuffed and the guard had left us alone. He angled his head toward the camera in the room. "It's off, so we can speak freely."

I slowly stood, planting my hands on the table. "Tell me you got Brambilla. Tell me he's off the streets." I needed the head of the crime family behind bars or dead. Dead would be preferable.

Lee's eyes met mine, and he nodded. "We located him at three in the morning, and he resisted. It turned into a gunfight. One of our snipers took him out, along with his right-hand man. He's not alive to order any retaliation hits against anyone."

Fuck, that was good news. Not that I believed my family would be targeted anyway. Any of the crime families would be too intimidated to come after us, given how we'd handled the Brambillas on Thursday. Plus, between my father and Giovanni, they had too much dirt on them. They wouldn't want to be next on the chopping block. Besides, no one ever really liked the Brambillas anyway.

"And Nico and Giovanni? Are they still in custody?" I asked.

"We're offering them immunity and new identities. I'm sure you want to have words with them, particularly Nico, but they've already been transferred to a safe location. I'm not privy to the details. But with what you gave us, their help, and whatever we find at Alice's home and office, I'm sure it'll be more than enough to ensure there'll be no new head growing back on the snake."

I *had* wanted to talk to Nico. To understand what the hell happened with him and my sister. But he'd been willing to die for justice for Bianca, and maybe it was thirteen years too late for him to stand up to Alice. I didn't believe he was complicit in her death, though. He had loved Bianca, but he'd feared his wife and father-in-law more.

Agent Lee reached out and offered a business card. "When my men are done combing through all of Alice's things, we'll let you know if we learn anything of value to you. Program my number so you accept my call."

I pocketed his number and nodded.

"And if you and your brothers decide to let us see what other names were on the cleaner's file, wait two weeks, would you? I owe my wife and kids a vacation after years of chasing the Brambillas."

"Copy that." I nodded and looked toward the door, anxious to see Maria and my family.

"Come on. I'll walk you out."

I quietly followed him. "Thank you again," I said after signing a few official documents for my release.

"Like I said, I owe you and your family. Could've used a bit more lead time than thirty minutes before hell broke out in Oyster Bay, but looks like you didn't need us," he replied when we made our way to the elevators. "Can I ask you something, though? Now that we don't have eyes?"

I knew what was coming, and as we waited for the elevator, I nodded and mentally prepared my answer.

"Killing your own cousin, even if she's a third cousin, couldn't have been easy. Was it so your sister could rest in peace? You think that—"

"No." I shook my head. "I finally realized Bianca's always been at peace. It was us who needed it." I frowned. "But that's not the only reason I killed her, and I think you know that."

Agent Lee palmed his smooth jawline, eyes falling to the floor in thought. "Because no one will dare fuck with you or those you love if you're willing to kill someone you're related to?"

I let go of a gruff breath. "Precisely." *Maria will be safe. My mom and sister.* "Untouchable again."

"By the bad guys, sure." He looked up. "But be careful out there if your family plans to exit retirement. Not everyone in the Bureau is a fan."

"Yeah, I can tell."

"But if you do start up again," he added as the elevator doors opened, "there're a few people I can recommend you look into who are off-limits to us and shouldn't be walking the streets." He opened his palm, motioning for me to head inside.

The fact he was letting me know we had an ally if we wanted one at the FBI was comforting, but I had no plans to be that guy again. No more going dark. If Maria was still willing to be in my life after this mess, I considered myself set for life.

"I'll pass that along," was all I said while stepping into the elevator, remaining quiet the rest of our way out, and then my heart shot into my throat at the sight outside the Bureau.

On the street, Maria was between Hudson and Constantine waiting for me, and I almost took a knee at the sight of her running my way.

"Ah, so you have a reason to stay retired," I overheard Agent Lee say on my way to Maria, and I lifted her in my arms.

Yeah, she was my reason. My fucking everything. Her and Chiara.

I guided her legs around my waist and held her tight, hugging her as she murmured my name repeatedly like soft pleas.

"I'm so sorry," I rushed out, never losing my grip on her. "Are you okay?"

"I was so worried about you," she cried.

"I'm okay, baby," I promised as her feet found the ground, and she kissed me, eliminating any doubts she planned to walk away after what happened. No, she was there. She was my girl. My fireball.

"Tell me you're coming back to Charlotte. Promise me you're getting on that plane today with me. No third-act breakup, right?" she asked, her voice trembling.

I wasn't sure what a third-act breakup was, but I bent forward and lightly sucked her wobbly bottom lip. "Breakup, are you kidding?" I pulled back to find her eyes, shaking my head. "I'm lost without you." I gulped at the emotion pushing up into my throat. "So no, no third-act breakup. You're my girl. Forever."

She reached between us, and it barely registered that there were people on the street, walking around us. "I love you, Lorenzo Costa," she said between soft kisses. "You didn't give me a chance to tell you that on Thursday. And maybe outside the FBI isn't the greatest place to say it, but I don't want to wait."

I replayed her words, waiting for the moment my brain would tell me I didn't deserve them or her love.

But nothing came.

The death grip of the past and that darkness didn't draw me back.

With narrowed eyes, she added, "But you knew I loved you, didn't you? You've always known."

"I've always known," I hoarsely admitted. "And I've always loved you, Maria Romano." I brought my hands to her face, thumbing away tears as I stared deep into her eyes. My own gaze a bit blurry.

"Then let's go home," she whispered while reaching into her pocket, producing my sister's rosary, and she placed it in my palm. "This belongs with you."

"Belongs with us," I gruffly said, hugging her again.

After a quiet moment passed, I stepped back and looked around, spotting Agent Lee talking to Hudson and Constantine by Hudson's truck.

"Ready?" Constantine called out when finding my eyes. "The family is waiting for you at your place."

The FBI office was in Lower Manhattan, situated between Tribeca and Chinatown, so we were closer to my home than my parents' second home by Central Park.

I had every intention of leaving with Maria today and letting my brothers and Hudson handle any potential damage control, because I trusted them to do it. But I needed to see my family before I left, especially Izzy.

I couldn't leave New York without ensuring she knew I loved her, too.

~

Maybe it was guilt at the fact Maria had witnessed me killing people on Thursday, but on the drive to Chelsea, a bad feeling planted roots in my gut.

The hugs from my family once at my place didn't ease the hard knot in my stomach that was beginning to squeeze without remorse. Nor the promises from Maria she'd be okay.

"What's wrong?" Alessandro asked, reading my thoughts.

I chanced a look at Maria at my side, and she tipped her chin to peer up at me. Her worried brown eyes shredded me, and I decided I couldn't share what was on my mind in front of her. She didn't need more stress.

"I'm fine," I lied. "But can we have a word in my office?" I focused on Constantine and Hudson. I squeezed Maria's hand, letting her know everything would be "fine." *Hopefully.* She returned my look with a soft nod, and I let go of her to join my brothers and Hudson in my office.

"What's going on?" Constantine cut straight to the point, perching a hip on my desk, and I went over to the fireplace and set a hand on the mantel. "Agent Lee say something to you we should be worried about that you didn't want to say in front of Maria on the way here?"

"No, it's not that." My free hand went to my chest as the pain in my stomach worked its way to my chest. "I feel like I'm missing something."

"Alice had us by the balls and we didn't know it until it was nearly too late," Constantine answered, and I looked over as Alessandro and Hudson took a seat on the leather couch.

"What you're experiencing is anxiety," Alessandro spoke up, and I wasn't sure if he was giving me a hard time or being serious. "Maybe guilt. It's all normal. You've been on edge all week, and we were blindsided on more than one occasion."

"You think that's all?" I wanted him to be right. God, did I ever. "No more loose ends?"

Hudson caught my eye next and gave me a serious look. "If you have concerns, then I'll take another look at everything and talk to Agent Lee. He still has people going through Alice's things and is trying to get more of her people to provide statements."

"Thank you." I nodded, and he was back on his feet and leaving the room, not wasting time.

When the door clicked shut, I let go of the mantel and looked at my brothers, both now on their feet, studying me.

Alessandro tipped his head. "You're having second thoughts about whether or not you're too dangerous for Maria, aren't you?"

No, I don't think that's it.

Constantine stepped forward, searching for my gaze. "Don't give up a love like you two have from a place of fear." He cut the space between us and gripped my shoulder. "She knows now the risks of being with a Costa. And yeah, our family should be untouchable after everything that went down, but no, there's no guarantees in life." He always gave it to me straight. No sugarcoating, and I appreciated that. "You can't protect her from everything, you know that, right?"

"But I want to," I rasped, my stomach still twisting like heated scraps of metal.

"Well then," Alessandro said, drawing closer, "you being in her life increases her chances of safety a hell of a lot more than if you're not. Because you'll be there to look out for her."

"He's right," Constantine said. "And you know how much it pains me to admit that."

A small, surprising smile slipped onto Alessandro's lips, but before he could come up with a clever response, Izzy opened the door and poked her head in, and Constantine let go of me and faced her.

"Hey, you." I motioned for her to come in.

"Can we talk?" she asked, eyes on me.

Constantine and Alessandro shot me a quick look, a plea to not be a dumbass about Maria, and I nodded my promise, and then they left.

Once we were alone, it was only then I noticed she had a folder in her hand, and in a small voice she said, "I thought you might want to read this. It's Bianca's original draft. Night and day different from what was published."

I gulped, my gaze clinging to the folder, uncertain what to say or think. The uneasy feeling in my stomach doubled at the sight of it.

"Can I confess something?" she whispered, and I peered up at her, not sure where this conversation was going to go. "Growing up, I was always jealous of the relationship you two had. You had the twin thing, and I felt left out. And then after she died, it was like you couldn't even look at me. And it hurt . . . a lot, if I'm being honest."

Her words deflated the air from my lungs. "Izzy."

She held up her palm, a request to let her continue, and I hesitantly nodded. "I look like her," she softly said. "And although we have different personalities, I understand how hard it is . . . because sometimes it hurts when I look in the mirror." Tears filled her eyes. "It fucking hurts."

I broke forward, dying to get to her. To ease her pain. But she kept her arm extended, a request to let her finish, so I did my best to stay back and respect that.

"But I also want to feel closer to her. And if I change myself and who I am, I'm scared I'll start to forget her. Lose her for good." She sniffled. "But she's gone, and you're not, and I—"

"Fuck." I couldn't stop myself; I hauled my sister against me, and she dropped the folder. I cradled her head to my chest and held her tight. "I'm so sorry. So damn sorry." I waited for her broken sob to slow before adding, "You do look like her. But I also see you for you. And I'm so proud of the woman you've become, and she would be, too."

She peeled back and gripped my forearms as if searching for help to stand.

"I wasn't there for you like I should have been. None of us was. We were focused on revenge. And we lost sight of . . ." I released a shaky exhale, my lungs hurting that time. "Let me be here for you now.

Please," I begged. "Let me prove to you that I do love you. And I'm here for you."

Izzy collapsed back into my arms again, and I cupped her head, and tears hit my face for the first time since the day I'd dropped to my knees at Bianca's church right before my arrest.

I lost one sister, and I nearly lost another, and somehow Bianca brought us back together. Saving me like always. Even from the beyond, she had my six.

"I love you, sis," I whispered once she'd untangled herself from my hug.

Her gaze slipped to the folder, to the papers that had fallen from it. "Bianca believed in forgiveness. Mercy. She believed in love. So I'm going to be like that, too." She knelt and picked up the folder, shuffling the papers back inside. "She didn't get her happy ending, but I know she'd want all of us to have ours. And we owe it to her to do it. To live in the now instead of the past. And I'm going to try hard to do that."

I tilted my head. "Does that mean no more dating men who don't deserve you?"

Her gaze shot to the door, and I was unsure why. "I promise, but if I lose my way—"

"I'll be there for you to guide you back."

THIRTY-THREE

Maria

I stared at Chiara asleep in her crib later that afternoon, my heart swelling in my chest at the sight of her. My parents, as well as Natalia and Ryan, had met us at the airport an hour ago. Chiara had nearly jumped free from Mom's arms to get to me. After I gave her a million kisses, Enzo stole her from me, and I'd swear that man held her as if he might never let go.

I'd sent Natalia and Ryan home, but my parents stubbornly followed us back to my place. My parents didn't know the entire story of what had happened, and they didn't need to know. But the Costas had assured them we were all safe and we would be protected.

"She always passes out on car rides." I folded my arms, continuing to stare at my beautiful daughter.

"Let's not wake her. Come on." Mom lightly grabbed my arm, urging me to leave, but it was hard to unglue myself from Chiara when I'd been away from her for far too long. But I supposed Mom was right, so we left her room, though I kept the door slightly ajar.

Dad was in the living room talking in private with Enzo and, from the sounds of it, in Italian.

"Give them a second more alone," Mom said, holding me back from entering the room.

"Don't tell me he's lecturing him? Threatening him that if something happens to me yada-yada-yada?" I asked her with worry, because that was the last thing Enzo needed right now.

"No, not at all. He's giving his blessing."

Well, that wasn't what I'd been expecting her to say, but I was all for it.

Mom looked over at the two men, then focused back on me. "Enzo was tasked long ago to keep you and your sister safe, and your father's worried Enzo may feel as though he's crossing some type of line by loving you, which he so clearly does. And who are we to stand in the way of true love?"

I needed to hear that. I hadn't realized just how much until now. "You're turning over that new leaf for real this time, hmm?"

She smirked. "A work in progress."

Her words brought me back to Enzo saying the same thing in New York. My man . . . my everything. I just wished I didn't get the feeling something was still bothering him and he was keeping it from me. "I thought we were done with secrets." *Shit, did I say that out loud?*

"What are you talking about?"

"Nothing. Ignore me. I'm tired."

"Mm-hmm. Well, I overheard Natalia talking to you on the phone yesterday, and you told her you're having nightmares. Bet you haven't told Enzo that."

"It was one nightmare. And now Enzo's back with me, so I'm sure I'll be fine." I hoped I would be, at least. But who could blame me? I'd had to watch Enzo take lives to protect us, and then he'd been ripped away from me by the FBI. That was the definition of "a lot."

"I'm just relieved Thomas wasn't part of whatever happened."

I folded my arms. "You really did a lot of eavesdropping on my conversation with Natalia Saturday, I see." I'd texted Thomas on my way home that I was back and had Chiara. He'd yet to answer, and I hadn't heard from him all weekend, which was shocking, so I had to assume he was still out of town.

"I think we should head out and give Maria and Enzo some privacy," Mom said a moment later, more than likely trying to dodge a lecture from me about her invading my privacy. So much for the new leaf.

Mom and I joined Enzo and my father, and my gaze landed on our luggage by the couch. Bianca's unedited story was inside Enzo's bag, but he said he wasn't ready to read it.

When I looked up at him, his eyes were on me, and there was that uneasy look from him again. What was going on?

"Well, we're glad to have you home." Dad came over and hooked his arm around me, pulling me in for a side hug. We all exchanged our goodbyes a few seconds later, and once they were gone, Enzo closed the door and kept his back to it.

"How'd it go with my dad?" I reached for his hand and threaded our fingers together, and he pulled me to him, our linked palms the only thing between our bodies as he dropped his focus to my mouth.

"It went better than I expected." He bent in and kissed me, and I wished it would have been enough to melt away my lingering worries, but nothing short of a promise from him everything was okay would do that.

When he lifted his mouth from mine, he palmed my cheek with his free hand.

"What's wrong?" I whispered, drawing my eyes closed as I waited for him to drop bad news on me, and I could feel it coming.

He slid his thumb over the line of my lips. "I just need to check something on my work computer next door."

"Your laptop for catering? Or are you planning to go into your Batman lair?" I opened my eyes while pulling away, searching his gaze for comfort and security, but I didn't find it.

"There's one possible loose end. I could be worrying for nothing. I hope I am. But I need to make a call and look into something, and there's no need to unnecessarily worry you if it's nothing." He lifted our palms and kissed the top of my hand. "I don't want to leave you alone, though. Maybe wake Chiara and you two come with me?"

"I'm just next door. Nothing will happen. And I think you're being paranoid, and there are no loose ends." I let go of his hand. "Please. The sooner you close the book on your concerns, the better for us all."

His shoulders fell. "Don't open the door for anyone but me. I don't care if it's a neighbor. No one. Got it?"

"Yes, sir." That was supposed to come across as sexy and teasing, to help ease his nerves and produce a smile, but he was clearly on edge, because his lips remained in a harsh line.

"The walls are thin," he went on. "You shout, call, scream at the top of your lungs if you have to if something is wrong. I'll try and be quick, but come over with Chiara if she wakes before I'm back."

"Okay," I responded in a softer tone despite now feeling on edge.

He leaned in and kissed me one more time. "Lock the door. Dead bolt," he ordered before leaving, and I did as he asked and went straight for Chiara's room once he was gone, needing to put eyes on my daughter.

I sat in the rocking chair by the crib, mindlessly rocking, doing my best not to think about the last few days, but memories kept popping up.

A few minutes later, there was a knock at my front door, followed by a ring. Chiara remained asleep. *That must be Enzo.* His key was probably in his luggage in my living room.

I carefully shut her bedroom door and went to let Enzo in.

But shit, it wasn't him.

Thomas stood outside my door in the hall, and he had Chiara's favorite stuffed animal tucked under his arm. *Great, you couldn't call first?*

I went for the knob, then remembered Enzo's directive not to let anyone in. But if I called Enzo to come over, with how edgy he was, there'd probably be another showdown between the men.

Thomas knocked again, so I reluctantly unlocked and opened the door.

"You're back." I frowned. "Thank you for bringing Stuffy. You could've called first." He handed me the bear and walked around me without an invite. "You don't live here," I reminded him as the door swung shut, and I turned to find him heading for Chiara's room.

"Yeah, well, I want to see my daughter. I've been away from her."

I set her bear on the chair in the living room as I followed him toward her bedroom. "So have I. And she's asleep. Let her rest. Come back when you're invited."

He stopped outside her room and faced me. "Where's Enzo?"

"He's next door. He'll be here any second." I folded my arms. "So don't do anything that might piss him off."

"What, like breathe the same air as you?"

"Funny that you mention that. Not funny ha-ha but like . . ." *What am I saying?* "You should go. Please."

"Fine." He leaned against the hall wall with no plans to budge from the looks of it. "You were with him in New York."

"He's the head chef of the restaurant, and we're considering a second location. Of course he went."

"You're a horrible liar." He pushed away from the wall, and I stumbled back a nervous step.

There was something in his eyes that triggered me to hold my hands up defensively, like I'd never once done during our marriage. "Someone had to let me in today. I lost my key fob, can you get me a new one?"

I stared at him for a moment as a memory from the attack last week resurfaced. "Key fob," I said under my breath. And then another thought crossed my mind. "Who told you about the attack? I never did ask you."

I knew it was Alice's handiwork to set Thomas up, but in all the chaos, I never stopped to wonder how she'd managed to let Thomas know. I doubted she played an old-school game of telephone, leaking the attack to someone at the restaurant, *hoping* it'd get back to Thomas.

Now he was the one taking a defensive step back. "I don't remember."

You're even worse of a liar. But then it hit me, and I realized Enzo's loose-end feeling was about Thomas, and he hadn't wanted to say anything to me without proof. "What'd you do?" I rasped.

"No clue what you're talking about." His voice was dead. Flat. A sharp contrast to the worried look in his eyes.

"I defended you. Told him you'd never do it. It was out of character," I went on, knowing I was right. No doubt in my mind now. "Why? You don't love me, that's not it."

He tore his hands through his hair, shot a look toward my bedroom, and then started that way.

"What are you doing?" I went after him, trying to yank his arm to stop him, but he didn't face me until he was inside.

"He doesn't know. Not yet," he muttered, jerking his arm free from my touch. "I wouldn't be alone with you if he did."

"Thomas." I shook my head as he paced alongside my bed, tears in my eyes at the fact my daughter's father would betray us by being involved. Cheating was one thing; this was something else altogether.

When I'd only thought he'd been pissed and hired the wrong people to beat up Enzo, even that had been hard for me to believe. But knowingly help the mafia? No.

"Talk to me. If you're thinking about doing something rash, remember you have a daughter down the hall. You're still her father," I calmly said, trying to maintain control of the situation. Talk him off any type of cliff of crazy. And hope I could do it before Enzo did show up and tear the man apart.

Thomas stopped walking and faced me, and he was barely recognizable to me right now.

"Maybe you hate Enzo." I shook my head. "But that's not why you helped them, and you did, didn't you?"

His hands landed on his hips, and now his boldness facing Enzo the day before the attack when he picked up Chiara made sense. He thought his time with him was short-lived because he'd been privy to Alice's plan.

"Your mother never had a heart attack, did she?" I took cautious steps closer. "Please talk to me." I showed my palms, letting him know I wasn't a threat. And hoped like hell he wasn't one to me, either. Not with his daughter down the hall, at least.

"Money." He shook his head. "Why else would I do it? I lost my shirt in the stock market last month, and the next thing I knew, I was being offered a chance to deal with my cash-flow situation."

Money. *That* I believed as an excuse. Not love for me.

"I figured if they wanted to beat the guy up, he probably deserved it," he rushed out. "I need to get out of here before he shows up." He came my way, and I blocked him.

"Beat him up?" I cried, my hands on his chest. "No, Thomas. They planned to kill him!"

"Move," he barked out, and he snatched my wrists and flung me away, but he'd done it with too much force, and I slammed into the dresser headfirst.

On my knees, breathing hard, a metallic taste filled my mouth. I wasn't sure where the blood was coming from, but I pivoted to look over at him staring down at me.

"Fuck. Shit," Thomas hissed. "That was an accident." He took a knee, and I reeled my hand back and slapped him.

THIRTY-FOUR

Enzo

"Alice must've had someone tamper with the footage," I told Constantine over the line after hacking the security cameras at my apartment building. "It's been erased."

My body was coiled tight, palms sweaty. But that uneasy feeling I'd had since New York had sharpened into a finely pointed knife now that I was back home, and I was getting cut with worry from every angle.

I'd yet to hear from Hudson, but my gut told me I was right. Everything had gone down so fast Thursday that I had missed something.

If someone had provided the three *idiotas* with a key fob, what if that someone had been Thomas? What if he was purposefully framed by Alice but also complicit in everything?

The key fob was a reach, but it was all I had to go on aside from a hunch until I heard from Hudson, and he was at the hospital attempting to get Jensen to talk. Well, write, since his jaw was wired shut.

"What if I hack the hospital records to see if Thomas's mother was ever a patient? If he lied about that as an excuse to take Chiara away to get out of town, then—" I let go of my words at the realization I had an incoming call. "It's Agent Lee. I'll call you back."

"I'm going to tell you something," Agent Lee started once I'd answered, "but first I need you to promise you won't act on your own."

"Tell me," I bit out. "Jensen knows something, am I right?" I had to assume Agent Lee had gone with Hudson to the hospital to question him.

A hard breath fanned out over the line. "Yes."

"Who?" My heart pounded as I waited for him to give me the name, knowing that bad feeling and worry were justified. There was one more loose end. But was it Thomas?

"I put together a team in Charlotte to pick him up. They're waiting outside his house, but he's not home yet. His plane landed an hour ago, though, so he's in Charlotte. I need you to let the Feds handle this one."

"Give me his name, damn it."

"Does the name Thomas—"

I never let him finish. I dropped the phone and rushed next door as fast as possible.

When I tested the knob, the door opened. *No, fuck, she had this locked.*

"Maria," I called out, and my stomach fell at the sight of Chiara's favorite stuffed animal in the living room.

I hadn't felt this empty, this scared, since the moment I'd known Bianca was gone from the world, hours before my family had called to let me know what had happened.

No, no, no.

I ran down the hall and went still in the doorway of her bedroom at the sight of Thomas pinning her to the dresser, trying to stop her from hitting him.

"Let. Her. Go," I hissed, taking slow steps with him near her, not wanting her to get hurt.

When Thomas shifted to the side, and I saw Maria's bloody nose, my world stopped. Everything went silent.

"She hit her head," he quickly rushed out in a panic. "It was an accident."

Maria relaxed her arms to her sides as Thomas backed away from her. "Enzo," she whispered.

"Go to Chiara's room and lock the door," I said in a low voice, staring at a man who knew he was seconds away from death.

Maria hesitantly moved around Thomas, but I couldn't rip my gaze away from him as she quietly passed me.

Once I was alone with him, I cocked my head, studying him. Deciding how I'd kill him.

"Please," he begged. "It's not what you think. I didn't know they were going to kill you. Just rough you up."

I kept quiet. The dark chaos inside me had been reignited, seeing Maria hurt. The demons I'd worked to lock up only this weekend were about to rage free.

Thomas lifted his hands and backed up, all the way to the window, as if he could save himself. But I was already painting the glass with his blood in my mind.

I prowled his way with slow steps, then snatched his wrist and twisted, dropping him to one knee as he whimpered. Reaching down, I squeezed his jaw so he had to look me in the eyes.

Freeing his wrist, I pulled my fist back, preparing to connect it with his face and every other part of him.

But my hand didn't move. Didn't budge.

The soft sounds of Chiara's crying in the distance had me going still.

Then Isabella's words punched through my mind, taking their toll on me: "Bianca believed in forgiveness. Mercy."

I blinked, trying to focus, to finish this man. But thoughts of Maria and Chiara shot through my mind, and my hand shook.

Thomas stared at me, confusion in his eyes, wondering why I hadn't hit him yet.

Fucking same.

"Maria," I yelled for her before I changed my mind.

"Enzo?" she whispered from behind me a moment later, more than likely surprised Thomas wasn't covered in blood.

"Do you want him alive?" I asked, my tone rough, anger still fiercely running its course through me.

"I . . . um." A pause. "Yes."

My shoulders fell. "Then I need a phone. The Feds are waiting at his house to arrest him." I shook my head, shocked at what I was doing. "They need to come here instead." I lowered my arm and leaned in closer to him. "You don't deserve mercy," I told him, "but I'm giving it to you. Consider yourself the luckiest son of a bitch on the planet," I added just before knocking him unconscious.

~

"I honestly don't know how you didn't kill him." Ryan had his arms crossed in his kitchen later that night.

I set the knife alongside the cutting board and looked at my two reasons why Thomas wasn't dead. Maria and Chiara. "I wanted to kill him," I admitted. "The things I wanted to do to that man are too vile to say aloud," I added in a low voice, thinking back to the text from Agent Lee after the Feds from the Charlotte field office arrested Thomas, and he'd thanked me for not painting Maria's bedroom walls with blood.

"I suppose it'd be hard to start a life with them if you killed Chiara's father."

I blew out a ragged breath. I was exhausted, in need of a shower and sleep. But more than anything, I wanted to hold Maria and Chiara and protect them and never let go.

I'd also wanted to give Maria a small sense of normalcy after the hell she'd been through, so I'd offered to cook a late meal for everyone.

But today was so far from normal, I doubted a home-cooked meal would change anything.

Maria had to witness the father of her child arrested by the FBI only three hours ago inside her bedroom.

"She'll be okay," Ryan said as if reading my thoughts, and I looked at her bouncing Chiara on her leg, sitting by Natalia in the living room.

Maria was tough, sure. But she wasn't a great actress, and I could easily see her struggling. She'd gone through far too much because of my past, and I had no idea how to reconcile the fact I was the cause of her pain.

I couldn't let her lie to me and promise me she was okay. What if she had nightmares? Post-traumatic stress?

"I should've told her my concerns were about Thomas." More guilt stacked on my shoulders.

"She's okay. She was the one trying to beat Thomas up when you arrived. She's strong."

Maria had admitted she'd hit Thomas a few times before I'd shown up, and he hadn't fought back. And that her bloody nose hadn't been by his hand.

That didn't change my disgust or hate for Thomas, though.

"The past is the past." Ryan slapped a hand to my back, trying to ease the discomfort I still felt, and I peeled my focus over my shoulder to look at him.

"And that past came back to haunt me."

"Thomas was the last loose end." He set a hand over his heart. "You know I'd be the first one to tell you if I thought you were a risk to my wife and her family."

"Yeah, I guess so," I hesitantly answered. "Also, thank you for letting us stay in the guest room until we can find a new place to live."

My apartment and hers were now full of shitty memories I didn't want surrounding her, and with Thomas more than likely going to prison for aiding the mafia, we had no reason to live in Uptown. It made more sense to be in Waxhaw by her family and the restaurant.

"Of course."

My eyes connected with Maria's from across the room, and she stopped talking and went quiet as I peered at her. And for whatever reason, this moment had me thinking back to Hudson's bar six years ago when we'd exchanged looks before that kiss.

She'd been a virgin then. Hadn't met Thomas. And still believed in fairy tales, searching for the kind of love she read about.

And I wanted that storybook ending for Maria, the one Bianca had written about just before dying. I blinked, realization hitting me at what I needed to do. "Can you watch the stove?" I asked without waiting for an answer, starting for Maria. She lifted her beautiful eyes and peered up at me as I said, "We need to talk."

Worry passed over her face, but she quietly nodded and handed Chiara over to Natalia. I took her hand, and we went upstairs to the guest bedroom.

Once the door was shut, I motioned for her to sit on the bed. Chiara's travel crib was set up by the bed, and I swallowed at the fact that what I was about to say would mean I wouldn't be sharing a room with them tonight.

"What's wrong?" she whispered, taking a seat. "I mean, aside from the mess of the last five days."

I let go of an uneasy breath and sat alongside her. She pivoted to face me, and I took her hand between my palms. "I want a do-over," I admitted. "A clean slate. Fresh start." I swallowed. "I don't want this to be how our story begins, because it feels fucking doomed if it does."

"Enzo." Her free hand went to my cheek, her eyes thinning.

I thought back to the edited version of my sister's story, the one published. The only version I'd read so far, which clearly lacked the behind-the-scenes details of my sister's life. "I wish I could edit out everything that's happened since Wednesday. But since that's not possible, I'm going to ask you for the do-over instead."

"What do you mean?"

I tightened my hold on her hand. "I want to take you out on dates. Flirt with you. Take things slowly. Give you the romance story you deserve."

Her glossy eyes shed a tear, and her lips crooked at the edges. I wasn't sure if that was a smile or frown she was fighting. "I don't need that. I already love you. Accept you. You don't need to do this. I just want us to be together." She palmed my cheek. "If you're in my life, my story is complete."

"I love you so much that it hurts," I confessed. "But that hurt is why I know we need to do this. The pain of my past is punishing, and I'm so damn terrified I'll mess up." My voice was rough. Emotions cutting through. The events of the week hammering my body, mind, and soul. Finally catching up with me. "Maybe it's me who needs a fresh start. The chance to truly move on from my past, and somehow this reset feels like I—"

"Then yes," she interrupted, both crying and nodding. "For you, yes. If you need this, I'll do it. If you're not trying to push me away because you think you're a danger or some insanity like that, then yes."

"You were right." *My brothers were right today.* "You're safer with me."

"Good." A heavy breath later, she shared in a shaky voice, "I promised you I'd be there for you to help you escape hell, and if for even a second you still feel like you're there . . . I'm here for you." She pulled her hand from mine and slipped her arms over my shoulders, drawing me in for a hug. "I've got your back like you have mine."

"Fuck," I cried against her neck, surrendering to every emotion I'd once battled to keep hidden. "I really am lost without you."

"But I'll always find you." She offered a similar promise to the one I'd made to Izzy. "Just like I know you'll always find me."

THIRTY-FIVE

Maria

One Month Later

"I'm in hell. I mean, there's no other way to put it." I pointed at the ground, frustration mounting, my body tingly all over. "Enzo's driving me insane."

"Mm-hmm." My sister tossed a few of her best dresses onto the guest bed for me to try on for my date tonight. "Yes, having a man like Enzo wine and dine you, be all charming and swoony for weeks, was the definition for hell when I looked it up."

I chuckled and dramatically collapsed onto the bed, probably wrinkling the outfits. "He's barely even tongued me."

"Because he knows he'll put that tongue elsewhere if he does, and he's trying desperately to take things slow. Give you some type of slow-burn romance."

I groaned and rolled to my back and let go of an exasperated sigh. "I don't want *slow burn*. I want action in chapter one. I want a whole book of hot scenes."

She laughed again, then tossed a little black dress on top of me. "I know you, missy. And you love the tension and anticipation. I see the looks you share at the restaurant. And I know whenever you get a text from him because your face lights up."

All true. I couldn't deny it. And we had exchanged some hot looks and some witty and sexy read-between-the-lines texts that left me super wet afterward. The man knew how to turn me on without using dirty words.

Towels. Freaking towel talk from the man debating the best thickness over a late-night call last night had even sent me over the edge.

"Also," my sister went on when I was lost in my thoughts, "not knowing when things will finally explode between the two of you is exciting and so, so hot. Trust me, I remember those days with Ryan."

I tossed the black dress aside and sat upright. "He's a walking book boyfriend, just like your hubby." I fake-pouted and crossed my legs, the pain horrendous between my thighs. Chiara had been sleeping in her travel crib by my bed in Natalia's guest room, so I was wound up tight without relief. My last orgasm had been in Long Island the night before hell broke loose.

Natalia smoothed a hand over her stomach. She was in a cute baby-blue dress with a bow beneath her breasts. "I really do think his request to do all of this is sweet and poetic. He wants to give your story a better beginning. And surely now that things are settled and the paint is dry on the whole mafia thing . . ." She wrinkled her nose. "Bad analogy, but the point is, I think enough time has passed, and he'll take things to the next level." She lifted one shoulder. "He is a chef, surely he knows how to turn up the heat."

"Oh, he does. And he has been. For four weeks, but without getting me off," I teasingly wailed, testing my drama skills. And yeah, they still sucked.

One thing I hadn't been able to hide from Enzo: the nightmares. When he'd pressed for me to share, worried I was dreaming about him taking lives, I finally admitted they weren't about him.

No, they were about Alice holding a knife over me by the bed. But I always woke up right before she could stab me.

Enzo had refused to take no as an answer when suggesting therapy. I'd told him I'd go if he agreed to see someone as well.

"I'll do anything for you," he'd said during our talk two weeks ago, holding my shoulders. "So yeah, if you'll only go if I do, then yes."

I'd had my fourth visit with the doctor last Friday and quickly realized I had a lot more to talk about than just Alice. Like the fact I'd ever let my mom pressure me into marrying Thomas in the first place. My doubts and insecurities about being a single mom. And on and on and on.

"I need to get out of your hair and move out," I said as she grabbed the black dress.

"Oh, please. I love having you here."

"I just don't want to go to Mom and Dad's, and why bother getting my own place when my hope is Enzo and I will move in together soon? At this rate, it'll be forever before I move out."

"Now that you don't need to live in Uptown by Thomas, when that day comes, you and Enzo can get a home near us."

Not that I'd seen Thomas since that horrific day last month, but he was back home and on an electronic ankle bracelet courtesy of the Feds. He was waiting to face a judge, where he'd plead guilty in exchange for a reduced sentence. Guilty for taking $50,000 from Alice to help them out.

"You think you'll ever let him see Chiara again?" she asked, and I was surprised she hadn't broached the subject sooner. "You think Thomas was telling the truth and he didn't know the real plan?"

"I don't know. Maybe." And that was another topic of conversation to tackle with the therapist. "But he won't be seeing Chiara anytime soon. He doesn't deserve to."

"You'll do what's best, I know you." She held the dress against her body, her cute belly popping out. She was nearly eight months pregnant now and their son was due mid-December. An early Christmas present.

"I'm honestly happy to have you here, though. Wish it was for a different reason, but still."

"Me too."

"And you're at the other side of the house, so it's not like I have to cover my face with a pillow during sex so you don't hear me." She shot me a funny look. "You don't hear me, right?"

"Still getting some at eight months, huh?" I playfully waggled my brows. "Good for you, Mama."

"Almost Mama." She handed me the dress, lifting her chin to let me know to wear this one tonight. "Did Enzo text yet? Is he back from New York?"

He'd flown home early that morning, but he'd promised he'd be back in time for a late dinner. "He texted thirty minutes ago his plane had landed, and after a shower, he'll be here to pick me up."

"He say why he had to go?" she asked as I swapped my sweatpants and tee for the black dress and zipped it up.

"No, and I didn't ask. I figure he'll tell me if I need to know." I studied myself in the mirror over the dresser. Enzo would have an excellent view of my breasts, and with any hope, his control would snap. "I kind of hate the fact that man has more restraint than I do. Shouldn't it be the other way around?"

"He spent years learning how to check his impulses. But don't forget, you attempting to date last month sent him over the edge and did have him making a move."

My body responded at the mere memory of him lifting my shirt that night to check if my panties were wet before he finally gave in and touched me for the first time.

"He's trying so hard to be the man he believes you deserve."

"He's always deserved me." I let go of a small breath. "Remember when I felt like something was missing in my life, so I took those classes, trying to figure it out?" I thought back to those days, which felt like years ago now. "But it's so easy to see now that what I was missing was him."

"Pretty sure he feels the same about you." She smiled, rubbing her stomach. "Has he, um, read Bianca's unedited story yet?"

"I don't know. I haven't wanted to press, but it's been a month, so maybe. He hasn't mentioned it, though." My shoulders slumped as I thought back to the story. "I only read the first two pages, so I don't know the details of what really happened myself. I just know Nico didn't tell her he was married until after she fell for him."

"And it wasn't like she'd been invited to Alice's wedding. I'm pretty sure the Costas didn't have family reunions with Angela's mafia side of the family for Bianca to have met him beforehand."

"Right."

"I hate to say it, and I don't want to ruin the glow you have going for you, so please don't let it, but I feel like Enzo needs to read it if he really wants to let go of the past. Maybe ask him about it tonight?"

I was on the same page. Like always. "I'll try," I said, nervous now, slipping on a pair of black slingback heels. "He should be here soon."

We went downstairs, where Ryan was on the floor in the living room, and he had Chiara over his head while she pretended to fly.

"Le sigh," my sister said at the sight. "He's going to be such a great father." She faced me, then tipped her head to the side, and I followed her gaze to see Enzo there.

The breath whooshed free from my lungs at the sight of him in the doorway watching us. Black dress pants and a black button-down shirt. Sleeves cuffed to the elbows showing his ink. A glimpse of the guardian-angel tattoo on his chest from the top two buttons undone. And his hair was styled off to the side in that sexy-messy way I loved.

"Hi." *Was that a pageant wave I just did?*

"Hi." Enzo removed his hands from his pockets and wet his lips, his eyes climbing from my heels up my legs. He spent a little extra time on my breasts as he started our way. *"Bellissima."*

God, I loved when the man spoke Italian to me. And his nickname for me, *Tesoro,* always had me melting.

"Don't stay out too late," Ryan called out, sitting up and placing Chiara on his shoulders. She clapped his cheeks and laughed.

"Dah-dah," Chiara called out, her eyes on Enzo, and that would never get old, especially the smile it produced from Enzo.

He went over and took her from Ryan, then lifted her up over his head, making that her second plane ride for the evening. "You going to be a good girl for your aunt and uncle, hmm?" Enzo asked her, and Chiara giggled before I hugged and kissed her goodbye.

Once we were outside, I leaned into Enzo and murmured, "But I might not be a good girl."

He snatched my wrist and spun me to face him. Arching into him as his hand traced along my silhouette, I heard him whisper, "Fire."

At the feel of his hard cock pressing against me, I had a feeling the chef was finally about to turn up the heat.

About.

Damn.

Time.

～

Sitting back on my heels on top of his hotel bed, I licked my lips and moaned as I finished my last bite of pizza.

Enzo stood in front of the bed, his eyes steady on me as I closed the pizza box and brushed a thumb across my lip, checking for crumbs. The steely, hard look in his eyes had me pinning my knees together.

Instead of dinner at a fancy restaurant, he'd surprised me with pizza delivery to his hotel room and a bottle of wine. I nearly blurted, *I love you*, at that fact, but I was trying to behave and take things slow. Pretend we were still in the early stages of our relationship and not say the words burning on my tongue that I'd last shared the day Thomas had been arrested four weeks ago.

"You barely ate." I frowned as he cupped his mouth, his gaze lifting to the ceiling, and that was never a good sign. "What happened in New York?"

I stood and set the pizza box on his dresser before returning to face him, hoping he'd talk to me. The therapist was supposed to be helping him on that front—not keeping secrets from a place of fear I wouldn't accept him.

"A lot happened back home." He gripped the nape of his neck and squeezed, his gaze returning to mine again, and I reached for his free hand and laced our fingers together. "With the Brambilla case pretty much over, my brothers and Hudson have decided to work together again. But in a different way."

"What do you mean?"

"Start a security company to help those in need." He paused. "Less vigilantism and more by-the-book-type stuff. Well, for the most part. They'll continue to work at the family business, too. Because their security work will be without pay."

"Oh, wow."

"I also saw Jesse today." He let go of his neck and motioned toward the bed, and we sat, hands still linked. "Now that Jesse's team is done with handling the rest of the clients from the cleaner's list, he was able to come up and chat. Offer some guidance on how things work at his security company, Falcon Falls."

"And you were part of that conversation because . . ." My heartbeat kicked up as I waited for him to answer.

"I'm not leaving here. Not leaving you." He shifted on the bed, cupping my chin with his free hand. "Don't worry."

"But do you want to help them? I mean, work with them from time to time?"

"I'm happy here with what I do."

That look in his eyes, though. "My inability to lie and hold a straight face is rubbing off on you." I took a second to gather my thoughts. "You spent so much of your life fighting bad guys, and I know you love to cook, but if you're meant to help others, too, I won't stand in your way."

"Maria." His broody look softened. "I love you, I . . ." His voice trailed off as he closed one eye, realizing he'd slipped up.

I couldn't help but smile. "And I love you, which is why I'll support you no matter what. If you want to go on missions here and there, save the world, then you should. The sous-chef at the restaurant has learned a lot from you. He can handle things when you're not here. You can have both." I shrugged. "You can have it all. I do."

"You do?" He tipped his head to the side.

"I have my daughter. My family nearby. A good job that I enjoy. And a man I love wholeheartedly. I feel complete. Happy." I chewed on my lip, knowing there was one thing I was missing. "I mean, I would like to make love again. I have a list I'd love to check off, and my patience sucks, but—"

He cut me off with his mouth, his tongue sliding between my lips as his hand went from my chin into my thick, curly hair.

"I have a list, too," he said after pulling back, our lips nearly touching.

"You do, do you?"

He smiled. "I do. But you'll have to wait a bit before I share it."

"Ugh." I groaned. "You love to torture me."

"Like you haven't done the same every hour of every day for the last month." A dark, sexy grin slipped across his face so fast, I nearly missed it.

"And you loved every second, don't lie." I let go of his hand to place my palm over his heart, finding it slow and steady. The beats a comforting rhythm.

"I'll think about the second job," he said after quietly staring at me. "We can discuss it again later. I don't need to say yes now. But there's more I want to share with you about my day."

He let go of me and was back on his feet. He went over to the uncorked bottle of wine and filled our glasses. Ryan's uncle owned a winery in Tuscany, and it was his label of Chianti Enzo had brought with him tonight.

"My family went to visit Bianca at the cemetery this afternoon before I flew home."

His words had me standing, my heart now feeling as though I were fighting for my life. "Are you okay?" *Dumb question. Why would you be?*

He turned, armed with the two glasses, his brows slanting as if unsure how to answer. "I think so, yes." He handed me a glass, and he took a small sip, and I did the same, hoping to calm my nerves. "I brought Bianca's unedited story with me and read it there."

Oh jeez. Now I was going to cry. But I did my best not to, because I didn't want him having to comfort me when I wanted to be the one there for him.

"You already know the parts printed in the magazine," he began, his eyes on the wineglass. "That she bumped into him at a coffee shop one Friday, spilling her coffee on him. They wound up chatting. And then he started going there every day at the same time hoping to run into her, even though it was out of his way and not his normal spot."

I thought back to the story, remembering her words. And how the "male lead" realized she was always there at nine in the morning on Fridays with her journal, jotting down her thoughts. And so, every Friday, they had coffee together, talked about life, and then they went their separate ways. Until one day he asked her out.

"It was three months until they went on a first date and he learned her last name." He paused. "He'd canceled the date they'd planned and hadn't told her why. Presumably because he panicked when he learned she was a Costa." He finally looked up at me. "But I guess he'd already fallen for her and decided to see her anyway. And so they dated. And eventually, she fell in love, and that was when he told her he was married, and to Alice."

"What happened?" I whispered.

"He promised her he was sleeping in a separate room from Alice and was miserable. It'd been an arranged marriage, and he feared his father-in-law, and he didn't know what to do." He shook his head. "But Bianca still ended things. And then in the unedited story, she wrote the ending she hoped for, that they bumped into each other years later and he was divorced."

"And it became a second-chance romance." Only, in real life, she never had that chance. "You blame him for her death now, don't you?" Had he been honest with her from the start, she'd more than likely have survived. "Does that mean you want revenge?" *Is the past not behind us?*

"Bianca wrote the ending she wished she had because she really loved him. Hoped she'd have another chance with him one day." His eyes fell closed as if visualizing his sister's words. "The last line in her story, what the guy said to the woman years later when they bumped into each other, was, 'Let me love you. If you give me a second chance, I'll spend my life proving I'm worthy of it.'"

"That was the original title of her story." I let go of a shaky exhale as he opened his eyes. "'Let Me Love You.'"

"So, as much as I want to kill him, I know she'd never want me to do that. And he was willing to die so I could kill Alice." He let go of a heavy breath, took my wine from me, then set both glasses down. "So no, I'm going to show mercy—*again*." His chiseled jaw relaxed, and his gaze softened. "I love you, and after today, I know I'm finally ready to move forward."

"You're finally ready to let *me* love you," I whispered, more as a statement than a question, knowing those words now had new meaning for him. For us.

"Yes," he firmly said, and he reached up and looped my arms over his shoulders, linking my wrists behind his neck.

"Then maybe we skip to the epilogue?"

"I don't know, I think we might have one more chapter in us before we get there."

"My chef. My hero. And my writer. You have a way with words, just like she did." I drew myself closer to him, feeling his body respond to me.

"Mm." He brought his mouth near mine. "The only story I want to write is ours."

THIRTY-SIX

Enzo

We'd made love. Soft and slow. Sensual and passionate.

Her whisper of, "I love you," as I'd plunged into her had rattled free emotions locked within my chest I hadn't realized had been stuck there.

But with my girl naked and tangled in the sheets on my hotel bed right now, I was ready to take her how I knew she wanted next. Hot and dirty.

"We skipped a few bases in taking things slow." She teased her tongue along the seam of her lips while circling her erect nipple with her nail.

"I was never much of a baseball player. Don't know the rules." I took my heavy cock in my hand, stroking myself in preparation to go again. I'd given myself a ten-minute break. A cold slice of pizza chased down by wine as an energy reboot. I was prepared to join her, but my phone buzzing on the nightstand had her gaze flying that way. "Ignore it."

"It could be important." She rolled over and snatched it. "It's a text from your brother."

I sighed. "Which one?"

She read the notification. "Alessandro, and it says, 'Have you asked her?'"

Shit. I lunged onto the bed, freeing the phone from her hand in one fast movement.

"Asked me what?" She chuckled while my fingers raced over the keys to respond.

Me: Not yet. And you almost blew it.
Alessandro: Just making sure you follow through.
Me: I swear, for a man who claims not to have a heart, you have the biggest one of all.

I set the phone on the dresser and silenced it like I should've done before, then focused back on the beautiful woman on my bed.

"So." She set her back to the headboard, sitting upright, holding the sheet to hide her nakedness. "What do you want to ask me?"

"Well." I joined her on the bed, going for the sheet, and peeled it free from her grasp so I could get a look at her.

Soft, supple skin I wanted to trace my lips over. Puckered nipples. A swollen clit from our lovemaking I wanted to taste for the second time tonight. And her mouth, God, did I want to kiss her, have our breaths become one.

She chewed on her lip as I lost myself in the moment, just taking in the sight of her. She reached out and swept her finger along the wings of the guardian-angel tattoo on my chest. "What do you want to ask me?"

I held her wrist and brought her hand up to my mouth and kissed her palm, never losing hold of her eyes.

"Don't make me wait." She fake-pouted. "I promise I'll behave if you tell me."

She wriggled side to side, moving her hips, and I laughed, knowing she didn't want to be good. My naughty girl wanted to feel the heavy weight of my hand on that ass of hers. The sting that I'd smooth my hand over and kiss away. And my balls tightened with anticipation.

"The guest room when my family visits needs to be far away from our bedroom," I said. "Like, on the other side of the neighborhood so they don't hear you scream my name."

"Oh, really?" She smiled as I lowered her hand and positioned it between her thighs, urging her to touch herself.

Her eyes slid down between us to her sex. "Touch yourself. Show me what you've been doing these last four weeks. Show me how you've been getting yourself off."

I let go of her hand to secure a grip on my cock, sitting on my heels, watching my woman slide a finger along the seam of her sex, spreading open her pussy for me.

"I haven't touched myself, actually," she whispered, and I drew in a ragged breath at her words. "Tonight was the first time I've gotten off since New York."

I wouldn't be able to say the same. "So you can be good, I see."

"I take it you were a bad boy?" Her smile met her eyes as she continued to touch herself.

"Oh, I was fucking horrible." I grinned, letting go of my shaft. "I jacked off at least three times a day. In my defense, you've been teasing the hell out of me for a month. And I couldn't stop thinking about this naughty little mouth taking every inch of me." I moved her hand aside to touch her myself, finding her soaked. "And how could I forget how tight and delicious you are down here?"

"You're playing dirty and distracting me from the question you've yet to ask." She removed my hand, and I grunted. "Don't leave me in suspense, mister."

My gaze fell to her full tits, and I smoothed her nipple between my finger and thumb, drawing it into a hard point, and she surrendered a little moan that time. Yeah, I was playing dirty, and my girl liked it.

"I think it's time you hear my list that's only partially checked off."
My heart was racing, but how could it not?

"Oh?" She angled her head, and I freed her nipple and shifted to
sit with my back to the headboard, and then I had her straddle me, her
pussy dangerously close to my cock. And so help me, if she moved an
inch, I'd fill her without anything between us. "What's on your list? Is
it like mine?" She teased her brows up and down a few times.

I reached around and squeezed her ass cheek, loving the feel of her
in my palm. "It's a little different than yours." I smiled. "A four-bed-
room house in your sister's neighborhood. Well, I already checked that
off my list. Made an offer last week."

Her eyes fell between us for a quiet moment, disbelief racing across
her features, and I shifted her thick hair to her back. "Wait, what?"

"I hope you don't mind, but houses there go fast. And I thought
you'd like to live in the same neighborhood."

"That cute place down the street that was on the market for only
an hour . . . that was you?"

I nodded, and she crushed her body against mine, throwing her
arms over my shoulders, hugging me. "So you don't mind?"

"I don't even know how to explain how happy you just made me.
I don't have words."

"Thank God I'm some great wordsmith, then, huh?" I answered
once she leaned back to find my eyes, and I held her chin. "Want to
hear more of the list?"

She quietly nodded.

"A sibling for Chiara." I paused. "And to be your husband. Still
need to check—"

"Are you asking . . ."

"I'm asking." I guided her face closer, drawing her mouth near mine.

"You know, for a man who doesn't know the rules to baseball, you're
pretty great at home runs." A few tears escaped down her cheeks as she
smiled.

"Is that a yes?" I hoarsely asked, hating I didn't have a ring. And although I'd asked her dad a week ago for permission to marry her without a specific timeline in mind, on the flight home today I'd decided it'd be tonight. I couldn't wait. I'd closed the book when it came to my past, and Maria and Chiara were my future. "Will you marry me?"

"Yes! Yes, I will marry you." No hesitation, not even a little. She eagerly nodded before kissing me. Soft and delicate before it turned bold and ravenous. When she broke away, she said, "I have a request, though."

"Anything, *Tesoro*." I slanted my brows, studying her. Unsure if I'd ever experienced a feeling of happiness like I was right now, knowing she'd be my wife.

"Well, since nothing about our relationship has exactly been conventional, what if we take our chances and go with the flow?"

I wasn't following, so I just smiled and waited for her to explain. Damn, I was so in love with this adorable woman.

"No condoms. If it happens before we're married, it happens," she finally said. "What do you say?"

"What do I say?" A hearty laugh fell from my lips, and I had this woman face down in a second, holding the weight of my body over her. "I'll show you, *cara mia*," I murmured against her ear, the head of my cock nudging her pussy.

She hooked her feet around my calves and pleaded, "Then show me."

I did as my girl asked, filling her deep. Slamming into her tight pussy over and over, holding her at the nape of her neck. "Fuck," I groaned, feeling her walls tighten around me, and I internally cursed at how phenomenal she felt. "You're going to get me in trouble if I get you pregnant before our wedding, aren't you?"

"Just with my parents." She lightly laughed. "You can handle them." Maria lifted her chin and mouthed, "Fire," before winking.

I wet my lips, shaking my head. "You're asking for it. You can't help but be bad." I slid free from her, and she moaned at the loss of contact.

"And you know exactly what to do with me."

My lips spread into a slow grin as I rasped, "Oh, believe me, I do." I stood and scooped her into my arms and tossed her over my shoulder, slapping her ass hard, and she squealed. I carried her toward the window and set her down, sliding open the curtains. "I'm pretty sure sex against a window, risking someone seeing us, is on that list of yours, right?"

"Yes," she confessed with her back to the glass. I hooked her leg to my side and hoisted her up just enough to position my cock at her center. "Give it to me. Hard and dirty," she nearly panted as her pussy swallowed my length in one fast movement, and she cried out.

Gritting down on my teeth, I slapped my free hand on the glass over her shoulder and leaned in and kissed her as I gave it to her just as she wanted. As we both needed.

I'd never get tired of her. She was mine. A real treasure. And I had truly been lost without her.

And now . . . I was finally found.

EPILOGUE

Maria

Six Months Later

"I just can't get enough of him." I rocked Dante in my arms at my sister's restaurant. Named after his late grandfather, he looked like a little man, dressed in adorable jeans with a blue button-up shirt.

"He's a ham, that's for sure. Already a charmer." Natalia smiled, staring at her son in my arms. She'd returned to work only last month, but she wasn't ready to have anyone else watch him yet. So, twice a week, she brought him to the restaurant, and Ryan would swing by after work to pick him up.

"Can I hold him?" our bartender Christian asked, already peeling him free from my arms.

It was almost five, so the restaurant would be opening soon. I'd had a catering gig earlier, but now I needed to head out and pick up Chiara. Standing alongside Christian, I folded my arms while I studied my handsome nephew. "I should probably head out. The day care closes soon."

Natalia checked the time, then asked Christian, "Can you keep an eye on him while I walk my sister out?"

"Absolutely." He grinned, and he looked like a natural, so hopefully one day he would settle down. He glanced at Dante. "Stick with me, kid, your uncle Christian will teach you how to get all the ladies."

Okay, so maybe not anytime soon. I rolled my eyes and kissed Dante's head. Grabbing my purse, I made my way to the parking lot with Natalia. It was almost too hot, even for North Carolina. The sticky kind of hot that slaps you in the face when you open the door.

We walked over to the black Escalade that Enzo had bought me a week before our wedding in January. We had a small ceremony in Charlotte with our families, since we hadn't wanted to wait any longer, and with Dante so young, we didn't want my sister traveling.

But I'd wanted to do something special at the Costas' home in the Hamptons as well, since it'd been Bianca's favorite place. So, in February, we'd had another small service there, and it truly felt as if she were with us that day.

Isabella and I had grown closer over the last few months, same with her and Enzo, which made my heart happy.

Plus, Enzo worked with her from time to time. Like right now. She'd shocked everyone with that decision, but her brothers and Hudson agreed to bring her on at their new security company, working behind the scenes only.

"You doing okay?" Ah, based on the nervous tone of my sister's voice, she had a reason to walk me outside.

My gaze flicked to my ring finger and the wedding set Enzo had picked out. "I'm good, promise. The first two times he went out were a little tough, just because of my overthinking brain, but I'm much better this time. I know what to expect."

Natalia reached for my arm and squeezed. "He'd stop if you asked him to."

Feeling her eyes on me, searching for my gaze, I looked up at my overprotective sister. "Enzo was meant for this life. I can feel it in my bones." I nodded. "For so long, he saw himself as the bad guy, and I think helping others is his way of finding redemption. Not that he needs it."

"He'll be back in time for your appointment tomorrow, I hope?"

"He better be." I reached into my purse for my phone. "But maybe I'll get an update now and make sure."

Natalia hugged me goodbye, and then I hopped into the Escalade and called Enzo, hoping I wasn't interrupting him in the middle of anything important.

He answered on the third ring with a breathy voice. "Hey, you."

"Timing okay?" I tossed my purse on the passenger seat, a Kate Spade bag, which had been a gift from Isabella.

"For you? Anytime."

My shoulders flinched at what sounded like . . . "It's daytime. Why do I hear gunfire? You don't normally operate when—"

"Friendly fire."

"Is there such a thing as friendly fire?" I hid a gasp of worry.

"Sure."

More gunfire.

"Enzo, oh my God, get off the phone. You shouldn't have answered. I was just checking in, making sure you wouldn't miss the appointment."

"Babe, of course I'm going to answer when you call. And I wouldn't miss tomorrow for the world. Which is why I'm handling things now."

I cursed at the realization Enzo was in the middle of his operation, and I was putting him at risk. And yet, the man had still picked up my call.

"It was on silent, stop worrying. I felt the vibration in my pocket," he went on, his words nearly lost to more "friendly fire."

"Lorenzo Costa, hang up on me right now. Be safe!" I ordered.

A light rumble of laughter left his lips. "Yes, ma'am. But I'm on high ground. Safe from direct action. I won't risk my life. You have my word, *Tesoro*."

"Okay," I whispered, setting a hand to my abdomen. "We need you."

I could nearly hear the smile slide through the phone as he murmured back, "And you have me."

~

"How'd Isabella do? You feeling better about her working with you all yet?" I asked Enzo as he captured my hand and laced our fingers together, walking into the office the next day. He'd kept his word. He'd come back to me and on time, thank God.

"We underestimated her. She's damn good at the tech stuff, and it's nice having her in our ears on comms keeping us safe when we all work together." An easy smile met his lips, and it was as if he were remembering something as he added, "A family affair." He stopped and peered at me. "Don't want you going on ops, though, so no ideas."

"I wouldn't dream of it. Trust me." I chuckled.

"And I promise this won't become a habit. They're just getting the company up and running and once they hire more people they trust, I won't be rolling out as often as I have been."

I set my other hand on top of his. "Hey, Isabella might have your six out there, but I have it here. And you do what you need to. Okay?"

"Mmmm." He leaned in. "How do you make military talk so sexy?"

I laughed. "You're crazy."

He closed one eye. "Am I, though?"

"Yes, but I love you anyway," I teased, and he set his mouth to mine for another hot kiss as his hand skated over my abdomen.

"You better," he whispered against my lips, and sometimes it was hard for me to believe this was my life.

That he was my husband. And now Chiara's father. On paper, too.

Thomas had allowed him to legally adopt her with the request that after his time in prison, he was allowed a few visits a month with

Chiara. They'd be supervised, though. I wasn't ready to leave him alone with her after what he'd done.

"This is happening, right?" I asked once he opened the door for me. "This is real? I'm not dreaming?" I also hadn't had a nightmare in months, but I'd kept up with therapy to continue working on myself, because why not?

Enzo let go of the door and held my cheeks. "Yes, it is." His brows slanted as he studied me.

I freed a deep breath from my lungs, which served as my own little pinch to let myself know I was awake. This was real. And then holding my hand again, he led me inside.

After checking in and going through the motions, I was finally about to hear our child's heartbeat for the first time. Chiara would have a sibling.

"You two ready?" my obstetrician asked, and Enzo squeezed my hand, standing off to my side, and I knew his heart had to be racing as fast as mine right now.

"Yes," I nearly choked out, and she began studying the screen, and my eyes were glued to it as well, not that I knew what I was looking at.

"Give me a second." Why'd that not sound great from our doctor?

I shot Enzo a panicky look, and he set a hand to my shoulder and lightly squeezed, a promise everything would be okay.

I nodded and gulped, praying he was right, and then the doctor looked at me, then over at Enzo.

"Two heartbeats," she shared after a dramatic pause of suspense, and little did she know we didn't need more suspense in our lives; we'd had our fair share already. "Looks like you're going to have twins, congratulations."

"I thought twins had to run on the mother's side," Enzo said, his gaze narrowed. Disbelief in his dark eyes. A smile slipped to his lips when he added, "I may have done a little research." He squeezed my hand, then pivoted back to the doctor, searching for confirmation we were truly pregnant with *two* babies.

"Having twins isn't always hereditary. But for fraternal, usually that's passed down through the gestational parent's side, yes. I take it you're a twin, though?"

Enzo nodded, and her smile broadened. "Well, looks like you're both lucky, then, to be blessed with two babies."

"Lucky," he said, eyes on me. "I am definitely lucky," he murmured, then kissed me.

And it wasn't until our appointment ended and we were back in the SUV that it truly hit me I was pregnant with twins.

Enzo was quiet from behind the wheel, not yet starting the engine, and then he twisted in his seat and stared at me.

"Are you okay?" I reached for his hand, and he leaned in and brushed his lips across my knuckles.

"Maybe I really am crazy," he softly said, meeting my eyes.

"Why?"

"Because I get the feeling she's somehow here with us. Her energy, at least? I don't know what you want to call it. But Bianca's here with us."

Chills peppered my skin, and now I was the one crying, and I knew it wasn't just pregnancy hormones.

I leaned across the console, careful not to crush my stomach, not that I was really showing yet, but I needed to get closer to him. I set my free hand over his heart. "She's been with you all this time. You've never been without her."

His hold on my palm tightened, and he let go of a heavy breath as if whatever weight he'd still been carrying was now gone from his shoulders.

Enzo brought our linked palms back to his mouth and kissed the top of my hand. "We're going to have three kids," he said a moment later, shaking his head, and then he cracked a smile. "We didn't plan for this. We can handle three, right?" Oh, my gruff alpha was now about to panic. Probably go overboard on babyproofing our house the way Ryan had before Dante was born. "And what if they're girls? *Three* girls? How many dates will I have to fight off and . . ." He let go of his words, realizing he was about to go off the deep end with worry.

"You'll protect them. Boys or girls. You'll keep them safe. And they'll know how loved they are," I reassured him.

Enzo focused on me, his smile meeting his eyes this time. "I'm not the only lucky one, by the way. Our babies will be, just like Chiara already is . . . because they have you as a mother."

Staring deep into his eyes, my heart never so full—and technically I had three heartbeats now—I wet my lips and reminded him, "No, they're lucky because they have *us*." It was my turn to kiss the top of his hand. "And, Enzo, I'm lost without you, too."

ABOUT THE AUTHOR

Brittney Sahin is a *Wall Street Journal* bestselling author of romantic suspense novels. She began writing at an early age with the dream to be a published author before the age of eighteen. Although academic pursuits (and later a teaching career) interrupted her aspirations, she never stopped writing—and never stopped imagining. It wasn't until her students encouraged her to follow her dreams that Brittney said goodbye to Upstate New York in order to start a new adventure in the place she was raised: Charlotte, North Carolina. In 2015, she published her first novel, *Silenced Memories*. When she is not working on upcoming novels, she spends time with her family. She is a proud mother of two boys and a lover of suspense novels, coffee, and the outdoors. For more information, visit www.brittneysahin.com.